HONORABLE
ENEMIES

HONORABLE ENEMIES

—

Joe Weber

G. P. Putnam's Sons

NEW YORK

—

G. P. Putnam's Sons
Publishers Since 1838
200 Madison Avenue
New York, NY 10016

LIBRARY OF CONGRESS CATALOGING-IN-PUBLICATION DATA
Weber, Joe.
Honorable enemies/Joe Weber.
p.   cm.
ISBN 0-399-13939-7
1. Intelligence service—United States—Fiction.   I. Title.
PS3573.E219H66   1994   93-45797   CIP
813′.54—dc20

Printed in the United States of America
1 2 3 4 5 6 7 8 9 10

This book is printed on acid-free paper.

Acknowledgments

For their advice, assistance, and encouragement during the creation of this book, I wish to thank those who helped see it to fruition.

I am grateful to Jeannie for her kind support and endless hours of work on the project.

A special thanks to John Flaherty for his excellent technical advice, Yukio Fujiwara for his priceless inputs, Berkley Publishing Group Senior Executive Editor Natalee Rosenstein for going above and beyond to assist me in my efforts, and Adele Horwitz for her patient guidance when I occasionally colored outside the lines.

I particularly thank my publisher, G. P. Putnam's Sons, and everyone involved in the metamorphosis of turning my manuscript into a book.

Because of the controversial nature of the novel, I wish to state that the work is the product of my imagination and should not be interpreted as expressing the views of anyone listed above.

Weapons are tools of ill omen. War is a grave matter; one is apprehensive lest men embark upon it without due reflection.

—LI CH'ÜAN
CHINESE MILITARY THEORETICIAN

Thought is one of the manifestations of human energy, and among the earlier and simpler phases of thought two stand conspicuous—Fear and Greed. Fear, which by stimulating the imagination, creates a belief in an invisible world; and Greed, which dissipates energy in war and trade.

—BROOKS ADAMS
AMERICAN HISTORIAN

Honorable Enemies is respectfully dedicated to the victims of Pearl Harbor, that "Day of Infamy," Sunday morning, December 7, 1941, and to the brave military men and women who vanquished the enemy.

AND

To the 200,000 Japanese citizens who were killed or injured by the Hiroshima and Nagasaki bombs. In conclusion, I wish to recognize the 120,000 Japanese-Americans who were unfairly incarcerated during World War II.

HONORABLE
ENEMIES

Prologue

HONOLULU, HAWAII

The passengers were relaxed as they leaned against the starboard railing on the spacious observation deck of the *Star of Honolulu*. Another perfect day of vacation on the picturesque island. They shielded their eyes and squinted into the dazzling early-morning sunlight, snapping pictures of each other and the majestic steel and glass towers sprouting from the colorful Honolulu skyline.

A few of them ventured aft to the fantail to watch the churning wake while their state-of-the-art tour vessel steamed from Kewalo Basin toward the entrance to Pearl Harbor. Other visitors shivered in the brisk sea breeze and walked to the port railing to photograph a large Hatteras sportfisherman as it dashed through the waves.

Overhead, an evenly spaced trail of brightly painted twin-engined sightseeing planes flew over the sand and sparkling emerald waters of Waikiki Beach. All eyes followed the airplanes until the last one approached Diamond Head, then disappeared behind the spectacular landmark.

In the private top-deck dining room of the $7 million, custom-designed tour ship, another group eagerly consumed a traditional Japanese breakfast of rice, miso soup, raw eggs, dried seaweed, salmon, soy sauce, and the ever-present green tea.

For this corporate-sponsored tour of Pearl Harbor and the *Arizona* Memorial, the vessel's disposable tableware and utensils were replaced with expensive opaque blue china, elegant cloth napkins, and ivory chopsticks.

A few daring souls deviated from their normal morning routine and helped themselves to a sumptuous continental breakfast. After tasting the assortment of delicate pastries and cold juices, their faces broadened with smiles and they nodded approvingly.

The sudden sound of a high-pitched whine caught the attention of those on deck seconds before an American Airlines jumbo jet passed over the bow. Some of the men raised their video cameras and photographed the airliner until it flared for a landing at Honolulu International Airport.

Chartered by a large consortium, the *Star of Honolulu* was crowded with the families of carefully selected executives and managers from several large Japanese financial institutions. Eight glorious days in beautiful Hawaii, with all expenses paid, including a suite with a private lanai, was the reward for performing in the top ten percent of their peer group.

The men were extremely proud of their accomplishments, as were their smiling wives, but no one dared mention their individual achievements in the harsh new financial and political era.

The wrenching collapse of Japan's stock and property markets had been a staggering blow to the nation's securities firms, and the employees connected with the brokerage firms had adopted a reserved image that was quite different from the garish boom days of the late 1980s and early 1990s.

Gone were the $1,000 steak and champagne dinners and the all-night parties in the Ginza bars. The nation's aptly named bubble economy had burst and the endless party was over. Japan, while dealing with the biggest restructuring of its internal politics since World War II, was retrenching and fighting desperately to overcome the humiliating financial setback.

Any display of self-importance or individualism threatened the new corporate unity and would be viewed as unacceptable behavior that could permanently sidetrack an otherwise promising career.

As the *Star of Honolulu* slowed near the entrance to Pearl Harbor, the general mood of the passengers grew noticeably somber. They returned the friendly waves from a handful of people near Hammer Point, then talked quietly among themselves while they passed Iroquois Point and West Loch.

Once inside the narrow entrance to the cloverleaf-shaped port, the tourists looked curiously at the sights while they listened to the recorded narration of the events that led to the surprise aerial attack on December 7, 1941.

Many of the younger Japanese managers, especially those who weren't knowledgeable about the history of Pearl Harbor, occasionally darted a glance at each other. The more senior executives appeared to be indifferent as the narrator explained how the attack climaxed a decade of worsening relations between the United States and an increasingly expansionist and militaristic Japan.

In a soothing voice, the man supplied a running commentary of the history that precipitated the entry of the United States into World War II. He talked about Japan's invasion of China in 1937 and the subsequent alliance with the Axis powers of Germany and Italy.

The sounds on the tour ship grew eerily quiet when the narrator talked about Japan's occupation of French Indochina in July 1941, which action prompted the United States to respond by freezing Japanese assets in the United States and declaring an immediate embargo on petroleum shipments and other materials vital to Japan.

As the *Star of Honolulu* cruised past Hospital Point and the southern tip of Ford Island, the narrator explained that during the final months of 1941 the United States severed most financial and commercial relations with the Empire of Japan. Though the two countries continued to negotiate up to the day of the Pearl Harbor attack, the government of Prime Minister

Tojo Hideki had secretly decided on going to war with the United States.

Now only the voice of the narrator could be heard. "In their attack upon Pearl Harbor, the Japanese simultaneously thundered in from several directions. A flight of dive bombers and fighters approached from the plateau between the Koolau and Waianae mountain ranges. They bombed and strafed Wheeler Airfield and Schofield Barracks before turning to come in from the east. With the sun to their backs, the fighter, dive bomber, and torpedo attack pilots struck Hickam Airfield, Ford Island, and Battleship Row."

Nobody commented while they viewed the entrance to Middle Loch and stared at the remains of the USS *Utah*, a former battleship that had been converted to a target ship before the attack at Pearl Harbor. The narration went on as they entered East Loch.

"Of the almost four hundred American military aircraft stationed on Oahu that Sunday morning, only thirty-eight were able to struggle into the air. Out of that number, ten were shot down by Japanese fighters and by American gunners who mistakenly identified them as enemy aircraft."

Everyone crowded the starboard rails of the *Star of Honolulu* as it passed the small islands of Mokunui and Mokuiki and cruised toward Battleship Row. The young American captain skillfully slowed the large vessel, stopping near the stark white memorial building that straddled the battleship USS *Arizona*. Timed to the second, the riveting narration continued without a pause.

The Japanese visitors were deathly quiet as they peered at the ghostly hull resting just below the surface of the water. Small black globules of oil rose from the innards of the sunken battleship, spreading in concentric circles before they floated toward Ford Island. Some of the passengers ventured aft to view the massive gun turret that protruded above the water.

While Nikons, Minoltas, Canons, and numerous video cameras recorded the sights and sounds at the famous war monument, the captain tossed a lei of fresh flowers on the water as taps quietly echoed across the harbor. The knowledge that 1,102 men were entombed in the watery grave registered on the faces of many of the tourists.

The solemn moment was suddenly interrupted by the clattering sound of a turbine-powered helicopter as it descended toward Ford Island and approached the long, white viewing platform over the *Arizona* Memorial.

Immediately, the Japanese vacationers began snapping pictures and recording videos of the Bell JetRanger. Resplendent in the intensely bright colors of a Honolulu television station, the noisy helicopter settled into a hover over the *Arizona*'s exposed number-three gun turret and turned to face the tour ship.

Waving and pointing at the pilot, the inquisitive Japanese smiled and continued to snap pictures. Moments later, they stood transfixed when the nose of the helicopter appeared to twinkle.

A fusillade of high-powered rounds ripped into the side of the *Star of Honolulu,* walking the entire length of the cruise ship as the nose of the JetRanger slowly turned first right, then back left.

Pandemonium erupted while the shocked crew and passengers reacted to the violent attack. Some of the panicked visitors screamed hysterically while others cursed and crawled across the deck in search of shelter. Bullets ricocheted off the hull and interior fittings as people stumbled over each other in the rain of debris.

After what seemed like an eternity of living hell, the two automatic weapons bolted to the helo's landing skids mercifully stopped firing. The pilot spun the vividly painted helicopter toward the northeast and dipped its nose to gain speed.

Initially paralyzed by the blazing assault, the captain gathered his wits and sent out a Mayday call, then immediately began rescue efforts to save the people who had either been blown into the water or had jumped out of fear of being killed.

Two National Park Service employees and a group of visitors, who were crouched in a corner of the memorial during the attack, hurried down to the pier to help three shooting victims and several other passengers out of the water.

A minute later, the Captain saw a Navy launch and two additional open motorboats hurrying to assist the stricken ship. He also heard sirens in the distance and saw flashing lights approaching the *Arizona* Memorial Visitor Center located across the harbor.

Anger now replaced shock on the main and upper decks as the uninjured passengers scrambled to assist the wounded. A woman yelled over and over that her husband and four other people were dead on the main deck. Cries of pain and anguish filled the air while the captain repeatedly radioed for medical help and passed along a description of the helicopter.

1

WAIMEA BAY, OAHU, HAWAII

The morning sunlight glinted off the water as the large, smooth ocean swells peaked into steep sets of waves. Theresa Garney slowed the descending helicopter while she watched a line of surfers paddle their distinctively colored boards out beyond the crests of breaking waves. With powerful strokes, the majority of the surfers propelled themselves to the prime position where the largest rollers were forming.

Once in place, they paddled swiftly toward shore to attain the speed they needed to catch the momentum of the wave. After the surfers had topped the crest of a huge breaker, they rose first to a kneeling position, then popped upright and coasted down the towering face of the wave until it went flat near the shoreline.

Theresa Louise Garney, who enjoyed surfing and scuba diving on her days off, studied the daring windsurfers further offshore before she shifted her gaze to the experienced surfers closer to the beach. The trim, athletic young pilot knew that only the best surfed diagonally toward the shore at Waimea Bay, especially under heavy surf conditions.

The hordes of spectators sprawled on the beach casually glanced up at the first sound of the colorful JetRanger. They were accustomed to having the "Sky Nine" helo film various surfing contests, along with other sporting events around the island. Many of the local sun-worshipers, who religiously watched Theresa's airborne reports on television, happily waved at the Channel 9 helicopter.

The blue-eyed brunette with the pixie haircut and impish smile was a popular island celebrity who was highly respected for having saved the life of a tourist who had been swept out to sea.

Fighting high winds and choppy waves, she had lowered the JetRanger's landing skids into the ocean next to the stricken swimmer. The exhausted man wrapped his arms and legs around the metal frame, clinging in desperation while Theresa carefully flew him to the safety of the beach and his grateful family. After the incident, she became the official ambassador of goodwill for the television station.

Theresa lowered the collective-pitch lever and maneuvered the helicopter closer to the breaking waves. Cliff Ackerman, the station's wizened veteran cameraman, continued to film the darkly tanned surfers while she skillfully flew sideways for a better camera angle.

Theresa placed the nimble JetRanger in a stationary hover while her cameraman panned the beach from the modified camera port.

The powerful rotor blade downwash whipped the surface of the ocean into a frothy gale, sending sheets of spray up through the tail rotor. She eased the helo back to keep the mist from floating over the surfers.

Finally, Theresa pressed the intercom button. "Have you got enough, Cliff?"

"Yeah, almost. I'd like to move up and away from the breakers so I can get a panoramic effect."

"Okay, here we go."

With the dexterity of a thoracic surgeon, she worked the cyclic-pitch lever, tail-rotor control pedals, and collective-pitch lever to execute a coordinated climb while the Sky Nine helicopter moved sideways. Theresa was a seat-of-the-pants natural, whether she was at the controls of a helicopter or an aerobatic biplane.

Ackerman let the video camera swing along the coastline and then leaned inside. "That's a wrap."

"Okay."

Canting the nose down, Theresa smoothly added power to accelerate. "Do you want to check Makaha before we head back?"

The world-famous four-meter waves that sometimes formed along Makaha Beach could propel expert surfers for over half a mile.

"Why not?" He popped a fresh stick of cinnamon gum in his mouth. "I've got a feeling that this is gonna be a slow news day."

Climbing to 4,400 feet to clear the Waianae Mountains, Theresa adjusted her headset and increased the volume on the mobile radio, selected the discrete switch, then raised the edge of her boom mike to her mouth.

"Sky Nine to base."

The instant response surprised her.

"Sky Nine," blurted the familiar female voice, "we've been trying to contact you. Where are you?"

Theresa looked down to her left and then glanced at the runway paralleling the shoreline on the right. "Sky Nine is a mile west of Waialua, just crossing the coast east of Dillingham Field."

"Stand by."

The radio remained silent for a few seconds.

"We don't have all of the information yet," the excited dispatcher continued, "but there's been some type of mass shooting at Pearl Harbor—actually, it happened at the *Arizona* Memorial about fifteen to twenty minutes ago."

"Sky Nine copies, and we're en route." Theresa glanced at Kaala Peak and then out toward Ford Island. "We should be there in approximately ten to twelve minutes if we can get priority handling from approach control."

Another pause followed the acknowledgment.

"Sky Nine, it looks like we'll be ready to go live—they want live coverage as soon as you're on the scene."

"We're set to transmit. Sky Nine out." Theresa turned to Ackerman and pressed the intercom switch. "Cliff, did you catch that?"

"Yeah. You want me to monitor base while you talk with approach?"

She nodded her thanks and quickly tuned the VHF radio to Honolulu Approach Control on 119.1 megahertz. She was about to press the transmit button when two Hawaiian Air National Guard F-15 Eagles streaked over the JetRanger, then snapped into punishing knife-edge turns. The fighters emitted streaks of grayish-white vapor from their wingtips as they rapidly decelerated.

"Well," Cliff drawled with his usual trace of sarcasm, "the Air Force is out burnin' up those tax dollars."

Ignoring the remark, Theresa kept an eye on the jets and keyed her radio transmit button. "Honolulu Approach, Sky Nine with a request."

"Sky Nine, squawk three-three-four-six," the radar controller shot back in a crisply detached tone.

"Thirty-three-forty-six," Theresa replied while she switched her radar transponder code to the appropriate setting.

Cliff Ackerman pointed to the Air Guard fighters. "The jet jockeys are slowin' and closing on us."

She nodded nonchalantly, but a warning bell was going off in her mind. Something wasn't right, and the controller had seemed unusually strained, almost hostile.

"Sky Nine is in radar contact," the staccato voice said, then went on in the same crisp fashion. "Sky Nine is hereby directed to fly to and land at Barbers Point. I repeat, you are instructed to proceed directly to Barbers Point and land."

An ominous feeling sent a chill down her spine. Except in the event of a declared emergency, Theresa knew that FAA regulations required that she comply with ATC instructions in an area in which air traffic control is exercised. However, she questioned if they could order her to land at the naval air station.

She breathed slowly and forced herself to be calm. "On whose authority?"

"On the authority of the Honolulu Police Department and the Federal Aviation Administration."

Theresa and Cliff exchanged disbelieving looks. Even though she was wearing dark-green aviator sunglasses, he could see the concern etched on her face.

"Sky Nine, do you copy."

Theresa glanced at the McDonnell Douglas F-15s and jabbed the transmit button. "Sky Nine copies," she answered with aplomb, "but I want an explanation about the fighters, and why I'm being forced to land at Barbers Point."

Her earphones remained silent.

Ackerman selected intercom. "You been skippin' out on your parkin' tickets?" he nervously asked.

Before she could answer, the approach controller issued new directions. "Sky Nine, contact Barbers Point Tower on one-three-two-point-six-five."

Now is not the time to argue. "Thirty-two-sixty-five," she said evenly, eliminating the first number since all VHF frequencies began with the number one.

"Cliff, give the station a call."

He snorted and shook his head in disgust. "They aren't gonna believe this."

"Something tells me they will."

Selecting the tower frequency for the Barbers Point Naval Air Station, Theresa reminded herself that she was a seasoned professional pilot. Besides, they would be on the ground soon and the mystery would be solved.

Ackerman gazed at the intimidating F-15s while the pilots let the sleek fighters drift apart.

"Sky Nine to base," he said hastily while he watched the landing gear extend from the flight leader's Eagle, then saw the wheels drop out of his wingman's aircraft. "Do you copy, base?"

The dispatcher's reply had been interrupted. "—ave received reports that a helicopter was involved in the shooting. Stand by."

Theresa made a slight course correction and waited to call the naval air station tower.

"Base—base to Sky Nine," the voice sputtered, then slowed after a moment. "The police have just arrived, and from what I understand, a helicopter fired guns at a Pearl Harbor cruise ship. They're saying—wait a second—they just said that the ship was full of Japanese tourists."

The woman paused while someone in the background spoke to her. "I've just been told . . . that witnesses claim it was our Channel Nine helicopter."

Stunned by the absurdity of the allegation, Theresa Garney arched her eyebrow and gave her cameraman a long look. Cliff Ackerman was incredulous, and it showed in his blank stare.

He laughed under his breath and then keyed his mike. "You might explain to the HPD that Sky Nine is not equipped with guns."

"They're right here," the mobile radio operator warned. "You might want to speak to them in person."

Theresa flashed Ackerman a disapproving frown and then started a slow descent. "Barbers Point Tower, Sky Nine is with you, fifteen north, negative ATIS." The JetRanger was not equipped with a UHF radio that could receive the Automatic Terminal Information Service.

"Sky Nine, Barbers Point Tower," the gravelly voice responded. "You're cleared to land on the numbers for runway one-one, next to the security vehicles. Winds are two-one-zero at eight. Altimeter two-niner-niner-one."

Theresa acknowledged the landing clearance and pushed the intercom button. "Cliff, what the hell is going on? Who would use a helo to gun down people on a tour of Pearl Harbor?"

"Someone with a vendetta and a sick mind," he answered uncomfortably, "who knows how to fly a helicopter."

She scanned the runways at Barbers Point. "Where do you figure our double is now?"

He thought for a moment, then gave her one of his infectious smiles. "I don't have a clue, but I can tell you one thing for damn sure."

Theresa gave him a knowing look. "We're in trouble."

He opened another stick of gum. "That's right, and we're gonna be the center of attention in Honolulu."

Her glance slid to Ackerman and then to the fighters as the pilots added power and retracted their wheels.

"No doubt," she agreed with a hint of irritation in her voice, "but the station's ratings will go up, and you know that's all that matters in this business."

2

NORTHWEST OF STEAMBOAT SPRINGS, COLORADO

Tadashi Matsukawa waded into his oversized spa and uncorked a bottle of wine from his French vineyard near Epernay, in the Champagne region. He selected a flute glass from the outdoor bar next to the bubbling water, then poured a liberal amount of the effervescent white wine and settled back to gaze across the meadows of his 1,780-acre ranch located at the foot of the Rocky Mountains. He was proud of the magnificent spread, but what he was most proud of was the fact that he had purchased the ranch with a sizable U.S. government grant.

A large man by Japanese standards, Matsukawa had wide cheekbones and a broad, slightly flattened nose. His piercing eyes were almond brown with a trace of pigment edging into his off-white eyeballs. The intelligent eyes behind the gold-framed spectacles seldom blinked when Matsukawa stared down a business opponent. His hands were soft, with puffy fingers and neatly manicured nails polished and shining from the protective clear coat. Not yet fifty, Matsukawa was a billionaire with a solid reputation for being ruthless and unforgiving.

He fervently believed in the Japanese tradition of Bushido—the feudal-military code that valued personal honor and proper action above the life of an individual. He admired the exploits of the kamikaze pilots so much that he had collected a number of expensive mementos from the families of the sacrificial aviators.

Tadashi Matsukawa, who had received his Master of Business Administration from Harvard, was programmed from early youth to be in the fast lane. Only the brightest young management trainees of Japan's most successful international corporations are allowed to apply to the oldest institution of higher learning in the United States. The remaining candidates, according to their initial performance evaluations and academic ranking, matriculate to Stanford, Columbia, or a host of other top-notch business schools.

After graduating with honors, Matsukawa had left Cambridge and returned to Japan, where he thoroughly impressed his superiors with his acute business acumen. His natural talent for commercial enterprises was highlighted by a shrewd knack for judiciously handling capital. Matsukawa's rapid rise to the top of the executive ranks surprised few of his colleagues, and he soon began forming his own corporation. Three days after his thirty-first birthday, the multimillionaire resigned from his parent corporation and devoted every waking moment to increasing his expanding fortune.

Matsukawa's vast empire was structured on the foundation of what he perceived to be rectitude. His decisions were made in accordance with what he believed, based on his logic alone. In his mind, business dealings were tantamount to waging war. More than anything, Matsukawa enjoyed the intellectual challenge of pummeling his opponents until their will to win finally evaporated.

He and his fellow business titans from Japan's six largest cartels, known as *zaibatsu,* took pleasure in laughing among themselves about dealing with the naive Americans and their self-important but faint-hearted trade representatives.

After years of business meetings with a number of chief executive officers of major American corporations, Matsukawa was still amazed at their ignorance of Japanese social realities and economic concepts. The Americans, who always acted like benevolent parents to wayward children, expected the Japanese business and political leaders to simply get in line and behave.

As one of the most powerful members of the Heiwa Shokai Investment Group, Matsukawa always relished debating U.S. leaders about the free-trade policy—until now. He was tired of trying to explain the Japanese business philosophy to the slow-witted Americans. They obviously could not accept the fact that controlling production, distribution, and prices, combined with a government that acted as a shepherd, was a more efficient system of capitalism than the U.S. model.

For the most part, everything had gone Matsukawa's way until the New York City building boom went bust in 1990. After paying over $1.2 billion for 85 percent of an expanding property-development company, the Heiwa Shokai Investment Group had lost over $550 million when the properties were devalued.

That was the beginning of a number of setbacks for the wealthy industrialist, including heavy losses in the Tokyo stock market. Next came the deflation of the real economy and the associated plunge of corporate profits.

When the stock market dropped over 27 percent, Matsukawa and members of the other cartels encouraged the Japanese parliamentary panel to create a securities watchdog to monitor the Nikkei. While they waited for the panel to act on the perplexing securities problem, Japanese economists nicknamed the downturn *baburu no hokai,* or explosion of the bubble.

Fifteen months later, Matsukawa barely avoided a major scandal when two bank officials who had approved loans for him were found to be involved in fraudulent transactions with the billionaire.

Matsukawa calmly lied about his involvement with the bankers while he diverted large sums of money from their banks to a banking company where the chief executive officer was on the industrialist's payroll.

Matsukawa also experienced significant losses from speculative art, real estate holdings in California, and from his investments in the automobile industry. He was astounded when the

U.S. Commerce Department ruled that Mazda and Toyota were illegally dumping minivans on the American market.

To Tadashi Matsukawa, dumping was merely good business that happened to be underwritten by the Japanese government. Matsukawa would flood a U.S. market with a quality product at a price below his competition's cost, wait for the various competitors to give up and go out of business, then raise the prices when he dominated the industry.

The business practice of dumping had worked fine until the Americans began to retaliate. People who knew the feisty Japanese businessman had learned not to mention the United States and automobiles in the same sentence.

His biggest single setback, which continued to consume him with rage, was the loss of $114 million in a patent dispute involving a video system for aircraft simulators. A federal jury in San Francisco ruled that one of his companies had intentionally infringed a patent held by an American inventor. Reluctantly, Matsukawa settled out of court to keep from tarnishing his corporate image, but the personal humiliation was indelibly imprinted in his mind.

Matsukawa was a volatile man with very little patience for people who didn't serve a useful purpose in his world. It was, however, painfully evident to anyone who knew him well that Matsukawa's character was, in one respect, fatally flawed. Unfortunately, Tadashi Matsukawa was born without a shred of conscience.

Although he was blessed with exceptional intelligence and unrivaled ingenuity, Matsukawa often fell victim to finding plausible reasons to circumvent his own logic. With a natural inclination to resist structure, he often let the explosive combination of superior intelligence and boredom lead him into bizarre schemes.

These traits became clearly apparent when the Liberal Democratic Party began to disintegrate. The violent conflict pitted the caretakers from the old guard against the ambitious young progressives. Matsukawa immediately saw a tremendous opportunity to take advantage of the turbulent process of political realignment. He smiled inwardly while turmoil swept through Japan's politics, knowing that the real power was still in the hands of the bureaucrats. The political chaos was a clever subterfuge to evade more pressure from the Americans.

The election upheaval, which was touted as the first step in a long campaign to reform the political process, was really a convenient smoke screen to alter Japan's course in history. Matsukawa, who laughed at the world for buying Japan's "stale-sake-in-new-bottles scheme," had his own grand design to help guide his country into a stronger and more competitive position.

His quiet solitude was interrupted when the English housekeeper stepped out to the pool deck. The middle-aged woman politely bowed before speaking. "Mr. Matsukawa, Senator Brazzell has arrived."

Matsukawa gave her a slow glance. "Tell him I'll be there in a few minutes," he said with a deep voice that cut through the cool air, "and fix him a double scotch on the rocks."

Senator Frank Brazzell, who had arranged for Matsukawa to buy a large share of a major U.S. investment firm, was the Chairman of the House Armed Services Committee. He was also the recipient of large under-the-table "contributions" from Matsukawa.

The unsmiling woman acknowledged the order and returned to the stately ranch home.

"Those lackeys in Congress will do anything for money," Matsukawa muttered to himself. He relaxed while he spent a few more minutes soaking in the warm water. The idea of keeping a U.S. Congressman waiting appealed to him.

Matsukawa and a number of other chief executive officers of Japanese mega-corporations had a great deal of influence over many Congressmen, including members of the House Science and Technology Committee, the House Appropriations Committee, and the Committee on Foreign Investment. The aggressive business leaders also had the Secretary of Commerce in their pocket and paid huge sums of money to former U.S. government officials to act as lobbyists for Japan.

Like Tadashi Matsukawa, most Japanese CEOs made sizable donations to many American colleges and universities. The ongoing endowments allowed the Japanese executives the privilege of arranging for the children or grandchildren of certain U.S. legislators to be accepted by the most prestigious universities in America, regardless of their academic qualifications.

The astute business leaders not only paid for the children's educations, they made sure the youngsters were offered well-paying jobs when they graduated. Most of the offers came from former American companies that were now owned by the large Japanese conglomerates.

If a legislator happened to chair an important committee, like the House Ways and Means or the Committee on Armed Services, Matsukawa quietly guaranteed the Honorable public servant's financial future in return for special consideration for his projects. The cozy arrangement, which provided a win for both parties, made perfect sense to the Japanese executive and the American politicians.

Matsukawa's worst fear was that some morning the American people would wake up and realize that the Japanese, in collusion with many of the elected officials on Capitol Hill, had economically raped their country.

Matsukawa believed that it was time to confront the arrogant Americans before the mood in the United States became both tougher and openly hostile. He viewed America as a debt-ridden nation in decline, plagued with crime and drugs and riddled with undisciplined minorities and a never-ending wave of undesirable immigrants.

He also bought protection from organized labor, and, through a distant third party, paid large sums to Japanese terrorist groups to stage anti-American attacks on U.S. facilities and citizens. Like the mythical Greek soldier who threw a stone in the midst of rival armies to get them to fight each other, Matsukawa relished fomenting trouble between Japan and the U.S.

In addition to his vast holdings and international influence in the business world, Tadashi Matsukawa was most pleased that he had access to the innermost chambers of the Central Intelligence Agency. His mole was a highly respected senior administrator in the Agency, but the American was afflicted with the common weakness of man—greed.

The career spook desperately wanted to retire and enjoy the largesse Matsukawa had provided, but the Japanese businessman kept upping the ante and the pressure. Now the billionaire wanted every thread of evidence the CIA gathered in connection with the assault on the cruise ship at Pearl Harbor. The worst fears of the lifelong bureaucrat were beginning to come true; he would never be able to retire while the ruthless Japanese executive held his future just out of grasp.

Rising from the water, Matsukawa paused to look at the pristine meadow at the base of the heavily wooded mountains. He watched a deer stop and cautiously drink from the stream running through the meadow. He glanced at his watch lying on the wooden bench, then sloshed out of the Jacuzzi and reached for a towel. The time had arrived to shove the good Senator's feet to the fire.

3

PIMMIT HILLS, VIRGINIA

Stephen Wickham sprinted the last seventy-five yards of his nightly four-mile run. Finally, with his lungs heaving for air, the former college track and field star slowed to a trot, then to an easy walk, and looked up at the star-studded sky.

The night was so flooded with moonlight that the attractive homes in the quiet subdivision looked like props from an old movie; the ones that had been filmed during the day, then filtered to look like it was dark. The shadows always stood out like neon signs blinking in the night.

The sweltering heat of the late afternoon had rapidly dissipated, and a slight breeze stirred the trees when the former Marine Corps captain reached his driveway.

A graduate of North Carolina State University, Steve Wickham had attended the Marine officer candidate school at Quantico, Virginia.

Commissioned a second lieutenant in the Reserve of the United States Marine Corps, Wickham completed the basic school, then reported to Camp Pendleton Marine Corps Base, near San Clemente, California.

During his tours of duty in Southern California, Okinawa, and Iwakuni, Japan, he constantly studied foreign languages and became fluent in German and French. Like his father, who had served with distinction in the wartime Office of Strategic Services (OSS) and then later with the CIA, Steve wanted a career in the national intelligence organization.

Shortly after he left Japan and reported to Camp Lejeune, he distinguished himself as a combat leader and became a highly decorated veteran of the Grenada invasion.

With a chestful of ribbons and a personnel jacket full of excellent fitness reports, Steve vacillated about leaving the Marine Corps. Sure, he told himself over and over, staying in the service offered a certain amount of security, but he knew that he would always wonder if he could have been a good intelligence agent. Besides, long-range security had always taken a backseat to Steve's desire for adventure.

Wickham made his decision after talking with two senior officers who had elected to make their careers in the Corps. Quite simply, they had explained over beers at the Lejeune O Club, they stayed in the service because they had families to support and the civilian job market was too uncertain.

After seeing the longing in their eyes, Steve knew what he had to do; what he was able and suited to do. Although he thoroughly enjoyed the Marines, he had always dreamed of a career in the CIA.

He was a bachelor who banked most of his paychecks in long-term savings, so in his mind he had nothing to lose and everything to gain.

Less than three months later, attired in a freshly pressed conservative gray suit and perfectly shined black shoes, he reported for work at Langley, Virginia.

Over a decade later, Steve Wickham was still handsome, with shallow furrows in his brow, sea-green eyes that exuded charm, and a square jaw which showcased his even teeth. At six feet one inch, trim and dark-haired, the senior operations officer for the Central Intelligence Agency looked younger than his age.

He was well liked and had established a solid reputation for successfully completing the most complex and hazardous assignments. Some members of the White House staff, along with a number of his associates, considered Steve a hero.

Wickham had recently returned from an extended period of service with the world-renowned British Secret Intelligence Service, known by the World War II designation of MI-6. The coveted assignment was reserved for the rising stars in the intelligence community.

During his fourteen-month stay in England, Steve enjoyed the opportunity to step away from the operations aspect of his profession. The Director of the SIS, an anonymous figure known as "C" in British governmental circles, had personally approved Wickham's request to work in the intelligence sector.

After years of being involved in various clandestine operations, Steve finally got the chance to hone his skills in gathering global intelligence and producing finished reports for his superiors.

Now that he was back at Langley, and still attached to the operations directorate, Steve was contributing to the definitive reports known in the Agency as National Intelligence Estimates.

The NIEs were closely reviewed by the Agency's Intelligence Board and then presented to the President of the United States. They represented the culmination of the CIA's work in tracking and forecasting world events.

When Steve reached his front porch, he grabbed the clean towel he had thrown across the railing and wiped the perspiration off his face. He entered his spotless home and went straight to the refrigerator for a cold beer.

After he popped the top off a chilled bottle of Miller Lite, he took a long drink and checked his answering machine. The blinking green light beckoned him to push the playback button.

Simultaneously, Steve clicked on the television and stabbed the play message button. He absently listened to a message from his former wife while he tuned the television. Steve stared at the screen while he listened to a second call, a short message from the Director of the CIA.

Mesmerized by the video he was seeing, Steve ignored the call from the ranking man in the Agency as he watched the riveting drama unfold on the screen. The amateur video, which was being replayed in slow motion, had recorded a scene of devastation that shocked Wickham.

He stared at the helicopter while two automatic weapons sprayed a barrage of fire straight at the camera. A second later, the picture tilted down and Steve could hear a tremendous commotion in the background. The picture became a series of blurs as he listened to a multitude of screams interspersed with gunfire, shouts, and yelling.

"Christ Almighty . . ." he said quietly while he turned up the volume. "This is unbelievable."

A different video camera recorded the departure of the helicopter as it turned and gathered speed. Wickham looked at the distinctive identifying symbol of a television station on the side of the JetRanger.

"What the hell is going on?" he said to himself.

The usual smile on the face of the familiar anchorwoman had been replaced with a grim set to her jaw.

"Tensions in Honolulu continue to escalate as authorities attempt to locate the pilot of the helicopter that opened fire on the Pearl Harbor tour ship.

"As word spread of the tragic attack on the Japanese-chartered tour ship, hundreds of outraged Japanese tourists protested at police headquarters, demanding protection. Another large group gathered at the Halekulani Hotel for an organized public demonstration.

"We have learned that a helicopter painted in the colors of Honolulu television station KGMB—a JetRanger similar to the chopper that opened fire on the tour ship—was forced to land at Barbers Point Naval Air Station shortly after the incident.

"Authorities have confirmed that the television station pilot and her cameraman were interrogated and released about an hour and a half ago.

"In related news, the reaction in Japan to the horrifying shooting spree has been described as a mixture of anger and hysteria. We hope to have a report from downtown Tokyo in the next few minutes."

The newscaster paused and glanced away from the camera for a brief second.

"I've been told that we now have a live report from our correspondent in Hawaii. Dave."

The picture went blank, then focused on a middle-aged reporter in a polo shirt. His hair and facial features suggested that he was a native Hawaiian. Behind him, across the harbor, a dozen boats surrounded the *Star of Honolulu* and the closed USS *Arizona* memorial.

"Helen, senior officials in the Honolulu Police Department have confirmed that seven people were killed during the brutal shooting at Pearl Harbor."

He glanced at his notes before continuing. "The latest figures that we have indicate that sixteen people were injured, eleven with minor injuries, and the others are described as serious or critical."

"Dave," she asked with a touch of sadness in her voice, "do the authorities have any leads at this point? Any idea who might have been flying the helicopter?"

A pained look crossed the man's rugged face. "No, Helen." He shrugged and cast a look at the war memorial. "From all accounts, witnesses to the shooting agree that the pilot appeared to be a Caucasian, but the police are simply baffled. An extensive aerial search is under way, including both military and civilian aircraft, but so far no trace of the helicopter has been reported." He heard his cue. "David Kaiulani, reporting from Honolulu, Hawaii."

Wickham finished his beer in three gulps, then pushed the mute button on the remote control and called the Director of the CIA.

The phone rang three times while Steve felt the anxiety build. He wasn't fond of the newly appointed Director, and he made every attempt to distance himself from Paul Holcomb.

Wickham, like many of his peers, wondered how the former Army major general had surfaced in command of the CIA. The man was reasonably competent technically, but his logic and social skills were not what one would expect of a flag-rank officer, let alone someone responsible for directing a sophisticated intelligence agency.

The truth of the matter, as Wickham discovered only weeks after Holcomb ascended to his position, was that his father had been a four-star general who used his wide-ranging influence to get his son through West Point. Although young Paul graduated near the bottom of his class, his father's extensive political connections carried him all the way to two stars.

Unfortunately for Holcomb, the Secretary of the Army finally pulled the plug on the major general's less-than-spectacular Army career. In order to smooth any ruffled feathers of the elder General Holcomb, the powers-that-be agreed to give his son a reasonable period of time as the Director of the CIA. The retirement agreement would look good on his résumé and biography. Besides, the President himself kept a firm hand on the Agency, so Paul couldn't do too much damage during his short tenure.

"General Holcomb," the hollow voice exclaimed. Paul Holcomb was using the speakerphone in his den.

"General Holcomb, Steve Wickham returning your call."

"Yes, Stephen," he said in his nasal Bostonian accent, "glad to hear from you. I suppose you've heard about the shooting—the incident in Hawaii?"

"Yes, sir. I just saw it on television."

"Well," Holcomb continued impatiently, "back when I was the C.O. of Schofield Barracks, we didn't have any trouble with the goddamned Japs in Hawaii. They stayed in their place—not like those overbearing bastards who cruise around Pearl Harbor like they own it."

Wickham seized the moment. "General, you asked me to call."

"Yes," he answered cryptically and cleared his throat. "The Chief launched two missiles late this afternoon."

Holcomb had an underlying contempt for the President and always referred to him as the Chief. Even though the President had appointed him to his post at the CIA and helped smooth his Senate confirmation, Holcomb still believed the former governor could have countermanded the Secretary of the Army and salvaged his career.

Holcomb coughed and raised his voice. "One of them landed on the FBI building and the other one landed in my office."

Unsure of how he should reply, Steve remained silent and glanced at the television. The network was replaying video of the helicopter assault on the tour ship.

"The White House has put a priority on finding the person, or persons, behind the attack before things get out of control." As he always did when he had important information, Holcomb paused for effect. "The Chief wants to clamp a lid on this before the Japs bomb Pearl Harbor again." Holcomb punctuated the statement with a hasty chuckle.

Caught off-guard by the remark, Wickham inwardly cringed. The few times he had been around Paul Holcomb, Steve sensed that he was a callous, intolerant man. But his open contempt for the Japanese people came as a surprise to Steve.

"I understand his concern," Wickham replied diplomatically.

"That's good, because you've been nominated to work on the shooting incident with two of the finest from the FBI's Criminal Division."

"Nominated?"

"By the Chief himself," he announced with undisguised sarcasm. "He's impressed by your previous accomplishments, and our records indicate that you have a working knowledge of the Japanese language."

"That was years ago, when I was stationed in Japan."

"Well, we don't argue with the Chief."

Steve reached for a pad and pencil. "When do I leave?"

"We're going to fly you from Andrews to Chicago tonight, and, let me see my notes . . . you need to be at Andrews by twenty-two hundred, and you've got a reservation on United in the morning."

Holcomb reached for his reading glasses. "United flight one eighty-seven, departing at zero-eight-twelve. One of the FBI people will be on the flight with you, and the other agent will join you during your stop in San Francisco. Any questions?"

"Yes, sir," Wickham answered while he viewed another replay of the cold-blooded attack at Pearl Harbor. "Do you happen to know the name of the agent in Chicago?"

"Marcus Callaway," he answered with a pronounced nasal accent. "He's a crackerjack ballistics expert and antiterrorism specialist."

Steve scrawled as fast as he could. "General, is there anything else you can tell me about the shooting incident?"

"You know as much as I do," Holcomb answered lightly, "but we'll have a full brief sent to the FBI agent in Chicago so you can go over it tomorrow during your flight."

"Yes, sir."

"Stephen." Holcomb paused for a moment. "The Chief told me that we—the CIA and FBI—had better close ranks and find out who's behind this incident, so I damn sure expect results."

"Yes, sir."

"We can't afford to have the situation spiral out of control," Holcomb stated flatly, "like that goddamn Rodney King fiasco."

Wickham forced his reply to be pleasant. "I understand, General. Have a nice evening."

"The same to you."

"Thanks."

Steve absently placed the receiver down and mentally replayed the Pearl Harbor video, then raised the phone and returned the call from his former wife. She was out for the evening, so he left a message and hurried to shower, pack, and drive to Andrews Air Force Base.

4

OSAKA, JAPAN

The small air-conditioned bus followed Shinsaibashi-suji Boulevard across the river into Higashi ward, then turned toward Osaka Castle.

An attractive, quietly gracious young Japanese woman gripped the handrail at the front of the cabin and continued her running commentary. "The original castle was built in 1586 by the Grand Chancellor—*Dajo-daijin*—Toyotomi Hideyoshi and was then the largest castle in Japan. Chancellor Hideyoshi, who paved the way for the feudal age, required his military commanders to contribute stones during the three-and-a-half-year construction effort."

The group of elderly couples paid close attention to the polite guide as the bus slowed near Osaka Castle.

"The largest rock"—her delicate mouth smiled—"is known as *Higo-ishi* and was brought here by the celebrated General Kato Kiyomasa from the island of Shodo. The rock is almost six meters high and fourteen and a half meters in length."

The driver brought the vehicle to an imperceptible halt while the lady finished her narration. "After Toyotomi Hideyoshi's son, Hideyori, was defeated at the Battle of Osaka by the forces of Tokugawa Ieyasu, the besieged castle was destroyed.

Hideyori, the last of the Toyotomi, committed suicide while the castle was being plundered."

She glanced at the historic building, then continued the commentary. "Later, for reasons of prestige, the Tokugawa Shoguns rebuilt the castle. When the Meiji Restoration forced the Shogunate to abdicate in 1867, the castle was burned down by the retreating Tokugawa forces. The present castle is made out of reinforced concrete and was constructed in 1931."

She placed the microphone on its hook. "If you'll please follow me."

The quiet passengers, some of whom were helping each other to their feet, suddenly heard an engine rev to a high-pitched scream. They turned to see an oncoming truck racing toward their compact bus. What shocked them most was the large flamethrower that was protruding from the top of the van behind the cab.

A split second after the driver leaped from the truck, the flamethrower shot a high-pressure stream of blazing incendiary fuel straight into the side of the small tour bus.

The American passengers and their Japanese guides screamed in panic and backed toward the far side of the vehicle. Their desperate efforts were in vain. Three seconds later, the large delivery truck plowed into the bus and exploded in a thunderous fireball. A huge pall of gloomy black smoke rose into the overcast sky while the melting tires exploded like shotgun blasts.

O'HARE INTERNATIONAL AIRPORT

Steve Wickham gratefully accepted a steaming cup of tea and looked around the crowded hotel restaurant. Most of the early-morning travelers were dressed for business, with a sprinkling of vacationers clad in a wide variety of casual attire. A steady stream of jets roared overhead as the air traffic began to build toward maximum capacity of the system.

Steve methodically stirred his tea while he patiently waited for his breakfast to be served. The harried waitress finally arrived with his ham and eggs at the same time the special agent from the FBI approached the table.

Wickham guessed the man's height at six feet even and his weight at 190 pounds. He looked like he was in his early forties, but he had the solid, muscular appearance of a collegiate running back. There was little doubt that he had been an athlete in his younger years.

"Marcus Callaway," the agent announced and motioned for Steve to remain seated. "Don't let me interrupt."

Steve thanked the waitress and offered his hand. "Steve Wickham."

"A pleasure," Callaway replied good-naturedly and shook hands before he seated himself. "I didn't even need your picture."

"Do I look that obvious?" Steve grinned and plunged his fork into his scrambled eggs. He looked ordinary enough to blend in with most of the crowd, but his cautious eyes never stopped surveying everything and everyone around him.

Marcus chuckled and ordered coffee. "Sitting with your back against the wall is a dead giveaway."

"That's an old habit I picked up from a gunnery sergeant," Steve admitted and cut into his ham. "Aren't you going to have any breakfast?"

Callaway leaned over and talked in a conspiratorial whisper. "Don't tell anyone that I told you this, but I honestly like airline food."

Steve laughed aloud and almost choked. "You must have spent some time in the Marine Corps."

"Close. I was an Army platoon commander."

A black man from Baltimore's inner-city projects, Callaway had been a member of a neighborhood street gang until a concerned teacher rescued him from the streets. Mrs. Schapiro used her considerable influence and various contacts to help a gifted youngster reach his full potential.

Marcus became one of the beneficiaries of a scholarship fund established for minorities with special aptitudes. Thanks to the generosity of a wealthy philanthropist, who had known adversity and poverty before making his fortune, Callaway was able to finish high school at a private institution and then graduated with honors from the University of Maryland.

He faithfully corresponded with the frail white woman who had intervened to give him and other deserving youngsters a fresh start in life. The few times he had tried to thank Mrs. Schapiro, she had given him the same advice. "Thank me by helping someone else."

A nineteen-year veteran of the Bureau, Callaway's experience with international terrorism had been invaluable during the lengthy investigation of the Pan Am crash near Lockerbie, Scotland. He also spent many years assisting numerous foreign officials to better understand the terrorist phenomenon.

Wickham and Callaway were anxious to discuss the tragedy at Pearl Harbor, but they knew from experience that it was impossible to carry on an in-depth conversation amid the constant interruptions in a restaurant.

Steve paid their tab and they grabbed their luggage, then caught the courtesy van to the airport terminal. When they reached the entrance to their concourse, Callaway held up his identification folder, identifying himself as a special agent of the Federal Bureau of Investigation.

The stodgy female attendant at the metal detector closely scrutinized his credentials and looked at the slight bulge under his jacket next to his left biceps, then reluctantly waved him around the metal detector and into the concourse. The security people always got nervous when anyone carried a sidearm onboard an airliner, even if the passenger was an FBI special agent.

Wickham, who flashed his identification and stated that he too was carrying a concealed weapon, also went around the metal detector, then rejoined Callaway in the concourse. They boarded the United Airlines jet and went to the last row of first-class seats that were reserved for them. No one was assigned to the two seats directly in front of the agents or across the aisle from them.

Steve and Marcus opened their magazines and began to leaf through the pages. A minute later they gave their beverage orders to the flight attendant and then noticed a last-minute passenger ease into the seat across from them. The scrawny Japanese senior citizen was wearing a wrinkled suit and his bow tie hung askew. Wickham thought he looked like a retired civil servant traveling on a mileage-plus upgrade certificate.

Callaway waited until the aircraft taxied from the gate before he leaned closer to Wickham. "Steve, have you been briefed about the terrorist attack in Osaka?"

"Not by the Agency," he explained and paused while the flight attendant checked to see if their seat belts were fastened. "I caught the gist of what happened while I was packing my bags this morning."

"The Chukaku-Ha has taken credit for the attack," Callaway announced. "Are you familiar with the Chukaku-Ha?"

Steve nodded and lowered his voice. "Oh, yeah. They're the most powerful terrorist faction of the Japanese New Left. From what I know, they have worked hard to abolish the constitutional democracy and do away with the monarchy, then scrap the U.S.-Japan Security Treaty and toss the American military out of Japan."

"Toss *every* American out of Japan," Marcus declared with a concerned look. "If you count all the organizations in the New Left, which we believe consists of twenty-four factions, you'll find approximately forty thousand radicals, including their sympathizers. They are definitely a growing threat—a deadly threat, as we've just witnessed."

Wickham glanced at the wingtip for a brief moment before he turned to Callaway. "So you think the Chukaku-Ha decided on swift retaliation for the attack at Pearl Harbor, even though no one knows who was flying the helicopter."

"They hate Americans," Marcus quietly explained while the pilot stopped behind the other airliners waiting for clearance to take off. "They are convinced that it had to be an American, especially after all the witnesses agreed that the pilot appeared to be a Caucasian."

Steve cast a look at Callaway, noting the fire in his eyes and the anger in his voice.

"This was vintage Chukaku-Ha tactics," Marcus stated harshly. "They've used front-mounted flamethrowers on trucks to attack everything from the political party headquarters to the Israeli Embassy to the Kansai International Airport in Osaka. It's one of their favorite weapons."

"Marcus, how do you stop a bunch of fanatics who have an irrational attachment to a terrorist group?"

"It's very simple. You can't stop them."

Wickham shook his head. "Terrorism is replacing Communism as the world's greatest threat."

"True," Callaway continued sadly. "And here's another example of how they use their technical proficiency to obliterate a busful of retired couples from California and the poor Japanese tour guides."

"It's just the beginning," Steve added.

"I'm afraid so," Marcus admitted with a touch of irritation. "The Chukaku-Ha is well funded, well organized, and they have continued to concentrate on overthrowing the political system and philosophy they abhor."

"Dedicated, they are," Steve agreed blandly. "Some of our people believe that the Chukaku-Ha has ties to major players in the Japanese political hierarchy."

"I've heard the same thing," Callaway confided and leaned closer. "We have firsthand information linking the group to the internal rebellion and the corruption scandals that tore the Liberal Democrats apart."

Both men remained quiet while the flight attendant chatted with a nearby passenger.

"The Chukaku-Ha," Steve said at last, "is deeply embarrassed by Japan's political strife and lack of leadership and accountability at the top. They're tired of the bowing-down, hand-wringing image that is symptomatic of Japan's sensitivity about its stature and future."

"And they have the means to do something about it," Marcus insisted with a sudden frown. "The tactical skills of the group are imaginative and they use mortarlike weapons and timed incendiary devices to augment the flamethrower trucks. These people are receiving clandestine training from some of the sharpest young officers in the Self-Defense Forces."

"Have the Japanese authorities had any success in stopping the group?"

Callaway tried to conceal his contempt, but the effort failed. "Are you kidding? The police are afraid of the Chukaku-Ha, and they have a right to be concerned."

"You mess with the boys," Steve suggested, "and you find yourself at the bottom of Tokyo Bay?"

"Close. Floating in the bay has more impact. They like to send a visual reminder to those individuals who might be contemplating messing with them."

"Marcus," Wickham began slowly while his mind shifted to the helicopter attack in Hawaii, "have you received an update from the CIA—about the incident at Pearl Harbor?"

"I haven't heard a word from your people," Callaway replied while the aircraft inched forward, "but I can tell you the latest from my people."

Steve suppressed his irritation at the lack of critical communications from the Agency. The unwieldy and inflexible CIA bureaucracy collected data so rapidly that the analyzers had information overload. Situations and events changed so quickly that real-time information occasionally tended to get shuffled aside.

"We've got over two hundred agents," Callaway said matter-of-factly, "converging on the islands. Our people have been told to get on board with the CIA and find the sonuvabitch who was flying the chopper."

"Yeah," Wickham said lightly, "I got the same message last night, straight from the head honcho."

Steve suddenly noticed that the elderly Japanese passenger was staring at a page of his newspaper, but something seemed amiss. Wickham observed that he never turned a page and wondered how slowly did the man read?

"Marcus," Wickham began while he kept an eye on the

eccentric-looking man, "I understand that we're going to be working with another specialist from the Criminal Division."

"That's right." Marcus grinned. "And she is something else, believe me."

Puzzled by the remark, Steve thought he detected a hint of pride in Callaway's voice. He studied the smiling FBI agent for a few seconds. "She? What do you know about her?"

Marcus laughed and shook his head. "Her name is Susan Nakamura, and she's a Japanese-American who was born in Oakland. Susan's one of our best agents. She specializes in criminal cases involving Japanese."

Steve was impressed so far. "Interesting."

"She sure is," Callaway answered with a chuckle. "Susan is serious minded and intelligent, but in a quiet, almost shy way. She has a dogged determination and the patience of Job—traits which have been noted by all of her supervisors."

Wickham gave him a quizzical glance. "If she's assigned to the San Francisco office, why is she working on the Pearl Harbor case?"

"The same reason they assigned me to the case. The director handpicked certain agents who specialize in particular areas."

Wickham covertly studied the quiet Japanese man across the aisle. "I assume that Susan is familiar with the islands."

"Hawaii," Marcus confided while the airplane swung onto the runway, "has been Susan's second home since she was a young girl. Her favorite aunt—her father's sister—lived in Honolulu, and Susan spent her summers with her from the time she was a small child until she graduated from college, so she knows the islands like the back of her hand."

"Not a bad place to spend your vacations."

"No kidding," Callaway continued as the captain jockeyed the throttles forward and released the brakes. "Her aunt died three or four years ago and left Susan the home, so she lives there when she's in Honolulu."

Steve nodded and looked out the window while the heavily laden jet accelerated to rotation speed, then lifted gracefully into the smoggy sky.

Across the aisle, the rumpled Japanese passenger appeared to be absorbed in his *Chicago Tribune*. From his relaxed pretense, it wasn't apparent that his pulse was racing from the tidbits of information he had overheard.

5

WASHINGTON, D.C.

The President, followed by his Secretary of State, Bud Tidwell, walked ramrod-straight into the renovated Oval Office and sat down behind his well-organized desk.

The stark difference between weekday and weekend Washington was clearly evident this morning. The cars and buses that choked the avenues were in sharp contrast to the empty parking lots and deserted streets of the weekend. The working citizenry of the nation's capital were flooding into the heart of the metropolitan area from all their widely scattered suburban homes.

"Okay," the portly Commander in Chief declared, "we've got to get a handle on this situation. The Japanese people need reassurances that we'll find and prosecute the person, or persons, responsible for attacking the tour boat at Pearl."

Tidwell nodded his agreement.

"By the same token," the President went on, "we expect them to show a sense of urgency in pursuing the sonsabitches who killed the retirees in Osaka. It's hard to believe that the Chukaku-Ha is still operating after they launched incendiary projectiles at the Imperial Palace and fired rocket bombs at the Narita Airport.

"What kind of idiots run their police force?" the President blurted. "They should have cleaned out the terrorists years ago."

Tidwell sat down in one of the three chairs that had been arranged in front of the cherrywood desk. The Japanese Ambassador and a special envoy, who normally dealt with the U.S. Ambassador to Japan and the Under Secretary of State, were waiting to meet with the President and his Secretary of State.

The American Ambassador, who was considered a has-been figurehead by many members of the Administration, had suddenly fallen ill and was recuperating during an extended leave of absence.

"I agree about taking a strong stance where the terrorist group is concerned," Tidwell replied in his usual confident tone, "but I would like to cover a few unrelated issues before we speak with the Ambassador."

"This ongoing flap about the trade issues?" the President shot back with a disgusted look.

"I'm afraid so," Tidwell lamented, "and the continuing plutonium shipments from France."

Robert S. "Bud" Tidwell was a consummate statesman who believed in a no-nonsense approach when dealing with foreign governments. "We need to talk about those problems, and the information and telecommunications infringement on the previous agreements we signed."

Tidwell removed his spectacles and allowed his shoulders to sag. "You've gotta know the lights in the Kasumigaseki district have been burning through the nights while their leaders are doing the same thing we're doing . . . debating the next steps to take in this latest standoff."

"I'm sure you're right, Bud," the President said emphatically. "Both sides are eventually going to have to face these things head-on."

He swiveled in his chair to look outside, then turned back to Tidwell. "However, the incidents at Pearl and Osaka have ripped open some deep wounds from the past, and the prevailing mood has the potential to set off a series of major international confrontations."

"No question about it," Tidwell cautioned and took a deep breath, then slowly let it out. "We're sitting on a giant powder keg, and I think it's time we push for a summit."

"Bud"—the President smiled approvingly—"I was thinking the same thing. These guys have continued to stonewall under the guise of political revolution. I thinks it's time to call their bluff."

A rare smile creased Tidwell's face. "This is an excellent time to bring up a summit."

"As good as any," the President replied firmly. He glanced at his daily appointment schedule lying on the middle of the desk, then moved it aside and thought for a moment. "What's the current situation?"

"Not good, I'm afraid."

Tidwell opened his flat carrying case and retrieved two pieces of paper. "We have received an avalanche of reports about the violent anti-American protests in many cities in Japan, and we're seeing a groundswell of Japan-bashing beginning to take shape in some of our larger cities, especially in California. The media has seized on the attacks and it's the current hot topic on the talk shows."

The seasoned statesman, who often soothed the bruised egos of those individuals who crossed swords with the President, slid the papers back into his portfolio.

"Sir, these protests and racial clashes are becoming a firestorm that is feeding on itself while the goddamn media fan the flames."

"We can always count on the media vultures," the President said with a touch of sarcasm, "to take a bad situation and make it worse."

"They're all falling over each other trying to compete," Tidwell offered.

The President paused to sort through his options. "Bud, we need to stop the violence before we tackle the other problems with Japan. If we allow this situation to get out of control, it could really hurt us domestically."

"That's true." Tidwell nodded. "We've got to get a grip on things or we'll be dead in the water. I just received confirmation of three drive-by shootings in L.A.'s Little Tokyo district.

"Four Japanese-Americans are dead," Tidwell went on sadly, "and three others are in critical condition. People are canceling athletic and entertainment events because of the potential for outbreaks of racial violence."

The President, who was convinced that relations with the Japanese would only become more acrimonious, didn't want to continue the discussion. "Bud, let's talk about our options during the Cabinet meeting, okay?"

"Yes, sir."

"Right now," the President went on with undisguised irritation, "I want to get this game of posturing with the Japanese out of the way."

Tidwell quietly acknowledged the statement while the President touched the button that signaled his staff assistant in the reception room. Less than half a minute later the administrative aide escorted the two Japanese diplomats into the Oval Office.

SAN FRANCISCO

FBI Special Agent Susan Nakamura glanced at her watch as she drove her white Toyota Camry southwest on Market Street. After working all night on the latest information about the Pearl Harbor attack, Susan was running late for her flight to Honolulu.

She reached forward and selected an easy-listening FM station as she neared Golden Gate Avenue. A few moments later she saw a large crowd of people moving into the street near the Civic Center.

She began to slow down when she saw the flashing lights

from four police cars approaching from the opposite direction. Another anti-Japanese demonstration was forming.

The traffic slowed to a crawl as the mob of angry Caucasians charged a group of young Japanese protesters.

Susan was attempting to turn around when she saw an assortment of bottles, sticks, rocks, and other debris fly through the air. Heavily outnumbered, the Japanese were defenseless as the police began to fire tear gas into the unruly crowd.

Blocked in front and back by other cars, Susan sat helpless as the enraged mob broke and ran in her direction. She made sure her windows were up and the doors were locked, then reached for the 10-millimeter Smith & Wesson in her purse.

Two scraggly men who appeared to be drunk stopped by the hood of her car.

Susan stared straight at them and slid her weapon next to her leg. "Move on and do yourself a favor," she said through gritted teeth.

"Hey, looky here," laughed a skinny man with a birthmark on his face. "We got us a stinkin' Jap bitch drivin' a Japmobile."

"Yeah, man," his pal chuckled and put his hands on the hood and leaned forward. "Hey, bitch, how about doin' us both for the price of one?"

Susan's temper flared and she gripped the Smith & Wesson with a renewed strength. "You morons."

The man with the birthmark reared back and kicked the left front fender as hard as he could, almost losing his balance. "Whad'ya think about that, Tokyo Rose?"

Susan flipped her badge on the dashboard where they could be sure to see it, then gripped her weapon with both hands and slowly raised it above the steering wheel.

"Shit, man!" birthmark exclaimed. "A fuckin' cop!"

Both of the vagrants ran through the traffic and disappeared into the crowd east of the Civic Center.

After the adrenaline shock wore off, Susan's heartbeat finally slowed to normal as she continued toward the airport. She turned the radio off and thought about the escalating conflict between the Japanese and the Americans.

THE OVAL OFFICE

Ambassador Koji Hagura was a short, rubbery-faced man who epitomized the etiquette of the Japanese lifestyle and ancient traditions. Always the polite gentleman, Hagura never directly contradicted anyone. Instead, he would go out of his way to find an indirect and conciliatory way to express his view.

Educated at Boston College and Stanford, Hagura would occasionally smile at a particularly amusing story or joke, but he never laughed in front of the Americans. His mission was serious, and he was a proud man who relished being the Japanese Ambassador.

Special Envoy Yamagata Isoroku was a younger and thinner version of the Ambassador. He had adopted many of Hagura's mannerisms, but not the stiff, formal public face. Isoroku was very active in the Washington diplomatic social circles. He enjoyed the less-pretentious social style of the Americans, and he had quite a reputation as a raconteur of anecdotes after a couple of stiff martinis.

Although Isoroku often grew impatient with the Americans, whom he considered short-term thinkers, he kept his feelings to himself. Like Hagura, Isoroku believed that any sign of impatience, or any display of irritation, would be regarded as a loss of face.

After they entered the impressive office, Hagura and Isoroku stopped and bowed.

The President and his Secretary of State, who were standing beside the desk, returned the polite gesture with bows that were almost imperceptible.

Although the Japanese occasionally shake hands, especially to save face when an unknowing Westerner thrusts out a paw, shaking hands remains for them an unusual and uncomfortable personal experience.

The President motioned for his guests to have a seat while Tidwell sat to one side.

"Gentlemen," the President began slowly while he seated himself, "we offer you and the Japanese people our deepest sympathy for the unconscionable incident in Hawaii."

He specifically avoided using the words *Pearl Harbor*. "Let me assure you that we're doing everything in our power to bring to justice the person who committed the heinous act."

The President looked straight into the Ambassador's widely set, soft brown eyes. He could see the sincere pain in Hagura's demeanor.

"It was a cowardly act, and we are using every resource available to find and apprehend the person who committed this abominable crime."

Koji Hagura's usual air of self-assurance had been replaced with a rather bland, expressionless look. He waited a proper amount of time before he delivered the short speech he had practiced for the past two hours.

"Mr. President," he said at last, "we sincerely appreciate your kind words and thoughts. On behalf of Prime Minister Koyama and the Japanese people, I offer our humble apologies for the regretable terrorist attack in Osaka."

Yamagata Isoroku lowered his dark eyes and nodded in agreement. They were honestly embarrassed by the brutal reprisal, and fervently hoped the authorities in the National Police Agency would soon track down the culprits of the grisly mass murder.

"I have been authorized," Ambassador Hagura continued with genuine compassion, "to offer a sizable amount of financial compensation to the families of the victims."

The President darted a look at his longtime friend. Tidwell gave him a slight nod. Hagura was going out on a diplomatic limb. If the tender was rejected, Koji Hagura would lose face and the refusal would further arouse resentment between the two feuding governments.

"Secretary Tidwell," the President advised gracefully while he fixed them with a stare, "will be happy to assist you in any way he can."

Before Hagura could respond, the President continued in a pleasant manner, sensing the suffering of the two men. "I know this is a painful time for all of us, but I need to discuss a few items unrelated to terrorist activities."

Seasoned diplomatic veterans, Hagura and Isoroku steeled themselves and mentally reviewed their standard replies to the standard complaints from the Americans.

"We have become concerned," the President said firmly, "about the insidious and continuing deterioration in the relationship between our countries."

He paused to allow time for the two diplomats to adjust to the sudden change in topics.

"We admire your efforts toward self-sufficiency," the President admitted with just the right amount of enthusiasm, "but the continued expansionism in the areas of strategic industries, especially nuclear, aerospace, and particularly the area of conventional weapons, has become alarming."

The President knew that many countries, including some U.S. allies, were deeply distressed by the ever-growing Japanese Self-Defense Force, known as *Jieitai*. Many U.S. military leaders, including the Joint Chiefs of Staff, regarded Japan as a mushrooming military power.

"Mr. President," Hagura said dryly while he attempted to keep his neck muscles from tightening, "strategic endeavors and military matters are not my area of expertise."

The President allowed a tiny grin to cross his face, then demonstrated some of his finely honed political skills.

"Ambassador Hagura"—he smiled, revealing his even white teeth—"I'm a straightforward guy who likes to cut through the obscurations. I like everyone to just throw it on the table, out in the open, so we can discuss our problems until we reach an agreement, then implement the plan and stick to our decision."

The President had his prey cornered. "Don't you think that's the best way to iron out our differences?"

Hagura maintained his composure and simultaneously nodded his head and lowered his eyelids. He was aware of the American's reputation for coming across as a simple, down-home country boy and then nailing his adversaries to the wall. The intelligent, well-educated President was a formidable challenge, and Hagura was always on guard.

"We've had all kinds of meetings, assemblies, come-togethers, diplomatic exchanges, and days and weeks and months of endless discussions," the President declared and slowed his delivery. "And we're still not out of the starting blocks."

The Ambassador cleared his throat. "I assure you that our government would be pleased to open channels of communication if you wish to address certain specifics."

Concealing his frustration, the President caught Tidwell's look of concern. "Ambassador Hagura, since you're the direct link to Tokyo, how about arranging a personal meeting between the Prime Minister and myself—say in Lake Tahoe, or here if he so desires—in ten to twenty days? I know it's short notice, and I know your country has major political changes taking place, but I believe you would agree that time is of the essence."

Hagura and Isoroku were clearly uncomfortable with the suddenness of the suggestion.

The new Prime Minister didn't like the American President, and he had made that point crystal clear in front of Japan's leaders of industry as well as the bureaucrats who operated the government.

As a rising political power, Genshiro Koyama had also been extremely vocal to the previous Diet, Japan's former members of parliament. As a result of the concern generated in the legislature, a small number of the senior and more courageous members of the House of Representatives, the lower house, known as *Shugiin,* and the House of Councillors, Japan's upper house, known as *Sangiin,* had attempted to soothe Koyama's temper, but to no avail. He couldn't ignore the way the American government had led them on about the possibility of Japan building a next-generation FSX jet fighter independent of the United States.

When a wave of uneasiness about giving away sensitive technology swept the U.S., Japan had bowed to American pressure and agreed to codevelop the sophisticated warplane.

Genshiro Koyama, who at the time of the incident had been a front-running candidate for prime minister, had been one of the most staunch supporters for codeveloping the FSX. He fervently believed that Japan needed the advanced technology, no matter the cost to nationalist egos.

After successfully lobbying members of the Diet's lower house to go along with the proposal, Koyama had been deeply embarrassed when Congress pulled the rug out from under a hapless Japan.

Fearing a hostile reaction from their constituents, who were apprehensive about relinquishing the aerospace technology, Congress had initially killed the proposal.

After Genshiro Koyama had been politically humiliated, the FSX project had finally been resurrected and approved. The net result was a late start with a price almost twice the initial budgeted cost.

Ambassador Hagura studied the President's expression, then spoke in a quiet, measured voice. "We will be happy to convey your desire to the Prime Minister."

"I'll be looking forward to hearing from you." The President rose from his chair.

The surprised diplomats quickly rose to their feet. There was no doubt when a meeting with this President was over.

Koji Hagura maintained his serene composure. "Thank you, Mr. President. I will be in touch with you as soon as I have an answer."

The President forced a conciliatory smile. "We appreciate your cooperation, and I assure you that we will leave no stone unturned until we find the person who attacked the cruise ship in Hawaii."

The President turned to Tidwell. "Bud, would you mind

escorting our guests out? And set a time for your staff to meet with them."

"Yes, sir," Tidwell replied and made a small gesture toward the entrance to the Oval Office. "Gentlemen."

The two men graciously bowed to the President and quietly followed the Secretary of State to the reception room.

The President reached for his fountain pen, then wrote himself a reminder to call the families of the California retirees who had been killed in the Osaka massacre.

6

SAN FRANCISCO

By the time United Airlines flight 187 landed at 10:37 A.M., the damp fog that had been covering the city was beginning to dissipate. A few rays of bright sunlight filtered through the cool haze and warmed the shivering tourists at Fisherman's Wharf and Chinatown.

When the lumbering jet stopped at the boarding gate, Steve Wickham placed his magazine in the seatback pouch in front of him and turned to Callaway.

"Marcus, how about some fresh seafood and San Francisco sourdough bread?"

Callaway looked at his watch. "What time are we scheduled to leave?"

"Eleven fifty-five," Steve advised. "We've got over an hour to kill."

"You twisted my arm."

Steve rose from his seat and stepped into the aisle. He glanced at the slight Japanese passenger who had been sitting across the passageway. The man turned away from Wickham and closed his briefcase, then patiently waited for the other travelers to walk past his seat.

"The restaurant we're going to," Steve advised, "is definitely above average for an airport slop chute."

"Sounds good." Callaway stretched his legs and flexed his arms. "If I can find Susan, we'll take her to lunch."

"Sure," Steve said as they walked off the airplane. "I'm anxious to meet her."

After they exited the jetway, Steve went to secure a table in the restaurant while Marcus stayed in the waiting area to see if he could spot Susan Nakamura.

Fifteen minutes later, while Steve was reading the *San Francisco Chronicle,* Marcus and Susan walked in and caught his attention. He rose to greet them and was surprised when she eagerly extended her hand. He shook hands and seated her next to him.

Steve found her very attractive. She seemed poised and mature and had captivating almond eyes. Her nose was thin and delicate, and her cheekbones were high. She wore very little makeup and only a trace of lipstick adorned her small, perfectly formed mouth.

Susan's dark brunette hair was arranged in a stylish bob that underscored her sense of authority. She had a friendly yet reserved air about her, but always displayed a quick smile.

Her grace and natural beauty made people look at Susan, glance away, then look again. There was some hidden quality, some spark in her steely calm personality that made both men and women want to seek her out, to talk to her, to try to find out what made her such an alluring woman.

With degrees in accounting and criminology, Susan Nakamura was a promising candidate when the FBI, confronted by a multitude of discrimination suits, was forced to hire more female and minority agents. She overcame the sexual harassment and formidable obstacles in the male-dominated environment and graduated in the top 20 percent of her class. Now, after twelve years of law enforcement experience, she was one of the most respected special agents in the Bureau.

•   •   •

When the threesome finished lunch, Marcus excused himself and left to phone his office. There was a moment of hesitation before Steve turned to Susan.

"Would you care for some dessert?"

"I'd love some." She laughed casually. "But I've disciplined myself to forgo the calories."

Steve glanced at her eyes and forced himself not to stare at her smooth face. "I wish I could be that disciplined, but I guess everyone has their vices."

She let the remark linger for a moment, then looked straight at Wickham. "You don't seem to have any bad habits, other than driving too fast."

Steve gave her a questioning look. "Excuse me?"

"Our files," she continued evenly, "don't indicate any abnormalities in your background. Just a couple of speeding tickets to your credit."

Wickham laughed aloud and then noticed that a few customers were looking his way curiously. He leaned closer to Susan. "My dark side has obviously been well concealed."

She arched her eyebrows. "I hear that you're a great asset to the Agency."

"Well, don't believe everything you hear."

She decided not to challenge his remark. "Who do you think was flying the helicopter at Pearl Harbor, and where do you think the pilot and helo are now?"

"I don't have any idea," he admitted and let his eyes linger on her face. "However, I think we should start by contacting the FAA and getting a complete list of past and present rotary-wing qualified pilots, along with a list of registered helicopters."

Susan raised her attaché case, zipped it open, then handed him the list of pilots that had been supplied by the Federal Aviation Administration. Many of the helicopter jockeys were also rated as fixed-wing pilots. She also had a copy of the FAA Register of Aircraft and a Bell Aircraft maintenance-support database for locating all their helicopters.

Wickham was impressed, and a bit embarrassed that he had

underestimated Susan's capabilities. "Excuse me while I wipe the egg off my face."

"You've been traveling," she said pleasantly and reached for her notes. "I've been working all night, and we've got a lot going on. We're currently tracking down every rotary-wing pilot and the location of each registered helo like the one used in the attack, but I think we're going to find a number of loopholes."

Steve nodded and thought about the helicopter assault. "It wouldn't be too difficult to take an airliner from the mainland, attack the tour boat, hide the helicopter, jump back on a flight, and be back on the West Coast in short order."

"Especially," Susan stated calmly, "if you came over on the red-eye, hit the tour ship early in the morning, then caught a midday flight back to the Coast."

She stopped to analyze her logic. "People on the mainland who had seen the pilot late one day would again see him late the following day.

"A perfect alibi," she said evenly. "If it appears that the pilot was on the mainland when the crime took place in Hawaii, then that's a pretty good defense."

Wickham studied the long list of pilots. "If someone was going to try the airline approach, an alias and a good disguise would make it virtually impossible for us to trail them."

"Correct," she declared with an underlying excitement in her voice. "I think the helicopter is still on Oahu, or one of the neighbor islands, but it's probably been repainted by now."

Steve handed the FAA list to Susan. "Let's discuss the possibilities—the 'what-ifs.' Do you have any information on what kind of helo we're talking about? I know it's a Bell, but I don't know the model or type."

"Right here," she answered and pulled out another folder. "A number of experienced helicopter pilots have viewed the videos, and every one of them agreed that the helo is a Bell 206B JetRanger identical to the one operated by the television station."

"What's the speed and range?"

Susan consulted the JetRanger performance section that her staff had compiled in the wee hours of the morning. "Depending on the altitude and conditions, the speed is approximately one hundred fifteen knots, with a range of around three hundred fifty nautical miles at low altitude."

After some mental calculations, Steve finally spoke. "The pilot could have flown nonstop to any of the islands, even down to the sparsely settled areas on the big island, and still had plenty of fuel to spare."

"You're right, Steve, but I feel that fuel wasn't the critical element in the escape. It was the exposure of being seen in a brightly painted helicopter."

"That makes sense." He was impressed with her reasoning and with the amount of information she had assimilated in such a short period of time.

"The longer the pilot placed himself in a position to be seen," she continued with a slight shrug, "the worse the odds became of a successful evasion."

"You're right," he admitted and placed himself in the pilot's position after the assault. "The pilot, who was going a little over two miles a minute, probably didn't stay in the air for more than ten to twelve minutes after the attack."

"That's basically what I've been thinking," she responded a moment before Callaway approached them. "It would have been easy to land in a remote place, camouflage the helo, repaint it, then fly it out later."

Marcus waited until she was finished. "Speaking of helicopters, I just saw the TV station pilot—the Sky Nine pilot—being interviewed."

Wickham had an intuitive feeling that they needed to interview her. "She might be able to give us some valuable information plus some background profiles of the helo jockeys on the island."

"I've already sent a request," Susan informed him with a level gaze, "to meet with Ms. Garney tomorrow morning." She observed the surprise in Wickham's eyes. "It would be good for all of us to talk with her, then compare notes."

Before Steve could respond, Marcus changed the subject. He knew that Susan's penchant for being organized could be intimidating at times, especially if you hadn't had time to do your homework.

"We've got people crawling all over the Hawaiian Islands," Callaway informed them with a dour look, "and we haven't found a damn thing."

Susan observed Steve for a moment, then softened her approach. "We don't have much to go on now, but I'm confident we'll make progress once we arrive in the islands."

"I know we will," he replied and pointed to the front page of the morning *Chronicle*.

Bold headlines described the Japanese/American civil unrest in the streets of San Francisco and other major cities. Related stories prophesied problems with workers and management in Japanese-owned, American-based industries in the aftermath of the senseless killings at Pearl Harbor. Some of the articles about the attack were biased against the practices of the United States, while other stories lashed out at the terrorist reprisal on the American tourists in Osaka.

Steve started to say something, then abruptly stopped himself. Susan was Japanese-American, and criticism from both the Japanese and the American sides was probably difficult for her to deal with. The thought made him uncomfortable.

Susan caught the subtle change in his disposition. "It's a shame, isn't it?"

"Yes, it is," he agreed. "I'm convinced that humans are the most vicious, predatory animals on this planet."

The stories under the headlines explained about the anti-Japanese protests in Japan Town, known as Nihonmachi, a few blocks east of Fillmore Street. San Francisco police had been forced to arrest protesters and break up skirmishes at the Japanese Tea Garden in Golden Gate Park and at the Japanese Cultural and Trade Center.

One of the saddest stories recounted how Japanese students at the University of San Francisco had been pelted with raw eggs and water balloons filled with paint. Some had even been hit with rocks and bottles during the clash.

Steve motioned for their check, but Marcus and Susan insisted on splitting the bill three ways.

As they walked to their gate, Steve gave Susan a friendly smile. "Since you know all about me, warts and all, I'm anxious to find out more about you."

She returned the friendly gesture. "That's fair enough, but I don't want to bore you to death."

"You're in trouble now," Marcus laughed quietly and slowly shook his head.

"Trust me," Steve said while Susan rolled her eyes at Callaway. "I can handle it."

MISAWA AIR BASE, JAPAN

The low, ragged overcast seemed to hang suspended in a dark-gray hue a half hour after the sun had risen. The warm air was oppressively sultry and there was a total absence of wind on the crowded flightline. The humidity was peaked at 100 percent and a fine drizzle continued to bathe the home of the 432nd Fighter Wing of the United States Air Force.

East of base operations and the control tower, a multitude of McDonnell Douglas/Mitsubishi F-15J air-superiority fighters from Japan's Air Self-Defense Force were being prepared for a practice mission. The Japanese Air Force controlled the airfield and adjacent air traffic, but coordinated all military activities with the U.S.

The air base was beginning to stir, and the smell of freshly brewed coffee permeated the muggy air. The quiet solitude of the sleepy morning was abruptly shattered when two afterburning turbofans belched hot air and roared to life. The high-pitched whine of the powerful engines cut through the air while the pilots went through their checklists.

After a radio check with the 432nd command post, known as

Falcon Ops, the two men switched to clearance delivery and copied their Chuhi Two Departure with a Miyako Transition. Shortly thereafter, the two General Dynamics F-16 Fighting Falcons began taxiing toward the active runway.

Major Tony Lavancia, a combat veteran of Operation Desert Storm, was the leader for the scheduled training flight. The highly skilled pilot was well liked by everyone, especially the younger pilots, who were the recipients of his wisdom and years of aviation experience.

Behind and off to the side of Lavancia's wing, Captain Jeff McIntire watched his flight leader taxi over a large puddle of water. The spray kicked up by the fighter's exhaust blew past his wingtip and disappeared.

Although new to the squadron, "Gentleman Jeff" McIntire was an experienced fighter pilot who had recently been a top scorer at "Gunsmoke," the USAF air-to-ground weapons competition held at Nellis Air Force Base, near Las Vegas.

Many of his peers were convinced that Jeff McIntire, with his chiseled good looks and engaging personality, would be selected to fly with the Thunderbirds when he completed his present assignment.

When the two F-16s approached the end of the rain-soaked taxiway, the pilots switched to the control tower frequency. Seconds later they were cleared for takeoff on runway 28. Lavancia glanced at the fighter alert hangar, then taxied into position and waited for his wingman to align himself in trail and off to the side.

After a final check of their cockpits, the fighter pilots advanced their throttles and checked their engine instruments. When McIntire signaled that he was ready to roll, Lavancia released his brakes, then lighted the afterburner.

McIntire watched the tailpipe of his leader's plane spew a tongue of red-hot flames as his own afterburner ignited. The rapid acceleration pressed him into his seat while he jockeyed the controls to stay welded to his flight leader. Moments later, McIntire rotated his fighter when Lavancia raised his nosewheel off the runway.

After the two jets were safely airborne, Jeff McIntire snapped his landing gear up at the moment he saw his leader's wheels start to move. Jeff would fly tight formation while his leader would concentrate on flying by instruments until the fighters broke out of the thick overcast.

The control tower personnel watched the sleek fighters lift off the 10,000-foot runway, then followed the flight path of the white-orange afterburners as the jets approached the low, uneven dark clouds.

McIntire was smoothly working his controls to stay in perfect position as the jets were engulfed by the gray, foggy haze. A moment later a blinding flash and violent concussion stunned McIntire. He fought the controls as the aircraft began rolling and the nose tucked down.

Without warning, the observers in the tower saw a bright flash, followed by a tremendous explosion. They stared in horror while one of the jets tumbled out of the gray sky. The Fighting Falcon had been reduced to a huge fireball spinning out of control.

I've got to get out! Jeff realized as he frantically reached for the ejection-seat handle. His last thought was two seconds too late to save his life. McIntire's heart pumped the last surge of blood into his circulatory system as the ejection seat fired.

The shocked men in the tower watched a blazing pinwheel of jet fuel spray in every direction before the aircraft smashed into the ground. The stunned witnesses could feel the tower shake from the impact and explosion.

Filled with anger and grief, Major Tony Lavancia slowly walked around the crash site. The light rain that continued to drench the base had extinguished the last of the smoldering fires. Only a few wisps of gray-white smoke rose from the charred debris that had recently been a sleek, multimillion-dollar fighter plane.

His lip quivered when he thought about Jeff McIntire. The humorous, good-looking young man with the superior intellect and raw flying ability never knew what hit him. McIntire had ceased to exist when the spinning fighter hit the ground at the same moment the ejection seat fired.

His neck muscles ached with tension, but Lavancia ignored the pain and replayed the accident over and over in his mind. One moment Jeff was there, tucked in tight against his wing, and a split second later he was gone. Something wasn't right. There was simply no reason, no history of F-16s blowing apart in flight.

Something strange had happened to McIntire's fighter, but Lavancia had no idea what. He was intimately familiar with every system in the F-16, yet nothing came to mind that could cause this kind of disaster if it failed.

The team of investigators who were probing the debris of the blackened, twisted wreckage knew who Lavancia was and paid little attention to him. They understood his desire to be left alone.

Lavancia was expected to report to the flight surgeon while the details of the flight were still fresh in his mind. Afterward he would attend a debrief to go over the sequence of events leading to the fatal crash. But that wasn't what the tormented pilot wanted to do, not by any stretch of the imagination.

All Tony Lavancia wanted to do was have a very stiff drink and purge his emotions. Still in his rain-soaked flight suit, he sat down on the perimeter of the deep crater and stared blankly into the scorched hole where his friend had perished less than an hour before.

Fifteen minutes later, Lavancia's commanding officer, accompanied by the base chaplain and the flight surgeon, walked to his side and helped him to his feet.

7

UNITED FLIGHT 187

When the dessert dishes were cleared and the movie began, Steve gave Susan Nakamura a fleeting look. She was sitting by herself across the aisle, reading reports from a stack of papers she had retrieved from her briefcase. The three of them would wait to discuss the incident at Pearl Harbor until they had complete privacy.

Susan looked at Wickham and subtly motioned to the seat beside her, then neatly stacked her reading material on the foldaway tray. Her soft brown eyes narrowed and sparkled.

He secured his tray and moved into the seat next to Susan. "He went to sleep," Steve said in a low voice, "like he'd turned off a switch."

She leaned around him and glanced at Callaway. "He's the only person I know who could sleep through an earthquake."

"He doesn't waste any time," Wickham observed and fastened his safety belt. Ensconced in his seat, Steve turned to the alluring young woman. "So, you promised to tell me all about yourself."

She gave him a questioning look. "What would you like to know about me?"

There was an awkward moment before Steve made the adjustment to her straightforward style of conversation. "Actually, at the risk of sounding too forward, I'd like to know everything about you. It's not every day that I meet a Japanese-American who happens to be an FBI agent."

"You mean a Japanese-American FBI agent," Susan said patiently, "who happens to be a woman."

He swallowed and looked her straight in the eyes. "You're right, but you'll have to admit that's not something people in my line of work see every day."

"I suppose that's true."

"What made you decide on a career in the FBI?" Steve inquired innocently.

She turned slightly sideways to face him. "It's a long and boring story."

Steve could see that she was masking something that was very painful. "I didn't mean to upset you."

Susan relaxed her facial muscles and gave him a wide smile. "It's okay, believe me. I don't normally talk about it, but if you're really interested . . ."

"I'm *really* interested."

"When Pearl Harbor was attacked," she began without any sign of emotion, "my parents were newlyweds. They didn't have much money, so they were living with my mother's parents in East Los Angeles. Shortly after the war started, the FBI took my parents and grandparents right out of their home and placed them in a temporary war-relocation center."

Tilting her head, she stared absently out the window at the puffy white clouds, then pulled the shade to block the bright sunlight. "The relocation center was a section of converted stables at the Santa Anita racetrack."

Steve closed his eyes for a second and slowly let his breath out. He could only imagine the terror and degradation the innocent Japanese-Americans had felt.

"The saddest part about the internment," she continued, turning her head to look into Steve's eyes, "was that no one tried to sort out who was spying for Japan and who wasn't. If you were of Japanese extraction, you were guilty, period."

Maintaining eye contact, Steve gave her a soothing nod. "I know, and it wasn't fair, but we——"

"Many of the Japanese-Americans were kindhearted," she quietly interrupted, "loyal U.S. citizens, including my grandparents."

There was a long silence as Steve began to understand why Susan had been compelled to join the FBI. He suddenly had the clear impression that she was reading his mind.

"Sometimes," she said steadily, "when an organization does something so grotesque to innocent civilians, you want to challenge the system, to join the organization and rise to the top so you can work toward seeing that it never again happens to anyone, regardless of race or creed."

Susan quietly sighed while a nagging protest tore at her nerves. "I know that sounds idealistic, but I really believed that I could make a difference."

"And now?"

"Well, I suppose I've matured over the years," she conceded. "I realize now that I can't single-handedly change the system, but I still like to think that I've made an impact—in some small way."

She noticed the uncomfortable, almost grim look on Steve's face. "I didn't mean to get so serious.".

"I'm sorry, Susan. I was just trying to imagine what your family must have gone through—the humiliation and absolute loss of pride and dignity."

"It was beyond belief," she replied sadly and looked down for a moment. "For years I lived with the psychological scars that my parents tried to conceal under a façade of smiles and happy talk. They pretended, for the sake of their children, that everything was wonderful, when deep inside they were living in mortal fear that a man with a badge might knock on their door at any moment."

Struggling to find the right words, Steve studied Susan's delicate hands and thin fingers. "How long was your family kept in the relocation center?"

"Almost four years," she answered sadly. "From December 1941 to September 1945. I'll never forget the dates.

"Actually," she continued, gathering her composure, "they were moved from the stables at the racetrack to another retention center—concentration camp is a more fitting description—in Amache, Colorado. They lived in cramped, partitioned compartments in rows of wooden barracks surrounded by sagebrush and barbed-wire fences."

Lost in her thoughts of the past, Susan looked down at the floor and recalled the afternoon her mother and grandmother unknowingly revealed the family's dark secret that had been kept from the children.

It was a warm spring day in Oakland when Susan's oldest sister discovered the awful truth. Sitting quietly under the open kitchen window, Betty Nakamura heard the two women alternately crying and talking about the atrocities of the detention camp.

Susan was six years old when she found out how her grandfather escaped the utter humiliation of being imprisoned in the wartime camp. He committed suicide by hanging himself with a strand of wire. Susan's grandmother awakened to find her husband dangling from a parallel beam that supported the pitched roof over their 8-by-10-foot room.

After a moment's hesitation, Susan glanced at the movie screen, then turned back to Steve. "At any rate, after enduring years of blazing heat and numbing cold, with hot dust storms in the summer and freezing blizzards in the winter, and suffering the embarrassment of sharing one bathroom with scores of other people, my family was finally released from Amache after the war ended."

Wickham frowned and shifted in his seat. He felt uncomfortable, as if he were prying. "That's when they moved to Oakland?"

"Yes. There was an American-owned company advertising jobs for the Japanese who had been detained in the wartime camps, so that's where my folks headed."

Susan paused. She liked talking about the close-knit family

she loved, but it still hurt. "My father got a job with the company and my grandmother moved in with them. My parents, who were afraid to even take a day off for seven years, finally decided it was safe to have children by the early fifties. I was the last of four daughters."

Steve cast a quick look at Susan's attractive face, noting the soft eyes. "That must have been about—"

"Nineteen-sixty," she answered frankly, "and I'll fast-forward from there."

He started to protest and Susan gently shook her head. "I grew up in a pleasant middle-class neighborhood in Oakland, attended the University of California–Berkeley, and you know the rest of my story."

Steve was intrigued, but decided against asking her any more personal questions. "Marcus said that the Bureau is going to provide a car for us."

"That's right," she replied, casting a glance at Callaway, "but you'll need to take a taxi to your hotel. Our people will pick you and Marcus up at seven-thirty tomorrow morning."

"Aren't you going with us?"

"No. A friend is meeting me at the airport, and I'll be staying at my home."

Steve grinned and let his gaze linger on her eyes. "I look forward to working with you."

Susan laughed in her polite way. "The pleasure is all mine. After what I've heard about your exploits, this should be an interesting experience."

He laughed and then excused himself and walked to the rest room in the first-class section, noting that the elderly Japanese man was not on this segment of the flight.

LOS ANGELES INTERNATIONAL AIRPORT

"Japan Air Sixty-Two cleared for the stadium visual runway two-four right approach."

The seasoned Japanese copilot keyed his mike and spoke

with a slight accent. "Japan Air Sixty-Two cleared visual two-four right approach."

On its fourth trip from Tokyo, the shining new 747 descended and passed over the Santa Monica navigational fix at 7,000 feet. Continuing eastbound, the captain banked to the right when they reached the Memorial Coliseum and Sports Arena.

The crew methodically went through their landing checklist while the airplane descended to 3,500 feet slightly east of the Harbor Freeway. Delayed three hours by a mechanical failure in the number-four engine, both pilots were fatigued and silently cursed the smog while they strained their tired eyes to locate the other airplanes in the busy skies over Los Angeles.

Sitting near the tail of the airplane, Mrs. Mayumi Fujitake surveyed the city and the sprawling coastal plain between the San Gabriel Mountains and the blue Pacific Ocean. On her first visit to America's motion-picture capital, the elderly great-grandmother was also enjoying her first ride in an airplane.

Her husband, Shozo, a more experienced air traveler, was still dozing as the 747 entered a shallow bank to intercept the final approach course to the runway.

Sweating profusely while he listened to the portable aircraft radio, Granville Penner sat in the back of the Chevrolet high-top conversion van and opened another lukewarm beer. When Japan Air Lines Flight 62 had not arrived on time, he waited approximately twenty minutes and then walked to a convenience store to call the airline.

After learning the new arrival time, the drug dealer with a felony record and two trips to the slammer bought a six-pack of Old Milwaukee and returned to the van.

The scintillating high from the crack cocaine was wearing thin, and the beer was giving him a throbbing headache, but Penner didn't care about the pain. Not today. He had $20,000 stuffed in his pockets and the promise of another $30,000 if he successfully completed his assignment. The money would be more than enough "talking cash" for a sizable down payment on a new burgundy Cadillac El Dorado and an extended vacation in New Orleans, the city where he was born and first went to jail.

Penner's newfound friend, a self-described affluent Japanese businessman, simply wanted the convicted rapist and burglar to use a .50-caliber machine gun to shoot a few holes in a Japanese airliner. Penner wondered why the small man with the gold and diamond Rolex wanted him to shoot at a Japanese airliner, but, then again, Penner never questioned motives when money was in front of him.

Granville "Big G" Penner figured that shooting a few rounds at a plane wasn't any crazier than some of the other things the Japanese did, like the guy who converted a lime-green eighteen-wheeler into a plush motor home, complete with sunken spa in the roof of the trailer.

Besides, Penner reasoned, he hadn't fired a machine gun since his days in the Army. He had always liked the feeling of power that a weapon gave him, and this would be a piece of cake since it was only two blocks to the warehouse where they would dismantle the van and bury the weapon. Easy money.

Parked next to a vacant storage facility east of the San Diego Freeway, Penner was in an excellent position between the two sets of runways at Los Angeles International. He had recounted his money and was daydreaming about the new Caddy when he heard JAL Flight 62 check in with the control tower. Startled into action, Penner turned up the volume control on the transceiver and prepared to swing the doors open and slide the tripod-mounted machine gun outside.

"Japan Air Sixty-Two," the clear voice replied in a routine, businesslike manner, "two-four right, cleared to land, wind two-two-zero at eleven."

"Japan Air Sixty-Two cleared for the right."

Penner crushed his cigarette on the floor and started scanning the sky for the big Boeing with the JAL logo. He rechecked the machine gun and the short belt of ammunition. He didn't have many rounds, so he had to make each one count.

• • •

The 747 was descending and slowing to the final approach speed as it passed near the Hollywood Park Race Track.

Mrs. Fujitake nudged her sleeping husband, then nudged him again when he didn't respond.

"Shozo, wake up. We're about to land."

"What?"

"We're landing," she said excitedly.

The retired chemical engineer grunted and slowly opened his puffy eyes. The sour taste in his mouth was a disgusting reminder of the raw sashimi and hot sake he had consumed during the long flight from Tokyo.

"Look at the ocean," she said with a rush of enthusiasm and pressed her face to the window. "We have to go to the beach!"

Shozo yawned and stretched his arms over his head. "After we get some sleep."

"Is that all you can think about when—"

Her response was cut short when she saw the streaks of reddish-orange tracer rounds curve upward and strike the left wing. The pyrotechnic bullets, combined with the incendiary rounds interspersed in Penner's ammunition belt, ripped into the fuel cells and ignited the raw fuel.

Penner was initially shocked when he saw the bright tracer rounds move steadily upward and strike the wing. A second later he was paralyzed when he saw a flash of yellow flames, followed by a steady stream of fire along the side of the aircraft. He had planned to put a few holes in the plane, not set it on fire.

"Shit!" Penner muttered when he realized that he'd been set up. Instead of scaring someone, the Japanese businessman wanted the airliner to crash.

Panic overcame him and he shoved the machine gun into the van and hurriedly slammed the door. He could hear the aircraft radio as he scrambled into the driver's seat and quickly started the engine.

"Japan Air Sixty-Two, you're on fire! Repeat! Japan Air Sixty-Two is on fire! Do you copy?"

Penner recognized the tower controller's voice.

"Sixty-Two copies!"

"We have the equipment rolling!" the controller exclaimed as he saw the first truck leave the fire station.

Penner yanked the transmission into drive, floored the accelerator, and screeched around the side of the building, then stomped on the brakes and came to a grinding halt.

Mesmerized, he watched the nose of the 747 dip lower as flames engulfed the fuselage and tail of the stricken airliner. Penner took one last look and jammed the accelerator down, hoping that the plane wouldn't crash.

Ashen-faced, Mayumi and Shozo Fujitake held each other close and tried to be brave. Chaos had erupted throughout the cabin, and the flight attendants were yelling for everyone to brace themselves for a crash landing.

Dutifully, the Fujitakes quietly followed the instructions and listened to the shrieks and cries from the other passengers. They momentarily grasped hands and then resumed the emergency position.

Seconds later, while traveling much faster than the usual landing speed, the Boeing jumbo jet slammed onto the runway and collapsed the left main landing gear. The engines on the left wing dug in, slewing the aircraft toward the edge of the runway before they were ripped from their mounts.

Trailing a long streak of fire, the JAL 747 skidded and bounced across a taxiway and runway 24 Left before bursting into a huge fireball. With the tail consumed by the billowing conflagration, the airplane shuddered to a halt as the forward evacuation slides began to pop out and inflate.

Of the 281 people on board, 67 died from burns and smoke inhalation, including the Fujitakes.

When he returned to the warehouse, Granville Penner was shot to death by his gap-toothed Japanese employer. After the small man recovered the $20,000 from the drug addict, an accomplice tossed Penner and the machine gun into a three-foot grave inside the building, then filled the hole with cement. When the man with the disfigured ear was finished, the final resting place of "Big G" Penner looked like the rest of the floor.

8

HONOLULU

A refreshing breeze drifted through the rear windows as the well-worn taxi approached Aloha Tower, the famous landmark near Honolulu Harbor. Marcus Callaway cast a look at the sun-drenched blue skies and turned to the friendly man behind the wheel. "You said you're from Samoa?"

"That's right," the beefy cabdriver replied with a cheerful smile. "I'm third generation in Hawaii. Got three kids—two of 'em got their degrees from the University of Hawaii, 'an my third kid is gonna be a freshman this year."

Wickham looked at the jovial face that kept darting glances at him in the rearview mirror. "Does your wife work?"

"Yeah, she works," he laughed good-naturedly while he deftly eased his way through the afternoon traffic. "She has her degree, too." His pride in his family was evident. "She works as an accountant during the day and takes care of the house at night. Everybody helps out, so it ain't too bad."

Without missing a beat, he swerved to avoid colliding with a lost tourist in a rental car, then continued his story. "Me, I drive a cab from seven to five, then load air freight from six to midnight." He laughed aloud and honked at another taxi.

"I figure this way, man." He looked at Wickham's reflection in the rearview mirror. "We ain't got time to have no more kids." He belly-laughed.

Steve was still curious. "Where are your kids now—the ones who graduated?"

"They're all living at home." His voice was suddenly serious. "They can't afford to buy a house, not even a little one. The Japs have taken over the real-estate market again, like they did back in the mid-to-late eighties. They come in, buy millions of dollars of property in a few weeks, real estate people jack up the prices, they buy more, and so on. The locals, we ain't got a chance, man."

His eyes focused on the rearview mirror. "They're turning the islands into suburbs of Tokyo."

Marcus turned and looked at the lush scenery and then shared a glance with Steve. Everything was not so wonderful in paradise.

"People like us—the ones who work and live here," the driver said glumly and poked his chest, "we can't afford to buy even a good, small house. The one we got—man, it's falling apart, I tell you—but we're damn lucky to have it."

Steve remained quiet. There had been major changes in Honolulu since he first vacationed in the islands as a newly minted lieutenant of Marines. The peaceful serenity and natural civility of years past had been replaced by jammed sidewalks, crowded streets, honking horns, rude people, cramped accommodations, and soaring housing costs.

He thought for a brief moment about his ex-wife, Becky. They had spent their honeymoon island-hopping from Oahu to Maui to Kauai. It seemed like only yesterday when he and Becky went snorkeling at Kaanapali Beach.

Steve's recollections came to an abrupt halt when the taxi slowed and stopped in front of the Hilton Hawaiian Village.

THE WHITE HOUSE

Bryce Mellongard was a straitlaced, no-nonsense reformed smoker who was known for his leadership abilities and attention to detail. Tall and reed-thin, he always wore a dark-gray suit and white shirt with a narrow, conservative tie.

Mellongard had made a career of positioning himself to fill the next-higher vacancy. He was a master of the game, a master who had a seemingly supernatural instinct for knowing exactly when the opportunity was ripe to move up a notch.

From the ranks of a midlevel civilian manager in the Pentagon, he steadily climbed the ladder. Always managing to showcase himself, then switch boats before the previous one began leaking, Mellongard carefully and skillfully worked his way through the treacherous rapids.

Now the wily, silver-haired veteran of the bureaucratic wars had reached his zenith: Secretary of Defense. Mellongard knew that being SECDEF could be a springboard to much bigger things. He just needed to slide through this obligation without committing any major blunders.

His biggest fear was that the unstable geopolitical situation would force the U.S. military into a position that could lead to catastrophic consequences. Even though Mellongard was a savvy political climber, he was honest with himself and knew his own limitations.

The chauffeur was just pulling away from the White House when Mellongard spotted Senator Frank Brazzell, the Chairman of the House Armed Services Committee. The trim, stylishly dressed senator was motioning for Mellongard's driver to stop.

Mellongard swore under his breath before he told the chauffeur to pull over. Brazzell walked up to the Continental and Mellongard lowered the window.

"Bryce, I'm glad I caught you," the Senator said hastily. "I need to discuss an urgent matter with you, if you've got a couple of minutes."

Mellongard knew that in Brazzell's time frame, a couple of minutes meant at least an hour of lobbying for his latest crusade. "Frank, I've got an appointment at the Pentagon," he said hastily and glanced at his watch. "Let's set up something for the first of next week, okay?"

Brazzell was not one to be placed on hold. "It'll only take a few minutes—I promise." He didn't give the Secretary a chance to answer. "In fact I'll ride over with you and then grab a cab back."

"Okay," Mellongard replied stiffly and reluctantly slid across the seat while Brazzell stepped into the car and quickly shut the door.

"Thanks."

"What's on your mind, Frank?"

"I'll get right to the point," Brazzell answered while the driver edged into the flow of traffic. "I've got all the ducks in order up on the hill, but I need you to apply some leverage on the President."

"You're talking about the carrier?"

They had had previous conversations about giving the Japanese the next U.S. aircraft carrier that was scheduled for decommissioning. The Japanese had asked for a large-deck carrier, ostensibly to be used as an antisubmarine warfare ship, but the last Administration had quietly rebuffed them.

"Absolutely," Brazzell shot back in his boldly confident manner. "Politically, the time is ripe for us to calm the waters and show some real confidence in the Japanese government. At the same time we can smooth some of the ruffled feathers about all this terrorist crap.

"I'm telling you," Brazzell went on without missing a beat, "that we're going to blow a major opportunity if we don't make the announcement now and follow through with our promise. Let's give them the next carrier on the list instead of turning it into a floating museum or cutting it up for the scrap dealers."

Mellongard let his head rest on the back of the seat. "Frank," he sighed heavily, "they've laid the keel for their second carrier. You know that's in violation of Article Nine of the constitution they are supposed to enforce. I think we should forget the idea."

The Secretary was referring to Article 9 of the post–World War II Japanese constitution that had been developed by General Douglas MacArthur and accepted and promulgated by the first postwar Diet.

The constitution included a thirty-one-article bill of rights, and Article 9 was the key to the foundation of the new Japanese government. Article 9 renounced war as a "sovereign right of the nation" and pledged that "land, sea and air forces, as well as other war potential, will never be maintained."

"Bryce," the Senator said patiently, "come on. We're well past that stage of the game. Besides, we've been encouraging them to provide their own defense for a long time, so why not help them?"

Brazzell waited for a response, but Mellongard remained silent. It was an old argument and the Secretary didn't want to discuss Japan and her burgeoning military power.

"Bryce, hear me out on this," Brazzell persisted. "You guys in the Puzzle Palace can't have it both ways. You tell the Japanese government to develop a stronger Self-Defense Force because we don't want to spend the money and use our assets to defend them."

Mellongard gave a warning look and Brazzell shifted to a softer approach. "Then, after conditioning them to that spiel, you question whether we should give them an old, worn-out carrier?"

"Senator," SECDEF countered and stared him down, "you know that's an oversimplification of the situation. Any of our carriers—even an older one—has the capability to project power anywhere around the globe."

Mellongard paused to gather his thoughts. "Frank, a seventy-thousand-ton carrier isn't what I would classify as self-defense technology."

"Sure it is," Brazzell shot back, remembering his discussion with the Japanese multibillionaire. The businessman had explained that Japan wanted to use the retired U.S. carriers for antisubmarine-warfare patrols. "They can use it for ASW work, and it's a great platform for rescue helos and reconnaissance aircraft."

The Secretary remained quiet and looked out the window.

"Bryce," the Senator gently prodded, "the Japanese are building their own blue-water carriers. China and North Korea scare the hell out of them, and they aren't going to sit around and twiddle their thumbs while they wait to get nuked again."

Mellongard bristled and turned to face Brazzell. "That's the goddamn point, Frank. They've gone from a total armed force of a quarter million men in '93 to well over one million in uniform today. They're building their own heavy battle tanks, armored personnel carriers, and artillery pieces."

Observing the restlessness in Brazzell's eyes, Mellongard carefully measured his words. "They've rapidly amassed a navy of over two hundred ships, including eighteen Aegis-equipped destroyers that are clones of our Arleigh Burke–class, and they've got a half-dozen new 767 AWACs, all while their economic and political upheavals are supposedly having a devastating effect on the country. Does that sound like a Self-Defense Force to you?"

Mellongard didn't wait for a response. "Frank, the Joint Chiefs are concerned. These Aegis ships are designed to provide protection for a carrier battle group, and they're building carriers that are designed for vertical takeoff and landing aircraft."

Both men shifted their eyes away from each other for a brief moment before the Defense Secretary turned to Brazzell.

"If they decide to preempt North Korea," Mellongard continued in a softer tone, "we don't want them to do it with one of our carriers."

"But I suppose we wouldn't mind if they clobbered North Korea with their own ships?" Brazzell countered while he planned his next avenue of strategy. He had to convince SEC-DEF to lobby for him, or the entire project would collapse, including his generous commission.

"You combine those ships," Mellongard observed, "with their twenty-eight submarines and support ships and you've got a world-class blue-water navy, not a coastal patrol. Add to that one of the largest ASW capabilities in the world, combined with an air force that has over seven hundred Japanese-made fighter planes, and we're talking about a major military power."

Mellongard looked straight ahead and took a deep breath. "Do you really think it's in our best interest to give them a carrier—even with the catapults removed—when our military is bare bones and getting smaller every day?"

"Yes. I honestly believe we should give them a carrier for ASW protection." Brazzell closely watched SECDEF for his reaction. "Especially for political reasons."

They remained quiet, each thinking about his own political interests.

"They'll have their own carrier soon enough," Mellongard finally said, "but they won't be launching the first one for another year or so." He didn't want to confront the issue on his watch.

"Don't bet on it," Brazzell calmly replied and shifted his gaze to the passing scenery. "The little shits are very industrious and motivated. Bryce, this is one hell of an opportunity to mend some fences."

"Let me think about it awhile," Mellongard answered with one of his classic maneuvers to consume time and obstruct issues, "and I'll get back to you."

Brazzell decided to use one of his hidden aces. "Bryce, we've been friends for a long time, and I'm telling you, for your own good, this is going to be a political coup."

Mellongard studied Brazzell's deeply set eyes. "There's more to this than politics, isn't there?"

"That's right," Brazzell admitted dryly and rubbed his thumb back and forth against his fingers. "Better than a gold mine."

SECDEF leaned forward and told the driver to pull over and stop near the Department of Interior. When the car came to a smooth stop, the two men got out and walked fifty feet away.

"Frank, you better level with me," Mellongard cautioned with his face set in a frown. "You owe me a big one, and don't forget it."

"I haven't forgotten." Brazzell smiled his thin smile. "I've got the votes lined up, and everyone cashes in if I have your support." He lowered his voice. "But you have to convince your man to go along with this."

Mellongard resented Brazzell's reference to the President as "your man," but the Senator had an uncanny ability to pull off surprises that no one could believe.

"Bryce, you're looking at a potential two million dollars in your personal portfolio if you can deliver. All you have to do is convince the man to play ball."

HONOLULU

"I can't believe this," Marcus said after he finished reading about the crash landing at the Los Angeles International Airport. He sipped his orange juice and glanced at Steve. "Eyewitnesses, including two commercial pilots who have combat experience, swear they saw tracer rounds hit the airplane as it approached the runway."

"I don't doubt it," Steve replied as he poured syrup on his pancakes. "There are thousands of machine guns on the market—anything you want—for a price. You mix all the proper ingredients, throw in a wacko who is about a half bubble off center, and presto—you've got a lunatic out shooting at a Japanese airliner that's on final approach to LAX."

Wickham reached for his hot tea. "Hell, most people would call that a normal day in Los Angeles."

Marcus shook his head. "It's crazy. This planet is being overrun by insane people."

"I think you're right," Steve declared while he accepted the paper from Callaway. "It's insidious, but day by day, year by year, decade by decade, this world *is* becoming more insane."

Wickham skim-read the front page and quietly placed it on the chair next to him. "The magnitude of these incidents with Japan is really frightening."

"No shit."

Steve gave Marcus a somber look. "It's much bigger than we

imagined, and I suspect things are going to get worse . . . because someone is really stirring the pot."

"Yeah," Marcus replied with a pained look on his face. "There's something going on," he trailed off, then caught Steve's eye. "Do you think that all of these incidents—the entire Japan/U.S. clash—are being orchestrated to take us from a trade war to a shooting war?"

Steve glanced toward Diamond Head before he faced Callaway. "Marcus, maybe I've become too cynical, but in this day and age, nothing surprises me anymore."

Callaway studied his colleague for a few seconds. "Well, tell me the truth and don't bullshit me. Is the CIA involved in this deal?"

"*What?*"

"Are you boys," Marcus asked and leaned back to study Wickham's expression, "trying to work us into a position to have a reason to kick the shit out of Japan?"

The question initially shocked Wickham until he took a moment to think about how plausible it sounded. It wouldn't be the first time the CIA had provoked a confrontation to enable the U.S. to take advantage of a situation.

"If the Agency was setting Japan up for a fall," Steve confided with an uneasy feeling, "I'd know about it."

"Are you sure?"

Steve chuckled and thought about his position at the Agency. His star was burning brightly, but he had a few more requirements to complete before he would be in a position to compete for the top post.

"Yes," he hesitated, "I'm sure the Agency isn't involved."

"That's good." Marcus's relief was clearly evident as he looked at his watch. "We better get going if we're going to be on time."

Wickham and Callaway were driven to the headquarters of the Federal Bureau of Investigation by a personable young agent who then gave them the keys to the four-door sedan.

When they entered the building at 300 Ala Moana, the place

was crawling with senior Bureau agents and local authorities who were attempting to coordinate their activities amid the chaos. Maps had hastily been taped on the walls, and radio chatter squawked above the din of noise in the crowded building.

Marcus looked through the open door to the main office and recognized Bureau friends from San Diego, Los Angeles, Seattle, Portland, and a number of other West Coast cities. He poked Steve with his elbow. "I've never seen this type of reaction before. If I didn't know better, I'd think the President had been shot."

"Well, no one can accuse the FBI of being lackadaisical," Steve commented while Callaway shook hands and exchanged greetings with two of his colleagues who were discussing the crash landing in Los Angeles.

Marcus introduced Steve to his associates as the two men moved toward the center of the office.

They spotted Susan Nakamura at the same time and worked their way through the throng of people.

"Good morning," she said briskly and motioned toward the open door. "Let's get out of the line of fire, then I'll explain what's going on."

Steve cast a glance at Marcus and shrugged. They followed her out of the main office and down the hallway to a storage room where a phone and two small desks had been hastily put in place.

"We can have some privacy in here," Susan said as she closed the door. "The Attorney General has issued a top-priority mandate to the Bureau. She wants us to get this case resolved as quickly as possible, and, as you have seen, she has pulled every available person."

Steve noticed that Susan had a moment of eye contact with Callaway. They were acutely aware of the tough reputation the hardworking Attorney General enjoyed.

"Basically," she confided with a trace of annoyance, "the Bureau is expected to solve these cases quickly or heads are going to roll . . . as they did after the Waco disaster."

She was clearly troubled by the implied threat from the Attorney General. "That's why this investigation has become a circus."

"Susan," Wickham said with conviction, "forget about the politics of the Bureau. What kind of leads do we have?"

"You're right," she acknowledged without any sign of irritation. "Since I have a number of contacts throughout the islands, I did some digging last night and found a few interesting bits of information."

Callaway was intrigued. "And?"

"There are two pilots—helicopter pilots—living on Oahu who have very checkered histories." She let her gaze linger on Steve. "Why they're still flying is beyond me."

Wickham started to ask a question, then decided it was best to hear her out.

"They both have DUI convictions," she continued evenly, "along with a string of violations and reprimands from the FAA. One of them even has a record of drug smuggling when he lived in Miami. He plea-bargained his way out of one charge, then got caught again and turned state's evidence against his co-conspirators."

"Have they been questioned?" Callaway asked, shifting into his role as a professional Bureau agent.

"Yes. One of them has an alibi for his whereabouts when the attack took place."

Susan sat on the edge of one of the desks. "We're checking his story, but the other pilot—the drug smuggler—says that he was on an overnight fishing and camping trip."

"By himself?" Steve asked, distracted by the glimpse of her legs.

"That's right," she answered serenely. "He's divorced and lives by himself. He's dual rated in helos and airplanes, but says that he hasn't flown helicopters in over a year. He makes a living as an interisland cargo pilot."

Steve looked at the phone. "I need to call Langley."

"Before you call, I'd like to add one other thing."

Callaway and Wickham gave her their attention.

"The pilot of the helicopter from the television station returned my call late last night and left a message. I just happened to walk in this morning when they were replaying the tape."

Steve's instincts told him the pilot's call was a positive aspect in the investigation. "What'd she have to say?"

"She was very guarded. I'm familiar with her personality—her on-the-air personality—since I occasionally watch her."

Susan placed her palms on the edge of the desk. "This side of Theresa Garney was very subdued. She started to explain something, then suddenly stopped. She left her home and business phone numbers and said it was urgent."

Marcus looked puzzled. "When was her initial interview?"

"I don't know, but she's been interrogated four or five times. I want to talk to her as soon as possible, so let's give her a call. She's probably at work."

While Susan placed the call to the television studio, Callaway and Wickham lowered their voices and stepped across the tiny room.

"I'm going to call Langley," Steve suggested, "and have a military helicopter assigned to us. I want to talk to everyone who watched the helo depart after the attack, then trace the exact route."

"You're convinced the chopper is still on the island?"

"Not completely," Steve admitted while he caught one side of the telephone conversation. "This was a well-planned, well-executed attack and disappearing act. Susan talked to me about her theory in San Francisco, and I think her reasoning has merit."

Steve lowered his voice to a whisper when Susan glanced at him. "The key to getting away with something like this is reducing the amount of time you spend in the air after the attack. The more time in the air, the higher the risk of being intercepted or seen."

"You don't think the pilot flew to another island or landed on a boat offshore? That seems probable to me."

Steve gave the options a moment of thought. "We have to

assume the pilot's highest priorities—after the strafing attack—revolved around not crashing and not getting caught."

Callaway wrinkled his brow. "I'd say that's a valid assumption, especially when the guy knows there's a boatful of people who wouldn't hesitate to kill him."

Wickham paused and studied his friend for a long moment. "You're convinced the pilot was a male?"

"No," Marcus responded smoothly, "but you know as well as I do that the probability of the pilot being female is almost nil. Besides, every witness has confirmed that he—the pilot—was a Caucasian male."

Wickham hesitated while Susan placed the phone receiver in its cradle. "For the moment let's just say that we don't know who was piloting the helo."

"Fair enough," Callaway replied evenly.

"She's flying at the moment," Susan announced and underlined the television station's phone number. "They expect her back in about an hour and fifteen minutes. I'll see if I can speak with her when she lands."

Callaway ran a finger through the dust on one of the desks. "I want to check out the drug smuggler and then go over the reports from the eyewitnesses."

Steve's glance slid to Susan. "I need to make arrangements for a military helicopter, then I'd like to sit in on your discussion with the—"

"Sky Nine pilot," she said easily. "Theresa Garney."

9

NEAR MARCO ISLAND, FLORIDA

Tadashi Matsukawa stood on the afterdeck of the *Gochi Nyorai,* his new 204-foot Feadship named after the five Buddhas of Wisdom and Contemplation. The gleaming white ship with the polished brass fittings and golden teak decks was considered the Rolls-Royce of superyachts.

Built in the Dutch seafaring tradition and hailed as a world-cruising masterpiece, *Gochi Nyorai* had been designed and equipped for any sea conditions, any season of the year. She could easily negotiate Drake Passage while rounding Cape Horn in the worst of storms.

Matsukawa was especially pleased with the absence of noise and vibration in the sturdy hull. With 38,000 gallons of fuel and 14,600 gallons of water in her bowels, the stately yacht had the ability to take the captain of Japanese industry anywhere in the world.

While Tadashi Matsukawa mingled with the 170 guests aboard *Gochi Nyorai* for the afternoon cruise, three chefs manned the huge barbecue on the afterdeck. The men slathered various sauces on the wide variety of meats while a second vessel trailed the yacht with freshly butchered livestock for the sizzling grill.

The CEOs of Fortune 500 companies chatted easily with members of Congress and professional influence peddlers. The core of lobbyists especially enjoyed the assemblage of female celebrities, well-known models, and highly paid call girls who were attending the extravagant party.

The primary topic of conversation centered around the ongoing investigation into the crash landing of the JAL flight at Los Angeles. A videotape taken by an amateur photographer near the airport clearly showed the highly visible tracer rounds impacting the airplane. Although the quality of the picture was poor, the frantic dive for the deck and subsequent hard landing and explosion had been captured on film.

Matsukawa was about to have another glass of champagne when Yoshio Okura, his aide for eleven years, stepped close to him and silently signaled to him. Okura never appeared in the midst of a social gathering unless the reason was extremely important.

Smiling and chatting cordially, Matsukawa slipped into a wide passageway and followed his assistant to the master suite. The lavish stateroom was connected to a private, state-of-the-art communications center.

"What is it, Yoshio?"

The chunky man backed toward the door for a quick exit. More than a dozen times, Yoshio Okura had borne Matsukawa's violent anger when the businessman had received bad news.

"The Ambassador is on your private line."

"Hagura?"

The nervous man nodded and inched backward.

Matsukawa thanked his aide and waited until Okura left the suite, then sat down in a leather chair by the phone with the blinking yellow light.

The billionaire had nurtured a friendship with Ambassador Koji Hagura in order to have another direct line of communication to the U.S. government. Considered a plodder by many, Hagura was much more than a dull functionary. Under the tutelage of Tadashi Matsukawa, the Ambassador had developed excellent politico-business instincts.

"*Konnichi wa, Hagura-san.*" Good afternoon, Mr. Hagura. Matsukawa never used the word "ambassador" when he talked with Hagura. "*Ogenki desu ka?*" How are you?

"*Genki desu. Arigatoo gozaimasu.*" Very well, thank you.

Matsukawa drummed his stubby fingers on the edge of the Chippendale desk. "What can I do for you, Hagura-san?"

"The President has requested a private meeting with the Prime Minister, due to our mutually strained relations."

Genuinely surprised, Tadashi Matsukawa switched the phone to his other ear. "*Yukkuri hanashite kudasai.*" Speak slowly.

Hagura paused, unsure if he had made a mistake by calling the leader of one of the strongest financial cartels in Japan. The Ambassador was deeply concerned about the deteriorating U.S.-Japanese relationship, and he knew that Matsukawa and the Prime Minister were close friends. Hagura fervently hoped that he had not overstepped his bounds.

"I forwarded the invitation to Tokyo . . . and moments ago, I received a curt message from Foreign Minister Katsumoto."

"Go on," Matsukawa prodded impatiently.

Hagura took a deep breath. "He instructed me to inform the President that Prime Minister Koyama will set the date and place of any formal meetings."

Matsukawa wanted Genshiro Koyama to take a strong stand against the Americans, but he knew the Prime Minister and the financial cartel members needed to proceed cautiously.

The opportune moment was rapidly approaching for an equal partnership between the two countries. Matsukawa and many other Japanese leaders firmly believed that it was past time to void all restrictions placed on Japan, including the size of its expanding military. They also believed that Japan would thrive like never before if it didn't have to placate the lazy Americans.

"I will make a call, Hagura-san." Matsukawa's mind was

racing. "You did the right thing, and I appreciate the information."

HONOLULU

The warm sun was high in the sky when Susan parked the Bureau's sedan near the First Hawaiian Bank. She and Steve locked the doors and walked down Kapiolani Boulevard to the studios of KGMB Television. After they entered the building and identified themselves, the startled receptionist escorted them to a conference room.

"Let's take her to lunch," Susan suggested while they waited, "so she won't feel so intimidated."

"I was about to suggest lunch," Steve said with an innocent smile. "Honestly."

"Sure," she teased with a doubting look.

Theresa Garney quietly entered the room before he could respond. She was dressed in white slacks with a blue and pale yellow aloha shirt. The former tomboy had blossomed into a blue-eyed beauty as well as a top-flight aerobatic instructor and helicopter pilot. Theresa was about to sit down when Steve suggested lunch.

"Sure," she replied with a nervous laugh. "I'd feel more comfortable if we had some privacy."

"We understand," Susan interjected smoothly.

While the trio drove to an out-of-the-way restaurant frequented mainly by local residents, Steve noticed a car following them. Constantly aware of his surroundings, he watched their "tail" as the driver maintained a set distance behind their sedan and made every turn they made. Steve started to say something to Susan, but decided against doing anything that might frighten Theresa.

When they reached the restaurant, Wickham casually glanced at the Chevrolet Corsica as the rental car made a right turn at the next intersection. He tried to see the license number of the dark-blue car, but his view was obstructed by a high hedge and other automobiles. He kept his secret to himself as they entered the restaurant and sat down.

The small, manicured lawn by the outdoor dining area was awash in colorful anthuriums, hibiscus, orchids, and red ginger. A mixture of furniture, including Filipino country antiques, carved Asian tables, and rattan chairs dotted the wooden floor.

After their fresh seafood lunches and iced tea were served, Susan turned to the pilot. "Theresa, you left an urgent message with our office. Is there something you forgot to add to the initial interviews?"

"No," she replied cautiously, "but there has been another development since I first talked with the local authorities and the FBI."

Theresa quietly cleared her throat and placed her fork on her plate. "It was by coincidence that you requested to talk with me a short time later."

Steve and Susan stopped and looked directly into her eyes.

"Just take your time," Wickham assured her, "and tell us exactly what happened."

"I had a call from an elderly lady," Theresa explained with a renewed confidence in her voice, "who watches Channel Nine and knows what our helo looks like. To make a long story short," she continued in a hushed tone, "quite a few people saw the helicopter after the attack—as I'm sure you've seen in your reports. By most accounts, the helo passed west of Aloha Stadium, continued toward Camp Smith Marine Corps facility, then was last seen over the Ewa Forest Reservation."

She glanced down at the table, then looked at Susan. "The woman who called me said that she and her granddaughter saw the Sky Nine helicopter after the attack, but on the windward side of the island. She is the only person to my knowledge who has reported seeing the helo after it went over Ewa Forest."

"Did she give you an exact location?" Steve calmly asked.

"And the time of the sighting?" Susan added, feeling the tingle that she always experienced when an important piece of the puzzle was falling into place.

"Mrs. Sakoguchi said they saw my helicopter flying close to the ridgeline of the Koolau Range."

"Where did they first see it?" Susan asked while she formulated a plan.

"The windward side, as I mentioned, near Kahana Bay. She said the helo was hugging the ridge, ducking in and out of the rain clouds." Theresa looked to Susan. "The ones that often settle along the top."

"I know," Susan replied. "The sun can be shining over Waikiki while torrential rains are falling on the tops of the mountains."

"What about the time?" Steve asked.

"She thinks it was about nine or ten minutes after the time of the attack—the time that was reported by the media."

Susan and Steve exchanged curious glances before he looked at Theresa. "Which way was the helicopter headed when they saw it?"

She looked slightly offended, but understood why he had asked the question. If Mrs. Sakoguchi was off on her time of sighting, the helicopter could have been on the way to Pearl Harbor.

"It was headed northwest, barely skimming the side of the mountains." Theresa took a deep breath, then slowly let it out. "Mrs. Sakoguchi is certain about the time. They left their home at a quarter to seven, and it was exactly eight when they saw the helo."

Susan lost interest in her meal. "Why didn't she go to the police or talk to us?"

Theresa glanced at Steve, then fixed her gaze on Susan. "Mrs. Sakoguchi, who is extremely shy, is of Filipino-Japanese ancestry and speaks only pidgin English. She was afraid that I might get in trouble or that she would somehow become involved in the investigation and have to go to jail."

Steve raised his hand slightly. "Theresa, we'll be happy to talk with Mrs. Sakoguchi and assure her that nothing will happen to her."

Theresa nodded and gave him a faint smile. "I would appreciate that, Steve. She's a nervous wreck, and I don't blame her for feeling insecure. It took a lot of courage to come forth with her information."

"What's your schedule for the afternoon?" Susan asked, thinking the same thing as Steve: a drive to see Mrs. Sakoguchi and reassure her that no harm would come to her could provide some useful information.

"I'm scheduled to fly during drive time, but we've got a contract pilot who could fill in for me." She looked at Wickham. "I'll have to check with our manager."

"After lunch," Steve suggested to Theresa, "let's go talk to your boss about borrowing you for a while."

"Good idea," Susan acknowledged and reached for her glass, then glanced at the pilot. "It would be nice if you would call Mrs. Sakoguchi and let her know that we'll stop in for a short visit this afternoon. We need to have her show us the exact point where she saw the helicopter."

Theresa openly smiled for the first time. "She'll be thrilled to know that she isn't in some kind of trouble."

"Quite the contrary," Steve responded, trying not to stare at the blue-eyed beauty. "We owe her a debt of gratitude."

ABOARD THE *GOCHI NYORAI*

After the final guests had left the moored yacht, Tadashi Matsukawa went to the communications center and sat down at the control station. He ground out his cigarette and flipped on the power switch for the Magnavox satellite terminal, then punched in the ship's latitude and longitude to align the large antenna mounted over the wheelhouse.

The terminal was certified to interface with the Inmarsat satellite network to provide telephone, fax, data, and telex communications from remote areas around the world.

Checking his wall-mounted brass clocks, Matsukawa noted the time in Tokyo. The Prime Minister would be preparing to have his usual light lunch of rice patties with fish, or broiled rice with slices of beef and fish. Genshiro Koyama was a regimented man who never varied from his strict diet.

Matsukawa looked at the signal-strength meter and tweaked a small lever to optimize the antenna elevation. He grabbed the secure-voice handset and tapped a special code into the sophisticated keyboard.

Waiting for his call to go through, Matsukawa lighted another cigarette and listened to the clicks and tones emitting from the handset. When the switchboard operator answered his call, he gave her his identification number.

The call was routed to a governmental agency in the heart of the Kasumigaseki district in Tokyo, then to an administrative assistant in the Prime Minister's Office. The aide asked Matsukawa his name, advised his boss, then put the call through to Prime Minister Koyama.

Matsukawa instantly recognized the unmistakable rasping voice of the man many Japanese felt was the strongest leader they had had in years. Outmaneuvering his opponents, Koyama had jockeyed to be at the right place to eventually ascend to the supreme position after the demise of the Liberal Democratic Party. The resulting political calamity had rocked Japan and caused many scars and strained relationships, but the crafty politician had waited patiently and emerged unscathed from the fracas.

Genshiro Koyama had received a degree in engineering from Japan's elite Tokyo University, then attended Harvard, where he took a master of business administration.

The sometimes caustic Prime Minister was a loner who rarely showed any emotion in public. Trim and always impeccably groomed, Koyama was capable of conversing freely in English. He firmly believed in maintaining his proficiency in English so that he would not embarrass himself in front of world leaders. Koyama seldom used his native language unless he was speaking with one of his closest aides or a member of his family.

"Ah, Matsukawa-san," the Prime Minister began slowly. "It is good to hear from you."

Tadashi Matsukawa exchanged pleasantries and steeled himself for the conversation. The Prime Minister had a well-deserved reputation for being blunt.

"Ambassador Hagura called me and mentioned that he had been in contact with you."

"That's correct."

"I understand," Matsukawa went on with a guise of nonchalance, "that you have been invited to a meeting with the President."

"Correction. I was summoned like a subordinate."

Taken aback, Matsukawa cautiously proceeded. "I sense that our breach in friendly relations with the Americans is rapidly widening, especially after the terrorist attacks."

"The terrorists from both countries," Koyama said curtly, "are making things more difficult for everyone."

"I know," Matsukawa replied glumly, "and it's very sad that the attacks are destroying the rapport we share with the Americans."

"Are you using secure-link?" Koyama asked while he opened the locked drawer in his desk.

"Yes."

Matsukawa learned the hard way not to leave anything to chance where sensitive communications were concerned. The top-of-the-line Magnavox satellite system was equipped with a secure-voice capability.

"I have recently been involved," the Prime Minister paused to spread his notes on the table, "in a number of meetings and discussions concerning the immediate and long-range planning for our country."

Tadashi Matsukawa perceived a dramatic change taking place in Tokyo. He could tell by the subtle difference in Koyama's voice that the politicians, bureaucrats, business leaders, and academics were awakening to the fact that they had to face up to the Americans—or become accustomed to being subservient to the powers in Washington.

"We are rushing toward the waterfall," Koyama continued in his raspy voice, "and we have to do something bold or we're going to be swept over the brink. Japan, unfortunately, is on a direct collision course with the United States."

Matsukawa gripped the phone. Was his government finally going to cleanse itself of the last stains of guilt about World War II? Was the Prime Minister finally going to break the shackles and confront the Americans?

Pressing the call button for his aide, Matsukawa reached for his fountain pen next to the console.

Yoshio Okura quietly entered the communications center and Matsukawa handed him a note. Okura nodded and hurried to tell the flight crew to have the corporate jet standing by for a flight to Los Angeles.

"This morning," Genshiro Koyama continued, "I met with the chairman of Keidanren."

Matsukawa was well acquainted with the man who headed Japan's most powerful business federation. Chihiro Yamashita always made any negotiation with the Americans as difficult and time consuming as possible. He generally succeeded in wearing down the U.S. business representatives until they collapsed.

"He implored me," the Prime Minister confided, "to stand up to the Americans and restore sovereignty and honor to our nation."

Matsukawa knew the core of the problems with Washington centered around the weakened American military and Japan's growing military capability. The key issue to the Japanese was the ongoing dispute over the constitutionality of the Self-Defense Forces and the fear that Japan would be left to defend herself if the U.S. failed to protect the islands if they were invaded. Most Japanese citizens simply didn't trust the fickle Americans to stand by what they promised.

Koyama sounded very troubled. "Yamashita reminded me about Nakasone and Takeshita. Especially about how they had been highly visible and outspoken advocates of dramatically increasing Japan's military capability."

Prime Minister Yasuhiro Nakasone had enraged many U.S. citizens by saying that America's intellectual level was lower than Japan's because America had too many blacks, Mexicans, and Puerto Ricans.

In 1988 Takeshita spoke to a group of cadets, telling them that Japan would need a defense force equal to its vast economic power. The message was clear: Japan had to become a global military power in order to protect her future.

"I've always believed that Nakasone and Takeshita were right," Matsukawa interjected. "We need to be able to defend ourselves, regardless of the potential enemy. At this period in time, we can't depend on the shrinking U.S. military."

"You are precisely correct," the Prime Minister confided.

Matsukawa was thrilled by what Koyama was saying. Indeed, the Chinese were flexing their muscles and filling the Asian power void. They had significantly increased their military budget, and Beijing was rapidly spreading her tentacles in many directions. Along with Matsukawa, most Japanese were afraid that the Chinese were going to envelop them if they didn't prepare to defend themselves.

The other wild card was North Korea, which already had produced enough plutonium to manufacture five nuclear bombs, and Pyongyang had successfully tested a ballistic missile capable of reaching Japan. The avowedly belligerent regime was slowly destroying the delicate balance of power in East Asia.

The Prime Minister sighed. "We're one of the richest nations on earth, Matsukawa-san, but we've left our soft underbellies exposed. Considering our growing differences with the U.S., we're going to have to expand our military even more rapidly than we have in the past three and a half years."

"I agree with you and Yamashita-san," Matsukawa declared and forged ahead with his proposal to begin preparations to confront the Americans. "In my estimation, it would be wise to convene the *gurupu*. We have to be totally committed or our efforts will be diluted."

"That suggestion has been made," the Prime Minister replied with a trace of hesitation in his coarse voice, "and plans are being made as we speak. Advise me when you will be returning to Tokyo."

Matsukawa smiled to himself. "I'll be leaving shortly." He checked the local time on a wall clock. "And I'll notify you when I arrive."

The Prime Minister spoke slowly. "It is time for Japan to rise and seek her destiny."

10

WAIAHOLE, HAWAII

When Susan, Steve, and Theresa arrived at the tiny cottage, Mrs. Sakoguchi was sitting in a porch swing, fanning herself. She rose and walked toward the car as the trio got out.

While Theresa introduced everyone, Steve surveyed the premises and spotted Mrs. Sakoguchi's granddaughter. The youngster was sitting on the ground near a small vegetable garden, digging a trench with a child-size spade. Behind her, in the midst of various pieces of discarded junk, sat a rusted and faded Chevrolet Malibu. A man who was sprawled under the car stuck his head out to examine the strangers, then returned to his work.

After helping the elderly woman into the car, they drove along the coast highway to a point near Kahana Bay Beach Park. Recognizing the familiar terrain where she first spotted the helo, Mrs. Sakoguchi asked Susan to slow down, then pointed to the area where she had seen what she thought was the Sky Nine helicopter.

"There," the frail woman said with a gesture of excitement. "Helly-copter fly 'long ridge—go north."

"Television helicopter?" Susan asked in a low-key, conversational way. "You're sure it was Theresa's TV helicopter?"

Mrs. Sakoguchi tensed and cautiously looked at the pilot.

"It's okay," Theresa assured her and patted her hand. "Just tell us what you saw."

"TV helly-copter," she muttered and looked up at Susan. "I sure it TV helly-copter."

"Okay, we believe you," Steve said with a reassuring smile. "We thank you for your cooperation, and rest assured that you have nothing to worry about, okay?"

She nodded and cast a nervous look at Theresa.

Steve and Susan carefully studied the ridgeline while Theresa continued to comfort the anxious woman.

Wickham turned and looked at the layer of clouds settling over the island. "It looks like that tropical depression is moving toward us."

"You're right," Theresa said with a quick glance at the gray clouds. "It's supposed to move onshore this evening."

After a few more questions, they drove Mrs. Sakoguchi back to her home and again reassured her that she had nothing to fear. The FBI and the CIA, Steve patiently explained, were thankful for the information she had given them. The small woman beamed when the sedan drove away.

When they reached Highway 83, Steve turned in his seat to face Theresa. "We really appreciate your help."

"I'm happy to help in any way possible."

Susan leaned her head to the side, keeping her eyes on the road. "I have to add my thanks, too. We finally have a solid lead to follow."

"I just hope you find the sonuvabitch," Theresa said without any sign of embarrassment.

"We'll find him," Susan assured her and glanced at Steve. "Were you able to get a helicopter?"

"All set. The Army is going to provide a helo for as long as we need it."

"When do we get it?"

"Tomorrow morning." He looked at the ominous clouds. "If the weather holds. They'll pick us up at Fort De Russey at oh-seven-hundred."

"It may be a long shot," Susan conceded, "but I'm anxious to start scouring the windward side of the island."

Theresa chuckled. "You and everyone else. This island is crawling with planes and helicopters."

"But they don't know what we know," Susan remarked and then noticed the question in Steve's eyes. "Before we tell the world what Mrs. Sakoguchi saw, we need to take a crack at finding the helo. Otherwise we'll be dodging every flying machine on the island . . . instead of searching."

"You're right," Theresa chimed in. "I've got an idea, if you don't mind flying with a civilian—"

"Can we use your helo?" Steve asked, anticipating her offer.

"It's already approved." She looked at her watch. "Our general manager has offered the use of Sky Nine in the search, so when it lands after drive time, we'll go refuel, then head for Kahana Bay."

MARCO ISLAND

Tadashi Matsukawa settled in his thickly cushioned chair as the Dassault Falcon 900B accelerated the length of runway 17, then smoothly rotated near the end of the pavement. He watched his brightly lighted *Gochi Nyorai* pass under the starboard wing before he reached for the Global Wulfsberg Flitefone.

The airborne telephone system incorporated a sophisticated voice scrambler and automatic channel-selection.

Matsukawa kicked off his made-to-order ostrich-skin shoes and propped his feet on the couch next to his desk. A minute later, his personal business manager was awake and taking notes at his home in White Plains, New York.

With unusual patience, Matsukawa explained that he wanted to quietly sell all of his American stocks and his real estate in the contiguous U.S., including the ranch in Colorado. He would keep his properties in London, Bermuda, Hawaii, Paris, Guam, and Singapore.

When his school friend from Harvard queried him, Matsukawa told him not to worry about anything. He explained that secrecy was paramount and that all proceeds must be sent through his holding company in Tokyo.

After his business manager copied and read back his instructions, Matsukawa abruptly terminated the conversation and reached for his drink. Next, he called the president of the firm that handled all of his travel arrangements when he was in the U.S.

Matsukawa punched on the VCR while he waited for the sleepy man to confirm that he had a reservation in the first-class section of the Japan Air Lines flight from Los Angeles to Tokyo.

The $24-million, three-engined corporate jet was too ostentatious for Japanese business standards, so Matsukawa always used JAL for his international travel.

Listening to the soft buzzing sound emitting from the Flite-fone receiver, Matsukawa's expression turned sour when he recalled the time he had been stranded in Los Angeles. The Transportation Department had ruled that Japan had violated the bilateral aviation agreement with the U.S. by restricting certain United Airlines flights from Toyko.

The open threat to take retaliatory action and impose sanctions against Japanese air carriers had forced Japan back to the negotiating table. Fearing the backlash of an aviation trade war with the U.S., Japan Air Lines had suddenly canceled many of their most popular and profitable flights to Los Angeles and San Francisco.

Caught in the middle of the dispute, Matsukawa had been forced to fly to Tokyo in the coach section of a Continental Airlines flight. The flight was a humiliating experience that he remembered with great contempt.

When he received confirmation of his seating assignment, Matsukawa finished his drink, then tilted his seat back and stared at the ceiling of the jet. He, along with the Prime Minister and the leaders of the *gurupu,* would have to proceed cautiously and not let nationalist sentiments cloud their judgment.

Matsukawa let his mind drift back to the attacks on the Pearl

Harbor tour ship and the Japan Air Lines 747. He smiled to himself and thought about his close ties to the Chukaku-Ha terrorist group.

A Matsukawa lieutenant had infiltrated the Kakumaru-Ha faction and helped plan the confrontation and subsequent split that had resulted in the Chukaku-Ha. Since 1983, when the leaders of the new terrorist organization instigated a mass struggle to change Japan's constitutional democracy, Matsukawa had had his finger on the pulse of the group.

Using his loyal aide, the wealthy businessman continued to funnel money to the terrorist group to support anti-American demonstrations and periodic attacks on U.S. installations. Matsukawa thought about the tour-bus explosion in Osaka and the downed American F-16 fighter at Misawa; every attack—anything that heightened tensions—was sweet music to his ears.

He snapped back to the present when the corporate jet flew through an area of moderate turbulence. Matsukawa sat up and cleared his mind.

Regardless of how they approached the Americans, he thought while he leaned back and closed his eyes, the days of *sumiwake*—the peaceful sharing with others—were coming to an end.

HILTON HAWAIIAN VILLAGE

Steve Wickham shielded his eyes when the brightly colored JetRanger slowed to a hover, then gently landed on the heliport by the beach.

"What a coincidence," Steve said to Theresa while the main rotor blades wound down.

She cupped her ear. "I couldn't hear you."

"It's nice that you operate from our hotel," he said in a loud voice.

"I have to be close to the studio," she explained with mock seriousness as the contract pilot removed his headset and opened his door, "in the event that I have to scramble for a breaking news story."

Steve looked askance. "Right."

"Actually"—she turned to include Susan—"it's great publicity for the station."

Susan nodded in agreement and followed Steve to the vividly colored JetRanger.

After Theresa talked with the relief pilot, she helped Susan strap in while Steve nonchalantly climbed into the left front seat of Sky Nine.

With a crowd of spectators watching, Theresa started the powerful turbine, checked her engine gauges, then brought the JetRanger to a hover and moved out over the clear water. A minute later they were racing toward Honolulu International.

When the helicopter was refueled at Air Service Hawaii, Sky Nine lifted off and headed directly toward Kahana Bay.

Once they cleared the top of the Koolau Range, Theresa slowed the helo and flew equal distance between the ridgeline and the shore. She studied the overcast, mentally noting the decreased visibility.

"We won't be able to stay long," she explained over the intercom. "The weather is about to clobber us and we don't have much daylight left."

"You're the boss," Steve said politely and cinched his restraint harnesses tighter. "Make it easy on yourself."

Susan was uncomfortable, but she decided not to question the pilot, at least not in front of Wickham.

Theresa handed Steve a tattered map of Oahu. "If you see anything suspicious, make a note on the chart."

"Will do."

"If you want to photograph anything," Theresa went on while she pointed to the metal container next to Steve's seat, "feel free to use the camera. We keep plenty of extra film on board, so shoot all you like."

"Thanks." He opened the case and removed the Pentax. "I appreciate it."

"No problem."

They continued along the coastline while Theresa pointed out two private residences that had heliports and small hangars. Steve photographed the lavish homes, then circled the locations on the map and made a check mark on the highway next to the shoreline.

He keyed the intercom and looked at Theresa. "Those mansions—the ones with the helipads—must be owned by Japanese."

"You're right," she confided with a wide grin. "They're in the twenty-five-to-thirty-million range, just in case you're interested."

"Not this month," Steve absently replied while he snapped photos of another massive home.

The opulent dwelling was new construction, complete with a huge free-form swimming pool with a large spa in the middle. A towering waterfall cascaded into a *koi* pond near a stone bridge that connected the marble spa to the large courtyard.

Next to the pool area was a tennis court surrounded by a row of tall trees and colorful flowers and shrubbery. Above the pool area was an elevated sundeck and wet bar with an unobstructed view of the ocean.

"Not a bad shack," Steve observed while he made a note and took a few more snapshots as they circled the home. He was surprised when he saw the camouflage-green landing aid near the tennis court.

"Down there." He pointed and Theresa banked the JetRanger. "That's a wind sock, right?"

She saw the conical, open-ended sleeve attached to a tall stand. The wind sock was connected to a pivot so it could swivel to indicate the wind direction.

"That's right," Theresa replied and began slowing the helicopter. "They're usually bright orange, so this seems a bit strange to me."

"Steve," Susan exclaimed over the intercom, "I just saw a man run around the back of the home and disappear inside. It looked like he was carrying a rifle."

"Where?" he asked and quickly shifted his gaze.

"By the side of the wing near the tennis court."

They circled the home once more before Theresa keyed her intercom. "We're going to have to hustle to get back before the weather goes down."

"Okay," Steve said and turned to look at Susan. "We need to check that place."

"First on the list," she agreed, still looking down at the large estate. "It seems odd to have a camouflage wind sock—with no hangar or helipad—and a guy with a gun running for cover."

Steve circled the location on the chart and then drew a straight line to the highway along the coastline. "We'll stop by tomorrow and pay them a visit."

When the JetRanger approached Puumahie Point, Theresa rolled the helo into a shallow turn and descended. Her uneasiness grew as the lack of visibility and diminishing daylight forced her closer and closer to the shoreline. A minute later the first splashes of rain smacked into the windshield.

"We may be in for a rough ride," Theresa announced while she added power and looked for a clear area along the ridge. She wanted to slip over the mountain range instead of having to fly all the way around the southeastern end of the island. "The visibility is dropping faster than I had anticipated."

Steve quietly nodded and watched the coastline flash under Sky Nine. He glanced toward the ridgeline and saw that the top of the Koolau Range was completely obscured by the dense clouds. He looked at his watch and estimated that darkness would swallow them in fifteen to twenty minutes.

Susan snugged her straps tighter and tried to concentrate on the scenery. She would have been more than happy to land while they could still see the ground, then hitchhike back to the Hilton.

Staying close to the shoreline, Theresa turned on her recognition lights and flew over the open water until she was abeam Kualoa Point. "We're going to have to stay VFR and see if we can work our way around the island."

"Whatever you think," Steve replied calmly while Susan

fought the urge to speak out and suggest landing before the rain intensified.

Theresa contacted the radar controller at Kaneohe Marine Corps Air Station and requested vectors around Mokapu Peninsula. She didn't want to risk flying low over the ground in reduced visibility. The high-tension power lines were too hard to see, especially in the rain.

When they were close to the southeastern tip of the island, the controller lost radar contact and Theresa was on her own. She tuned in the Koko Head VOR, a navigational aid known as a very-high-frequency omnirange station, and circumnavigated Kawaihoa Point.

Proceeding outbound on the Koko Head 230-degree radial, Theresa detected a grayish-white glow ahead of the JetRanger. A fraction of a second later, she yanked up on the collective, and Sky Nine cleared the tall mast of a sailing ship with inches to spare.

"That was a tad close," Steve exclaimed while he slowly let out his breath.

Susan slumped in her seat and closed her eyes.

With her heart in her throat, Theresa set her navigational aids to intercept the 110-degree radial of the Honolulu Vortac. When the needle centered, she turned inbound on the radial, knowing that it would keep her from hitting Diamond Head as she made her way to the heliport at the Hilton Hawaiian Village.

Theresa took a deep, silent breath when the distance-measuring equipment indicated that she was directly offshore from the hotel. As the driving rain pounded the helicopter, she hovered low over the water and air-taxied Sky Nine toward the beach.

A minute later Theresa and Steve simultaneously saw the beach emerge from the wall of water. She made a slight correction to the left and guided the helo to a smooth landing at the heliport.

Susan still had her eyes closed. "Are we on the ground yet?"

"Finally." Theresa sighed as she shut down the turbine. "I need to buy the two of you a tall drink."

11

WASHINGTON, D.C.

The Chairman of the Joint Chiefs of Staff and the Air Force Chief of Staff looked uneasy when they walked into the home of the contentious Secretary of Defense. They were not anxious to confront Bryce Mellongard with the unnerving fact that had recently surfaced, especially not at this hour of the night.

When the distinguished-looking Chairman of the Joint Chiefs first contacted Mellongard at his residence, the former nuclear-submarine commander explained that the nature of his call was extremely sensitive.

The Admiral mentioned that he was with the Air Force Chief of Staff and suggested that it might be prudent to have the CIA involved from the very beginning.

In turn, the Defense Secretary invited them to his home and immediately called Paul Holcomb and requested that he attend the informal meeting.

Mellongard always insisted that every detail be spelled out, with logical solutions for any problems, before he approached the President with perplexing issues.

The Director of the CIA was already seated in the study when Mellongard rose and offered a perfunctory handshake to the two senior officers, then motioned them to a large sofa.

Bryce Mellongard sat down and leaned forward with his forearms on his desk. "Well, Clay," he said to Admiral Clayton Biddle, "I can tell from the look on your face that you're not bringing me any good news."

"Mr. Secretary," the submariner began sadly, "the Air Force has conclusive evidence to prove that a surface-to-air missile knocked down the F-16 we lost at Misawa."

Mellongard and Paul Holcomb were stunned by the disclosure. The Secretary shifted in his chair and stared at Fred Dunwall, the lanky Air Force general. "What did you find, Fred, and how long have you known about this?"

"Sir, I was informed about the missile approximately fifteen minutes before Admiral Biddle called you. Well-qualified eye-witnesses have claimed they saw a flash on the ground before the jet exploded."

Dunwall looked at Paul Holcomb before he continued. "Our team of investigators found debris which clearly indicates that the aircraft was hit by an explosive weapon."

"If I may, Fred," Admiral Biddle interrupted as politely as possible. "Mr. Secretary, the key element in the crash investigation is the fact that Air Force personnel found remnants of a Soviet-made SA-7 surface-to-air missile near the perimeter of the base."

Mellongard's eyes widened and he leaned back in his seat. It was hard for him to comprehend that a shoulder-launched antiaircraft missile had downed an American jet fighter in the middle of Japan.

"The weapon apparently malfunctioned when it was fired," the Chairman of the JCS continued. "The Air Force investigators found pieces of the SA-7, and there were splatters of blood on the fragments."

"They didn't leave the entire weapon behind?" Paul Holcomb suddenly interjected.

"No, sir," Biddle answered. "They apparently gathered what they could and got the hell out of there."

Mellongard turned to the self-serving director of the CIA.

"Paul, what do you make of this? Do you think this was another terrorist attack?"

Holcomb cleared his throat to give himself time to formulate his response. He was aware that international arms brokers were selling large quantities of the SA-7 Grail infrared-homing missiles as fast as they could get their hands on them.

"It could very well be the Chukaku-Ha," Holcomb suggested, remembering the latest terrorist brief he had received. "We're aware that the *Organizatsiya*—the Russian organized-crime element—is supplying terrorist groups with the latest military hardware, including mortars, AKM assault rifles, rocket-propelled grenades, incendiary devices, and shoulder-launched antiaircraft missiles."

Mellongard grew more uncomfortable as he thought about discussing the situation with the President. He fixed his gaze on Holcomb. "What are the real capabilities of this group—the Chukaku-Ha?"

It was the Director's time to squirm. "I—we simply don't know. But they are definitely a formidable and violent group. I see no reason to count them out."

Holcomb attempted to control the conversation by taking the offensive. "Our latest intelligence reports confirm that members of the Russian underground, accompanied by Soviet military officers, have been selling weapons-grade uranium and small, low-yield nuclear bombs to agents who regularly supply weapons to various terrorist factions."

Mellongard tugged at an earlobe. "Nuclear bombs?"

"That's correct. The nukes are small, but they're remotely controlled and they can reduce a small town to a pile of rubble. If they had used one of the smallest nukes on the World Trade Center, the twin towers would no longer exist and lower Manhattan would be polluted by radiation."

The Secretary's growing concern prodded him into being cautious. "What kind of confirmation do you have?"

Holcomb paused and glanced at the officers, then framed his

answer and looked at Mellongard. "Our agents have secretly filmed the exchanges, and federal police inspectors in Frankfurt and Stuttgart have recently arrested representatives of several terrorist groups—with the uranium in their possession. They even snagged one buyer who had a nuclear weapon in the back of a panel truck."

Mellongard was thinking ahead to his upcoming meeting with the President. "Are you telling me the Chukaku-Ha might have nuclear weapons?"

"It's impossible to know for sure." Paul Holcomb had mastered the art of dodging questions. "If a terrorist group has the means—the money and the contacts, and the Chukaku-Ha has both—they could conceivably get nuclear weapons from underground arms-brokers."

Unsure of how much he should reveal, Holcomb decided to be conservative and discuss only unclassified information. "We have confirmation that international arms dealers—mainly the crime bosses in the *Organizatsiya*—have set up cafeteria-style armories where agents for the terrorist groups can stroll through and pick out anything on the market."

When the Secretary didn't respond, Holcomb quickly continued in a defensive posture. "If the local authorities can't control the spread of weapons—even small nuclear weapons—we certainly can't do anything about the proliferation."

Giving himself time to weigh a few options, Mellongard cast a long look at the Chairman of the Joint Chiefs. "Clay, what's your recommendation about the situation in Misawa?"

Living up to his reputation as a straight shooter, the Admiral spoke freely. "Sir, my concerns are more broad. I'm concerned about all of our bases in Japan."

The Defense Secretary tensed. He felt like he was being manipulated out on a limb. "Explain your concerns."

"From a military standpoint, if we continue to keep forces in Japan, we have to substantially increase our security system at every base. My recommendation is to use the Marine Corps to provide perimeter security at all our military facilities over there."

Clay Biddle continued after he saw the slight nod of approval from the Secretary. "From the other side of the coin, however, I believe we need to decide whether or not our military forces should even be in Japan."

"That's definitely something we should take into consideration," SECDEF lied. He didn't want to become embroiled in that issue. Leave it to the next Secretary.

Mellongard turned his attention to the Air Force Chief of Staff. "Fred, how do you feel about our presence in Japan?"

"I agree with Clay about security. Faced with the growing tide of animosity between our countries, my main concern is preventing the loss of any more lives or aircraft, regardless of who is shooting at us."

Mellongard was more uncomfortable then ever, but he sounded dispassionate when he spoke. "Do you think we really need a fighter wing at Misawa?"

The General, still troubled over losing a bright young pilot to terrorists, finally answered. "Sir, I think the forward presence of our military keeps problems to a minimum in various areas of the world. In my opinion the North Koreans would be more aggressive if we pulled out. However"—he rotated the academy ring around his finger—"whatever is decided, my personal responsibility is to take appropriate measures to protect the men and women in the Air Force."

The room suddenly became quiet while Mellongard leaned forward on his desk and rubbed his eyes. "I'll meet with the President as soon as I can."

HAWAII

Susan and Steve finished dinner and were walking across the large, airy breezeway by the registration desk when they saw Marcus Callaway. He had changed into shorts and a knit pullover that complemented his muscular physique.

"Where have you two been?" Callaway asked with a straight face.

Susan chuckled dryly. "We've had an exciting afternoon—one I won't soon forget."

"Any news?" Steve asked.

"Nothing very significant," Marcus admitted and lowered his voice. "I went to inspect the tour ship and then talked to some eyewitnesses and the lab people. The ballistics guys showed me some of the 5.56-millimeter projectiles they dug out of a seating area. The cartridges are the standard NATO brass-jacketed rounds used by a number of countries, so we're reasonably sure the weapons were assault rifles that were probably bolted to the side of the chopper."

"Like an M-16?" Susan asked.

"Yes," Callaway answered quietly, "but they could have been Belgian FNCs, German G41s, or British L85A1s. We may never know unless we find the helo or the pilot."

"Speaking of pilots," Steve said quietly, "did you find out anything about the drug runner?"

"The pilots—including the former drug smuggler—have solid alibis from credible witnesses."

"What's the story," Susan asked, "on the pilot who was supposedly fishing when the attack took place?"

"There were several people," Marcus explained, slipping into his professional role with ease, "including a police officer who saw the pilot repairing a flat tire at a gas station at the time of the assault. He claimed that he had been camping on the beach overnight and noticed the flat tire when he was fixing breakfast. The guy has bright-red hair, and all the witnesses are positive that it was him."

"It sounds like a tight alibi," Wickham agreed, concealing the skepticism he suddenly felt. "However, let's keep him under surveillance and see what develops."

"I've already arranged it," Callaway said.

The subtle message was crystal clear to Wickham and he wisely nodded.

"Well, I've got to get off a report," Susan announced and turned to Marcus. "Steve can fill you in on our interesting day."

"Okay," he said and flashed his friendly smile at Steve. "I'm anxious to hear about it."

Susan handed Wickham a business card. "My home phone number is on the back if you need to call me. Otherwise why don't we meet here at seven in the morning."

"That sounds fine to me." Steve put her card in his shirt pocket. "I think we should investigate the homes we saw today."

"I agree." She smiled with anticipation. "And you need to tell Marcus about the car that followed us to lunch."

"Would someone clue me in?" Marcus asked with a blank look. "Who was tailing you?"

"I don't know," Steve informed him with a measured quiet to his voice, "but someone followed us to lunch this afternoon—and it rang a bell."

"And?" Callaway prompted.

Steve hesitated while he tried to reconstruct the picture in his mind. "Do you recall the elderly Japanese man sitting across from us during the flight from Chicago?"

"Vaguely," Marcus admitted. "Wasn't he wearing a bow tie?"

"Yes," Wickham stated emphatically, "and there was something about him that seemed unnatural, don't you think?"

"Not really." Callaway shrugged. "Other than the fact that he never moved."

"Never moved," Steve remarked in a flatly serious tone. "And, if I recall correctly, never turned a page of his paper the entire time he was supposedly reading it."

Marcus paused and a weary sigh came from him. "Now that I think about it, you're right."

Steve glanced at Susan and noticed the question on her face. "I think the guy was listening to our conversation and gleaning every scrap of information he could absorb. Whether he was following us today, or it was one of his associates, the fact remains that someone knows who we are and what we're doing."

"Then we've got a leak somewhere," Marcus grumbled, "because only a handful of people know about our assignment."

"That's what bothers me the most," Susan cautioned with a look of uncertainty. "We don't know who to trust, and we're obviously being watched. Not what I would call a good sign."

Steve suddenly felt uncomfortable with the conversation. "Susan, would you like for one of us to drive you home?"

"No." She laughed unconvincingly. "But thanks anyway. See you in the morning."

"Good night," Callaway and Wickham said in unison.

They watched Susan walk away before Steve turned to Marcus. "I've got some beer on ice in my room, unless you want something stronger."

Marcus grinned. "A cold beer would hit the spot."

After they settled on the lanai, Steve recounted the story about the car that had followed them and what Susan and he had discovered during their airborne search. Both agreed that it would be wise to reconnoiter the house where a man with a rifle had been spotted.

When Marcus retired to his room, Steve called the Army liaison officer and canceled the helicopter he had reserved for the following morning, then opened a fresh beer and stepped out to the lanai. He sat in one of the chairs and watched the rain fall at a steady pace while he thought about the car that had tailed them to lunch.

There was something else in the back of his mind that was haunting him, but he couldn't quite identify what it was. He listened to the steady splash of the waves and tried to relax.

A knock on the door brought him back to the moment. When Steve answered the door, he was pleasantly surprised to see the Sky Nine pilot.

"Hi, Theresa." He noticed that she had changed clothes and brushed her hair.

"Hi. I hope I'm not interrupting anything."

"No, not at all."

"I had your photographs developed and I thought you might want them as soon as possible."

"Thanks. What do I owe you for this?"

"They're complimentary," she countered with a radiant smile. "The lady who handles our station's photo needs was happy to rush these through."

"That's great." He put the pictures on a counter. "I really appreciate your efforts."

"No problem."

There was a moment of awkward silence.

"Would you care to come in?" Steve said at last.

"Are you sure I'm not intruding?"

"Not at all. May I fix you something to drink?"

"That sounds good. White wine, if you have any."

"I think I have a couple of bottles in the bar. Have a seat. I'll only be a minute."

Theresa walked to the open sliding-glass door leading to the lanai. "Do you mind if we sit outside?"

"Make yourself at home."

When Steve finished pouring a glass of wine, he joined her on the covered deck.

"Thanks," Theresa warmly responded as she accepted the Sauvignon Blanc. "I don't know about you, but the sound of the waves helps me wind down."

He let his gaze take in her lips and eyes. "Yeah, like watching a flickering fire in a snow-covered cabin."

"Exactly." She sipped her wine and turned to face him. "Steve, I really apologize for the rough ride this afternoon. It was an unusual situation, but I'm not going to make any excuses."

"Forget it. You were just trying to cover the most ground in the short time we had available. Don't worry about—" He stopped in midsentence when the elusive thought that had escaped him all evening flashed into his mind.

"Steve—what is it?"

"Excuse me, Theresa—I'll be right back."

He hurriedly opened the packet of photographs and flipped through them until he reached the one he wanted. He studied it for a long moment, then reviewed a similar snapshot from a different angle.

How could I have missed that unless I was concentrating on the wind sock?

12

THE WHITE HOUSE

When the Secretary of State entered the private dining room, he could see the President was in a foul mood. The curt response from the Japanese Foreign Minister had cast an ominous cloud over the relations between the two countries. The tenuous situation was further exacerbated by the increasingly violent anti-American demonstrations throughout Japan and many other countries opposed to U.S. foreign policies.

All the major television networks were providing blow-by-blow coverage of the growing unrest, while many members of the international news media were howling for answers to their myriad questions. The White House Press Secretary was fielding the mostly confrontational questions by promising to respond when the Administration had a better grasp on the situation.

"Mr. President," Bud Tidwell began slowly as he seated himself at the dining table, "Secretary Mellongard will be here in a couple of minutes."

"That's fine, Bud. Go ahead and dig in."

The tall man with the lined, once-handsome face dabbled with his salad and remained quiet. He had learned early in his long association with the President that the Commander in

Chief didn't like to repeat himself. He never began a meeting until everyone was in place and paying attention.

After his first year and a half in office, the restless President had become an elusive mystery to most of the members of his staff. The warm smile and folksy comportment that was prescribed by political necessity during the presidential campaign disappeared almost overnight.

A constant frown had replaced the smile, and he had developed a tendency to change his mind impulsively. Sometimes witty and charming, his personality could suddenly become brittle and aloof. However, there was one trait about the President that remained a constant: he didn't suffer fools well.

When the Secretary of Defense entered the room, the President noticed the somber look that always signaled a problem. Although he was a shrewdly expedient politician, Bryce Mellongard was incapable of camouflaging his feelings.

"Give it to me straight," the President said while Mellongard sat down and unfolded his napkin.

Bud Tidwell looked at Mellongard, then quietly placed his fork on his plate. After years of diplomatic service, he knew when trouble was brewing.

When the President heard Mellongard's report on the attack at Misawa, he became livid. "What kind of missile are we talking about?" he hissed.

"A Soviet SA-7."

"You're positive?"

"Yes, sir."

"Sonuvabitch," the President swore under his breath and tapped a button on the leg of the dining table. "When did you talk to Biddle and Dunwall?"

Mellongard had dreaded this moment since his conversation with the two officers. "Late last night."

"Why the hell didn't you immediately contact me?" the President exclaimed and tossed his napkin on the table.

Mellongard winced inside. "Sir, I wanted to confirm a few details before I discussed the situation with you."

"For Christ's sake, Bryce—I want to know about these things when they happen! Not the next day."

Mellongard's reply was interrupted by a military aide who entered the dining room.

"Sam, cancel my appointments until three o'clock," the President ordered, "and call the Director of the CIA. I want him in my office as quickly as he can get here."

The young officer acknowledged the instructions and quickly left the room.

"Bud," the President continued briskly, "you do whatever you have to do to get their attention in Tokyo. I want you to confront them with this. If they can't ensure the safety of our military personnel at Japanese bases, then I'm damn-sure not going to let them use our people as clay pigeons. Make goddamn sure they understand that point!"

"Yes, sir," Tidwell responded in an expressionless voice. "But I suggest we proceed cautiously."

Tidwell was thinking about the ramifications if the Japanese took umbrage and used the issue to force a confrontation. "We've got over half a million Americans who collect paychecks from over two thousand Japanese companies in this country."

"I understand that," the President countered, "but what is it going to take to get them off high center? We've been patient with them on almost every issue, from business and trade relations to the questions about their mushrooming military power. In fact, we've been too patient and too easygoing for too long— and that's why we're sitting here having this conversation while they continue with their business-as-usual routine."

Tidwell sipped his water. "If it appears that we're threatening them—forcing their hand—they may pull the plug, which is going to have staggering consequences."

The President sat quietly for a long moment, trying to calm himself. "Bud, we've known each other for a long time."

"Yes, sir."

"In all that time I've never heard you suggest that another

country could hold us hostage. Is that what you're telling me?"

Bryce Mellongard's heart sank. He knew he was witnessing the start of a confrontation that could only end in a face-off between the United States and Japan.

Tidwell took a deep breath and began speaking in his diplomatic voice. "Sir, if we wade in with both barrels blazing, they may revert to *kaizen,* or, worse yet, sever diplomatic relations with us. Then we're dead in the water."

"Bullshit," the President snapped. "They've been practicing *kaizen* since the last pieces of debris stopped raining down on Nagasaki, and," he said venomously, "they can't *afford* to sever ties with us."

The Japanese business principles of *kaizen* called for slow movement and painstaking analysis. It was a great ploy to buy precious time to study the opposition and then take the most advantageous position.

"On the other hand," the Secretary of State calmly continued, "there are a number of indicators pointing to an inevitable showdown with Japan if we pursue this course. I think it would be better to keep our relationship with Japan as cooperative as possible, and quietly settle the issues in a peaceful manner."

Bud Tidwell watched for a reaction, but the President appeared to be impassive.

"The Japanese," Tidwell warned, "don't respond well when they're being threatened."

The President sat motionless while the seconds ticked away, then propped his chin on his balled fist. "Bud, we're not talking about Armageddon."

The President studied the surprised men for a brief moment. "There aren't going to be any nuclear weapons landing on the White House lawn."

"Sir," Bryce Mellongard finally said, "why don't we give it some thought before you make your final decision."

"Bryce, I've *made* my final decision," the President declared with a trace of sarcasm. "The Prime Minister has said that he'll make the decision when and where he will discuss the issues with me. That sure as hell doesn't indicate any respect for the United States."

"Mr. President," Bud Tidwell persisted, well aware of the President's fragile ego. "Why don't I initiate some dialogue, then we can discuss this in more detail when I have a better feeling for their position?"

"Bud, hear me out, okay?"

"Yes, sir."

"I respect the Japanese people on the whole, and I don't underestimate them. My bone of contention is not with the people."

There was a growing level of anger and impatience in the President's tone of voice. "It's a very simple concept. I want assurances from the Japanese government, in writing, that Japan will take immediate measures to ensure the safety of our military personnel who are in Japan to defend their country. That, in my opinion, is not too much to ask."

Tidwell showed no emotion. "Sir, I'll contact the Foreign Minister and relay your request; however, I want to go on record about my concerns."

"Speak freely."

"I think we're setting ourselves up for some very difficult problems in the near future."

The President didn't try to conceal his irritation. "Bud, let me allay your concerns. You can have all the money in the world, but if you've got a gun barrel jammed against your head, you get into compliance posthaste."

Tidwell darted a glance at the Secretary of Defense before he answered. "Yes, I see your point."

HONOLULU

After an early-morning jog in the drizzling rain, Steve Wickham showered and dressed in slacks and a sport coat, then went down to the restaurant to meet Susan and Marcus. He found them having coffee and gazing out at the miserable weather.

"Good morning," Steve said and slid the packet of photographs on the table.

"You're bright and cheery," Marcus observed and automatically turned to look at the large envelope.

"Theresa had these developed last night," Wickham informed them and pulled a vacant chair toward the table. "After looking at them, I discovered another interesting anomaly about the home with the camouflage wind sock."

Callaway opened the envelope and spread the enlarged photos in front of him while Steve sat down and ordered his usual hot tea.

Susan leaned over for a closer look. "Considering the weather, these turned out a lot better than I expected."

"Look at these two prints," Steve said excitedly and shoved them directly in front of Susan and Marcus. "Have you ever seen a tennis court without a fence around it?"

The Bureau agents carefully examined the photographs and then exchanged glances. The tall, imported trees that surrounded the court were bunched together, but the trunks were too far apart to stop a misguided basketball, let alone a tennis ball.

"You're right," Callaway finally agreed, "but you would never know it from the road. The trees block everything except the view from higher up on the ridgeline."

"And no one lives up there as far as we know," Susan Nakamura added, remembering the terrain that sloped upward behind the isolated home.

"That's right," Steve commented and turned the photo around for a better view. "The tennis court is a perfect helipad, and it's totally concealed except from above."

Marcus had a sudden thought. "Think about all of the fly-in communities from California to Florida. Many of the homes have attached hangars that are cleverly disguised as part of the main structure."

Susan and Steve nodded in silent agreement.

"I remember one case in particular," Callaway went on enthusiastically. "A guy we finally put away, who happened to be involved in an elaborate counterfeiting operation, owned a gigantic home at a fly-in subdivision in Florida. The place had a hangar that appeared to be part of the home. The hangar doors—one on the front and one at the back—were operated by remote control from the airplane. He could taxi in the back after he landed, then taxi out the front when he was ready to fly."

Thinking back to the arrest of the eccentric forger, Marcus grinned. "The front door—the doors were the bifold type—had windows that matched the ones at the other end of the home. That hangar was really elaborate."

Steve tilted one of the photos upward and then looked at Callaway. "Do you think there's a hangar concealed in this home?"

"I wouldn't bet against it."

Susan carefully inspected the photographs and sat back in her seat. "Why would someone have two jackhammers near the pool area? The house appears to be finished as far as I can tell."

"To mask the sounds of a helicopter's rotor blades," Marcus casually offered without looking up. "Throw in the screech of a power saw, or something equally loud, and it sounds like you're still building the house. The racket might not conceal the sounds of a big military chopper, but it sure would disperse the noise from a JetRanger."

Steve paused to look at the prints and form a mental image of the view from the highway. "You can't tell what's happening from the lower terrain, so who would question the sounds of a construction crew?"

Susan glanced at Wickham and gave him a lazy smile. "It does look suspicious, doesn't it?"

"Yes," he answered and hesitated while a customer walked past their table. "When you put everything together, including the guy you saw carrying a rifle, the oddities do raise a few questions."

She studied him with wondering curiosity. "More than a few questions, in my view."

"I may be wrong," Steve conceded, "but we won't know until we investigate."

"Let's take both cars," Susan suggested while she pointed to the tennis court, "and begin with this place. If we don't find anything there—or at the other two homes with heliports—we can split up and start canvassing the area."

"I'm ready," Steve declared while he finished the last sip of his tea and shoved the photographs into the packet.

After the trio walked out of the airy restaurant, a slight, nondescript Japanese diner who had been sitting with his back to the agents slowly adjusted his bow tie and reached for his check.

13

NORTHEAST COAST OF OAHU

Steve and Marcus slowed to a stop along Highway 83, north of Punaluu Beach Park, and examined the dog-eared aerial chart Theresa had given Wickham.

Susan followed them to the side of the road, then raised her binoculars and carefully studied the steeply rising terrain. The monotonous rain had finally stopped and the clouds were dissipating, leaving only the top of the slopes obscured. She examined the general area they had previously flown over, but was disappointed when she couldn't find a trace of the grand estate.

"I'm sure this is the right spot," Steve said confidently, pointing to the circled area on the map. "I guess we're going to have to do some reconnoitering to find the road up to the house."

Callaway studied the chart at length and then looked up toward the distant ridgeline. "If we're at the right place, which I'm sure we are, that house is definitely well concealed."

"This is the right place," Wickham said quietly. "I remember that point of land that juts out into the ocean, and I know the lot for the homesite had been leveled by a bulldozer."

"Okay," Marcus said. He placed the car in gear. "Let's go take a look."

Susan fell in trail while Steve and Marcus tried two different roads that went in the general direction of the hilltop home. Each promising avenue eventually turned into a narrow, muddy path that abruptly ended.

Wickham listened to the constant chatter over the FBI radio frequency. Susan and Marcus had agreed not to add to the communications problems unless it became a necessity.

"Dammit," Steve swore to himself. "I wish I'd paid closer attention when we flew over the place."

"Don't worry about it." Callaway gave him a cheerful look. "We'll find it in a few minutes."

Steve was about to suggest they call Theresa and see if she could fly to the house, then trace the road to its origin, when he noticed a secondary road leading into a thick forest. Many of the trees had been cut and were piled along the side of the road.

"Marcus, let's try that one."

Callaway cast a cautious look at the muddy trail. "I hope we don't get stuck in that mess."

"Have faith."

"Right."

With Susan close behind, Marcus negotiated the steeply rising drive for three quarters of a mile. At that point the soft surface widened into a paved roadway.

"It looks like we're onto something," Callaway suggested and glanced in the rearview mirror. Susan was right on their bumper.

A half mile farther they spotted the elegant home after the winding road suddenly turned into a long, stone and brick driveway.

"This is it," Wickham announced. He reached into his battered canvas bag and extracted a 9-millimeter M9 Beretta.

Callaway casually glanced at the handgun. "Let's hope we don't need any weapons."

"Yeah," Steve said while he checked the fifteen-shot magazine and slid the pistol into a specially made holster that attached to the back of his belt.

With the Beretta resting snugly against the small of his back, Steve straightened his sport coat. "Marcus, since this is your bailiwick, why don't you and Susan go to the door and I'll provide backup?"

"Actually," Callaway answered while he stopped the car, "I think it would be better if you and Susan go to the door."

Steve gave him a curious look. "How's that?"

"If they're Japanese," Marcus explained, "Susan can deal with them. If there's any hesitation or resistance, the initials CIA generally have more of an impact than FBI."

Wickham gave him a skeptical glance. "Whatever you think."

Steve and Marcus got out of the car and looked around the lushly landscaped grounds while Susan walked to the front of the sedan. From their vantage point, there didn't seem to be anything that appeared suspicious or any indication that a helicopter had operated from the premises.

After they discussed what Marcus would do in the event something went wrong, Steve and Susan approached the huge home. Their adrenaline levels were elevated, but they didn't let it show. In their professions, image was almost as important as experience and training.

Wickham saw a small surveillance camera mounted near the apex of the wooden roof, then spotted the microwave sensors hidden in the shrubbery on each side of the wide yard. The monostatic sensors transmitted and received radar signals to detect intruders.

"They've got a fairly sophisticated security system," he said under his breath as they approached the ornate mahogany double front doors.

"I suppose I would too," she replied without moving her lips, "if I lived in a palace like this."

They stepped on the porch and Steve rang the doorbell. Then they noticed the small square of tinted glass recessed in the irregularly colored marble wall. "Another camera."

"They're everywhere."

A few seconds later the intercom speaker came to life.

"How may I help you?" the hollow voice asked in clear, unaccented English.

"Susan Nakamura, Federal Bureau of Investigation," she stated evenly and pressed her identification badge near the camera port.

Steve flashed his credentials and announced his name and position with the CIA.

"Are you the owner of the home?" Susan politely asked.

"No," came the quick response. "I am house-sitting while the owners are traveling."

"Then you're the one we need to speak to," Susan continued in an authoritative voice, "if you'll be kind enough to open the door."

A long silence hung in the air.

"I'm sorry," the empty voice finally responded, "but this is a very busy time for me."

Wickham's patience was rapidly dwindling as he turned to face the surveillance camera. "Sir, we only need ten to fifteen minutes of your time, so let's make it easy for everyone, okay?"

Another awkward silence caused Steve and Susan to question each other with their eyes.

"If you insist," came the curt reply a second before the intercom went dead.

Steve darted a look at Callaway, then turned to Susan. "I don't think we'll get very far with this guy."

She gave him a reassuring smile. "I'm afraid you're right."

A moment later, one of the massive wooden doors swung open. Susan and Steve were surprised to see a gap-toothed Japanese man who appeared to be in his early forties. Slight of stature, bespectacled and prematurely bald, the man was attired in an expensive silk suit and sported a gleaming watch that was encircled with diamonds.

He gave a small courtesy bow before he spoke in the same precise English.

"My time is extremely limited," the man stated with a distinct frown of displeasure, "so how may I be of assistance to you?"

Susan took the lead. "May we step inside for a few minutes?"

The man stiffened and glanced at the black agent standing in the driveway. "I'm sorry, but I am not allowed to let anyone in the home during the absence of the owners. What is it that you are inquiring about?"

"We would like to ask you a few general questions," Susan explained in a smooth, professional manner, "in regard to the recent incident at Pearl Harbor."

"Unfortunately," the small man quickly countered, "I cannot help you. The only thing I know about the tragedy is what I have seen on television and read in the paper. Now I must return to my duties."

Susan and Steve noticed a hint of nervousness in the canned response. The delivery was too fast and there was a jumpy, apprehensive sound to his voice.

Steve's calm appearance belied the growing hostility he felt. "Sir, you speak excellent English. Obviously you've been in the United States long enough to know that we have a job to do, one way or the other."

The pinched eyes turned cold and he took a half step back. "Yes," he snapped, "I am familiar with your agencies. But I have nothing to offer."

Wickham tried to hide his irritation. "Sir, you can either cooperate with us now or we'll be forced to do it the hard way. It's your decision."

The man's growing animosity was clearly evident in his voice. "You surely must understand the concept of orders. You have your orders," he almost hissed, "and I have mine. I am not permitted to allow *anyone* in the home during the absence of the owners. It really is quite simple." He finished with what passed for a disdainful look.

"Who are the owners?" Susan politely interjected when Wickham went rigid. "And where are they now?"

The Japanese man displayed his most exasperated expression. The effect was diluted by his restlessness. "I am not at liberty to divulge that information."

"That's fine," Steve said evenly as he noticed a tall, muscular Oriental man with a crew cut and horribly scarred ear step into sight fifteen feet behind the house-sitter. "We'll make this as easy as possible. If you'll be kind enough to telephone the owners and explain the situation, we'll be happy to wait."

A look of pain crossed the nervous man's face. "I'm afraid that is impossible at the moment. The owners are on an extended cruise and I don't have an itinerary."

Steve was boiling inside, but he forced himself to appear undisturbed.

"Perhaps we could approach this subject from another angle." Wickham smiled easily, then stopped in midsentence when he caught a glimpse of two armed men who were quietly approaching Callaway from the side of the expansive grounds. *It's time to pull the rip cord.*

Steve quickly decided to take a different course and grabbed Susan by the back of her arm. "As soon as you have an opportunity to contact the owners, please give Miss Nakamura a call at the local FBI office in Honolulu."

Susan followed Wickham's lead and handed the fidgeting man her business card while Steve shifted his look to the area where Callaway waited for them. Marcus would be a sitting duck if the men in the foliage decided to take him out.

"If Miss Nakamura doesn't hear from you in the next twenty-four hours," Steve continued firmly, "we'll be forced to resort to another option, but we *will* accomplish our objective. If the owners have nothing to hide, there'll be no problem."

Susan and Steve caught the brief moment of genuine fear in the man's dark eyes. It was the kind of look that a terrified animal gets when it's penned into a corner by a ravenous predator.

When the massive door shut, Steve spoke in a hushed whisper as they turned to leave. "Don't react to what I'm about to say, but there are two armed men kneeling in the shrubs near Marcus."

Susan looked out across the driveway and never glanced toward the edge of the yard. "Steve, I think maybe we've hit it. Did you see the look on his face when you mentioned that we *will* accomplish our objective?"

"Yes," he replied out of the side of his mouth. "Did you see the enforcer with the mutilated ear?"

"How could I miss him?"

"I think we've seen enough to confirm our suspicions," Steve said under his breath.

As they walked toward him, Marcus sensed that something was wrong. He sagely got into his sedan while Susan slipped behind the wheel of her car. When Steve shut his door, Callaway made a U-turn in the wide driveway and gave Susan a fleeting look. She was right on their bumper.

"What the hell is going on?"

Steve gave him a detailed but succinct account of what had transpired on the front porch, adding that at least two men with handguns had slipped down the side of the property to a point near Marcus.

"You're shitting me . . ."

Steve let his eyes shift toward Callaway. "They would have nailed you in a New York minute."

"Okay, so I'm a little rusty," Marcus said. "We need to throw a net over that place as quickly as we can get everyone organized."

"I agree that we need to move fast," Steve said hastily and shot a glance at Susan. "If there's a helo hidden somewhere on the property, they'll try to fly it out before we come back with a search warrant."

Callaway kept his eyes on the road while he spoke. "If these people were part of the Pearl Harbor attack, even if the chopper is gone, they'll want to get rid of any other evidence that could link them to the assault."

"Marcus, if we're right about this, you can bet that they're in the process of sanitizing the place right now."

Callaway gave him a concerned glance. "We need some backup, like now."

Steve looked back at Susan's car. "Marcus, pull over by the slope up ahead."

"Okay."

When both cars came to a stop, Wickham and Callaway leaped out and hurried to Susan's door.

"We've got to move quickly," Steve advised, "but we can't risk using the radios. Those people are sharp, and I have no doubt they have the equipment to monitor radio calls from both the air and the ground, including the FBI."

"Hell," Callaway snorted, "everyone listens to us."

"Susan," Steve continued, planning for what he believed to be inevitable, "I can use my secure phone and have Langley contact your office."

"That would be great."

"Steve," Marcus said and looked up the road toward the imposing residence, "I'll find another approach to this place while you and Susan stake out the home."

"Good idea," Wickham replied, "but be damned careful. These people aren't clowns."

Susan nodded in agreement. "Marcus, keep your distance and if anything develops, call my code name over the radio."

"I'll do it."

"Steve," she said hastily, "I think we should move closer to the house."

"Yeah," Wickham agreed while he watched Callaway grab a pair of coveralls from the trunk of their car. Then Marcus handed him his SecTel secure phone.

Steve energized the discrete communications system. "I've got to coordinate some air cover since we can't completely surround this place."

Steve jumped into Susan's car and she turned it around while Callaway drove down the road.

"What do you think?" she asked as they made their way slowly up the long drive. "Is the helicopter there?"

"I don't know." He sighed and opened the phone case. "But something is definitely wrong when two armed men are sneaking around in the yard."

She gave him a quick glance. "Especially with two FBI cars sitting in the driveway."

14

U.S. NAVAL BASE, YOKOSUKA, JAPAN

The bridge of the aircraft carrier USS *Independence* (CV-62) was quiet at this time of the morning. The sailors and officers were asleep, except for the early risers and members of the ship's company, who were standing watch.

Belowdecks, the mess cooks worked against the clock in order to be ready to serve a savory breakfast when reveille sounded. They had fourteen peaceful minutes remaining before the hungry, sleepy-eyed men would begin forming a chow line.

Outside on the long carrier pier, two food-vending trucks were preparing to serve the civilian "yardbirds" who were reporting for work. The vendors also did a booming business with the multitude of sailors who opted for a change from the usual navy fare.

The hushed solitude of the cool morning was suddenly shattered by a deafening explosion. The thunderous report echoed across the base as the rocket-propelled grenade burst in a blinding white flash when it detonated against the carrier's bridge.

Three panes of glass blew inward, seriously injuring one of the sailors on the bridge. Everyone in the area dropped to the deck and scrambled for cover as the violent concussion reverberated through the big flattop.

The majority of the crew sat up in their bunks and looked at each other with questioning eyes. Whatever it was, it wasn't good news.

On the quarterdeck, confusion reigned while a seasoned chief petty officer talked the young officer of the deck out of sounding general quarters. The salty boatswain's mate grabbed a phone and called out the Marines, then ordered medical corpsmen to go to the scene of the explosion.

OAHU

Marcus Callaway drove to a narrow road a quarter mile from the path leading to the mansion, then followed it up the incline until he came to a dead end. He grabbed his binoculars and stepped out in the muddy path.

After locking the car, he placed the strap over the 10-millimeter Smith & Wesson in his shoulder holster and started making his way to higher ground. The going was tough in the dense vegetation, but he made steady progress and finally reached an area where he could observe the sprawling home.

Perspiring profusely, Callaway dropped to a prone position in the thick foliage and raised the binoculars. He guessed the distance to the home at 300 yards.

A quarter of an hour passed without any sign of life around the exterior of the stately residence. Marcus was beginning to wonder if they had overreacted, but he steadfastly kept observing the grounds.

Shortly thereafter, he noticed some activity near the back of the home, but nothing that looked out of the ordinary. Two men in casual clothes were working on something near the tennis court while the well-dressed man who answered the door stood nearby.

Marcus dried his forehead with the sleeve of his coveralls and continued to watch the men by the tennis court. He could see that one of the workers was Asian, undoubtedly Japanese, but the other man was definitely a Caucasian, with sandy blond hair.

The minutes passed slowly while the heat and humidity forced Callaway to slip out of the top half of his coveralls. He was tying his sleeves around his waist when he froze and stared at the home. Were his eyes deceiving him?

He rolled over and snatched the binoculars from the ground. Marcus let out a barely audible whistle while he watched the end of one wing of the spacious home swing open next to the tennis court.

"I'll be damned," he muttered when the tail rotor blades and pylon of a helicopter emerged from what appeared to be the guest living quarters.

It looks like bedrooms with a bath in the middle, but it's really a narrow hangar for the helo.

When the helicopter was rolled clear of the house, Callaway could see that it was indeed a Bell JetRanger. It was painted in military olive-drab camouflage and looked like any other Army or Marine helo. The average person wouldn't have any idea that U.S. forces on Oahu didn't operate dull-brownish, grayish-green JetRangers.

With the two blades of the main rotor in line with the fuse-lage, the helicopter slid through the tree-lined opening to the tennis court.

You've got to get moving!

Marcus cursed himself for not bringing his portable radio from the car. He crawled backward on his stomach until he couldn't see the house, then rose and thrashed his way down the hillside to his sedan. Winded and gulping air, he unlocked the car and started the engine, then flipped on the air conditioner and reached for the radio microphone.

Susan and Steve stopped seventy-five yards from the edge of the stone and brick driveway. They were out of sight of the home and far enough away that no one could hear their conversations.

Steve tried to call Langley a number of times before he received an answer tone. He impatiently waited while his key code went through a National Security Agency computer for validation. The seconds slowly ticked by while an encoding algorithm was selected for his particular conversation.

At last Wickham heard an authentication code and finally a friendly voice on the other end of the line. He quickly explained the situation, described the location, and requested that military air support be standing by to assist them if they needed it.

Once that effort was under way, he asked the operations coordinator to notify the Honolulu FBI office. Steve gave Susan the phone and she calmly explained the circumstances and requested that more agents be sent to the scene as quickly as possible.

Wickham took the phone and was in midsentence when Callaway's excited voice startled them.

"Tiger Paw, Tiger Paw!"

She snatched the mike from the retainer. "Go, Marcus."

"The stadium is full and the kickoff will be in a matter of minutes! The bird is on the court in camouflage. Copy?"

"Copy," she replied, making eye contact with Steve. "We have players on the way."

"Make it fast," Callaway exclaimed.

The Bureau radio conversations suddenly became a series of strange comments and unanswered questions.

Susan started the car. "I just thought of something."

"What?"

"We had better go down to the highway entrance and mark it so they can find us."

"You're right," Wickham replied tersely. "They'll have a helluva time finding this place if we don't show them a marker."

"Hang on," Susan warned and shifted into drive.

While they hastily made their way to the highway, Wickham asked the nameless voice at Langley for two helicopters from the Kaneohe Marine Corps Air Station.

The instantaneous communications network with the Hawaiian military installations had been implemented by the Agency while Steve was en route to Oahu. As an emergency backup for his secure telephone system, Wickham could use his transportable cellular phone to contact the coordination center in Virginia.

Less than a minute later, he had confirmation that helos from nearby Kaneohe would be airborne in five minutes.

Acting on Wickham's request, the field operations coordinator asked the helo pilots to orbit a mile offshore, then told the agent that he would keep the line open for further instructions.

"The helo was right under us," Steve protested, pounding his fist on the dashboard for emphasis, "and we spooked them into getting it out of there."

"Spooked is right," Susan said with a look of determination. "Let's just hope we can keep a lid on things until we can secure the place."

AIR FORCE ONE

The specially configured presidential Boeing 747 cruised in light turbulence at 35,000 feet after the crew had tried 39,000. Finding the ride at the higher altitude even more bumpy, the Air Force colonel received an immediate clearance to descend to his original flight level. As was customary, Air Force One always received kid-glove treatment from air traffic controllers when the Commander in Chief was onboard.

Stocked with a fine assortment of excellent wines and fresh food, the flying White House was also a gourmet restaurant. The specially trained military chefs prepared delicious meals that were talked about at cocktail parties from one end of Washington to the other. Carrying enough supplies for 2,000 meals, the two galleys could easily accommodate the needs of the seventy passengers and twenty-three crew members.

With a range of over 7,000 miles, along with an inflight refueling capability, the customized blue and white jet could stay airborne for days.

Although many of the presidential perks were under fire, especially the need for a jumbo jet during a time of shrinking budgets and increased taxes, the Chief Executive had not altered or downsized anything where Air Force One was concerned. He considered the sophisticated airborne command post a necessary tool to his Administration.

The President was changing into his fishing clothes when the Secretary of State knocked on the door leading to the executive suite.

"Come in."

Bud Tidwell slipped into the spacious stateroom and quietly shut the door, then reluctantly faced his boss when he came out of the dressing room. "We just took another broadside—literally."

The President shook his head but continued to button his plaid shirt. "The Japanese?"

"I'm afraid so," Tidwell announced and sat down in an overstuffed chair. "I just received a preliminary message from Yokosuka indicating that someone fired a grenade launcher at *Independence*."

After the Secretary of State explained the incident, the President walked across the suite. Feeling a sense of rage swelling in his chest, he sat down in his favorite chair and stared for a long moment at his friend and confidant. "What about *Belleau Wood*?"

"She's fine," Tidwell answered with a feeling of relief. "The Marines are guarding her and we haven't seen anything out of the ordinary."

Belleau Wood, the assault aircraft carrier that was serving as the flagship of Amphibious Squadron 11, was at its home port in Sasebo, Japan.

The President seemed to go limp. "Do they have the people responsible in custody?" he asked in a soft voice.

"No, sir," Tidwell answered bitterly. "They're sure it was another terrorist attack. The shot came from a food-vending truck that was parked on the pier."

The President absently tapped his fingers on the small table at his side. "How did they get away with it, for Christ's sake?" His voice rose in pitch. "We're talking about a goddamned naval base, not some dimly lighted back-alley."

"The investigators," Tidwell patiently went on, "said the driver of the truck had a set of valid credentials. They believe he got away before the base was secured after the incident."

"Valid, my ass."

Tidwell was not intimidated by the President's temper.

"As you know, sir, the strategy of terrorist activity is simple. They always attack when you *least* expect it, and when you're *not* looking."

The men exchanged a tense glance.

"We cannot guard against random terrorism," Tidwell explained in his smooth diplomatic style and watched the President's irritated reaction. "That is its basic effectiveness . . . the random hit-and-runs."

They felt a slight power reduction as the pilot began a shallow descent toward Missoula, Montana. The President's trip was carefully planned to include a number of excellent photo opportunities, including the chance to go fishing in the Flathead National Forest with a Japanese guide.

The President reached for his phone and punched in the code for his Defense Secretary. The sensitive communications equipment could reach the SECDEF anywhere, anytime.

Bud Tidwell sat quietly and listened to the one-sided conversation. After Secretary Mellongard told the President what he knew about the attack on the aircraft carrier, the tone of the discussion changed.

"Bryce, I want increased security at all military facilities in Japan. Most importantly, I want the *Independence* to be heavily guarded around the clock."

The President looked at Tidwell before he gave SECDEF his final orders. "I don't care what you have to do, or who you have to use—find the instigator of the terrorist attacks. Any questions?"

The cautious Secretary knew that it was not in his best interest to have any questions or suggestions. Not when the President started giving orders. It was time for action, not words.

15

HAWAII

Susan brought the Bureau car to a smooth stop at the highway entrance to the driveway leading to the mansion. She and Steve wrapped bright-yellow crime-scene tape around a clump of trees to mark the entrance for the other FBI agents.

When they were finished, she made a brief call to Callaway to find out his location in relation to the house. He disguised his answer, but Susan read it clearly. Three hundred yards south and ready to move in when he received the signal.

Steve instructed the CIA field-ops coordinator to inform the FBI about the yellow crime-scene tape. When the senior Bureau agent advised that he had received the message, Wickham told the OPSCO to have the Marine helo pilots ready to orbit the area on his command. He would direct them to his location when the FBI was ready to storm the home.

If the Bell JetRanger managed to get airborne, they were to force the pilot to land at the nearest suitable facility, preferably Kaneohe Marine Corps Air Station, since it was only a short distance away. FBI agents and other law enforcement officers were assembling at the air station and other airfields around the island.

Unfortunately, the communications stalkers in the news

media had already detected the unusual activity from the FBI and local law enforcement officials. The word of an impending police action was spreading like a flu epidemic. If the people in the mansion got wind of the situation, the operation would be jeopardized.

Steve told the Langley operations coordinator to again stress an important point to the Marine aviators: don't let the JetRanger get away, regardless of what action they had to take. Wickham was shocked when the OPSCO told him the Huey Cobra gunships were not armed. The helicopters were not allowed to fly over civilian-populated areas while carrying live ammunition.

Driving back to the house, Susan reached into her small purse and extracted her stainless steel Smith & Wesson. She carefully examined the magazine and placed the compact semiautomatic on the seat between them, then glanced at Steve. "Are you armed?"

"Yes. I've got a Beretta tucked away if I need it."

"Good," she replied evenly and closed her purse. "I noticed in your Marine Corps files that you fired expert in both pistol and rifle."

Steve looked surprised. "Well, that was a helluva long time ago."

Suffocating in the heat and oppressive humidity, Marcus Callaway held the damp binoculars steady and watched the sandy-haired man crawl into the cockpit of the camouflaged JetRanger. He appeared to be approximately six feet tall and had a slender build.

The main rotor blades slowly began to turn as the pilot went through his takeoff checklist.

"Damn," Marcus cursed under his breath. "Where's our backup?" He raised his portable radio to his lips. "Tiger Paw, they're about to punt. We've gotta take the field. I repeat, we've gotta go for it *now*!"

•　　•　　•

"Move out, Marcus," Susan replied in clipped fashion. "We're on our way!"

Wickham listened to the surge of radio conversations while he called Langley. "Tell the Cobra pilots to come ashore. I'll give them final directions as soon as I have a visual on them."

He paused when the car slid into a turn. "I should be able to see them as soon as they're feet-dry."

Susan drove with a vengeance while Steve braced himself whenever the car swerved on the slippery road. As they approached the edge of the paved portion of the road, he spotted the two gunships.

"The target—a camouflaged JetRanger—is sitting on a tennis court at their one o'clock," he explained. Seconds later the pilots spotted the civilian helicopter and began a steep descent.

When Steve and Susan neared the circular brick driveway, a Nissan Pathfinder barreled straight at them. Susan locked the brakes and slid the sedan sideways, partially blocking the driveway.

"Get down," Steve shouted while he reached for his gun. He recognized the well-dressed Japanese "house-sitter" and the crew-cut enforcer a split second before the rugged Pathfinder plowed into the front of their sedan.

Glass shattered and metal screeched as the car violently spun around, coming to a stop facing down the driveway. Recovering from their initial shock, Susan and Steve leaped out of the car and opened fire at the accelerating Nissan. The blue and cream vehicle lurched from side to side, then disappeared around a bend in the road.

Susan gave her colleagues at the Bureau a quick description of the Pathfinder and tossed the microphone onto the seat.

"Take the right side!" Steve called to her as he ran toward the left side of the home.

Halfway between the driveway and the tennis court, Wickham paused to watch one of the Marine Cobras smoothly maneuver to a position directly over the JetRanger. The civilian helicopter was trapped by the surrounding trees. If the pilot tried to lift straight up in the hurricane of wind, his main rotor blades would disintegrate when they hit the landing skids of the gunship.

Cautiously, Steve started toward the JetRanger and aimed his gun at the pilot. He was prepared to shoot the man if he didn't shut down the turbine and climb out.

Without warning, an assault rifle opened fire. Steve dove for the ground as he heard more high-powered rounds whine through the air.

Marcus stumbled over a rise and spotted the man with the rifle at the same time the Asian saw him. They were about eighty yards apart. The agent dropped to a firing position, but he knew the distance was too great to be very accurate with a handgun.

With great deliberation, Marcus aimed at the man and began squeezing off rounds. He watched in frustration as the gunman fired toward Wickham, then turned his rifle on Callaway.

Hearing high-powered rounds impacting near him, Marcus took careful aim this time and gently pulled the trigger twice. He was about to fire again when he was staggered by a burning blow. Callaway dropped his weapon and felt the moistness of his blood.

Steve belly-crawled toward the side of the house in time to see the rifleman spray the hovering Marine helo with the last rounds in his clip. Clouds of black smoke belched from the stricken Huey Cobra.

Wickham watched in dismay. "Pull up and get the hell out of there," he said to himself.

As if in slow motion, the damaged helo tilted sideways and drifted toward the slender, manicured trees. After passing over the tall barrier around the tennis court, the gunship suddenly rolled on its left side and crashed in an exploding fireball.

Shrapnel from the main rotor blades ricocheted in every direction, forcing Wickham to clasp his hands over his head.

After the jagged shards stopped impacting the side of the house, he tentatively looked up.

Horrified by the disaster, Wickham paused for a moment, then sprung to his feet and started toward the JetRanger. Twenty steps later he rounded the side of the house and confronted the bare-chested man who had decimated the Cobra with his assault rifle.

The slender Asian, who had slipped in a fresh magazine, saw Steve at the same time. He fired two short bursts at him and then raced for the helicopter.

Showered by puffs of dirt and grass, Steve sprawled on the ground and fired seven rounds between the tree trunks. He saw the small man nosedive into the JetRanger as the pilot simultaneously lifted the craft into the air.

Susan quickly joined Steve while they watched in amazement as the second Marine helicopter bore down on the accelerating JetRanger.

The civilian helicopter tried several wild evasive maneuvers to elude the faster gunship, but the Cobra pilot was as tenacious as a pit bull terrier.

"Pray that he doesn't get away," Susan exclaimed and gripped Steve's arm.

Wickham thought about calling for a pair of armed fighter planes as the civilian pulled his helo almost straight up and rolled 90 degrees to the right. The pilot was obviously talented and highly experienced.

The gunship shot straight up beside the JetRanger and hung directly over the helicopter until both craft lost their kinetic energy and quit flying. They plunged toward the ground to gain airspeed, and the Cobra sliced directly over the tail rotor of the civilian helo. The lethal contest went on for another paralyzing minute while the civilian frantically tried to escape.

Steve cupped a hand to shield his eyes while he watched the deadly aerial duel. "The gunship driver is deliberately trying to ram him."

"It's not worth the Marines' lives!" Susan declared and gripped his arm tighter. "Can't you do something?"

"You're right," he conceded while the two adversaries yanked their helicopters into a tight, low-speed turn. "I'll call him off and have the Air Guard scramble some armed fighters."

Wickham was on the verge of running for his SecTel when the two helos appeared to collide. The JetRanger's tail rotor blade struck the gunship's right landing skid, then shattered into a dozen pieces while the Cobra pulled up and moved off to the side of the damaged helo.

"He's going in. He's losing it," Steve said stiffly while the fuselage of the civilian helicopter slowly began to rotate under the main rotors.

Without the stabilizing tail rotor to counteract the powerful main-rotor drive torque, the helo turned increasingly faster in the opposite direction of the main blades.

The pilot of the JetRanger was desperately trying to salvage an autorotation to a crash landing, but the aerodynamic forces induced by the unique situation were causing the helo to oscillate out of control.

Steve and Susan witnessed the craft tumble over and plummet nose-first toward the ground near the coast highway.

Holding his bleeding shoulder, Marcus staggered up to them as the helicopter impacted with a spectacular explosion of jet fuel.

"Judas Priest, how did things get out of control?" Callaway asked while he panted for breath.

16

NEAR MISSOULA, MONTANA

There was a hushed sense of excitement in the rustic, woodsy restaurant nestled alongside a winding brook. The President of the United States was going to have a late lunch at the unpretentious café before he and his entourage continued their tour of northwestern Montana.

Two Secret Service agents closely watched the preparation of the food and beverages in the kitchen, while other agents interviewed and carefully selected several "customers" who would have an impromptu, spontaneous chat with their Commander in Chief.

CNN and NBC elected to tape the folksy luncheon for their prime time newscast. The combined noise of two generators, coupled with the rows of cables and the battery of satellite dishes, spoiled the otherwise tranquil valley.

As the President's motorcade approached the quaint eatery, a Cable News Network reporter hurried over to one of the stone-faced security agents. After a short pause, the unsmiling agent walked straight to the President's limousine and informed him that CNN was preparing to broadcast a special report about the Pearl Harbor incident.

The President smiled broadly and waved to the small crowd

before he entered the CNN truck to view the news report with his top aides. A technician quickly slid a chair on rollers to the President as the "CNN Special Report" graphic flashed on the television screen.

The familiar anchorwoman fumbled with her earpiece and looked into the eye of the camera. "Thanks for joining us. We have a breaking report just in from Honolulu, Hawaii. At least two helicopters have crashed during a joint exercise involving the FBI and the military. The details are sketchy at the moment, but we will update you as quickly as we receive the information.

"I'm being told," the reporter continued, "that a team of agents from the CIA and FBI located the helicopter that was allegedly used in the assault on the tour ship at Pearl Harbor. During the attempt to capture the pilot and his passenger, a Marine Cobra helicopter crashed, killing its two-man crew. The names of the two crewmen have not been released pending notification of next of kin."

Out of habit, the woman cleared her throat while the news director talked to her. "We now go live to David Kaiulani in Honolulu. Dave."

The native Hawaiian correspondent was standing near the blackened wreckage of the JetRanger. The crash site had been roped off, and armed guards surrounded the mangled helicopter.

"Loraine, I'm standing by the remains of what authorities believe was the helicopter used in the assault on the *Star of Honolulu*. Both people aboard the JetRanger perished in the fiery crash after their helo collided with a Marine gunship that was accompanying the downed military helicopter."

The reporter turned sideways to allow the cameraman a good shot of the accident site.

"Everyone is being cautious about what they say," Kaiulani continued, "but officials at the scene, who wish to remain anonymous, have told me they are certain this is the chopper that was used in the attack."

Rising from his chair, the President thanked the CNN team

and stepped outside with his Secretary of State and Scott Eagle-hoff, his recently appointed Chief of Staff. The President waved everyone away while the three men walked to the edge of the street.

"Scott," the President said with a grim set to his face, "I want all the particulars on this goddamn mess as soon as you can sort it out. Who was the pilot? Who owned the helicopter? And what the hell went wrong?"

Eaglehoff nodded. "I'll turn the screws."

Swarthy and morose, Scott Eaglehoff was by nature a reserved man, but the plump, pigeon-toed former federal judge enjoyed a unique reputation in Washington. He made things happen.

THE MANSION

Bureau laboratory personnel and photographers documented and analyzed everything in and around the estate before Steve and Susan were allowed to explore its interior.

Marcus had been transported to the hospital and was reported to be undergoing surgery.

The Bureau experts found that an entire section of the guest wing had been constructed with hinged walls.

One person could quickly and easily swing the high wall partitions open, move the light pieces of furniture, then cover the wooden parquet floor with a heavy canvas.

The final step in the transformation required two people to open the cleverly constructed entrance to the combination hangar/guest quarters.

When the civilian helicopter was not concealed in the guest wing, the rooms looked perfectly normal, including the large, immovable bathing suite. Because of plumbing constraints, the bath and water closet were built long and narrow to allow room to work on the JetRanger.

After the luxurious home—sans guest quarters—had been

built by local crews, a special team of Indonesian construction workers was hired to build the hangar and make it appear like part of the original structure.

The trio of men and their female interior decorator disappeared after a postconstruction drinking party. A week after the group was expected to return to Indonesia, law enforcement authorities in Jakarta asked the Honolulu Police Department to investigate. The HPD looked into the matter, assuming foul play, but they never found a single clue.

Only two men knew the last whereabouts of the construction workers. By the time the authorities were consulted, the four-some was a long way from where they had last been seen. Sharks make unpredictable course changes in their ongoing quest for food.

"Well," Steve observed as he inspected the interior of the guest quarters-*cum*-helicopter hangar, "they were in a helluva hurry to get out of here."

"Max panic mode," Susan deadpanned and looked behind one of the numerous drop cloths that was used to protect the walls, furniture, and fixtures during the hasty repainting of the JetRanger. "They apparently sprayed the camouflage design directly on the other paint scheme."

"A quick makeover and out the door," Steve mused while he looked at the spray gun and paint containers. "They must have been on the verge of slipping the helo out of here when we paid our first visit."

"No question about it."

He glanced at her and then frowned. "Why do I have a feeling they knew we were on our way here?"

"I don't know," Susan replied, careful not to jump to conclusions, "but I think you're right. And there's something else that puzzles me."

"Me, too," Wickham confided, then turned to his attractive friend and focused his attention on her eyes. "I want to know where they planned to hide the helicopter."

"Exactly," Susan answered and caught Steve's tense, restless look. "They were mighty anxious to get that helicopter off the premises."

"So anxious that they were willing to take major risks to get it out of here because they somehow knew that we had them nailed to the wall."

"Someone"—she let her suspicions rise to the surface—"has been feeding them information about us. . . ."

Wickham took a moment to review his thoughts about the strange turn of events. "That's a distinct possibility. We're going to have to be very cautious about everything we do from now on."

Susan offered him a vague smile. "And not trust anyone until we know if our suspicions are correct."

Steve nodded in agreement. "It looks like our basic logic has been on track, for the most part, so I think we have to continue following our instincts."

"True," she remarked quietly and tilted her head to the side. "Where does your instinct think the pilot was headed?"

"Well, someone threw a hell of a lot of money and effort into setting up the assault, so nothing is beyond the realm of possibility."

Steve walked over to the window and looked out to sea. "I'd have to guess that the pilot was heading offshore . . ."

"Headed for a ship or barge?"

"That, or maybe he planned to dump the helo in the drink after he was out of sight of land."

"With someone standing by to pick him up," Susan replied coolly.

"Or kill him." Steve looked at his watch. "Dead men don't tell tales."

"True."

"Right after the crash, my ops coordinator asked the military to search the ocean around the island. I want to know the name and origin of everything big enough to land a helo aboard."

"How soon will you have the information?"

"They've promised to do a thorough job—low flybys for

photos, et cetera—so I'm not sure when I'll get the final results. Probably sometime tomorrow."

Susan gave Wickham a questioning look. "How'd you get so much influence with the Pentagon? You're the only person I know who can get the military to jump through hoops with a simple request."

"Well," Steve replied with a faint grin, "I got lucky on a couple of difficult field assignments, then unlucky enough to get some notoriety in high places."

"Amazing," she responded with a shake of her head. "You make it look easy."

"Trust me, it isn't as easy as it seems. Getting the military to move on a moment's notice takes a lot of groundwork and a few persuasive words from the White House don't hurt."

"Clean," a laboratory technician announced as he entered the room. "This place is antiseptically clean. They were well organized and didn't leave much to go on when they split."

"The only glitch in their plan," Steve offered with obvious satisfaction, "was that we stumbled across their hiding place before the helicopter was gone."

"That's true," the technician chimed in and looked around the unique hangar. "Once this place was restored to the guest house façade, you'd never know, with just a casual look, that it was once used as a hangar."

Steve nodded in agreement and looked around the interior of the hangar. "They may have had plans for more airborne attacks—under the cover of darkness or in military camouflage—until someone tipped them off that we were on the trail."

"Yeah, you're probably right." The man smiled and wiped the sweat from his brow. "Somebody has been dreamin' in Technicolor, big time."

"The thing that just doesn't fit," Susan began slowly and looked at Steve, "is why would these Japanese be involved in shooting innocent Japanese? Who would go to all this trouble and risk this expensive home to kill their own people?"

Steve watched her jaw muscles tighten. "If you're right, and

I think you are, they used a Caucasian to actually commit the attack. So I think—"

"They did it," Susan interrupted with anger in her voice, "to set the Japanese people against the Americans."

Wickham saw the anger in her eyes.

"Susan," he said compassionately, "we should know who owns this place fairly soon. I expect the pieces will start falling into place in a couple of days."

"I sure as hell hope so," she said with a trace of skepticism. "Because we don't have much to go on. We have the remains of the helicopter that we *believe* was used in the attack, we have the body of the pilot we *think* flew the attack, the other guy in the helo shot at us, this place looks suspicious as hell, and it wouldn't surprise me if we never see the 'house-sitter' again."

"Relax," Steve said lightly and looked around the room. "He'll turn up."

She ignored the comment and walked to a window overlooking the tennis court.

"With what we have right now," Susan complained, "a good lawyer could shoot holes through the whole scenario."

"You may be right," he reluctantly admitted, "but we've got to focus on the loose ends and pursue them until we get some straight answers."

"You're right," she asserted with renewed enthusiasm. "Why don't you follow up on the air search while I see what I can uncover through the island grapevine?"

Steve saw that special gleam return to her eyes. "What have you got in mind?"

"I want to locate the son of—" Susan paused to select a more ladylike response. "I want to locate the individual who rammed my car and find out who owns this place."

17

TOKYO

Tadashi Matsukawa awakened with a start, then closed his eyes and let the events of the previous evening slowly drift through his aching head. After the exhausting eleven-and-a-half-hour flight from Los Angeles, he had been totally inebriated when he lurched out of the first-class section and made his way to his limousine.

His chauffeur, who had learned not to attempt a conversation with Matsukawa when he was drunk, silently drove him to the hotel. A second car would bring his luggage while his driver left to fetch Matsukawa's usual lover.

He clearly remembered the sensuous and attractive *hosutessu* from the exclusive and very private *kara oke* bar. Michiko was a lithe and sexually stimulating hostess who always made herself available for Matsukawa. He had tried to persuade her to be his only sexual partner by offering her an expensive apartment to live in and a generous allowance, but Michiko, who thoroughly enjoyed the wild nightlife and her wealthy boyfriends, had repeatedly turned down the industrialist's offers.

Although Michiko knew Matsukawa was a selfish lover who sometimes manhandled her, she always returned to his bed in the lavish suite he maintained at the Imperial Hotel. Spending a night with the wealthy businessman provided her more income than she could earn in a week at the exclusive club.

He looked at the lighted clock on the nightstand and rubbed his aching temples while the memories and sensations slowly returned. Michiko had left a few minutes before sunrise and Matsukawa's weary chauffeur had driven her home.

Between the jet lag, Michiko's boundless sexual energy, and the endless sips of warm sake, Matsukawa had slept longer than usual. There was much to accomplish today, and he was getting off to a late start.

In less than a week he would be entertaining some of the most powerful and affluent businessmen in Japan. A quartet of young, carefully selected geishas would relax Matsukawa's guests with songs, dances, and conversations ranging from history to contemporary gossip. Geisha means "art person," and training for the unique profession, which has been a part of the Japanese culture since the 18th century, begins early with a demanding apprenticeship.

The attractive women also play a string instrument known as a *shamisen,* and they serve rice wine to help the men unwind. After an appropriate period of time, the geishas would quietly slip away, and the power brokers would be free to discuss the future of Japan.

Matsukawa intended to focus on the concerns of the present and former prime ministers in regard to the escalating fears about the United States. He felt confident that he could convince the leaders of Japan to coalesce and back the Prime Minister in his upcoming discussions with the Americans.

Matsukawa knew that he would have to pound home his message to a few of the fainthearted: Japan must chart her own course and be accepted on an even keel by the United States, including militarily. The Japanese could no longer afford to be the junior partner to the lazy, illiterate, and inefficient Americans.

Once he convinced the cartel members, including the leaders of the Big Four Japanese securities firms, to follow his vision of the future, it would be easier to persuade Prime Minister Genshiro Koyama to take a firm stand and not back down from the arrogant Americans.

After he called room service and ordered vinegared octopus and broiled chicken with rice, Matsukawa opened the drapes and gazed at the Marunouchi business district, where his main offices were located.

He turned and started for the bathroom a moment before the phone rang. Not in the best of moods, he snatched the phone from its cradle. "Matsukawa."

"This is Mishima. Are you alone?"

"Yes," he replied with a visceral feeling of apprehension. "What's wrong?"

"I'll be there in ten minutes."

Matsukawa started to reply and the connection went dead.

Mishima Takahashi was his closest and most loyal business partner. He was the man responsible for structuring the resort hotels along Tumon Bay on Guam, then overseeing them to completion. Takahashi was a key ingredient in the tremendous growth and success of Matsukawa's vast empire.

WAIKIKI BEACH

The warm, yellow-pinkish sun was just beginning to peek over the lush mountaintops when Steve Wickham reached for his copy of the *Honolulu Star-Bulletin & Advertiser*. Bold headlines and pictures of the crashed helicopters dominated the front page and most of the first section.

Opening to the second page, Steve's eye caught another article capped with bold type.

FIGHTER AIRCRAFT TO BE MOVED
Associated Press

WASHINGTON — The Air Force said Wednesday it was temporarily relocating the fighter squadrons of the 432nd Fighter Wing attached to Misawa Air Base, Japan. The F-16 aircraft will be dispersed to the 18th Fighter Wing at Kadena Air Force Base, Okinawa, and to the 8th Fighter Wing at Kunsan in South Korea.

Pentagon sources indicated the sudden move was due to security reasons stemming from the recent crash of an F-16 at Misawa. The air-superiority fighter reportedly was hit by a surface-to-air SAM missile shortly after takeoff. White House officials have yet to deny or confirm the story.

"You're up bright and early." Susan smiled as she approached the outdoor table near the swimming pool.

Steve quickly folded the paper and rose to greet her. "Good morning."

"*Ohayoo gozaimasu,*" she replied and sat down across from him. "Marcus is doing well and resting comfortably."

"Great. Can we see him today?"

"I'm sure we can," she answered and looked at a note she had scribbled for Callaway. "His wife will be arriving later today, so he'll be in good hands."

"That's a relief."

"It sure is. The doctor told me that he'll be able to return to Chicago in a couple of days."

"I'll miss him," Steve said with a glimmer of emotion, "but I'm just glad he's okay. It could have been a lot worse."

"True. He was lucky this time." Susan eyed Steve's handsome face for a moment. "Any news about the military search?"

"Not yet, I'm afraid."

He offered her a cup of hot tea from the urn sitting on the table. "Have you made any headway?"

"A little." She sipped the warm tea. "But I have a strange feeling about this entire incident."

Steve gave her a knowing look. "Like we're caught in a house of mirrors, and someone—someone close enough to reach out and touch us—is watching our every move?"

"Exactly." Susan was surprised by Steve's perception. "The real ownership of the house is totally submerged in a sea of corporations and assorted holding companies. Someone has gone through a tremendous amount of trouble and expense to disguise the actual owner."

Steve shoved his cup aside and leaned forward. "Someone who has so much money that they could afford to walk away from a mansion in Hawaii. . . ."

Susan nodded and looked him in the eye. "Someone who wanted to incite the Japanese people and stretch to the limit the already fragile U.S.-Japanese relationship."

He could tell that something was bothering her. She was tense and preoccupied.

Steve let his gaze travel to the paper. "I see that the car that rammed us was found near the entrance to the Polynesian Cultural Center."

"That's right," she replied and reached into her attaché case for her copies of the FBI reports. "Their suits were found in the car, so they obviously changed into casual clothes and probably blended in with a tour group to get transportation back to Honolulu."

"Yeah," Steve said to himself, "that makes sense."

"After that it was easy. Just a routine cab ride to the airport and they were off to Tokyo."

Steve was puzzled. "The law enforcement officials had their descriptions. They couldn't miss the guy with the mangled ear, and the airport was swarming with cops and FBI agents. Didn't they check any IDs?"

"No." The tone of resentment in her voice was tempered by her usual pleasantness. "Our people were told not to inconvenience any Japanese tourists unless they were absolutely certain they had the individuals who were in the Nissan."

Steve closed his eyes and slowly shook his head. "No, we sure wouldn't want to inconvenience anyone."

"The local police," she went on without showing any emotion, "were even more touchy about offending the Japanese."

"Money?"

"Yes. On the average"—Susan paused while two Japanese women and their children walked past the table—"a million dollars is pumped into the economy every time a Japanese airliner touches down here, so most local people are sensitive about maintaining good relations with the people who happen to have the money."

Steve decided to keep his thoughts about the local economy to himself. "Why are you so sure they went to Tokyo?"

She slid some photocopies to him. "Our people have done a great job, but they ran into a dead end. The car lease was signed by the same person who signed the papers for the house. The handwriting was identical. Everything was handled in cash and they used phony names. However, the certified funds for the house came from a bank in Tokyo, so that's where I think we should concentrate our efforts."

"Interesting."

Susan glanced toward Diamond Head before she continued the conversation. "The account at the Tokyo bank, which was under another bogus name, was closed the day after the attack on the tour ship."

Steve leaned back in his chair and wearily shook his head.

"This whole thing is bizarre," he said, thinking out loud. "Who would go through all the associated risks involved in attacking a tour ship in broad daylight at Pearl Harbor, especially when it's full of people of the same nationality? It just doesn't track—at least in my mind."

"You don't understand the Japanese culture," Susan explained as pleasantly as possible. "Steve, busy Japanese executives hire actors to stand in for them at family reunions, birthdays, and other gatherings. You may think that's really bizarre, but the Japanese who rent the actors think it's efficient and increases their productivity."

He smiled wanly. "I must be losing it."

"No, you just need to think in a different spectrum. This whole thing wasn't as exotic and elaborate as many Japanese projects are, but it was designed to look reasonably simple and straightforward."

"Americanized," he offered.

"You said it." She shrugged in agreement and continued.

"The key is Pearl Harbor and the Caucasian pilot. You could do a number of things to inflame the tenuous relationship between the two countries, but memories of Pearl Harbor gave this assault a life of its own."

"No question about that."

"After the attack," Susan went on, "we've seen a series of escalating incidents, including the JAL crash in Los Angeles and the attacks on the U.S. military."

Susan cocked her head and studied his face. "These attacks could be the catalyst that causes everything to spin out of control between us and the Japanese."

She waited for two giggling children to run by on their way to the beach. "The attack here was an efficient, well-planned operation that was almost flawless. Even with their bad luck, the person or persons who planned the attack had enough good luck to leave only a lukewarm trail."

"And you think that leads to Tokyo?"

Susan arched her eyebrows and gave him a self-assured smile. "There's no question in my mind."

"I hope you're right, but we're going to need something fairly solid to go on."

She nodded in agreement. "Let's take a minute to talk about the helicopter."

"Okay."

"The two men who were in the JetRanger didn't have any identification on them and they were burned beyond recognition. Because the crash was so violent, there is some doubt about trying to match dental records. So we can only hope that we can trace the helicopter to the owner."

"I checked on the JetRanger," Steve said glumly, "and that's another dead end. The helo was purchased from a Brazilian mining enterprise called Vale do Rio Doce. The corporate entity that purchased the JetRanger paid cash, the company no longer exists, and the FAA and Bell Aircraft files indicate the helo was destroyed five months ago near Lima."

He let his glance drift to a bird that was feasting on crumbs at an adjacent table. "I just can't put any of the pieces together.

This is one of the craziest cases I've ever heard of, let alone been involved in."

She followed Steve's gaze to the colorful crumb-snatcher hopping around near them. "It only sounds crazy because you don't think like a Japanese."

Steve nodded and turned his attention to Susan. "Maybe you're right."

Susan smiled warmly. "Let me give you some background information about the Japanese and how they think?"

"Sure," he agreed and noticed her assertion of pride.

"When I was a child, my grandmother read to me on a daily basis," she explained, touching his hand for emphasis. "She spent many hours instilling the history of Japan in me. What became clear was that the Japanese people have always been a determined race with strong motivations and traditions. They are a sensitive people, and emotions sometimes play a greater part in their actions than rational reflection."

Steve gave her a questioning look.

"Think about it," she said convincingly. "They've displayed suicidal tenacity, superhuman intensity, unfailing courage in the most adverse conditions, and a zealous capability to withstand the pain and suffering necessary to make their country strong, efficient, and profitable."

He gave her a slight nod. "I understand what you're saying, and I admire them for pulling together as a nation, but what does that have to do with this situation?"

"Steve, there are a number of powerful Japanese leaders who have deep-seated desires for Japan to be an empire again—both economically and militarily—and I think someone may be trying to accelerate the growing rift between the U.S. and Japan."

"Susan," he began tentatively, "I don't mean to question your intuition, but the empire philosophy is what led Japan to disaster in World War Two. Surely the Japanese people haven't forgotten that significant piece of history."

"That's true," she conceded, "and they haven't forgotten—but it doesn't make any difference."

He furrowed his brow. "It doesn't make any difference?"

"No, it doesn't," she said sadly and glanced down. "The Japanese leaders—the core of men at the center of power—still want to dominate the world, including China and the United States."

The statement brought the conversation to an awkward halt for a few seconds.

"There's a big difference," Steve finally replied, "between wanting to dominate the world . . . and facing the reality of your real capabilities."

"That may make sense to you," she explained evenly, "but you can't convince the warrior mentality. They're a very proud people and they don't like being number two to anyone, especially to people who they consider to be intellectually and morally inferior."

Susan paused when she saw Steve's jaw muscles tighten.

"Now," she said more softly, "they're so close to being a major empire, both economically and militarily, that they can taste and smell the victory."

He cast Susan a fleeting look. "Victory—as in a shooting war with us?"

"Yes," she replied calmly. "The United States is the only thing standing in the way of Japan becoming a colossal military power again."

"Susan, are you suggesting that Japan is going to provoke the U.S. into going to war?"

"It's inevitable," she answered evenly, "at some point in the near future. As their money and military grow, the warriors' egos continue to swell at an accelerated rate. Japan is not going to bow and smile to the Chinese or the Americans much longer—and I think someone wants to speed the process along."

Steve was momentarily speechless. He knew that even though the Japanese could now field a formidable military, they couldn't compete with the American aircraft carriers and nuclear submarines. "You're really convinced that we're going to see Japan and the U.S. engaged in combat?"

"Sure. The Japanese have strong warrior traditions. From the Heiji and Gempei wars in the mid to late 1100s, to World

War Two, the Empire has been involved in so many wars it's hard to recall all of them."

Steve indicated that he had a question. "You're talking about the Medieval Period?"

"Yes," came the dry response. "The civil wars took quite a toll on the losers, but they consistently regrouped, rearmed, and attacked again. Many of the losing factions rose from total defeat to strike down their former victors."

Susan gave Steve an icy look. "Believe me, the Japanese state of mind hasn't changed."

"I don't know what to say," Steve replied in his respectful way. "It's just difficult for me to understand Japanese thinking, especially after the horrors of World War Two."

"Steve," Susan countered with a smile, "the two cultures are polar opposites, with different foundations of logic and reason.

"The brave warrior of past battles," she went on with conviction in her voice, "is surfacing in the Japanese males who control the country. Japanese history is again coming full circle, and the U.S. is in the way, along with the military threat from China and North Korea."

Wickham was reminded of a recent briefing at Langley. "A number of knowledgeable people agree with your prediction."

"Probably more than you think."

"Some of the analysts"—Steve let his eyes drift to the beach—"are convinced that an Asian Cold War would renew Sino-Japanese rivalry and lead to a shooting war . . . with the U.S. being drawn into the battle."

"That's why," Susan explained firmly, "the Japanese have quietly been rebuilding their military."

Surprised by the urgency in her voice, Wickham turned to see the intense look in Susan's eyes.

"Steve, when Japan capitulated to General MacArthur in 1945, it was the hardest blow the warriors had ever taken. They knew if they didn't surrender unconditionally that the Japanese race might be totally destroyed."

"That's why it's so difficult for me to understand," he explained and looked away for a few seconds before facing her.

"Why anyone in Japan would even think about armed conflict with the U.S. is beyond me. If things got out of control, which they would very quickly, the Japanese would run the risk of replaying the end of World War Two."

"True." Susan lowered her voice. "The Japanese look at our declining military and compare it with their growing forces. Some of the leaders in Tokyo believe the two military powers will soon be equal, except for nuclear capability—and the Japanese are secretly working on their nuclear equalizers."

"I hope you don't take this the wrong way," Steve began, "but I think the Japanese don't know when they're well off."

"Many people don't know when they're well off," Susan replied with a hollow voice. "But let me go back to the end of World War Two."

"Okay."

"The Bushido code demanded that Japan congratulate the U.S. for having the genius to invent the atomic bomb. That's the warriors' way of saving face after they've been beaten into submission. How could a victorious nation refuse a mandatory Bushido call for congratulations from their battered and defeated enemy?"

He agreed and saw the hurt in her eyes. "It also provides the loser with the option of not being annihilated."

"You hit the nail on the head!" she exclaimed. "Over the hundreds of years of traditional Japanese warfare, it has sometimes taken forty, fifty, sixty, or more years to rebuild to again fight and invade other countries. There were always cries for peace and reform, but the machismo warriors always prevailed—and they will do it again."

Her face reflected the pain she felt. "It's in their blood, and they *will* surface, regardless of whether it's the age of samurai swords or nuclear weapons. Steve, it's a tradition that is hundreds of years old, and you've seen how traditional the Japanese are. The warriors still believe the Bushido code will carry them to victory or protect them in defeat so they can rebuild to fight again."

"Unfortunately," Steve admitted sadly, "I have a feeling

you're right. It's a frightening thought when you see how fast they've reconstituted their military forces."

"Their naval power"—she glanced at the ocean—"is what I'm most concerned about because it forces other nations into an Asian arms race."

Steve thought about the multitude of international problems that had intensified as the U.S. military was downsized and fractured by the fierce debate over force structuring.

"Susan, we know our government should have managed the growth of the Japanese Self-Defense Forces, but they didn't pay attention and Tokyo hoodwinked them."

"You don't have to remind me," she said with a disgruntled look.

"Now that we've gutted our military," Steve went on with a touch of sarcasm, "the Japanese are taking full advantage of the opportunity to build on our weaknesses."

"Why wouldn't they capitalize?" she responded with enough of a smile to be polite. "Our politicians have selective amnesia where the lessons of history are concerned, especially when it's an election year and they're stuffing lots of money in their pockets from Japanese lobbyists."

18

YOKOTA AIR BASE, JAPAN

Towering more than 12,000 feet, Mount Fuji dominated the horizon as the giant Lockheed C-5B Galaxy turned off the runway and taxied toward the parking ramp at the Air Mobility Command Post. The flight crew was completing their after-landing checklist while the seventy-two members of the special operations forces from Fort Bragg, North Carolina, were gathering their gear and personal belongings.

The highly trained and uniquely equipped soldiers from the Army's 1st Special Operations Command were trained to deal with insurgency and international terrorism. Being the first ground forces to arrive at Yokota Air Base, the elite troops would be supplemented by their comrades from Fort Lewis, Washington, and Okinawa, Japan. The mission of the combined forces was to protect the air base during the period of heightening tension between Japan and the United States.

After the Galaxy lumbered to a smooth stop on the parking ramp, the engines on the mammoth transport spooled down and a hushed quiet settled over the airfield. The tranquillity was suddenly shattered when a mortar shell arced through the air and exploded next to a C-141B Starlifter parked beside the Galaxy.

Another round ripped through the air as the soldiers scrambled from the upper deck of the C-5B. The impact-fused shell found its mark near the center of the fuselage at the right-wing root. Within a microsecond the detonation process began while the round penetrated the passenger compartment and instantaneously killed thirteen men. The shrapnel and shock wave injured or maimed another thirty-four soldiers as they fought to get out of the smoking aircraft.

A half second later the strategic transport burst into flames as the soldiers scrambled from every exit. The ensuing inferno quickly consumed the aircraft while the firefighters worked feverishly to prevent the flames from reaching other airplanes on the ramp.

QUEENS MEDICAL CENTER

Marcus Callaway was quietly dozing when Susan and Steve walked into his private room. He opened one eye and the familiar smile spread across his rugged face. "I thought you guys had gone away and abandoned me."

"No way we would let you off that easy," Susan told him with mock seriousness and handed him a strawberry milk shake. "How are you feeling?"

"Oh, a little weak," he confessed and eagerly took a sip, "but I'm ready to get out of here and go home."

"I'll bet." Steve chuckled.

"Thanks for the shake," Marcus said and sucked on the straw.

Susan winked at Callaway. "I remembered how much you like strawberries."

"Where's your wife?" Steve asked as he walked to the opposite side of the bed.

"She went to get a bite to eat," Marcus answered and then changed the subject. "What's the latest?"

Susan sat down in the chair next to the bed. "The investigation is going slowly, but we're making progress. We'll keep you updated, I promise."

"I appreciate it."

She glanced up at the television mounted on the wall. CNN was on, but Callaway had pressed the mute button on his remote control switch.

"Have you heard the latest news?" Susan asked.

Marcus had indeed seen the live broadcast from Yokota Air Base. "Yes. I guess the attack on the C-5 blew the lid off this latest dispute with Japan. The last report I saw mentioned that one member of the Chukaku-Ha mortar team was killed by our special forces, but his partner got away."

Callaway puffed up his pillow and sat up. "From what I understand, the military believes that the Chukaku-Ha is responsible for the crash at Misawa, the tour bus massacre, and the explosion on the carrier at Yokosuka."

"That's what they're claiming, and there's more," Wickham said and glanced at Callaway's bandaged shoulder. "The White House and Tokyo have opened up with both barrels, and the accusations are flying back and forth. The Marines are guarding our ships at Sasebo and Yokosuka, plus the Third Marine Division and the First Marine Aircraft Wing are gearing up to move out. It looks like the President intends to turn up the heat."

"Yeah." Marcus grimaced when he moved his shoulder. "And I heard that things are popping at Camp Pendleton."

"So I've heard," Wickham said dryly. "Our relations with Japan have really degenerated in the last twenty-four hours, and I suspect it's going to get ugly."

Callaway slid his shake onto the tray over his bed. "This afternoon the White House apparently leaked a rumor about sanctions against the Japanese, and Tokyo fired back with some broadsides of their own."

"They sure did," Susan observed with a look of concern. "We've got a brushfire going on, and I think everyone is reacting too harshly. JAL has stopped flying to Los Angeles and San Francisco, and a spokesman for the Prime Minister said that

Foreign Minister, but time was growing short and he needed Nagumo Katsumoto on the team; that, or make him unavailable for comment.

"The vast majority of the heads of our enterprise groups," Matsukawa said slowly and clearly, "are in agreement that we should terminate the Treaty of Mutual Cooperation and Security and announce that Japan is going her separate way, including militarily. It is in the best interest of our country—and I suggest that it would be in your best interest—to endorse the idea and look into the future."

Katsumoto shifted his gaze to the powerful and wealthy industrialist. "Sometimes it isn't wise to peer into one's future."

HONOLULU

"We may have something here," Steve exclaimed when Susan Nakamura walked into the brightly lighted room at Hickam Air Force Base.

The FBI agent examined the aerial photographs spread around the table. The rest of the military reconnaissance photos were stacked on a desk next to Wickham.

"I've gone through all of these ships," Steve declared, "and we can eliminate everything except this one."

"It looks like a regular freighter to me," Susan murmured, "but I'm not an expert on ships."

Steve tapped a pencil on the bow of the merchant vessel. "I thought the same thing until the photorecon experts pointed out the crane strapped to the deck."

Susan studied the picture. "Oh yeah, I see where it's normally mounted."

"You can't see it from an angle, but from directly overhead it's easy to spot."

She looked up at Steve. "With the crane out of the way, you could easily land a small helicopter and then camouflage it with a tarp or something."

"Exactly."

Susan squinted at the picture of the ship's stern. "I can't make out the name."

"It's the *Matsumi Maru* number three," Steve explained. He handed her a sheet of information about the vessel. "I called the Coast Guard Port Operations and they put me in touch with the people who oversee the arrivals and departures."

"Let me guess," Susan said as she slumped into a chair. "The ship was docked in Honolulu until shortly before the JetRanger took off?"

Steve gathered the photographs together and shoved them over to Susan. "It sailed on the tide the day before they attempted to fly the helicopter offshore. The freighter and a skeleton crew had been in port for almost two months with purported mechanical problems."

Susan glanced at the pictures. "Where was the ship when they spotted it?"

"Approximately forty-five miles northeast of the northern tip of the island. About a twenty-minute flight if they had managed to pull off the escape."

"Do you have any idea"—she paused to examine the information page—"what course the ship is on or where it's headed?"

"Not really," Steve admitted, "but after a few conversations with some of the people who work at the docks, I found out she's registered in Singapore, *and* it's also her home port.

"I called the Port Authority in Singapore," Steve continued. "They told me the *Matsumi Maru* number three generally plied the waters of the South China Sea, but they wouldn't tell me who owned the ship. Something about not having the authority to supply any information about ownership."

Susan remained quiet for a few seconds. "It does seem coincidental that the ship left hours before they tried to fly the helo to another location."

"That's the way I see it," Steve agreed, then reached for another picture of the merchant vessel and studied it for a moment. "I think the next missing piece to this puzzle is in Singapore, and I'm heading there to see what I can find."

"I think you're right," Susan said and looked at the freighter. "I'll bet the *Matsumi Maru* three will show up there before too long."

Leaving Hickam Air Force Base, Steve followed Susan as they made their way toward Honolulu. He replayed the entire series of events relating to the attack on the tour ship and felt that he was overlooking a critical piece of evidence.

Steve turned off the air conditioner and rolled the windows down. He breathed in the fresh air and relaxed, letting his mind drift.

The afternoon traffic was beginning to become congested as they approached Ala Moana Park. Steve was intermittently glancing at Susan's car and watching the people in the park when he heard two loud reports.

Snapping back to the moment, he was shocked to see Susan's sedan swerve to the right and skid to a stop. He saw a silver Continental Mark VIII almost collide with a panel truck as the car turned in front of oncoming vehicles and sped down a side street.

Steve mashed the brake pedal and screeched to a halt behind Susan's car. He leaped out and immediately saw the shattered glass on the pavement. Susan had her Smith & Wesson drawn and was crawling out the passenger-side door when he reached her.

"What happened?" Steve exclaimed at the same time he saw the small cuts on Susan's neck.

"I was wrong," she gasped, "about the enforcer at the mansion—the guy who was driving the Pathfinder."

"You're talking about the bodyguard with the crew cut and chewed ear?"

"You got it," she declared wide-eyed. "Crew cut didn't go to Tokyo. He just tried to kill me!"

Steve looked in the sedan and saw that the window on the

driver's side had been blown inward. The front seat and dashboard were covered with glass particles.

"Folks, please move along," Steve said to the onlookers and took Susan by the arm. "Are you okay?"

She dabbed at her neck and looked at the traces of blood on her fingertips. "I think so."

Susan cautiously looked over the hood and turned to Steve. "I only had a quick glance before I hit the brakes, but I'm positive it was the same guy."

"The enforcer," Steve said while he examined Susan's neck, "knows that we're the only ones who can identify him."

"That's right. He must have followed me to Hickam and never had an opportunity to get a clear shot until we left the base."

"Susan, did you drive to the ba—"

"That's it!" she interrupted when she remembered where she had seen the Continental. "The same car—the silver Mark eight—was pulling to a stop across the street from my home as I was getting into my car."

"You were set up by someone," Steve said caustically and looked up and down the boulevard. "Susan, call your office and give them the details, then have someone guard your home until we get there. We need to have a couple of agents stay at your place while we get hotel rooms under different names."

"No argument from me." She breathed heavily. "Something is very wrong with this picture."

"Yeah, and crew cut is getting information from someone, so we can't afford to tell anyone where we're staying."

"What we need to do," she declared in a firm voice, "is catch that sonuvabitch."

"I think we'll get our chance," Steve replied, then cautiously surveyed the streets and surrounding areas. "Only a high-risk taker would attempt something like this in broad daylight. The guy may not be very bright, but he's a professional hit man who won't give up."

"Well," Susan replied while she brushed herself off, "you certainly have a reassuring way about you."

He noticed long trickles of blood on the back and left side of Susan's neck. "The first thing we need to do is take you to the emergency room."

"No," she said emphatically, "I don't need to go to the hospital."

He gave her a disapproving look. "You have slivers of glass embedded in your neck."

Susan started to touch the nape of her neck, then stopped. Inside, she was criticizing herself for being so stupid. She had been carefully trained to pay attention to everything happening around her, and she had let her guard down.

"Okay, I'll go." She reached for her purse. "If I hadn't slammed on the brakes when I did, I could have rammed that sonuvabitch."

"Or," Steve countered softly, "he could have shot you."

19

THE WHITE HOUSE

The President was vigorously pedaling his stationary bicycle when his Chief of Staff walked into the well-equipped exercise room. "What have you got?" he asked breathlessly.

Scott Eaglehoff took his usual seat near the rowing machine. "Holcomb told me the Agency is getting indications from many of their Asian sources that the hierarchy of Japan's industrial and financial giants are getting together for a major meeting in Tokyo."

The President flexed his legs. "I'm not surprised."

"The planning for these assemblages," Eaglehoff went on, "is usually extremely detailed, but this appears to be an emergency meeting of the enterprise group."

"What do you figure is on their agenda?"

"My guess," Eaglehoff answered gruffly, "considering the festering hostilities between us, is that Japan will opt to put us in a monetary bind to get our attention."

"You really think so?"

"It's a real possibility," Eaglehoff answered without showing any emotion. "The world has changed a lot since September of '45. I think the Japanese are finally fed up with playing second fiddle."

The President lowered his head and stretched his neck muscles. "Did you read the article in the *Post*?"

"About our crime and decay?"

"Yes," the President answered with a disgruntled look.

"Yeah, I read it," Eaglehoff replied. "The Japanese have a point. Their kids don't carry guns to school, they can walk the streets at night without looking over their shoulders, and their subways operate safely and on time."

"The ethics issue," the President said bitterly, "made my blood boil. Ethics, my ass. They have the unmitigated gall to talk about ethics when they repeatedly violate the Buy-American Act and then lie about it."

The enactment required the U.S. military to give preference to goods made by American companies.

"They ship tens of thousands of crates of Japanese-made products to their companies here," the President said venomously, "then relabel the containers 'Made in the USA,' slap a Machine Tool Association sticker on the side, and then sell the products to our military.

"Hell," he went on, "we've got billions of dollars' worth of Japanese-made equipment at our air bases, naval installations, and even in our nuclear facilities."

He looked at his Chief of Staff and lowered his head. "We can't get anyone to do a goddamn thing about it," he said contemptuously, "because the Japanese have the most powerful lobby in Washington—most of whom are former U.S. trade officials or members of the Department of Commerce."

Eaglehoff sighed. "When Tokyo has over twelve hundred lobbyists in Washington, and spends over 140 million annually in this city, a lot of influential people get on the gravy train."

"Scott," the President began sadly, "the Japanese are absorbing us like a sponge, and we're sitting here with our heads up our asses."

"It's the same old argument," Eaglehoff suggested. "If we could ever get government and business to work hand in hand instead of bashing each other over the skull, we'd be the epitome of capitalism again. The Japanese look at us and wonder how such incompetent people rose from our apathy to crush them during World War Two."

"I'll admit," the President responded uncomfortably, "that we have some improvements to make, but the Japanese aren't doing themselves any favors by poking us in the eye. They should take a long look in the mirror and be grateful for the position they're in today."

"In their minds," Eaglehoff added, "they've suffered the consequences of their sins long enough, and I don't think they're in the mood to pay further penance to the United States. The Japanese now own the home, and we're the renters."

The President gave his Chief of Staff a curious glance. "So you think they'll squeeze our financial balls until we learn our lesson?"

Eaglehoff loosened his tie. "Financially, they could put us on our knees. If the Japanese pulled the rug out from under us, we'd have a national bankruptcy on our hands."

"The wizards at the think tanks," the President said with false indifference, "have been discussing that scenario for the past several days. They have come up with some interesting possibilities . . . and I think it's time to give Japan something to consider."

"A wake-up call?"

"I would classify it as a visual reminder," the President responded cryptically. "Something to think about while they're puffing out their chests."

EAST CHINA SEA

Commander Hayama Shimazaki stood on the bridge of the Aegis destroyer *Kongo* and watched the jet fighters being catapulted from the deck of the Nimitz-class nuclear-powered carrier *Abraham Lincoln*.

Shimazaki was the commander of a small detachment of Japan's Maritime Self-Defense Force ships operating near the southern extremity of the Ryukyu Islands. The *Kongo* was flanked by the replenishment oiler *Tokiwa* and the destroyer *Asagiri*.

Shimazaki had received orders to cruise in close formation with the American carrier battle group after the crew of a Shin Meiwa flying boat radioed the position of the huge flattop to Tokyo.

The orders explained that the high command wanted Shimazaki's flotilla to solidify the Japanese presence in the East China Sea until more Self-Defense Force ships and submarines could reach his position.

Shimazaki and the officers in his command surmised that the latest instructions came about because of the degenerating relations between their country and the U.S. They were concerned about the worsening situation and talked in private about the possibility of a military conflict.

Although Shimazaki was uncomfortable about shadowing the Americans, the career naval officer carried out his orders as he expected his men to do. However, with tensions on the high seas ripe for hostilities, Shimazaki had elected to interpret his orders in a cautious way and give his ships plenty of room to maneuver.

Dusk was settling over the carrier group when Lieutenant Commander Peggy Rapoza taxied her F/A-18 Hornet onto the number-one catapult. She carefully checked her flight controls, then watched the cat officer give her the full-power signal.

Shoving her throttles forward, Rapoza felt the sudden adrenaline surge, verified her engine gauges were normal, snapped a salute to the "shooter," braced her head against the top of the ejection seat, and sucked in a breath of cool oxygen.

Seconds later, Rapoza was nailed to the back of the seat as her vision blurred under the excruciating g-forces. The punishing catapult shot abruptly ended with what felt like a sudden deceleration as the Hornet went off the end of the flight deck.

Although Rapoza's powerful fighter was still accelerating at a tremendous rate, the first few seconds down the catapult track felt like she had been shot out of a cannon.

With her heart rate finally slowing, Rapoza flipped the landing gear lever up, waited for the speed to increase, raised the wing flaps, then checked her engine instruments and caution lights.

Satisfied that all systems were normal, the seasoned flight leader eased back the power and waited for her wingman to rendezvous on her right side. After a brief air-combat-maneuvering session, the pilots were scheduled to practice refueling from a KA-6D Intruder tanker before making a night landing.

When the last fighter plane raced down the catapult and climbed into the darkening sky, Captain Perry Wiggins gave the order to turn the group to their reciprocal heading and steam downwind until it was time to recover aircraft.

While the mammoth carrier was turning to the new course, the flight deck personnel were repositioning aircraft in preparation for the next recovery period. Clad in various brightly colored pullovers, the sailors performed their demanding tasks with a degree of finesse that was honed by experience and constant training.

Once the ships had steadied on course, Wiggins went to his at-sea cabin for a quick dinner and a short chat with his executive officer.

Peggy Rapoza's F/A-18 Hornet was accelerating through 430 knots when she heard a bang and felt a tremble in the airframe. Something was wrong, and her intuition told her to slow down and evaluate the situation.

"Flash," she radioed to her wingman, Lieutenant Charlie Gordon. "Let's knock it off and join up. I'm slowing to three hundred indicated."

Her partner could tell from the inflection in Rapoza's voice that all was not right.

"Roger," came the terse reply. "I'm at your eight o'clock and closing. What's the problem?"

Rapoza glanced over her left shoulder and spotted the pulsating anticollision light on Gordon's fighter. "I'm not sure what's happening. Ah, I heard a strange noise, and then the fuselage shuddered. I think something may have broken in the engine compar—"

At that moment an engine right caution light illuminated, followed by a fire-warning light. Her eyes widened as she gawked at the engine gauges.

"Flash, I've got a fire-warning light!"

"Any secondaries?"

"Yeah. I'm shutting it down," Rapoza exclaimed while she secured the engine, fired the extinguisher, and then jettisoned her external stores and started dumping fuel.

"Peg, you've got a steady stream of black smoke pouring out of the right engine."

Rapoza stared at the glowing fire-warning light like it was a coiled rattlesnake. The extinguishing system had not controlled the raging blaze.

"Flash, switch to Pri-Fly."

"Switchin'," he said excitedly while they turned for the nearby carrier.

Primary Fly was the carrier's control tower where the Air Boss and his assistant "Mini-Boss" coordinated all aviation operations in the air and on the carrier.

"Boss," Rapoza radioed Pri-Fly, "Stinger Three-Oh-Three has an engine fire and I need an emergency pull-forward."

Seconds passed before anyone replied. "Say again."

"Stinger Three-Zero-Three has an engine fire and I need to return to the boat. I need to trap immediately!"

"Copy." More time passed. "We're clearing the deck and getting ready to turn into the wind."

"Roger that," Rapoza said while she descended and quickly covered the checklist items. She flinched from the sudden tightness in her chest and then reviewed her single-engine emergency procedures. A night carrier-landing was difficult enough with two good engines and no distractions, but this situation was the toughest she had ever faced in her flying career.

• • •

The navigator aboard *Kongo* stepped next to Commander Shimazaki and spoke softly. "Sir, we need to make a course change before we get too close to the islands. We don't want to get squeezed between the Americans and *Ishigaki*."

The skipper agreed and told the officer who had the conn to cross behind the carrier battle group and take up station on the opposite side.

Peggy Rapoza was having difficulty seeing the curved wake of *Abraham Lincoln* as the big carrier heeled over in the turn. She set up for a downwind approach so she could roll on short final once the ship completed the turn.

Before she was abeam the flattop, she stopped dumping fuel and lowered her landing gear and tailhook. After configuring the aircraft for a single-engine landing, she checked her ejection seat fittings, then said a silent prayer.

"Peggy, you've got flames!" Gordon bellowed. "I see flames comin' from the tailpipe!"

A cold shiver ran down Rapoza's back. "Stinger Three-Oh-Three needs a clear deck! I've got visible flames!"

"You've got a ready deck," the Air Boss instantly replied. "Paddles is up."

Paddles was a nickname from the days when Landing Signal Officers used bright-colored paddles to "wave" pilots aboard the carriers.

Rapoza started her unconventional approach to the ship while it was still turning and called the LSO when she saw the bright "meatball" on the primary optical landing aid. "Hornet Three-Oh-Three, on the ball, seven-point-eight."

Something in her peripheral vision caught her attention and she glanced up for a split second. Rapoza thought she saw the lights of another ship on a collision course with the carrier, but there wasn't time to confirm her suspicions. She had to concentrate on getting the Hornet down in one piece.

"Roger ball," the LSO said calmly from his platform on the aft portside of the ship. He could see bright, reddish-orange flames licking around the tail of the fighter, but he wasn't going to say anything to the pilot at this stage of the emergency. "You're lookin' good, Stinger. Keep it comin' and give me a little power."

Rapoza tweaked the left throttle forward and concentrated on making the approach the best she'd ever flown. "Come on, Three-Oh-Three, stay together just a little longer."

Captain Wiggins stepped into the bridge of *Abraham Lincoln* at a moment when utter chaos was erupting around him. The officer of the deck had turned toward the Japanese vessels to avoid the U.S. ships on the other side of the carrier. He felt confident that *Abe* could safely make the 180-degree turn without jeopardizing any of the vessels. He hadn't anticipated the *Kongo* turning toward the carrier.

The radar operators had been the first to notice that both warships were rapidly closing on each other. Everyone on the flattop's bridge was shouting when Wiggins told the helmsman to tighten his turn and then stared at the oncoming navigation lights of the Aegis destroyer.

"Sound the collision alarm!"

Hayama Shimazaki had already caught the blunder and was attempting to turn away from the enormous carrier. He stood transfixed as feelings of confounded amazement and sheer terror flashed through his mind.

Everyone on the bridge silently stared as the bows of the two ships crossed head-on for an instant. To a person, they knew the supercarrier could crush them like a rowboat. The sailors cringed as the huge flattop suddenly grew into a massive image.

Seconds later, *Kongo* collided with a flight-deck elevator on the side of the carrier as the ships brushed sides.

Working hard to keep the bright "meatball" even with the green datum lights, Peggy Rapoza concentrated on lineup as the blazing jet flashed over the carrier's ramp and slammed into the steel deck.

She was thrown against her shoulder straps when her tail-hook snagged the number-three wire. After the aircraft came to a sudden stop and rolled back a few feet, she opened the canopy and quickly secured the left engine.

Peggy saw the fire truck and the silver-clad "hot-suit" rescue personnel racing toward her while the aircraft handlers hurried to chock her wheels.

Rapoza was halfway out of the cockpit when she was engulfed in a sea of thick foam as the firefighters hosed down the burning jet. She hurried out of the way, then stopped to thank God as the medical corpsmen surrounded her.

20

The FBI office was crowded and noisy when Steve walked in to meet Susan. He waited patiently while she finished her conversation with another agent, then greeted her with a friendly smile. "Good morning."

"It *is* a good morning." She beamed and picked up her coffee cup. "We've got some information about crew cut."

"That sounds promising."

"It is. The car he was driving was stolen," she explained. "The HPD found it abandoned next to the Punahou High School."

"Maybe I was wrong," Steve admitted.

"How's that?"

"A professional hit man wouldn't steal a car to go eliminate someone. It's too risky."

"Maybe he doesn't operate like other hired guns."

"That's the scary part."

Steve pointed at the neatly arranged bulletin board containing the FBI composite drawings of the well-groomed, gap-toothed Japanese "house-sitter" and the young assailant with the grotesque ear. "These came out better than I thought they would."

"Everyone has a copy of the composites," Susan went on, "so the enforcer shouldn't be too difficult to locate unless he finally left the island. Not too many people have a right ear that looks like it's been partially chewed off."

Susan greeted another associate and turned to Steve. "Let's go to our private office."

"Lead the way."

They walked down the hallway to the storage room Susan had been using since they first arrived on the island.

"Steve," she began sadly, "I just talked to another agent who works in our office in San Francisco. There's an epidemic of Asian-bashing spreading across the country."

"I know," he said ruefully. "Some of the National Guard units are being called out."

"This isn't the usual Japan-bashing," she continued gravely. "All Asians are being harassed. People are shooting Asians— and they're shooting back, especially the Koreans."

Steve shook his head. "It's going to get worse as long as these terrorist attacks continue."

Steve and Susan stared at each other for a few seconds, realizing how close they had become.

"Are you going to Tokyo?" he asked.

"I sure am. I still believe the answer to the attack on the cruise ship lies in Japan. However, I'm not going in an official capacity."

"What?"

She tore the top sheet of paper from her legal pad and looked at her notes. "There's a major controversy raging in the National Police Agency—they supervise all of Japan's law-enforcement services—and they've reversed course in regard to allowing the FBI to work with them on this particular investigation."

"Are you saying," Steve asked with a perplexed look, "that you can't even get access to any of the information they may have uncovered?"

"That's correct. Our Attorney General is really steamed, but the official protests to the NPA are being handled by the Department of Justice and the State Department."

"This is crazy," Wickham protested. "Both countries are clubbing each other to death, and we can't get law-enforcement agencies to cooperate with one another. Totally fucking insane."

"That may be true," Susan conceded with a degree of surprise at Steve's outburst, "but the fact is that the Japanese feel very strongly about this, and they made it clear that we are not welcome to join them in the investigation."

She folded the piece of paper. "I don't know what the reason is. It could be the open antagonism between our countries, or maybe they know something we don't.

"Or," she speculated, "it could be a matter of saving face if they believe Japanese citizens were involved in the scheme. We know there were at least three Japanese linked to the crime here. We know one died in the helicopter crash, but can we solve the case?"

"We will eventually," Wickham answered with a sense of determination. "I guess we need to make some travel plans and get under way."

"I took the liberty of making travel arrangements for both of us," Susan admitted with a slow smile. "I'm going to Singapore before I go to Tokyo."

"Great," he exclaimed and instantly wished he could retrieve the word. His enthusiasm had not been overlooked and Susan was obviously embarrassed.

She maintained her composure while a sense of uneasiness settled over her. There wasn't any doubt that she was attracted to the handsome agent, but the files she had reviewed indicated that he was married. Susan was also well aware of the difficulties associated with an interracial relationship.

If she had learned anything worth remembering in her adult life, it was to stay away from married men and interracial relationships. Susan bore the scars of experiences in both arenas.

"Well, I better get busy," she suggested and caught Steve's eye. "Our flight leaves at eleven-oh-five."

THE OVAL OFFICE

The President glared at his Secretary of Defense and then gave Admiral Clayton Biddle a cold look. "The Japanese are placing the blame on us," the President blurted and held up a front-page headline from *The Washington Post*. "How could such a thing happen?"

"Sir," Admiral Biddle cautiously answered, "the Japanese have the right to operate in international waters. If you or Secretary Mellongard so desire, we can take every precaution to avoid other ships, but I don't think that's the best solution to the problem."

The President bristled and leaned forward against his polished desk. "We're not going to go out of our way to avoid anyone, including the Japanese. Period. I want the people in command of our ships to pay attention to what the hell they're doing. It's that simple."

"Yes, sir," Biddle responded somberly.

"What's the status of the carrier?" the President asked in a tone laced with irritation.

The Admiral maintained a calm exterior while he examined the idea of taking early retirement. "*Lincoln* is operational, but the tempo of flight ops is hampered anytime a deck-edge elevator is inoperable."

The President looked at Biddle's service medals. "What's your recommendation, Admiral?"

"Secretary Mellongard and I believe the carrier needs to go to the naval shipyard in Philadelphia. They've got the facilities to do the job right."

The President thought about the idea and rejected it. "Is there someplace closer?"

"I'm afraid not, sir. The other yards are in use, and Philly happens to have a slot open."

"How long would it be tied up?"

"Thirty to forty days, sir."

Glancing at the small globe on his desk, the President made his decision. "Gentlemen, let's keep *Lincoln* on station for the present time. If Japan even attempts to muscle us around, I want the biggest stick on the block."

Clayton Biddle remained his usual calm self. The Admiral had learned to expect anything from the unpredictable Commander in Chief.

The President gently spun the globe and watched it revolve for a moment. "We've seen a sudden increase in Japanese warships in the South China Sea. I want them to think about the overwhelming power that is sitting in the middle of their shipping lanes."

Biddle nodded. "Yes, sir."

"And I want to take another step," the President continued and let his glance slide to Mellongard. "Bryce, you and Admiral Biddle work out the logistics, but I want *Independence* out of Yokosuka and on station somewhere in the South China Sea as quickly as possible.

"I want *Lincoln* in a position to block the Lombok and Sunda straits," the President continued, "and—where's *Kitty Hawk*?"

"She's in the Arabian Sea," the Admiral told him, beginning to feel uncomfortable. "Sir, the threat of closing Japan's main sea-lanes is going to infuriate the Japanese people and cause global repercussions."

"We'll place her in the Strait of Malacca," the President went on, ignoring the advice, "as a reminder that we mean business if the Japanese become rambunctious."

Admiral Biddle started to protest, but Mellongard spoke first. "Sir, with all due respect, I don't think this is a good course of action. The waters of the Malacca Strait are extremely congested and difficult to navigate. As many as fifteen hundred ships pass through there each day, and a number of nations would be extremely upset if we cruised in there with a carrier group."

The President gave Mellongard an angry look and turned to

his Chief of Staff. "Scott, set up a meeting with Bud Tidwell and have an airplane standing by. I want him out there calming the fears of our allies, and I don't give a damn about anyone else.

"We've got a problem with the Japanese," the President said curtly, "and I want them to think things through before they do something irrational."

Mellongard slowly exhaled. "Sir," he said as calmly as he could, "placing a carrier group in the straits would be extremely intimidating. We've got enough problems with the Japanese, and we don't need to provoke them at this stage of the game."

Admiral Biddle nodded his agreement, then looked at the floor.

The Japanese rely on the straits and shipping lanes for the vast majority of their oil and raw goods. Without the ability to import raw materials, Japan would quickly grind to a halt.

"Bryce," the President said evenly, "you know as well as I do that large, highly maneuverable and powerful forces are likely to make the Japanese think twice before they want to confront the U.S. I want them to have a very clear picture of what they're facing if push comes to shove."

"Sir"—Mellongard tried another avenue of reasoning—"this type of action has the potential for open warfare, and we've got thousands of military people in Japan."

"And they're going to stay right where they are," the President said firmly. "At the present time we have an obligation to Japan, and we're going to honor that commitment."

"Mr. President," Mellongard pleaded, "we have people and weapons in Japan to *defend* their country. To reverse course and threaten the possibility of cutting off their economic life-blood is not what I would recommend. There is no mutual trust in the region, and our military forces are the only security mechanism that governments from Tokyo to Canberra can count on. We can't afford to switch from policeman to bully."

The President hesitated, then gave him enough of a smile to be polite. "I understand your concerns, but my job is to focus on the problems at hand and make the tough decisions, and now is the time to prepare for a confrontation with the Japanese. I don't want them to have any doubt about our resolve."

Bryce Mellongard was dismayed and needed time to sort through the possible effects of this threatening action. "At a minimum, it's going to set back our relationship with Japan a long way."

"I don't care," the President continued in a steady voice, "if it sets our relations with Japan back to 1945. The days of the U.S. being their benevolent protector are almost over, and the alliance with Japan is shaky at best. We're not going to continue to spend billions of dollars to defend a country that is an economic competitor and attempts to skirt every issue from trade to exchange rates."

The men dutifully nodded.

"Their military is mushrooming," the President said bitterly. "Mark my words—at some point in the *near* future, Japan's growing military power in the Pacific Ocean is going to eclipse our shrinking forces and ships."

He idly twirled the globe. "Then we're right back to rebuilding a huge military force to cope with an Asian Cold War. Gentlemen, I know it may sound implausible to you, but it's right over the horizon, believe me."

The President watched the surprised reactions on the men's faces before he went on. "If we're going to confront Japan, which I believe is inevitable at some point, I'd just as soon do it now and sharply decrease the size of their Self-Defense Forces in the process."

Pausing to wait for a response, the President leaned back in his chair and observed his SECDEF.

"I realize," Mellongard began slowly, "that we're on a collision course with Japan, but using our military power to hold them hostage economically is going to send shock waves around the world."

"That's fine," the President replied in a calm voice. "Everyone, including the Japanese, needs to take a close look at the situation that prevails today. We're the only superpower on the planet, and that status has an upside, which is obvious, and a downside.

"The downside is that our nation spends a lot of money to provide a great deal of stability to this world. Many people look to us for leadership, and they're grateful that we use our power in a responsible manner . . ."

The President let his remarks hang in the air for a brief moment. "That's why we're obligated to place a cap on Japan's military forces, forcibly if we have to, or we'll get to repeat history—and that's the last thing we want to do."

21

TOKYO

Tadashi Matsukawa looked down at the Babasaki Moat from his imposing office in the Mitsubishi Building. He turned and walked back to his glass desk and sat down in his custom-made chair, which was covered in mink fur.

Mishima Takahashi, the man who had been in charge of the Pearl Harbor and JAL operations, sat in front of the large desk, nervously smoking a Camel. Through Matsukawa's mole at Langley, they knew that the U.S. investigators were gaining ground in their search for Takahashi and his accomplice.

Takahashi was furious that his protector had not killed Wickham and Susan Nakamura, even though the CIA snitch was providing information concerning their whereabouts.

"I have to be patient and have faith," the senior executive told himself over and over. What the crew-cut, barrel-chested bodyguard lacked in intelligence and innovation, he made up for by being fearless and aggressive. Takahashi was confident that his stooge would kill the government agents, eventually.

Matsukawa studied the small, bespectacled man for a moment. Takahashi looked haggard, and his eyes were red and puffy from smoking and from drinking vodka the previous night. He was slowly succumbing to the overpowering fear of being exposed as the ringleader of the brutal attack at Pearl Harbor.

"Mishima," the billionaire said at last, "you've got to pull yourself together. Everything is going to be fine, honestly. We've covered our trail—so relax."

Takahashi knew better after hearing the report from the Langley informant who was keeping Wickham and Nakamura under constant surveillance.

Matsukawa thought about sending the executive on a vacation aboard his yacht, but changed his mind. He wanted to keep a close eye on the troubled man.

"We were within minutes of flying the helicopter out," Takahashi said glumly and lit another unfiltered cigarette, "when they came to the door."

Matsukawa had never seen the usually urbane man break down and become emotional. "You've got to calm down and think in positive terms."

Takahashi's hands shook and ashes drifted to the carpet. "It is my fault for not making them work faster. We would never have been discovered if I had pushed harder."

"Mishima, listen closely to me . . ." the industrialist said, with most of his thoughts on the upcoming meeting with the corporate groups.

Matsukawa waited until the worried executive finally looked at him. "I'm going to be extremely busy with the *keiretsu* and the Prime Minister the next few days."

Takahashi absently acknowledged the statement but couldn't stop thinking about the consequences if his involvement in the attacks were discovered. It would be a scandal that would rock the entire world. The more he thought about the assaults, the more he couldn't believe that Matsukawa had convinced him that it would be foolproof. *Shigeki must find and kill the two agents who could recognize us.* Takahashi had promised the Japanese mercenary 7 million yen for proof of the agents' deaths.

"I want you to study the projects that we have on our schedule," Matsukawa said, "and prioritize the best eight. Also, we've got to shift some of our focus to our aerospace and defense efforts. I've got a strong feeling they're going to be producing more products very shortly."

Takahashi gave his boss a blank look and rose from his chair. "I will do the best I can." He ground his cigarette in the crystal ashtray on the desk and quietly walked out of the elegant office.

Matsukawa swiveled his fur-covered chair around and gazed toward the Imperial Palace. He knew what he would eventually have to do with Mishima Takahashi. An accident while cruising aboard *Gochi Nyorai* was a relatively safe way for him to sever his ties to the Pearl Harbor attack.

NEW TOKYO INTERNATIONAL AIRPORT, NARITA, JAPAN

Susan and Steve studied the unique interior of the Japanese specialty restaurant and smelled the simmering food being prepared in the tiny kitchen. Though small and crowded, the tidy restaurant provided a pleasantly cozy atmosphere while they waited for their connecting flight to Singapore.

When Steve raised his glass of cold beer to take a sip, he noticed that many of the Japanese patrons were staring at him. Not one of them had even the hint of a smile, and some were openly scowling at him.

Always keenly alert to her surroundings, Susan noticed the antagonistic looks, but attempted to ignore them. She glanced at the beer Steve was sampling. "How do you like it?"

He raised the glass and mused for a moment. "When I was stationed here, my friends and I always drank Kirin, but the Sapporo is good, too."

Susan knew she had to acknowledge the unfriendly situation. She felt badly about having suggested the restaurant. "Steve, if you'd like to go somewhere else, I understand. I didn't expect this kind of treatment."

"It's okay, really," he replied with an encouraging smile. "From the looks I'm getting, they must think I'm the guy who invented taxes."

"No." She allowed a tiny smile. "The looks you're getting are worse."

"Thanks a lot," Steve said and let his gaze linger on her pleasant features. "We're going to have a nice meal and mind our own business."

She gently lifted her glass of plum wine in an impromptu toast. "I admire your spirit," she said firmly and clinked her glass against his. "To our success."

He noticed a couple of Japanese customers frowning in disgust, but he forced himself to ignore them.

"What did you manage to find out"—she smiled and leaned slightly toward him—"from the mysterious depths of the legendary CIA?"

He had been in contact with the Intelligence Directorate at Langley to have the analysts work on researching the ownership of the *Matsumi Maru* number three.

"Not much for the moment, but I'm hoping they'll have something for us by the time we get to Singapore."

She could see that he was ill-at-ease. "Do you know what you want to order or would you like me to select one of my favorites for you?"

"I'll defer to you." He quietly laughed. "I have absolute faith in your judgment."

After Susan ordered *mizutaki* for both of them, she looked at him for a long moment. "May I ask you a personal question?"

He gave her a slow glance. "You want to know if I'm married, right?"

She blushed slightly, embarrassed that Steve had anticipated her question. "Well, your file indicates that you're married, but you don't wear a wedding ring. I was just curious, since I've never heard you say anything about your wife or family."

"I was married," he said matter-of-factly, "but my divorce was final about five weeks ago."

Susan felt a strange sense of relief sweep over her.

He gave her a friendly smile. "You'll have to bring your files up-to-date," he teased and sipped his beer.

"If you don't mind telling me," she asked delicately, "what happened?"

"I'll make a long story short." He chuckled and slid his empty glass to the edge of the table. "She was a flight attendant for Pan American, and when the airline went under, Becky had a hard time dealing with the loss of her job.

"She finally managed to get another flight attendant position with TWA, but she had to start at the bottom of the seniority list. After she had become adjusted to starting from the bottom again, the airline started downsizing and she was laid off."

"That would be tough on anyone," Susan commented with a concerned expression. "Is that when the problems began?"

"Yes, basically. She never liked my career choice, so when she left TWA, she wanted me to quit my job and move out west with her. I didn't want to do that, so things escalated to the point where we decided to go our separate ways."

"Do you have any children?" Susan asked as their meals arrived at the small table.

"None that I'm aware of," he replied in an attempt to lighten the conversation.

Susan gave him a look of mock disgust. "I'd kick you in the shin"—she laughed softly—"if we weren't in a public place."

"This crowd would love that," Steve responded, then stopped dead cold when he saw the familiar Oriental man with the crew-cut hair and mutilated ear. The tall, ruggedly built hit man was standing about 150 feet down the concourse, pretending to read a magazine.

"Susan, look at me," Steve insisted, "and don't make any sudden moves."

She went rigid as the color suddenly drained from her face. "He's stalking us, isn't he?"

"Yes," Steve uttered under his breath and observed the small kitchen at the back of the restaurant. "Go into the kitchen and see if someone can contact security."

"Okay, but please be careful."

"Susan," Steve quietly went on, "stay in there and cover me if something goes down."

"You can count on it." She reached for her purse, gracefully rose from her seat, and walked in the direction of the kitchen.

When Susan reached the back of the restaurant, Steve looked away from the hit man but kept him in his periphery.

What's that bastard going to do? he had just asked himself when the man tossed his magazine to the side, pulled a handgun from his jacket pocket, and headed toward the restaurant.

Steve glanced around. *I can't wait for security. The place is crammed with people.*

He was reaching for his Beretta when Susan yelled a warning. "Steve, watch out!"

He jumped to his feet and aimed his Beretta at the hit man. "Freeze! Drop to your knees and put your hands over your head!"

The man stopped and raised his gun.

"Now, goddammit!" Wickham ordered and fired a round over his attacker's head. "Drop your weapon!"

People started screaming and running in every direction while others dropped flat on the floor and scrambled for any cover they could find.

The hit man turned and raced down the concourse, knocking down passengers and visitors like bowling pins.

Steve started after him and then stopped. It was too dangerous to get boxed into a position where he might have to exchange gunfire in the middle of a crowd.

He returned the Beretta to the small of his back and walked over to Susan. "This guy is crazy."

"Or very stupid," she said as she watched the airport security personnel hurrying toward the restaurant.

"If he's this overt in public," Steve said as he reached for his identification, "he isn't going to give up. Anyone who would try to kill someone in a busy airport is either a complete mental case or really desperate."

"Or both." Susan frowned. "That's what concerns me."

"Same here," he openly confessed. "It's like someone is telegraphing him our every move."

Susan couldn't conceal her ire. "You're right. We're traveling under assumed names, and only a few people know where we're going."

"And even fewer"—Steve paused to slow his breathing—"had access to our flight itinerary."

"Someone," Susan fumed, "is setting us up. There's something bigger going on than what we see on the surface."

"If we're careful," Steve said with a look of concern, "we might be able to trap this nutcase—which could possibly lead us to the person behind the attack at Pearl."

"And to the person who is selling us out," Susan added bitterly.

"That's right," he agreed. "We've got to set a trap for this psycho."

She reached for her badge as the airport security team surrounded the front of the now-empty restaurant. "Which one of us is going to be the bait?"

22

STRAIT OF MALACCA

USS *Kitty Hawk* and her carrier battle group slowed to a leisurely pace and entered their assigned patrol area southeast of the Nicobar Islands, near the northern mouth of the Strait of Malacca.

This hazardous strait, 550 miles long, varies in width from 155 miles in the northern section to 40 miles in the south. Named after the port of Malacca on the Malayan coast, the crowded strait provides the shortest sea route between the Persian Gulf and Japan.

Located between Malaysia and the Indonesian island of Sumatra, the strategic waterway connects the Andaman Sea in the Indian Ocean to the South China Sea. The shallow, pirate-infested bottleneck, which is the main shipping route connecting Europe and the Mideast to Eastern Asia, narrows tightly near the port city of Singapore.

Along with the English Channel, the Bosporus Strait in Turkey, and the Strait of Gibraltar, the Strait of Malacca shares the infamous reputation of being one of the most dangerous, collision-prone channels in the world, and the congested channel is a natural chokepoint to stem the constant flow of raw goods and petroleum that Japan so desperately needs.

A constant stream of giant petroleum tankers traverses the waterway during around-the-clock operations between the Middle Eastern oil fields and ports in eastern Asia. The twenty-one-hour journey through the main section of the strait is difficult to navigate and features tricky tides, unpredictable local traffic, and the ever-present gangs of modern-day pirates who board ships to rob and sometimes kill the crews.

An airborne warning-and-control aircraft orbited high above the Seventh Fleet carrier and her six escort ships from Cruiser Destroyer Group Five. The Grumman Group Two E-2C Hawkeye provided the radar eyes for the warships and the fighter planes. The "Hummer" rotated with three other Carrier Air Wing 15 Hawkeyes to supply around-the-clock surveillance for airborne threats. If the early-warning aircraft spotted unidentified planes, the "bogies' " position and altitude would be sent by digital link to *Kitty Hawk* and to the air-warfare officer aboard *Chancellorsville,* one of the carrier battle group's two Aegis cruisers.

Miles from the center of the carrier group and operating in separate quadrants, two Lockheed S-3B Viking jets patrolled for submarine activity. The pair of antisubmarine-warfare aircraft, known as Hoovers because their engines sound like vacuum cleaners, also provided the capability for visually searching the surface of the ocean. The crews of the jets from the VS-37 *Sawbucks* took pride in knowing that they were the best of the best in the ASW business.

Beneath the choppy waters leading to the Strait of Malacca, a Los Angeles–class nuclear-powered attack submarine quietly prowled the depths in search of stealthy threats to the battle group. Limited by the shallow waters of the southern end of the narrow strait, which varies from 90 to 120 feet in depth, the submarine had to stay in the northwest area, where the bottom gradually deepens until it reaches approximately 650 feet at the boundary of the Andaman Basin.

With the threat from Soviet ballistic-missile submarines now history, the American attack-submarine community had shifted its focus to detecting and countering diesel subs in shallow coastal waters. The challenge is particularly difficult because the latest generation of diesel-electric boats is extremely quiet and has the endurance to "sleep" on the bottom of the ocean for extended periods of time.

In the crowded Strait of Malacca, the problem of detecting enemy submarines is exacerbated by the mixed propeller noises generated from the multitude of vessels plying the busy shipping lanes.

The commanding officer of *La Jolla* acted primarily on his own and seldom communicated with the battle group. Like all fast-attack skippers, he didn't like any type of communication that might reveal his presence and location. His mission, like the responsibility of the commanding officers of the surface ships, was to protect the vulnerable aircraft carrier. He would quietly attempt to find and kill any submarine that dared to stalk the battle group.

On the massive flight deck of *Kitty Hawk,* two Grumman F-14D Tomcats from Fighter Squadron 111 were sitting on the bow catapults in an Alert Fifteen status. They were armed with Phoenix long-range missiles and Sidewinder heat-seeking air-to-air missiles.

The Tomcat pilots and their radar-intercept officers were resting in their squadron ready room, waiting with a degree of apprehension for the order to scramble. If any type of threat materialized, the "Sundowner" crews would have to be airborne in fifteen minutes or less.

Like everyone else, the pilots and RIOs weren't sure why they were in the strait, but they suspected that it had something to do with Japan. The escalating tensions caused by the fractured relations between the two countries was the lead story on every news program beamed to the ship.

Seated at a chart table in the flag bridge, the battle group commander, Rear Admiral Isaac Landesman, fully understood why his ships were taking up station in the Strait of Malacca. The order to raise the group's defense-readiness condition from DEFCON FIVE, the level of normal peacetime activities, to the status of DEFCON FOUR was a surprise for the entire battle group. The upgraded defense condition mandated an increased intelligence watch and an increase in security.

TOKYO

The luxuriously decorated hospitality suite overlooking the Marunouchi business quarter was crowded when Tadashi Matsukawa gave the quiet signal that it was time for serious matters. The attractive young geishas silently prepared to leave the softly lighted room. After the quartet of talented hostess-entertainers were politely escorted away by a member of the large-scale security detail, Matsukawa followed the Prime Minister and Chihiro Yamashita to a small platform and podium.

Yamashita, the resilient chairman of Keidanren, Japan's powerful Federation of Economic Organizations, thanked Matsukawa for providing the entertainment and the spacious meeting facilities for the important business conference.

Afterward, Prime Minister Genshiro Koyama thanked the cartel members for rearranging their schedules on such short notice, and they all adjourned to the large soundproof conference room on the top floor.

The building was guarded by sixty specially selected uniformed guards and forty-five civilian-clad security specialists. The entrances were locked and guarded, and seven men with automatic weapons patrolled the roof. Fifteen people had spent over four hours checking from floor to floor for anyone hiding in the building. In addition, a sophisticated monitoring system relayed television pictures to a central command post, and pairs of armed sentries roamed each floor.

The elevators and stairs were guarded, and the elevator doors could be electronically sealed from the command post. Security was extremely tight for the "brain trust"—the experts concerned with planning the ongoing economic and military strategy of Japan.

When the men were comfortably seated, Prime Minister Koyama stepped behind the lectern.

"Japan," he began solemnly, "as you are painfully aware, has reached another crossroad in our long and proud history."

The room was deathly quiet.

"As our country has rapidly approached this historical intersection," he continued glumly, "we have attempted to steer clear of confrontations with the Americans and concentrate on prosperity and growth. Unfortunately, the course we have chosen often finds us at odds with the United States."

The Prime Minister paused a brief moment to make eye contact with many of his friends and associates. "Today, Japan faces an intractable situation. Even though our current relations with the U.S. are strained, we must confront Washington and announce our independence . . . and we must be steadfast about our intentions."

Koyama closely studied the audience and saw the looks of understanding. He also saw reactions of doubt from some, including Foreign Minister Nagumo Katsumoto. The short, stylishly dressed statesman, who was perpetually bent at the waist, appeared impassive. As Koyama knew from years of friendship with Katsumoto, the expressionless look on his face meant that he was not pleased.

"Many of you have discussed the situation with me privately," Koyama observed as he gazed at the sea of faces, "and many of you have suggested that it is in Japan's best interest to give notice to the powers in Washington."

He looked squarely at Tadashi Matsukawa and saw the slight nod. "Notice that we are going to henceforth make our own decisions regarding our country's future, including the size and scope of our military."

The Prime Minister saw the looks of agreement from the majority of the attendees. What bothered him was the sour looks on the faces of the chief executive officers of Japan's Big Four securities firms. The leaders of Daiwa, Nomura, Nikko, and Yamaichi were sitting together and obviously disagreed with the idea of approaching the Americans with any type of proposal.

"We must be united in our cause," Koyama declared and

noted the suddenly grim expression on the face of the Foreign Minister, "or we run the risk of dividing our own country. Our political parties are in agreement that now is the hour for discussing our independent future with the Americans.

"If we approach this subject with a well-organized plan, I believe we can minimize any negative reaction from Washington and achieve the results we desire and need."

He looked at Matsukawa for a moment and turned back to the audience. "I would like," he said in his raspy voice, "one of our widely known and esteemed business leaders to speak to you, then we'll discuss the subject in detail." He motioned to Matsukawa and introduced him to the *gurupu,* then quickly walked to his seat.

"Many of you," Matsukawa said clearly, "have visited with me, agreeing that we can no longer afford to have the Americans influencing Japan's future. Prime Ministers Nakasone and Takeshita began this movement, and now we need to bring it to a conclusion."

He raised his hands when a few of the cartel members started to speak. "Let me finish and then I want to listen to what the rest of you have to say."

Matsukawa took a sip of water from the glass under the wide podium. "You know many of the key issues at stake: the continuing trade disputes, the argument over the size and constitutionality of our Self-Defense Forces, America's shrinking military presence in the Western Pacific, and our lack of confidence in their desire, or ability, to come to our defense if someone attacked us."

He impatiently waited for the murmur to die down. "Now that the presence of the U.S. military is not felt in East Asia, China's Congress has passed a law claiming Taiwan, the Senkaku Islands, and most of the South China Sea, where there are thought to be rich oil and gas deposits.

"Beijing's territorial claims are explosive issues that place China in a confrontational position against Japan, Taipei, Vietnam, Malaysia, India, the Philippines, and Brunei. Chinese military leaders have even been quoted in the *China Business Times* as saying they consider the United States a developed nation in decline while China is a developing nation on the rise."

Matsukawa reached for his water glass. "So we can see that Beijing is not terribly worried about the American reaction to China's ventures. The situation that exists today in our region of the world could change very quickly and very dramatically. Since the Americans abandoned Clark Air Force Base and Subic Bay Naval Base in the Philippines, the Pacific Ocean is not America's lake anymore. They are no longer there to protect us."

Matsukawa looked at the chairman of Keidanren before continuing. "We have over seventy-five billion dollars invested in Asia, from Indonesia to Hong Kong, and we must be able to protect it. That's why we must continue to expand our military forces, especially the naval presence throughout the Pacific Rim."

The chief executive of Yamaichi Securities made a slashing gesture with his hand. "Matsukawa-san, I disagree with continuing to allow our military forces to grow at the expense of our economy. Besides," the troubled man said more excitedly, "over fifty-five percent of all Southeast Asians, let alone the majority of Americans, have deep-rooted fears about Japan's reconstituted military and what we're planning to do with it in the near future."

The deceitful billionaire gave the business executive a disdainful look. "It's time to face some facts," he began with a touch of sarcasm. "Don't you see the big picture? Japan is a political dwarf. We're going to have to have a world-class military that equals our economic power or continue to cower in fear of the Americans and anyone else who wants to step on our toes.

"We have rebuilt our country," Matsukawa rushed on, "from the shambles of 1945 to a world economic leader, and today we are building collateral to protect our vast investment."

Matsukawa fixed his eyes on his adversary. "Surely you wouldn't risk an investment without something to underwrite your money. Our collateral *has* to be our military—or Japan is going to remain a political dwarf to be slapped around."

The securities executive grunted and gave Matsukawa a look of pure hatred. "You"—he pointed his finger at Matsukawa—"and the rest of you who believe in alienating the Americans are making a major mistake."

"Let's think about that for a moment," Matsukawa persisted, attempting to conceal his growing irritation. "China now has a rudimentary aircraft carrier, a large complement of Russian-built naval Su-27 jet fighters and Yak-141 supersonic vertical-takeoff-and-landing fighter-bombers. In the meantime they have been turning out vast quantities of MiG-31s from their own plant in the Guizhou province . . ."

Before he continued, Matsukawa listened to the buzz as the men talked quietly among themselves.

"The Chinese," he informed the *gurupu,* "also have a number of MiG-29s with stowable in-flight refueling probes and a large number of Ilyushin-76 transports that have been converted to tankers and airborne warning-and-control aircraft. These modified airplanes are capable of escorting the fighters and bombers over extended ranges.

"As you know," he continued, "P'yongyang also has an arsenal of Nodong-1 missiles that are capable of carrying nuclear warheads to Kyushu, Shikoku, and the lower regions of Honshu. With those threats staring us in the face, we have no choice but to increase our military forces."

Matsukawa was encouraged when he saw a few of the men indicate that they were in agreement with him. He could tell that he was getting the reaction and support the Prime Minister needed to carry out the plan.

The disgruntled man from Yamaichi Securities shook his head in disgust. "Democratic nations don't make war on each other. We're not going to see wars like we have in the past. Warfare has essentially become irrelevant. Our long-range goals should be to increase trade because the 'little tigers' are nipping at our heels."

"Unfortunately you are clearly wrong about war," Matsukawa countered. "Man will never change. The only change will be the weapons available to him at any given time."

The chief executive of the securities firm scowled in anger and again pointed a finger at Matsukawa. "You, and all the people like you, are the reason we can't have a stabilized, sensible, compassionate, merciful world."

A low, continuous series of hushed whispers floated through the room while Tadashi Matsukawa tried to control his temper and his tongue. He was not used to having *anyone* talk down to him. This was an insult that caused him to lose face in front of the most powerful body of men in Japan.

"As long as the Americans"—Matsukawa gazed menacingly at the securities executive—"continue to be the lawmen for the world, we have a reasonable chance of escaping warfare. But look at the situation that prevails. The Americans, at some date in the foreseeable future, are going to have to pay their multi-trillion-dollar debt—which means they're going to have to continue shrinking their military forces."

Matsukawa locked the man in his icy stare. "When the U.S. Congress becomes financially desperate—when they're on their knees and completely insolvent—they will attempt to raise taxes and slash every budget in sight."

Hunching over the lectern, Matsukawa's voice became a low growl. "The deep cuts in domestic spending and huge taxes will pit the rich against the poor, the young against the old, the healthy against the sick—basically, the haves against the have-nots. Chaos and calamity is America's future, and we can't afford to sink with them. That's why we must continue to prepare ourselves to defend our country."

He took another sip of water to moisten his dry mouth. "If the American people," Matsukawa continued more lightly, "ever figure out how to get their nation and themselves out of debt, then I wouldn't be so worried.

"However," he said with sudden intensity, "that isn't the case. The U.S. is headed for national bankruptcy and their politicians are too frightened to admit it to the people—or to themselves."

Matsukawa took a deep breath and tightly gripped the sides of the podium. "It is best for Japan. It is the only course for Japan. We *must* go head-to-head with the U.S!"

Matsukawa paused to sample the mood of the audience. He sensed that almost everyone agreed with him: Japan had to abolish further dependence on the United States and her wilting military.

Scanning the faces in the packed room, Matsukawa felt the heady rush of knowing that he was spearheading a dramatic change in the history of Japan. "All the indicators point to a showdown with the Americans, and we need to do it very soon. The timing couldn't be better, especially after the savage attacks on our people at Pearl Harbor and Los Angeles. Those assaults have prompted us to take action, and the Japanese people are looking to us to restore the dignity and respect Japan once commanded."

Three and a half hours later, after everyone who wanted to make a statement had had the opportunity to do so, the majority of the cartel leaders elected to back the Prime Minister in restructuring Japan.

Genshiro Koyama stepped behind the podium and donned his simple, wire-framed spectacles. In spite of all his associates and friends, the Prime Minister was by nature a loner. This was a bold step for the man who rarely demonstrated any emotion in public.

"I know that some of you are hesitant," he began in his gravelly voice, "about the course of action that we have decided to follow, but I strongly encourage you to stand by the decision of the majority. This is an extremely important period for Japan, and I thank each and every one of you for taking the time to convene on such short notice."

His eyes glistened as his thoughts turned to the future of Japan and her people.

"It may be painful in the near future"—he paused to look around the conference room—"and we may have a fairly hostile reaction from Washington, but we can't put off the inevitable any longer."

The Prime Minister let an enthusiastic smile crease his lined face. "History will record"—he paused to allow the words to register—"when we again became our own masters."

23

CHANGI INTERNATIONAL AIRPORT, SINGAPORE

"We're finally here," Steve observed when the captain smoothly stopped the jet and the engines began to spool down.

"That we are," Susan replied in a tired voice. She gathered her personal belongings and closed her thin attaché case. "When do you think crew cut will get here?" she asked in a conversational tone.

"I don't know," Wickham admitted and released his seat belt. "He's got the book on us, so he's probably on his way here as we speak."

"No doubt."

Steve checked his watch. "It's almost midnight. Why don't we check into the hotel and order a late dinner from the room service menu?"

"Do you think they're still serving?"

Steve reached for the overhead storage locker. "Sure. Most of the hotels here have twenty-four-hour room service."

"That sounds good to me," she replied with an exhausted yawn. "I've been on guard the entire flight, waiting for crew cut to leap out of an overhead bin or something."

"I know."

Susan noticed how tired Steve looked. "I don't know about

you, but I just want to kick off my shoes, fix a drink, and relax for a while."

"I'm with you," he said in a voice laced with fatigue, then slung his carry-on bag over his shoulder.

After they cleared customs, retrieved their luggage, and exchanged American dollars for Singapore currency, Steve hailed a taxi and they arrived at the Westin Stamford twenty minutes later.

The spotless skyscraper, the world's tallest hotel, stands out handsomely from the British colonial architecture and the Chinese shophouses. Located at the crossroads of Singapore's tourist and business districts, the Stamford is famous for its high tea on the 70th floor, where guests have a spectacular view of the lush greenery of the "Garden City" and its vast deepwater harbor.

Susan went to her room to change clothes while Steve ordered dinner for them and called an Agency analyst at Langley. He was still on the phone when Susan tapped their private code on the door. Steve stretched the phone cord to let her in, then quickly concluded his conversation while she closed the door and locked it.

"Any news?" she asked while she sat down on the couch and placed her Smith & Wesson on the table.

"Not really," he confessed uneasily, "but they're tracking a number of leads. I'll tell you about it over dinner."

"Okay," she said at the same time she saw the glass of wine on the table. "Is this for me?"

"Yes. I noticed that you ordered white wine on our flights, so I took a chance on the Chablis."

"Perfect." Susan sighed. "Thanks."

"You're welcome."

Susan looked at him for a long moment, prompting Steve to turn and face her.

"You're staring," he said with a curious smile.

She covered her mouth and softly laughed. "I'm sorry. I know it's very impolite."

A knock on the door interrupted his response. He cautiously opened it while Susan concealed her Smith & Wesson behind her back. Steve signed the check while the young Malaysian woman carefully removed the plates of food from the warmer.

Susan stuck her handgun under a throw pillow and stared at the tantalizing array of delicacies on the room service cart. "There's enough food here to feed a professional football team."

"You told me to use my imagination," Steve teased while he opened the door for the woman to leave, then locked it behind her. "I think the best way to do this is buffet-style, then we can sit by the balcony and look at the lights of the city."

"Sounds good."

After they rearranged the furniture to accommodate the coffee table between them, Steve proposed a toast and they started sampling the specialties of Singapore.

Susan finished a few bites and reached for her wineglass. "What's your hunch? Do you think the owner of the freighter is the person behind the attack at Pearl Harbor?"

"I don't know," he said thoughtfully, "but there's something we're missing in this whole equation."

"What do you mean?"

He placed his fork on his plate. "That's what I was going to tell you. Our people at Langley are basically stumped about this deal, but they did come up with some information."

"Oh?"

"A few years ago a U.S. Navy destroyer, the USS *Ingersoll,* had a minor collision with a merchant vessel while it was returning home from a deployment in the Persian Gulf."

She stopped eating and quietly placed her utensils on the plate. "The *Matsumi Maru* number three?"

"No," he answered and reached for his wineglass. "The *Matsumi Maru* number seven, which is also registered in Singapore."

Susan felt that special tingle of excitement. "Do you think they're owned by the same person?"

"They aren't now."

He stared out the window for a moment, conscious of the speculative look she was giving him. "That's the problem. Our folks at the Agency discovered that six of the original eight *Matsumi Maru* freighters have been sold to various companies during the past eleven months."

"Including the one that we have a question about?"

"No," Steve answered, "which doesn't come as a surprise to me. Number three was sent to a salvage yard and then sold at auction when the owner didn't pay the bill to refurbish it."

He watched her closely. "They—our analysts at Langley—tried to track down the former owner of the ship, and there's no trace of the company. It dissolved—vanished into thin air the same as the bank accounts and holding companies associated with the mansion in Hawaii."

Susan's eyes narrowed. "The same pattern."

"That's the way I see it."

"What about the other ship? The one that isn't accounted for?"

"Number five went down during a typhoon about two years ago. That's the angle I want to pursue."

"You want to go after the insurance company."

"Exactly. If the ship *was* insured."

Susan looked bewildered. "Steve, think about the liability factor. It would be crazy to operate on the high seas without some form of insurance."

He refilled their glasses. "Maritime law, or admiralty law as some refer to it, has a characteristic feature that allows a shipowner to limit liability in most cases to the actual value of the ship."

"You're kidding."

"No." He shook his head slowly. "Most shipowners carry hull insurance to cover any damages to the vessel, and to protect themselves against claims by third parties, they carry protection-and-indemnity insurance."

"Are you saying that shipowners have liability limitations?"

"To a degree. Shipping was an extremely risky business long before they had even primitive forms of insurance. The idea of liability limitations is an ancient one that protected the ship-owners from losing all their assets."

Steve's words had little conviction. His mind was on Susan, and he knew it would be impossible for him to remain emotionally indifferent toward her. She made him feel relaxed and comfortable.

"If an owner was found negligent," Steve continued half-heartedly, "he could satisfy his responsibility by turning over the ship and cargo to the claimants. Obviously, the laws have been modified over the years, but the basic maritime rules are still in effect."

"Where do you suggest we begin our investigation?"

"Well," he answered slowly and raised his glass, "I'd say the Port of Singapore Authority is a good place to start."

Susan smiled in her seductive way, then raised her glass to meet Steve's toast. "First thing in the morning."

CHIYODA WARD, TOKYO

Tired from the lengthy discussions with the enterprise groups, Prime Minister Genshiro Koyama felt groggy as Defense Minister Yutaka Isida and three members of the civilian-controlled National Defense Council entered his residence. They were served green tea while Koyama finished dressing and received a sketchy brief from an administrative aide.

The clear, star-studded sky was beginning to turn light when Foreign Minister Nagumo Katsumoto, looking like the model of neatness even at this early hour, was ushered into the elaborately ornamented meeting room.

A moment later, Koyama walked in and invited everyone to be seated. Yutaka Isida and the National Defense Council representatives appeared to be apprehensive and tense, while Katsumoto presented himself as calm and low-key. He had been anticipating a problem with the U.S. military since the terrorist episodes at Yokosuka Naval Base and the air bases at Misawa and Yokota.

After the initial pleasantries were concluded, Koyama asked the senior defense official to explain the latest incident in the clash with the Americans.

The rumpled-looking bureaucrat in a black business suit appeared to be weary and needed a shave. Isida nervously fingered a small stack of reports and papers while he addressed his remarks to the Prime Minister.

"We have been monitoring the movements of the U.S. carrier groups in the western Pacific," he began awkwardly, "and we have become increasingly alarmed at the implications of their operating locations."

After glancing at his Foreign Minister, who showed no outward reaction, Koyama coughed. "Where are the carriers, and what are your primary concerns?"

Uncomfortable in front of the Prime Minister, the Defense Minister hesitated a moment to shape his answer. "The *Independence* group is operating in the South China Sea off the northwestern coast of Borneo, and *Lincoln* and her escorts are in the Java Sea between the Lombok and Sunda straits."

Genshiro Koyama frowned and thought about the collision between the American ship and the Aegis destroyer *Kongo*. "I thought the carrier was going back to the States for repairs. That's what I saw in my morning summary."

"That's what we thought," the worried man answered anxiously and shifted in his seat, "based on their normal operating practices. But she has been positioned in the Java Sea. We think they are trying to send us a strong message."

"Where's their other carrier group?" Koyama suddenly interrupted. "The . . ."

"*Kitty Hawk*," the defense expert offered, then went on when the Prime Minister nodded. "Her group is in the northern area of the Strait of Malacca. Again, the implied message, as far as we're concerned, is that U.S. forces can strangle our supply lines at their leisure."

"That's *exactly* what the Americans want us to believe," Nagumo Katsumoto said in his quiet and restrained manner. "They are as frustrated with us as we are with them, and they're demonstrating their military strength. Many experts think the American President is like tofu—nothing in the middle—but we can't afford to underestimate him and their Joint Chiefs of Staff."

Koyama examined carefully the look on the face of the Minister of Defense. "Isida-san, what is your recommendation in regard to the carrier groups?"

"We have discussed the issue at length," Isida explained in a halting voice, "and it is our recommendation that we increase our military visibility in the South China Sea and the straits of Lombok and Malacca."

The Prime Minister let his glance shift to Katsumoto. "What is your assessment of our predicament, Katsumoto-san?"

The Foreign Minister tasted his green tea before he spoke. "The situation is not unlike that of a child who is more intelligent than his or her parents. At some point, when the child is strong and not dependent on the mother and father, he or she will stop smiling and agreeing to the parents' every wish and order."

Katsumoto placed his tea on the table. "Japan is ready to step away from American influence, but we need to continue to be a friend to the United States because of China's growing military threat and the unpredictable nature of North Korea's communist regime. We can accomplish this if we keep everyone's interest in mind."

Koyama gave his friend a disgruntled look. "We have to stand up for our rights, but we've got to be careful. Our parent has an arsenal of nuclear weapons."

"They aren't going to use nuclear weapons on us," Katsumoto said calmly, "and you know that as well as I do."

Koyama reacted with angry defiance. "Tell that to the survivors of Hiroshima and Nagasaki."

Katsumoto slowly turned to the Defense Minister and the

delegation from the defense council. "If you'll excuse us for a few minutes. . . ."

After the men left the room, the Foreign Minister turned partially sideways to rest his curved back. "I agree that Japan has to become independent at some point in time, but I am firmly convinced that we can reach a reasonable solution with the United States if we're patient and don't provoke them."

"I don't agree with you," Koyama bluntly replied. "There is too much animosity and mistrust between our nations, and I don't think the deep-seated antagonism is ever going to evaporate completely."

Katsumoto pondered the statement. "Let's think about what you just said, and examine our conscience with regard to our motives and values."

Koyama gave him a disgusted look and shook his head. "You know my feelings about the matter, so let's look at reality."

"I'm asking you to hear me out," Katsumoto said. "This is a pivotal point in our history."

Koyama tossed him a suspicious look.

"There are many factors and dynamics in play," Katsumoto quietly continued, "that have worked to place Japan in this difficult position. We, as a unified country, must begin to address these issues face-to-face and be brutally honest with ourselves and the rest of the world."

He saw the look of irritation in the Prime Minister's eyes.

"We can't afford to put bandages on our problems," Katsumoto went on as he returned the stare from Koyama, "then shove them under the rug and lie about everything like the Americans do. We need a fundamental change in our attitudes if Japan is going to be accepted and trusted by the global communities."

Koyama frowned. "I don't like what I'm hearing. What are you trying to say?"

Katsumoto was straining to keep his emotions from spilling over. "Face the truth and it will be much easier to deal with the Americans."

"What truth?" Koyama shot back with open indignation.

Without blinking, Katsumoto glared at the Prime Minister. "We have been deceiving the world, ourselves, and our children. As a nation, the Japanese people have been programmed to believe that we are the victims of the war with the United States."

Katsumoto's perpetual smile had been replaced with a grim set to his mouth. "Because of the shock of Hiroshima and Nagasaki, our people have consistently refused to look at ourselves as the perpetrators of the war."

"I'm not going to listen to any more of this tripe," Koyama declared and rose to his feet, then looked down at the stooped man struggling to get up from his chair. "Furthermore, I strongly advise you to keep those kind of thoughts to yourself if you want to have a political future."

"Think about what I said," Katsumoto countered and abruptly turned to leave. "Facing the truth about Japan's past is the first step in winning our total independence from the United States."

24

SINGAPORE

When Steve walked into the hotel's executive center, Susan was having a spirited conversation with someone in her San Francisco office.

He called Langley and received an update on world affairs and the current status of the Pearl Harbor and Los Angeles cases. He scribbled a series of notes on a small hotel pad, then cupped the receiver when Susan completed her call and turned to him.

"Two minutes." He smiled and jotted a phone number on the writing pad.

She finished her coffee and nervously watched everyone who entered the business center. The encounters with the muscular Asian who was stalking them had forced Susan to be constantly on guard. She had even resorted to wearing her Smith & Wesson in a special shoulder holster under her jacket.

When he finally placed the receiver down, Steve looked at his homespun shorthand. "The Agency is still looking for the needle in the haystack, and they have focused on our ship."

"Number three *Matsumi Maru?*" she asked with a surprised look on her face.

"That's right. One of our people interviewed a dockworker

who swears he remembers that the crane—the one lying flat on the deck in the photos—was upright the entire time number three was in Honolulu."

He looked at his scrawled words. "The man has twenty-two years of experience around ships, and he said there wouldn't be any reason to lower the crane to go to sea."

Susan tried to quell her growing excitement. "Do they know where it's going?"

"Not yet," he admitted and tore off the slip of paper. "But they've got a number of military reconnaissance aircraft scouring the Pacific."

"Steve"—Susan suddenly changed the subject—"did you see the report about the Japanese man who was shot while a television crew was filming him?"

"Yes," Steve confided and rubbed the bridge of his nose. "I saw it on television first thing this morning."

The Japanese protester had been standing on a packing crate yelling through a megaphone at San Francisco commuters. A group of male Caucasians were taunting him from across the street. When the young man shouted, "Japan must never apologize for the war! We don't owe America anything, and we will not pay any reparations!" a single shot rang out and the crowd scattered, leaving the wounded protester writhing on the sidewalk. He died three hours later at San Francisco General Hospital.

"Do you think," Susan asked, "that relations between Japan and America are irretrievably doomed?"

"I wish I could give you an answer," Steve temporized, "but in my opinion there's a high probability that our two nations will never get along."

"Do you really think that's what the future holds?"

"Yes, I really do." He glanced down. "I doubt if the Japanese, who are a fairly pure race, and the hodgepodge of people we call Americans, will ever be close to each other."

Susan looked at the entrance when an Asian businessman walked in.

"Many of our core values," Steve went on, "including our

ideology and a number of other things, are diametrically opposed to the Japanese . . . and then we have the matter of their sneak attack and the two atomic bombs we dropped on them. So I don't see much hope for a warm, friendly relationship between our two societies."

"I'm afraid you're right. And, as I said before, I think we'll go to war. The people of both countries—for the most part—don't like or trust each other. If I had been born and raised in Japan, I probably wouldn't trust Americans either."

They remained quiet until Susan checked her watch. "Well, now that you've brightened my morning, are you ready to go to the Port Authority?"

THE WHITE HOUSE

The President was conferring with his Chief of Staff when an aide brought Japanese Ambassador Koji Hagura and Special Envoy Yamagata Isoroku into the Lincoln Sitting Room. The quiet space was the President's favorite environment to contemplate difficult situations. He felt more organized and disciplined in the historical surroundings, and often said he got most of his best ideas in the room.

The men had dismal looks on their faces, and the Chief of Staff had coffee stains on the front of his white shirt and blue silk tie.

"I'd like you to sit in on this," the President said hastily when Scott Eaglehoff started to leave.

"Yes, sir."

Evening was settling over the city as the formalities were exchanged and the men took seats.

"Mr. President," Hagura began glumly, "I apologize for bothering you and your staff at this hour; however, due to the present difficulties our two nations are experiencing, my government has instructed me to initiate an immediate dialogue with you and your staff."

The Ambassador's polished etiquette and decorum were

clearly evident, but the occasional half-smile was missing. Although Special Envoy Isoroku was more woodenly expressionless than the President had ever seen him, the young diplomat didn't seem as depressed as Hagura.

"We are extremely pleased," the President replied when he noticed Eaglehoff give him the *take it easy* look, "to sit down with you and Mr. Isoroku. We have serious problems that we're confident can be resolved if we work together."

Hagura allowed the slightest of smiles.

"What would you suggest we do first," the President continued in a conciliatory manner, "to rectify the situation and gain the trust and confidence we once shared?"

Hagura pursed his lips. "Our first concern is the placement of the U.S. carrier groups in the South China Sea."

You should be concerned, the President thought. "We can understand how you feel, Ambassador Hagura, but the United States must take the steps necessary to protect our vital interests as well as those of our allies."

Hagura showed no emotion and neither diplomat made an attempt to communicate. The Ambassador knew he was in a position that was controlled by the Americans. He struggled to maintain his patience and not display any sign of irritation. The worst thing he could do was lose his self-control, thus losing face on behalf of his country and his government.

"Mr. Ambassador," Scott Eaglehoff said in a friendly tone, "I would like to make a suggestion, if you don't mind."

Hagura solemnly nodded his head.

"I think it is extremely important," Eaglehoff said with conviction, "for the President and our Secretary of State to meet with Prime Minister Koyama and Foreign Minister Katsumoto as soon as possible.

"We feel a great sense of urgency," Eaglehoff continued firmly, "about the escalating friction between our two countries, and we trust that it is a priority to your government and to the Prime Minister."

Out of habit, Koji Hagura raised an eyebrow. "We deeply share your concerns, and Prime Minister Koyama is prepared to offer the first step toward normalizing our relationship with the United States."

The President was caught off guard, but he didn't outwardly convey his elation. This was by far the toughest game of international stud poker he'd played since taking the oath of office, and the outcome was indeed unpredictable. He and Eaglehoff shared a quick glance and remained quiet.

"Our Prime Minister"—Hagura looked at the President while Yamagata Isoroku stared straight ahead—"has suggested that he and Foreign Minister Katsumoto meet with you and Secretary Tidwell in Anchorage, Alaska, as quickly as the necessary security arrangements can be worked out.

"Our leaders," the Ambassador went on in a grave and formal manner, "have agreed to a collective plan we feel will be in the best interest of both great countries, and Prime Minister Koyama wishes to personally present it to you."

"That sounds like an excellent beginning." The President smiled broadly and turned to his Chief of Staff. "Scott, I'd like you to work out the details with Ambassador Hagura, and then let's get under way as soon as possible."

25

STRAIT OF MALACCA

Kitty Hawk steamed slowly downwind eighteen miles north-west of Langsa, Sumatra, while the pilots and naval flight officers emerged from their quiet, air-conditioned ready rooms to preflight their aircraft. All appeared to be in order, business as usual, but a strange sense of foreboding had spread among the officers and sailors.

As the aircrews spread out among the F/A-18 Hornets, A-6 Intruders, S-3 Vikings, E-2C Hawkeyes, and F-14 Tomcats, the tempo of operations rapidly increased. Helicopters, planes, white tractor tugs, and flight crews crisscrossed in a surrealistic ballet of moving aircraft and imminent danger. People ducked under moving wings and simultaneously dodged wheels and other obstacles while they went about their hazardous jobs.

The studious-looking aircrews, encumbered by their green flight suits, boots, g-suits, torso harnesses, oxygen masks, and helmets, scrutinized their airplanes for any structural damage and checked the security of the external fuel tanks, missiles, and bombs. Next, they looked for fuel or hydraulic leaks, then peered into jet intakes to assure that nothing would be sucked through the engine's fragile innards.

Because of the aircraft carrier's relatively slow speed, everyone on the flight deck was breathing the dense, acrid black smoke from the funnels used to vent the exhaust gases from the ship's oil-fired boilers.

When the external checks were completed, the aircrews climbed into their cockpits and began the familiar task of helping the plane captains strap them to their ejection seats. This was an extremely important ritual for each person because their lives might depend on the explosive seat to propel them clear of a doomed airplane.

After they were secured to their ejection seat, each crew member went through the routine of checking the multitudes of dials, switches, buttons, knobs, circuit breakers, levers, and gauges. One small item missed, whether it was overlooked or out of place, could spell instantaneous disaster for the aircrews or the individuals who worked on the perilous flight deck.

Once the prestart checklists were completed, the pilots started their engines and checked all the systems for any anomalies. After satisfying themselves that all the temperatures and pressures were normal, the aviators carefully checked their flight controls and waited for the carrier to turn into the wind and increase speed.

Shortly thereafter, the conventionally powered *Kitty Hawk* and her array of escort ships commenced a sweeping turn to prepare for the first launch of the day. The flotilla of escort ships executed the course reversal at precisely the same time as the flattop.

Although the carrier provided an airborne knockout punch, it rarely operated alone. Armed with Sea Sparrow missiles to shoot down high-flying threats or surface-skimming targets, and automatically fired Vulcan Phalanx cannons for close-in protection, the floating airfield was still vulnerable to attack and relied heavily on the escort ships.

While the Aegis guided-missile cruiser *Cowpens* took up station off the starboard side of the 80,000-ton carrier, the plane-guard guided missile cruiser *William H. Standley* eased into position two miles astern the *Hawk*.

The Belknap-class cruiser would be responsible for working

in harmony with the carrier's designated plane-guard helicopter. Together, they had the responsibility for search and rescue missions during flight operations. The small Sikorsky SH-60 helicopter, which had a specially trained rescue swimmer on board, would fly near the starboard side of the flattop.

The pace on the flight deck increased even more as the aircraft began to taxi forward toward the catapults. The flight-deck personnel had to avoid the searing heat from the powerful jet exhausts while they sidestepped the propellers from the screeching turboprops of the E-2C Hawkeye. Others kept an eye out for the jet intakes, which could suck an unwary deck-hand into the gaping openings leading to the engines.

Operating in international waters, the air group could launch warplanes in international airspace without permission from local authorities, hostile governments, or capricious politicians. The mammoth *Hawk,* as a sovereign United States territory, is capable of projecting tremendous power with a flexible mobility unknown to other countries.

Although the huge aircraft carrier is highly visible during daylight hours in clear weather, the ship can disappear in bad weather, especially on stormy nights. The aircraft can launch and recover, in almost any conditions, with the ship's radars and communications systems completely shut down to conceal the carrier's position.

The Group Two E-2C early-warning command-and-control aircraft was positioned on the number-two catapult while the carrier's four screws accelerated the flattop to thirty knots. The all-weather surveillance and strike-control airplane would launch first in order to relieve the Hawkeye that was currently orbiting high above the carrier group.

The yellow-shirted catapult officer gave the Hawkeye aircraft commander the full-power signal, returned the pilot's snappy salute, then gave the deckedge operator permission to shoot the straining airplane.

After the E-2C blasted down the catapult and clawed for altitude, the Tomcats, Hornets, Vikings, Intruders, and a radar-jamming EA6-B Prowler taxied forward to be launched.

From a standing start, each jet rocketed the length of the catapults in approximately 2½ seconds, reaching speeds up to 170 knots as they flew off the bow.

From his large, comfortable chair perched on the left side of the flag bridge, Rear Admiral Isaac Landesman scanned the expansive flight deck and then focused his attention on a single Grumman F-14 Tomcat as it approached the number-two catapult track.

When the primary emphasis in carrier aviation strategy shifted from the Cold War open-water tactics to littoral concerns, some of the F-14s were fitted with racks for Mk-80 series bombs. The newly configured fighter/bombers were quickly dubbed "Bombcats" by the aircrews.

The swing-wing, twin-engined Mach 2 air-superiority fighter, which had been plagued with a mechanical problem during the frenzied launch sequence, was finally fixed and ready to fly its mission.

With the variable-sweep wings extended for maximum lift, the pilot shoved the synchronized throttles forward to military power, then into afterburner. The nozzles on the aft section of the powerful turbofan engines squeezed the superheated thrust into a screeching, white-hot tongue of flame that scorched the jet-blast deflector.

After a thorough check of the engine instruments and a full sweep of his flight controls, the young aviator gave the catapult officer a casual salute, braced his helmet against the ejection-seat headrest, and held his breath.

Suddenly, the sleek fighter squatted down and shot forward while the pilot and his radar-intercept officer were instantaneously shoved back into their ejection seats. The heavy g-forces rendered the crew helpless until the Tomcat hurtled off the bow and into the air.

Landesman reached for the ringing phone that was his direct link to the command-and-control facilities. "Landesman."

"Admiral," the senior watch officer said, "Square Dance Seven-Zero-Three reports at least five Japanese Aegis destroyers, along with various support ships, have entered the strait . . . and Square D confirms two Chinese guided-missile destroyers are about to enter the strait."

Square Dance was the call sign of an S-3B Viking antisubmarine aircraft that was on a low-level reconnaissance flight to check out the military traffic in the southern section of the Strait of Malacca.

"Keep me informed of any new developments," Landesman advised and placed the receiver back in its bracket. He then called the ship's captain and invited him to the admiral's bridge.

While the carrier and her escorts slowed and changed course, the short, stocky former attack pilot went into his private dining room for a late breakfast with Captain Carl "Jinks" Witowski.

After both men were seated and served the first course, Landesman spoke softly to his longtime friend. "Jinks, we've got five Japanese destroyers in the strait with us. We've got to make damn sure we don't do anything to provoke a bad situation."

Hawk's popular skipper nodded in agreement. "I just heard about it as I left the bridge," the lean, graying fighter pilot confided while he tasted a freshly baked pastry. "The Japanese have slowly extended their patrol areas well beyond their original thousand-mile limit, but this is unprecedented. We'd better stay on our toes."

The Japanese Maritime Self-Defense Force was originally obligated to provide Japan's security out to a 1,000-mile limit, but they had roamed well past the limit in order to develop an effective force to protect the shipping lanes and defend their homeland.

"What really concerns me," Landesman said with a touch of frustration, "is being caught in this type of situation—where we have a military power vacuum."

"I couldn't agree more," Witowski conceded. "With Clark and Subic closed, and fewer of our ships in the RimPac, I don't know how we're going to effectively keep a rein on the ambitions of Japan, China, India, and to some degree, what's left of the Soviet Navy. Everyone wants to get into the act, now that we're spread too thin."

Landesman slipped a message across to Witowski. "I received this just before the launch. The Australians are sending two missile destroyers and three frigates to augment *Lincoln* and her escorts, and Taiwan has dispatched three Cheng Kung–class frigates to operate with *Indy*."

Witowski studied the detailed message and handed it back to Landesman.

"That's good," the skipper replied, "but I sure as hell hope Tokyo and Washington can work things out. I don't like placing *Kitty Hawk* in this kind of predicament."

"Yeah," the Admiral grumbled under his breath. "I don't like the idea of having this carrier running around in a crowded, brown-water shipping lane. It's a sitting duck in a small pond."

SINGAPORE

Steve and Susan felt pangs of disappointment when they walked out of the Port of Singapore Authority building. After countless questions and researching a number of documents, they had gained little more than what they had already learned about the former owner of the *Matsumi Maru* number three. Someone had cleansed the evidence of the previous ownership.

"Well," Steve said at last, "it wasn't a complete loss."

Susan covered her eyes to protect them from the bright sunlight. "That's true. We basically know where number three and number seven dock, but we don't know when number three will make port."

"When *Matsumi* seven collided with the destroyer *Ingersoll*," Steve replied while he waved at a passing taxi, "all of the *Matsumi Maru* fleet was owned by one person, or so we believe."

"And you think"—Susan finished his thought—"that

maybe someone is still around who might be able to give us the former owner's name or some information that will lead us to him."

"We don't have anything else to go on," he mused and opened the door to the cab, "so we might as well go to the harbor."

They remained lost in their own thoughts during the drive to the thirty-six-square-mile port along the Keppel Harbor. The sprawling deepwater channel, which is home to miles of docks, warehouses, berths, and associated facilities, runs between the main island of Singapore and the islands of Sentosa and Pulau Brani.

Steve asked the taxi driver to slow down while he and Susan took a windshield tour of the major shipping gateways of Telok Ayer, Keppel, Sembawang, and Pasir Panjang. After surveying the world's busiest container port, they finally returned to the array of Keppel wharves, which contain major docks and large storage spaces.

After paying the cabdriver, Steve looked around the immediate area. "Since this section of the port is Southeast Asia's primary transshipment point, I would think that someone knows where the *Matsumi Maru* number seven is docked."

Susan glanced at a nearby oil tanker and turned to Steve. "I'm wearing my walking shoes, so press on."

"First"—he reached into his jacket pocket—"take a few of these to hand out."

Susan studied the ordinary-looking business cards and smothered a saucy laugh. "Insurance agents?"

"That's right," Steve answered with a slight grin. "We're representatives of Royal Continental Insurance Company, and we're looking for a ship that belongs to one of our clients. You're the seasoned pro, and I'm new to the company—just tagging along to gain experience."

"Steve"—she held the card in front of his face—"these don't even have names on them. Just the company name."

He gave her a knowing smile. "The company is changing its

logo, so we won't have our personal cards for a while. You can sign a fictitious name if someone asks for it."

"Working with the CIA," Susan confided while she pocketed the generic cards, "is definitely interesting to say the least."

Steve glanced at a crew of men loading cargo onto what appeared to be a rusted tramp steamer.

"If you flash a badge around here," he quietly cautioned her while they started walking toward the freight handlers, "the news will shoot through this place like a lightning bolt and we probably wouldn't get another peep out of anyone. Plus, we don't have any jurisdiction in Singapore."

His statement made her realize that showing her credentials was routine in her profession, but Steve's world was very different.

"Since you're the expert in clandestine operations," she respectfully replied, "I certainly defer to your judgment."

"Don't get me wrong," he said as they approached the sweating men. "There are certain places, or situations, where we have to be . . . let's say, creative."

"I can only imagine," she whispered and looked straight ahead at the wizened man who was obviously in charge of the dockhands. "He looks like a mixture of Chinese and Malaysian."

"Just relax," Wickham said as they reached the small man.

"Excuse me, sir," Susan began and casually handed him a business card. "We're insurance adjusters and we're looking for one of our client's ships—the *Matsumi Maru* number seven. Do you happen to know where it's docked?"

A smile that revealed shiny gold teeth creased his round face. "It near big warehouse." He beamed and pointed down the busy terminal. "At end of dock."

"Thank you," Susan happily replied while she and Steve hid their surprise. "We appreciate your help."

The man looked Steve over a couple of times, then smiled at Susan. "I happy to help."

Across the dock, Shigeki Okamoto slipped into the shadow of a warehouse and brushed the sweat from his crew cut. Even though he was very close to his prey, the athletic mercenary killer knew he had to be extremely cautious. The former British colony at the tip of the Malay Peninsula enjoyed the reputation of having no crime for a very good reason.

The authoritarian politics of Singapore vigorously enforced severe penalties on violations ranging from drugs and pornography to eating on the subway or failing to flush a public toilet. If you murdered someone and got caught, the penalty was an automatic sentence of death.

Okamoto would do anything for the millions of yen Mishima Takahashi had promised him for killing the agents, but the martial arts expert had no desire to die an agonizing death.

THE JAPANESE EMBASSY, WASHINGTON, D.C.

Unable to concentrate on the stack of messages in front of him, Koji Hagura reached for the remote-control unit to the television. He clicked it on and rapidly flipped through the channels until he reached CNN. A live news report from the Pentagon was in progress and a senior spokesman was fielding questions from a large crowd of journalists. He recognized the intelligent woman correspondent from NBC when the camera focused on her face.

"Can you tell us," she asked evenly, "why the United States is operating three carrier task forces in such a confined area? Is the White House trying to intimidate Japan because of the friction between our countries?"

The White House spokesman rested his hands on the sides of the podium and looked straight at the news reporter. "No, the President isn't trying to put any pressure on Japan, or anyone else, for that matter."

A low, continuous buzz of disbelief spread throughout the crowded room.

"Because of the current fears of instability in the Southeastern Asian region," the man went on with a placid look, "the

Secretary of Defense and the Chairman of the Joint Chiefs felt that it was prudent to lend a stabilizing hand in the area. The President endorsed the idea and the Secretary of State is visiting our allies to assure them that we don't expect any trouble in the southeastern sector."

The spokesman pointed to a *Washington Post* reporter who was sitting on the front row.

"We have been told," the reporter began in his combative style, "that satellite- and aircraft-reconnaissance photos indicate a large number of Japanese warships and support vessels are in the South China Sea or on the way to join the rest of the fleet. Why aren't you and your cohorts at the White House leveling with the American people?"

The reporter's voice suddenly rose. "They have a right to know what our military is doing sitting in the middle of some of the busiest shipping lanes in the world!"

"The United States has a vested interest," the Pentagon official serenely continued, "in the security of the Pacific Rim region and in the safety of our allies in that area. We are simply taking the necessary precautions to ensure long-range stability in that part of the world."

"That's a bald-faced lie," Koji Hagura muttered to himself. "The U.S. government is holding a guillotine in front of the Japanese people and daring them to put their heads on the chopping block."

There was a loud commotion in the back of the briefing room and the camera panned to an agitated Japanese journalist. A moment later he was bathed in the glare of the bright television lights.

Hagura quickly reached for the remote control and turned up the sound. He felt a deep sense of empathy for the angry feelings of the man.

"This is what we think!" the Japanese reporter shouted while he held up an enlarged facsimile of the front page of *Yomiuri Shimbun,* Japan's largest newspaper.

Hagura could clearly read the headline.

UNITED STATES PREPARES
TO ATTACK JAPAN

"Why don't you tell the truth?" the man yelled while two security guards moved toward him. "America will pay for this! Mark my words, you bastards!" He spat contemptuously as they roughly escorted him from the room.

The CNN Pentagon correspondent immediately seized the silence to address a question to the spokesman. "A reliable source informed me that our carriers in Southeast Asian waters are operating at a higher-than-normal defense-readiness condition. Will you confirm that statement?"

The speaker paused a moment and looked at a briefing note he had scribbled earlier. "Our carriers are conducting routine training flights, and we consider that normal operations. Next." He gestured to a friendly face.

"Wait a minute," the CNN reporter snapped. "One question—since you won't answer the last one—what about the reports that China and India have warships in the same area as our battle groups. Is that true?"

The spokesman showed a trace of irritation as he answered the pugnacious correspondent. "There are some Chinese Luda-class destroyers and Jianghu-class frigates currently conducting maneuvers near the Spratly Islands, and that isn't a new development.

"As far as the Indian Navy is concerned, we are aware of only one Delhi-class destroyer in the vicinity, which we do not consider a problem."

"So the basic *problem*," the reporter hurried on, "is clearly with the Japanese?"

"Our situation," the Pentagon spokesman countered with a trace of exasperation in his voice, "is one of maintaining stability in a sensitive part of the world. We are there to enforce the rights of our Pacific Rim allies."

A woman journalist who represented *Newsweek* rose from her chair. "Do you in all good conscience expect us to believe that, when there is so much evidence pouring in about our preparations to confront the Japanese?"

Her voice turned brittle. "Why won't you be forthright, when it's obvious to the world? Allow us to do our jobs in a responsible manner."

The spokesman smiled wanly and squeezed the sides of the podium. "You can believe whatever you want, and, like the rest of you, I have a job to do."

Feeling a sudden revulsion, Koji Hagura clicked the remote control unit and the picture went blank. *We must never trust the Americans.*

26

KEPPEL HARBOR

As Steve and Susan neared the end of the congested dock, Susan spotted a colorful cable car suspended high above the ship channel. She pointed skyward. "Do you know where it goes?"

Glancing up at the car, Steve followed the path of the cable system. "It connects Mount Faber and Sentosa Island, which has an amusement park, a fantastic golf course, and some really nice beaches and picnic areas."

"It's too bad we aren't here on vacation," Susan complained and turned to examine one of the wide variety of merchant vessels in port.

Steve directed his attention to her unexpected remark. "Let's plan one," he responded enthusiastically as they began to feel the first sprinkles from an afternoon shower.

"You've got my vote."

"We better go for it," Steve hastily suggested, "or we'll be soaked to the skin."

She darted a glance at him. *Let's plan a vacation. Interesting.*

They jogged the last hundred yards to the gangplank of the *Matsumi Maru* number seven. The dilapidated cargo ship was rusting and badly in need of paint.

"I suppose if it's seaworthy," Steve reasoned as they started up the ramp, "it doesn't make any difference what it looks like from the outside."

"Well," Susan protested, "I wouldn't want to go very far in something that—"

"Hold it right there!" a loud voice boomed from the entrance to the main deck. "Sorry, folks. Ain't no visitors allowed aboard—company policy."

"Wait a second," Steve quickly countered and displayed his calling card to the short, heavyset boatswain's mate. "We're with a subsidiary of the ship's insurance company, and your parent company may be eligible for additional funds stemming from the accident with the American destroyer . . . the collision back in ninety-two."

Steve saw the look of surprise cross the man's beefy face. "Do you mind if we step in out of the rain until the shower passes?"

Confused by the unexpected news, the crusty deck crewman waved them up the ramp.

"C'mon in here," the sailor instructed while he opened a hatch to expose an unkempt, greasy working space.

"Thanks," Susan and Steve said in unison as they stepped out of the light rain.

She handed the grizzled man her business card and noticed the array of tattoos on his arms. "We're investigators with Royal Continental Insurance, and we need to know if there is anyone currently in the crew who was on board this ship when the accident happened."

The grease-stained bos'n studied the card while he gave a size-up of the two insurance representatives.

"Yeah," the salty veteran said at last, "we got one hand who was on the *Whiskey Maru* when the U.S.-goddamn-Navy run us plum over, but he ain't aboard just now."

"Where is he?" Steve asked with a pleasant smile. "We need to interview him as quickly as possible, before the statute of maritime limitations expires, which would result in a loss of money to your company."

The boatswain mate's eyes widened with suspicion. "When he's off duty—Grover Bodeker's his name, but everybody calls him Stinky—he generally hangs out at the Cat and Fiddle. If he ain't there, he'll be sleepin' it off next door at Chigger's stop-and-flop."

Susan turned on her enticing charm. "Would you be kind enough to give us a description of Mr. Bodeker?"

The brusque seaman belly-laughed, then quickly stopped. "Sorry, ma'am, but I ain't never heard no one call Stinky that before, if ya know what I mean."

She gave him an understanding look.

"At any rate," the sailor innocently explained, "Stinky—he's 'bout average in height and weight, with reddish-blond hair and lots of freckles. Got him a scar 'cross his nose. Can't miss him, believe you me."

"Just one more thing," Steve said as he tugged open the hatch and glanced at the passing rain shower. "Where is the Cat and Fiddle located?"

"It's too hard to explain, man," the stocky sailor snorted. "Just ask a cabbie, 'cause most of 'em know all the harbor joints around here."

"Thanks," Steve replied and followed Susan out the hatch. "Since the rain has stopped, it must be time to go."

"It must be," Susan said and carefully surveyed the dock area.

Shigeki Okamoto stepped back in the shadow of the warehouse and watched his prey walk past his hiding place. He pulled a dark-blue knit cap out of his pocket and snugged it over his head and ears. It was time to stop toying with the two agents.

The Cat and Fiddle tavern, while not the ideal example of tidiness, was a hushed and reasonably clean bar with a distinct Oriental flavor. A replica of an old-fashioned Wurlitzer glowed in the back corner, waiting for another customer to plunk a token into the slot.

Behind the well-stocked bar, a number of eye-catching neon display lights advertised various brands of beer and liquor. The afternoon customers in the long, narrow room were confined to the bar or to a row of small tables lined against the wall. The regular patrons at the Cat and Fiddle were perched on the same barstools they always occupied.

Susan and Steve sat at a table near the entrance and waited for their eyes to adjust to the dim light. The drastic change from the bright tropical sunlight to the darkness of the tavern made them partially blind for a few moments. Slowly but surely, the people and objects in the bar began to take definite forms.

"May I bring you something to drink?" Steve finally said as he rose from the wobbly chair.

Susan grinned and looked down the bar, then turned to him. "In a place like this, I think a beer would do just fine."

He winked. "Good choice."

Wickham stepped over to the curved end of the polished counter and waited for the bartender to approach him.

"What'll it be?"

"Two Tigers," Steve replied and immediately recognized Grover Bodeker sitting near the middle of the bar. *The man was right—you can't miss Stinky.*

"Here you go," the bartender cheerfully said and glanced at Susan. "You're new here, so the first one's on me."

"Thanks. We sure appreciate it," Steve replied while he scrutinized the coarse-looking young man with the thatch of carrot-colored hair.

He handed Susan a cold beer and sat down. "The guy we're looking for is sitting at the bar," he quietly informed her. "I'm going to go introduce myself and see if he'll join us for a short chat."

"Okay," she said with a touch of reticence and reached for one of her business cards, "but you better be the seasoned insurance veteran, while I play the part of the new girl on the block."

"Will do."

A man with a navy blue knit cap tugged over his ears entered the bar and plopped in an empty booth near the entrance.

"Enjoy the beer," Steve said lightly and rose from his seat, then walked up to the side of the seaman and waited until there was a slight pause in the conversation the sailor was having with a young Malaysian woman.

"Excuse me, Mr. Bodeker." Wickham smiled like a Cheshire cat. "I'm with Royal Continental Insurance company, and we may have some good news for you and your company."

The man swung his head around to reveal a pink gash across a nose surrounded by a sea of freckles. "What the hell you talkin' about?"

"Don't get me wrong," Steve said while he kept the smile plastered on his face and extended his hand. "We're not here to sell you anything. We're here to see about refunding money that may be owed to your company."

Bodeker looked bewildered. "Man, I think you got the wrong person here."

"You *are* Grover Bodeker, right?" Steve queried while the merchant seaman mechanically shook hands. "You were on the *Matsumi Maru* number seven when it collided with the American destroyer in ninety-two."

"That's right," Bodeker cautiously admitted, "but what's that got to do with insurance?"

"Relax," Steve said in a soothing tone and handed him a business card. "This is good news. Have you got a couple of minutes to talk with us?"

Bodeker still looked skeptical. "Well, me an my ol' lady was just fixin' to go over to a friend's house."

"All we need"—Steve beckoned the bartender to give the reluctant seaman and his girlfriend another beer—"is five or ten minutes of your time."

"All right," Bodeker acquiesced and faced the young woman. "I'll be back in a few minutes."

Wickham threw some money on the bar and accompanied the sailor to where Susan was sitting. After introductions, Steve pulled up an extra chair while she smiled and gave Bodeker a business card.

"Mr. Bodeker," Steve began slowly, "do you have any idea what insurance company covered your ship when the collision occurred with the Navy destroyer?"

The seaman quickly lit a cigarette and gave Wickham a strange look. "The same one we've always had, 'cept for a couple a months after she was sold."

Susan and Steve were taken aback by the unexpected revelation, but they managed to conceal their exuberance.

"Our records about your ship," she earnestly confided, "are incomplete, and we certainly appreciate your cooperation." Susan opened her pen. "What is the name of your ship's insurance company?"

"Tokio Marine and Fire," he answered and blew a ring of smoke toward the ceiling.

"Are you positive about the name?" Steve asked in a friendly way and sipped his beer. "We have a lot of incomplete information in our records."

"Yeah, I'm positive," the sailor countered with a surly look. "I 'member because they—them insurance guys—spelled Tokyo with an *i*. T–O–K–I–O."

Steve decided to go for the grand slam. "Mr. Bodeker, do you know who owned your ship when the collision happened?"

"No," Bodeker admitted and nervously puffed on his cigarette. "It was one of them weird deals, man. Our orders used to come from somewheres up in Japan, but I ain't got no idea who owned the shit bucket."

"We really appreciate your help," Susan said with a smile and got a whiff of the sailor's foul body odor. *We know how he got his nickname.*

"Don't get me wrong, ma'am," Bodeker hurriedly explained. "I just do my job, and that's all I know about this whole thing . . . honest to God."

"No problem," she replied casually. "You've made our job a little easier, and for that we're grateful."

Bodeker grinned and crushed his cigarette in the ashtray. "Glad to help ya out."

The seaman returned to his girlfriend and Susan and Steve finished their beers and decided to leave. The moment they walked out of the entrance, Shigeki Okamoto followed them and shoved the barrel of a 9-millimeter Taurus in Susan's ribs while he grabbed her by the arm. "Don't do anything stupid," he said, "or I'll blow her in half. Go down the alley," Okamoto ordered and jerked Susan sideways when they entered the narrow passageway. He yanked her jacket open and pocketed her Smith & Wesson. "Stop," he growled and pushed Susan against the side of a building.

"You," he said to Wickham. "Throw your gun behind the trash cans and spread out on the ground."

Okamoto pointed the Taurus at Steve while the agent reached behind his back to retrieve his Beretta.

Susan seized the moment to spin around and grab Okamoto's weapon. Steve reacted instinctively and slammed the man's head against the wall while Susan wrenched the gun out of Okamoto's grasp. The hit man lashed out, knocking Susan to the ground and kicking Steve in the groin.

Dazed, Susan struggled to get to her knees while Wickham lunged at Okamoto and both men fell against the rubbish containers. Steve regained his balance and smashed Okamoto in the face at the same instant the assailant hit him in the head with something heavy.

Steve saw only a blur as Okamoto leaped to his feet and ran toward the street. Steve reached for his Beretta, then jammed it back in the holster and hobbled over to assist Susan.

27

ARMY-NAVY GOLF COURSE, ARLINGTON, VIRGINIA

Swinging his new club with wild abandon, Tadashi Matsukawa's senior Washington lobbyist solidly whacked the golf ball high into the early-morning sky. The sweet sound of a well-hit tee shot carried across the course while Gichi Ebata paused to follow the flight of the ball.

The small white sphere soared down the right side of the fairway, bounced twice near the edge of the rough, then left a straight trail in the dew as it rolled to a stop near his partner's first shot.

"You're definitely getting better," Senator Frank Brazzell commented in his quiet, servile manner. "There's no question about it, you've cured your slice."

"At least it's on the fairway," rejoiced the Japanese influence peddler, flashing his mechanical smile.

"That's always a good sign," Brazzell replied with his own unctuous smile, then added a small chuckle. Everyone was pretending that relations between the U.S. and Japan were pleasant.

The slender lobbyist and the Chairman of the House Armed Services Committee waited for another Matsukawa lobbyist and Bryce Mellongard to tee off, then Brazzell drove the electric cart toward Gichi Ebata's golf ball.

Brazzell could feel his anxiety reaching a peak as they cruised down the fairway. He had worked hard to accommodate Matsukawa's special request to have the Secretary of Defense meet with the créme de la créme of Japanese lobbyists.

After Brazzell and Mellongard had agreed to talk with the President about giving the Japanese the next decommissioned aircraft carrier, Matsukawa had loudly demanded that his representatives meet with the Senator and SECDEF.

"Senator Brazzell," Ebata began pleasantly, "Matsukawa-san would like you to express to the President another primary reason for acquiring an aircraft carrier, other than antisubmarine warfare."

"The piracy problems along China's coast," Brazzell suggested with a nervous laugh.

"Yes," the polished lobbyist declared through his perpetual smile. "The pirates are a growing menace that could easily trigger a military and diplomatic flash point between the major Asian powers. We believe a Japanese carrier with a complement of vertical-takeoff attack aircraft would be a strong deterrent to the marauders."

Brazzell beamed as he formulated a more persuasive argument to present to the President. "I can definitely see the merit in that idea. Excellent proposal."

"We think so," Ebata went on. "As soon as the American presence wasn't felt in the South China Sea, the cowardly pirates began taunting and attacking merchant ships from the border of China and Vietnam to the waters off North Korea. Matsukawa-san believes it's time to stop them."

"I agree, and to my knowledge," Brazzell said as he shifted into his sedate and reserved role, "most of the attacks have been taking place between Hong Kong and Vietnam."

Ebata nodded in his charming way. "You're right. The Russians have a number of the Pacific Fleet ships protecting their freighters and fishing vessels in both the East China Sea and the

South China Sea. We feel confident, after our Asian neighbors become used to our involvement, that a Japanese carrier can project a stabilizing influence on the high seas off the coast of China."

Glancing up at the hazy sky, Brazzell inhaled a breath of fresh air. *Beijing won't be thrilled, but who gives a shit what those clowns think?* "I couldn't agree more, and as I promised Matsukawa-san, I'm going to take the lead in recommending that Japan receive the next carrier that is scheduled for decommissioning."

Ebata pursed his lips and smiled. "Matsukawa-san will be most pleased with your enthusiasm."

Frank Brazzell watched the progress of the other golf cart as it approached Mellongard's ball. Brazzell slowed to a smooth stop and watched the Secretary of Defense address his ball.

"What worries Matsukawa-san," Ebata quietly confided, "is the uncertain security environment surrounding Southeast Asia and the real potential for armed conflict in the near future.

"The Chinese," he went on while Brazzell studied Mellongard's swing, "even after Emperor Akihito went to Beijing and apologized for the occupation of China, still don't trust us . . . and we can't trust their intentions."

"It's very unfortunate," Brazzell sighed with a glum look plastered on his face. He was still trying to master the fine art of Japanology—trying to figure out what was going on in the minds of the Japanese.

Ebata turned to the Senator. "I'm sure you remember when Akihito was on his historic visit to China, and the Chinese bungled a nuclear-bomb experiment that blew the side out of a hollowed-out mountain?"

Brazzell absently nodded. "How could I forget?"

The Chinese test that went awry spewed radioactive gases and dust into the atmosphere. Upper-air winds subsequently transported the deadly emissions from Xinjiang province to Japan, where the vast majority of the fallout settled over the Nipponese Islands and the Sea of Japan.

After taking two practice swings, the seasoned lobbyist hit a solid shot that flew straight toward the pennant on the back of the green. "Senator Brazzell, Japan doesn't want to do anything that would radically alter the balance of power in Asia; however, China has nuclear capability, and we would like to take a step to counter that threat."

"What are you suggesting?" Brazzell asked skeptically.

"Japan," Ebata said confidently, "would like to investigate the possibility of acquiring one or two of your ballistic-missile submarines to counter the Chinese."

Brazzell was dumbfounded. "Well, I . . . I'm not sure this—"

"It means millions and millions in your pocket," Ebata persisted with a sudden intensity, "and everyone wins."

SINGAPORE

Steve and Susan stood at the hotel window and looked down at the sights of the spectacular city, then turned to each other and shared a knowing smile. They had reported the incident outside the waterfront bar to the local authorities and had given them a description of the assailant and the serial number on Susan's Smith & Wesson.

"We were lucky this time," Susan said. "He caught us totally off guard . . . and we survived."

"That's because he didn't want to bring attention to himself. He knows how they deal with crime here."

"In most other places," Susan ventured, "he would have just gunned us down and walked off."

"We'll get him," Wickham said boldly, "because he *will* try again. I think the people behind the attack at Pearl know we're on the right trail, and they're becoming more desperate by the hour."

They quietly soaked in the sights of Marina Bay and the Singapore River while they watched the shimmering sun dip below the horizon.

Susan studied an ominous squall line of churning dark clouds approaching their hotel. "I believe our sightseeing time is about to come to an abrupt halt."

Steve moved his chair aside to have a better look at the windstorm and heavy rain as the system moved toward the city.

She picked up her notepad. "I think the information about the ship's insurance company—Tokio Marine and Fire—is the link we've been missing.

"The company has confirmed the coverage and the dates," she went on. "When we get to Tokyo, I'm sure we can get the insurance company to tell us the name of the former owner of the shipping line."

Even though he was still outraged by the brawl outside the Cat and Fiddle, Steve hadn't lost his professional perspective. "What makes you so confident?"

She gave him an innocent look. "A couple of years ago—three to be exact—I was in charge of investigating a series of sabotage attempts at an aerospace company involved in U.S. government contracts."

The wind and rain suddenly blasted against the windows and momentarily interrupted her.

"The case centered around an internal-security problem," she said loudly over the howling wind, "and one of the experts I consulted was, and still is, a Japanese investigator for a pool of Tokyo-based insurance companies."

She noticed the surprised look on Steve's handsome face. "So I figure if anyone can help us pin things down, it'll be my friend from the sabotage case."

He stared into her eyes while the violent storm raged outside. "You're really amazing."

"Oh, I wouldn't go that far," she teased him with a quick glance, then watched in fascination as the torrential downpour obscured her view of the bay and river. "If you had been incapacitated, that son of a bitch would have killed us . . ."

"Susan," Steve responded calmly in an attempt to change the subject, "we need to find out who is selling us down the river."

Susan's features hardened and she pulled her feet up under

her. "Like we discussed, it appears as if someone has a direct connection to what we're doing and how the investigation is proceeding."

She looked at Steve and saw a smile slowly spread across his face. "What's wrong?"

"Nothing." He suddenly took her by the shoulders. "Susan, contact your office and tell them that we're going to check into the Hyatt Regency at noon tomorrow."

She beamed with understanding.

"I'll call Langley," Wickham hurried on, "and tell them that we're going to meet representatives of a Japanese insurance company at noon tomorrow in the Port of Singapore Authority building."

Susan reached for a writing pad. "I'll set up a phone watch and surveillance at the hotel and you can stake out the Port Authority."

Steve seemed to hold back, then gave her a cautious look. "Susan, we're going to have to be damn careful."

USS *KITTY HAWK*

Leaning back in his cushioned seat on the flag bridge, Rear Admiral Isaac Landesman had a commanding view of the approaching warships. He raised his binoculars and observed the Japanese Maritime Defense Force flagship *Hayasa* pass the carrier group on the portside.

He carefully examined the Aegis destroyer from bow to stern, noting the numerous missiles, guns, and radar systems sprouting from the spotless man-of-war. Landesman blew on his hot coffee and watched an SH-60J antisubmarine-warfare helicopter lift off the fantail of the flagship and commence a slow turn away from the carrier group.

Following his long look at *Hayasa,* the battle-group commander scanned two Asagiri-class destroyers, the replenishment oiler *Tsukeru,* and the minesweepers *Yurishima* and *Hikoshima.* When the last Japanese vessel passed the carrier,

Landesman felt the ship list to starboard as the flattop turned into the wind in preparation to recover aircraft.

Shortly after *Kitty Hawk* steadied on course, a flight of two F-14 Tomcats thundered over the ship and snapped into a gut-wrenching break as they turned downwind. Landesman was watching the airplanes decelerate when his aide stepped up to his chair.

"Admiral," the youthful-looking officer said as he peered down at the flight deck, "we just received confirmation from CINCPACFLEET. *Bremerton* has entered the southern end of the strait and is expected to rendezvous with us in approximately thirty hours."

"Very well," Landesman replied without taking his eyes off the lead Tomcat. "If we get into a skirmish in these waters, it's going to be like a knife fight in a dark closet."

"Yessir," the aide automatically responded and left the bridge.

Isaac Landesman had twice made his case to the four-star commander of the Pacific Fleet, but to no avail. CINCPAC was going to do *precisely* what the President wanted to do, even if it didn't make sense, and even if the tactics unnecessarily impeded the capabilities of the carrier battle group.

ANCHORAGE, ALASKA

The large conference room in the Hilton was a madhouse of bewildering actions and uproarious confusion. Japanese Special Envoy Yamagata Isoroku, who had been dispatched by Ambassador Koji Hagura to coordinate the schedule for the upcoming meeting between Prime Minister Koyama and the President, was attempting to deal with an overbearing U.S. State Department representative who continued to ignore him.

Isoroku, like Ambassador Hagura, sorely missed the pleasant American Ambassador to Japan. They had stayed in touch with the recuperating statesman and wished for his speedy return to Japan.

Emotionally strained, Isoroku knew the stage was being set for a less-than-harmonious session if he didn't seize control of the situation. The Americans were clearly attempting to dominate the meeting and they showed open disdain toward his Japanese delegation.

In total frustration, Yamagata Isoroku telephoned Ambassador Hagura and explained the situation.

"Ambassador," Isoroku said with a combination of embarrassment and anguish in his voice, "I came here under the impression that we would make all final decisions. After all, Prime Minister Koyama initiated the meeting."

"That was my understanding," Hagura answered bitterly and gave instructions to his special envoy. "Keep our people away from the Americans until you hear from me."

Isoroku fought to maintain his composure. "I understand."

"We simply cannot afford," Hagura said firmly, "to be responsible for causing any incidents that might jeopardize the conference."

28

NEW YORK CITY

Bud Tidwell felt exuberant after his whirlwind trip to gain support for the Administration's position toward Japan. The only opposition had surfaced in France, and the Secretary of State had diplomatically twisted some arms to obtain the backing of the less-than-comfortable French government.

However, Tidwell's expectations for resolving the dispute with Japan had become abysmal after he spoke to the members of the United Nations Security Council. The coalition of permanent and nonpermanent members was not willing to immediately address the maintenance of international peace and security.

He thought about the preamble to the United Nations Charter while he walked to the room reserved for the U.S. Secretary of State. The introduction to the formal document declares that the representatives of the United Nations are determined to save succeeding generations from the scourge of war.

Nice verbiage, Tidwell thought when he entered the suite, *but no one wants to play their hand when big money and massive power are at stake.*

Chief of Staff Scott Eaglehoff, whom the President asked to

accompany Tidwell to New York, was waiting impatiently in the room. While Bud Tidwell coped with the reluctant Security Council, Eaglehoff was busy making final arrangements for the trip to Anchorage. He was also lobbying select members of the General Assembly for their support on behalf of the United States.

Eaglehoff saw the look of deep concern etched in Tidwell's face. "How'd it go?"

The Secretary of State loosened his tie and opened his collar before he sat down and sighed. "In a nutshell, not so good. The Chinese are extremely concerned about their most-favored-nation trade status, or being slapped with more human rights conditions, so they've gone straight into their normal ostrich position."

Eaglehoff in turn loosened his tie and adjusted his collar. "What's the position of the Japanese member?"

"Surprisingly, he hasn't said much thus far," Tidwell answered, "but there's something mighty strange blowing in the wind."

"Oh?"

"I can't remember his name—"

"Fukushima," Eaglehoff prompted.

"Yeah, that's the guy."

Eaglehoff remembered an exchange with Fukushima when they met during a trade show reception at the Four Seasons Resort at Wailea, Maui. "He's a smooth operator."

"At any rate," Tidwell paused, "he stays glued to one topic, and that's the parent-child relationship we've had with Japan since the occupation after World War Two. However, there's something much bigger under the surface."

"Like what?"

"I'm not sure," Tidwell grumbled, "but he's obviously been ordered to mindlessly repeat the same message."

"So you think at Anchorage they're going to tell us to kiss their asses and they don't want it to come as a complete surprise?"

Tidwell glanced at his close friend. "I wouldn't doubt it, and they've got a lot of monetary and military power to back up a stand against us."

Eaglehoff shrugged. "Who knows? They may have finally developed enough backbone to cut the ties with the parent, as Fukushima refers to us."

"I wouldn't doubt it," Tidwell warned, "not for a second."

"What's your plan," Eaglehoff asked, "if the Security Council won't take steps to pave the way to Alaska?"

Tidwell laced his fingers, turned his hands backwards, then stretched his arms and hands. "Use the Uniting for Peace Resolution and play some hardball with these weenies."

The statement elicited a crooked smile from the Chief of Staff, but he didn't interrupt his friend.

"Which means," Tidwell continued, "that if the Security Council, because of a lack of unanimity of the permanent members, fails to exercise its primary responsibility, the Peace Resolution provides an avenue for the General Assembly to immediately consider the issue."

Eaglehoff gave him a skeptical look. "Do you really believe they'd do anything, since we're talking about the U.S. and Japan? This isn't Bosnia or Somalia . . . where they can put up a smoke screen and howl in protest."

"If it seems like a threat to the peace," Tidwell answered slowly while he contemplated the options of the General Assembly, "which the Japanese feud with us certainly does, or an act of aggression, which it isn't yet, the General Assembly *should* invoke the clearly stipulated obligation to do something to correct the problem, including the use of armed force."

Tidwell looked at Eaglehoff and chuckled self-consciously. "End of lecture."

Eaglehoff didn't appear to be convinced. "You're right about one thing: when you deal with the General Assembly marshmallows, one of the key words is *should.*"

"Scott, if we take this to the edge," Tidwell continued in a pleasant tone, "it will force the U.N. to establish a Peace Observation Commission to observe and report on our situation. By definition, the current circumstances—international tension that is likely to endanger global peace and security—is exactly what the commission was designed to deal with."

Eaglehoff thought about all the ships crowding the Strait of Malacca. "It would definitely buy us some time to work with the Japanese on a one-on-one basis without having everyone label us bullies."

"True." Tidwell cracked a smile. "And you know how slow a commission moves."

The telephone rang and Scott Eaglehoff answered it, then handed it to Tidwell. "It's someone from your staff." The recently installed phone was connected to the White House switchboard.

"Thanks."

Eaglehoff watched his friend's face turn crimson. Whatever the problem was, the news wasn't good.

"Patch me through to him," Tidwell blurted and cupped the receiver. "We've already got a problem with the Anchorage team—my understudy is being his usual asinine self."

The Chief of Staff listened to only one side of the brief conversation, but there was no doubt about the outcome. Bud Tidwell, the consummate statesman, was a firm, calm man most of the time—but this was not one of those times. The experienced academic and political expert, who normally exercised leadership with a great deal of self-discipline, was enraged at the man who had been forced on his staff.

"I'd fire that pompous ass," Tidwell said curtly after he terminated the call, "if the President didn't owe him a political favor."

Eaglehoff wasn't fond of the Under Secretary of State either, but he kept his thoughts to himself while the White House operator connected Tidwell with the Japanese Ambassador.

When he heard Koji Hagura's voice, Tidwell tried to sound pleasant.

"Ambassador Hagura, Secretary Tidwell," he announced

lightly. "I deeply apologize for the misunderstanding with Envoy Isoroku, and I assure you that we will fully cooperate with your advance team in Anchorage."

After the brief conversation, he placed the receiver down and turned to Eaglehoff. "I'm already extinguishing fires in Anchorage—and the meetings haven't even started."

SINGAPORE

Promptly at 11:30 A.M., Steve parked the rental car in a position to view the main entrance to the Port of Singapore Authority building. He placed a Tiger Beer windshield sunscreen over the dashboard and checked his Beretta, then glanced in the rear-view mirror and studied the area around the building.

Alternately looking at his wristwatch and peeking through two small holes he had punched in the sunscreen, Wickham grew more apprehensive as noon approached. With each sweep of the second hand, his anxiety rose to match his doubts about whether or not this whole thing was such a good idea.

His thoughts turned to Susan and he wondered what was happening at the Hyatt Regency. In an effort to avoid a one-on-one confrontation if the stalker appeared at the hotel, Susan and Steve had enlisted the aid of two private security officers. They had also asked two members of the Hyatt management team to monitor the switchboard for any inquiries about the arrival of the American agents.

Steve stretched his arms and legs in an effort to ease his tension, but it merely increased. As the minutes ticked off, he grew more impatient and began to question his own logic about a leak in the FBI or CIA.

At ten minutes after the hour, Wickham decided to enter the building and see if crew cut was inside. He leaned over to grab his sunglasses and Wallaby sun hat, then glanced in the rear-view mirror and froze.

"Sonuvabitch," he said under his breath as his pulse quickened and he felt a fleeting stab of pain from the sudden adrenaline surge.

The Asian with the short haircut and mangled ear had just stopped his rental car twenty meters behind him.

With feelings of outrage about the breach of security at Langley, Steve shifted into survival mode. *Did he see me?*

Wondering if the stalker was waiting for him to make a play, Wickham eased his Beretta across his lap and flipped the safety to the off position. He couldn't afford to allow his thinking to be clouded by his desire to find the weasel in the Agency. He would have to deal with that later. His sole priority had to focus on defending himself and capturing the hired killer.

He obviously doesn't know I'm here, Steve thought as the hit man cautiously looked around. *I'm going to have to confront him while I have the element of surprise on my side.*

Wickham breathed deeply and slowly exhaled. *Be aggressive, and if he tries to escape, take him out.*

Without a moment's hesitation, Steve shoved the driver's door open and leaped out. He grasped the Beretta with both hands and placed the sight on the driver, then realized he'd made a tactical blunder. The Asian's engine was running and the man had already reacted to the unexpected assault. With the rear tires screeching, crew cut was barreling straight toward Wickham.

Steve took quick aim and squeezed off two shots before he dove back into the front seat of his car. He was scrambling out the passenger-side door when the hit man's car slammed into the open driver's door. The grinding impact tore the door off the car and blew out the left front tire.

Wickham belly-crawled to the front of the badly damaged vehicle and got off one shot before the stalker careened around a corner and vanished.

Shaken by the incident, Steve had calmed down externally by the time the local authorities arrived. He absently went about discussing the incident with the local police while his insides boiled. He vowed to capture or kill his assailant, then find the traitor at Langley and the bastard who was paying for the information.

From behind her concealment near the registration counter, Susan watched Steve walk into the spacious lobby of the Hyatt Regency. She could tell by his impatient stride that something had gone awry.

She rushed out to meet Wickham and gave him a faint smile. "Are you okay?"

"Couldn't be better," he joked feebly.

Her concerned gaze quickly sobered him.

"Susan, our leak is at Langley," he confided with a look of disdain etched on his face. "I'd have to bet that he's in a very senior position. Access to almost anything."

"What happened?" Susan asked and cautiously looked around the hotel lobby.

"He showed up at the Port Authority."

"And . . ."

"I blew it," Steve said with a disgusted shake of his head. "He's still out there . . . waiting for us—me—to make another dumbass mistake."

"Steve," Susan began with genuine concern in her voice, "let's arrange for a couple of agents—FBI, CIA, or a combination—to join us as backup."

"Susan, I don't want to run anything through the Agency," he said emphatically. "We've got a spineless weasel locked on to every move we make."

Feeling a little awkward, she sighed and nodded her understanding. "I know you feel rotten and betrayed, and I don't blame you, but we need to get to Tokyo and track down the lead about the insurance company."

"You're right," Steve conceded with a long face. "If you want to bring in more FBI agents, that's fine with me."

"It's the safe thing to do," Susan suggested.

"I know it is. But just one favor, okay?"

"Sure," she replied and hesitated a moment. "If it's within reason."

"I want to personally capture the sonuvabitch who is stalking us," Steve said contemptuously, "and find out who his Agency connection is."

CAMP DAVID

The bright rays from the late-morning sun filtered through the trees as the gleaming Marine helicopter approached the sprawling presidential retreat, then flared for a smooth landing on the helo pad. After the Sikorsky VH-60's main rotor blades began slowing, Scott Eaglehoff hurried from the helo to the President's private quarters.

The Chief of Staff had had a lengthy breakfast meeting with the Secretary of Defense, the Secretary of State, the National Security Advisor, the Director of the CIA, and the Joint Chiefs of Staff.

The President was ending a conference call when Eaglehoff was ushered into the richly appointed study.

"Well, Scott," the President said glumly as he dropped the receiver in its cradle, "our media watchdogs are saying that the proverbial shit is hitting the fan in Japan, and that I'm going to have splatters all over me."

"I'm afraid"—the President's closest adviser grimaced—"that we're going to take some heat, sir."

"No doubt," the President replied with a crooked smile, "but I'm not too concerned. I look forward to getting to Anchorage and facing Koyama, the snide sonuvabitch."

Eaglehoff, known as a two-fisted gunslinger around the Beltway, was disappointed by the President's drift toward a casual, contentious personality. Uncharacteristically low in spirits, Eaglehoff had even thought about tendering his resignation in order to salvage his future prospects in Washington.

"Scott," the President went on and propped his feet on an upholstered footstool, "the stakes are getting higher. I think we've got to take some bold steps if we're going to head off a confrontation in Anchorage and a possible military clash with Japan."

"Sir," Eaglehoff began tentatively, "I recommend that you convene the Cabinet as soon as possible and take a strong stance about the course you wish to pursue. Otherwise no one has any idea which way you want to jump or how far you'll go to force the Japanese to back down."

The President rubbed his temples. "Yeah, I've been thinking about it since I woke up this morning."

Eaglehoff frowned and blew his nose. "We're facing an ominous, challenging situation where our adversary could become unpredictable. Once bloodied, Japan may lash out and ricochet in many directions."

The President tossed the remains of his cheeseburger on the plate. His mood turned dark. "How'd the meeting go this morning? Any worthwhile ideas?"

"We had a productive session," Eaglehoff dutifully reported. "I think we're making progress in understanding how to deal with the Japanese."

The President glanced away. "What's the situation at the moment?" he snorted.

"Not exactly good," Eaglehoff said stiffly, and nervously cracked his knuckles. "There have been a number of bomb threats directed at Japanese and American airlines, the Japanese are fleeing from Oahu and the other Hawaiian islands as fast as JAL can provide flights, there's a tremendous exodus of all races from the Los Angeles area because the Asian protest has turned into an open rebellion, North Korea is rattling swords and flying reconnaissance missions close to Japan, and the Joint Chiefs and Bud Tidwell believe we should immediately withdraw our military forces from Japan and advise U.S. citizens to do likewise."

"Okay. Now tell me the bad news." The President grinned and walked to the liquor cabinet.

Eaglehoff sat in startled silence while he watched the President do something he hadn't seen him do before: drink straight whiskey out of a water glass.

29

TOKYO, JAPAN

Precisely one minute before the scheduled arrival time, the spotlessly clean train came to a smooth stop in the railway station. The forty-mile trip from Narita International Airport to Tokyo had been smooth and comfortable, with the exception of the offensive looks Steve continued to receive from the Asian passengers.

During the flight from Singapore, Steve and Susan had discussed at length his altercation with the Asian hit man and concluded that it would be best to keep quiet for the time being. They had no idea who the CIA informer was, and one miscalculation could easily get them killed.

They were relieved to know where the leak was originating, but Wickham was humiliated that the information was coming from someone in the Agency.

Steve had thought about calling the Director on his SecTel secure phone, but he had reservations about discussing the breach of security at the Agency. He didn't trust Paul Holcomb, and he had begun to wonder if the Director had lied about the President requesting him for the unusual case.

When the train doors opened, Steve and Susan quickly hoisted their luggage and stepped out of the crowded car. They cautiously looked around, ready to react to any threat. Both had no doubt that the stalker had observed them board the airliner in Singapore.

"One more lap," Steve said with a determined look, "and we'll have it made, if we can catch a cab."

"I don't want to hurt your feelings," she responded with a self-conscious smile, "but *I* had better hail us a taxi, then you can slide in with me."

He hesitated a brief moment, unsure if she was putting him on. "You're serious, aren't you?"

"Unfortunately, yes," she replied quietly and walked toward a waiting cab. "The animosity toward Americans is reaching a fever pitch."

Steve glanced around before he followed her. Many of the unsmiling strangers wouldn't even look at him, while others cast looks that made it clear that he was unwanted.

During the ride to the hotel, Wickham was surprised to see the crowds of militant protesters who were waving banners and shouting anti-American slogans through bullhorns. Steve made a mental note of the shouted sentiment characterizing Japan's part in World War II as a holy mission to liberate their Asian neighbors from the grasp of Western colonialism.

They had canceled their original hotel reservations and checked into the Keio Plaza Inter-Continental Hotel under assumed names.

While Susan contacted her friend, a fraud investigator for various Japanese insurance companies, Wickham went to a pay phone and called the Agency. He received an updated briefing on world events, including the meeting in Anchorage and the current global military situation. He kept the conversation light and never gave the slightest hint that anything was wrong.

Steve also had a message from the director of the CIA. Paul Holcomb wanted results and he wasn't being subtle about his demand. What Wickham didn't know was that his supposedly secure-link conversation was being traced in a quiet room at Langley.

Steve was walking around the uncrowded 7th-floor swimming pool and garden terrace when Susan joined him. They sat down at an empty table and he looked around at the other non-Asians. No one seemed to notice them, or at least no one indicated any sign of disapproval of the mixed-race couple.

"Is your friend going to work with us?" Steve asked while thinking how else they might solve the mystery of the ownership of number three *Matsumi Maru*.

"He said he'd help us," she explained with a shrug. "He seemed rather uncomfortable when I explained the circumstances and the need for total secrecy."

Steve grew cautious and lowered his voice. "Are you sure we can trust him?"

"Yes, I'm sure."

"One hundred percent?"

"I can't be one hundred percent sure," she admitted. "Why are you so jumpy about my friend?"

"We don't know how far the tentacles from Langley may reach," he remarked in a relaxed manner. "Your friend may already know something we don't, and we could be setting ourselves up for an unpleasant surprise."

"Steve, don't take this the wrong way, but I think you're starting to see shadows behind every corner."

"In this business"—he forced a smile—"it only takes one mistake to buy the farm."

Susan bristled at the implication that she was a novice. She raised an eyebrow and gave him an icy look. "I'm quite aware of the risks involved in *this* business."

Taken aback by the sudden personality change, Steve gazed steadily into her eyes. "I apologize if I offended you, but someone is trying to kill us, and they're getting information about our whereabouts from the CIA."

"No apology needed," she replied in a mildly derisive manner, then softened her tone. "Steve, I fully understand the gravity of the situation. I respect you very much, and I trust that you have the same respect for me . . . and for the way I perform my job."

"Of course I respect you," he proclaimed and reached for her hand.

Susan had doubts about her friend, too, but she didn't want to expose them. Hiroshi was their best bet to find the owner of the ship, and they had to have faith and follow through, no matter what.

Her brief flash of irritation quickly subsided and she smiled when Steve grasped her hand.

"Hiroshi Okubo," she explained, "has a solid reputation and was highly recommended when I worked with him. I don't think we have to worry about Hiroshi."

"Fair enough."

"Besides," Susan went on, "he has his honor to protect, and that is very important to the Japanese. I don't think he would risk his excellent reputation by doing something stupid."

"Like I said before," Steve responded with a serious look, "I trust your judgment."

"At any rate," she quickly finished, "Hiroshi said that he'll have an answer for us by tomorrow afternoon—one way or the other—on who owned the *Matsumi Maru* fleet."

Wickham studied the impressive skyline in the busy Shinjuku ward. "That sounds good to me if it works out."

Steve would have to be content to wait. Squinting to see through the hazy sky, he looked at the Century Hyatt Hotel and the other modern high-rise buildings, then turned to face Susan. "If you investigated fraud for a group of well-heeled insurance companies and discovered something really bad about one of your best clients, would you be willing to blow the whistle?"

"I seem to recall," she said with a friendly wink, "Steve Wickham, a legendary CIA agent, once told me that 'sometimes you have to roll the dice and take your chances.' "

Steve nonchalantly glanced around the swimming pool and garden terrace. "Speaking of chances," he said with a trace of tension in his voice, "I have a feeling crew cut is watching us."

STRAIT OF MALACCA

Moving quietly through the water at a speed of 3½ knots, the Japanese submarine *Harushio* was rigged for supersilent running. All noisy machinery and unnecessary activities had been silenced, including the showers, galley equipment, and laundry facilities. The public-address system was immobilized, which required the crew to use a single phone circuit and communicate their orders by whispering to each other. No one was allowed to open or close any hatches or use any tools.

The crowded and complex interior of the eerily silent diesel-electric sub was bathed in a soft hue of red light. The off-duty submariners, who were relegated to their cramped living spaces, were waiting for a cold snack to be served.

The Yushio-class submarine was creeping through the depths at 220 feet when the sonar operator noticed an unusual trace on his screen. The towed array sonar trailing the *Harushio* provided acoustic waves to detect and locate submerged objects. He studied the input for a moment and then selected a display that provided a range of sound frequencies to analyze.

Working rapidly and carefully, the technician examined the range of graphs produced by the narrowband processors. The system blended the incoming sounds for a number of minutes to make sure they were not background noises from the vast number of vessels traversing the busy waterway.

Finally, a spike emerged on the graph and the operator immediately recognized the unique signature. The sound was emitting from an American Los Angeles–class fast-attack submarine. The nuclear-powered boat wasn't even attempting to mask its noise.

The sonar technician checked his tonal data one more time. *The Americans are too arrogant.* He keyed his microphone and spoke softly. "Bridge, sonar."

"Bridge," came the instant reply.

"I have a Los Angeles–signature bearing zero-six-five—overtaking us at a high rate of speed."

A long pause followed the announcement.

"Sonar," the officer of the deck said excitedly, "confirm type of signature."

"The contact," the operator explained clearly, "has the signature of an American attack submarine."

"Los Angeles–type?"

The technician stared at the graph. *"Hai."*

A few moments later the sonar operator heard a different voice in his headset.

"Sonar, this is the Captain speaking. I want a time-bearing plot every five minutes until the target is abeam us."

After the man acknowledged the order, the Captain turned to his second-in-command. "When the attack sub passes us, we will slowly increase speed and fall in behind the careless Americans."

Most submarines have a blind spot astern where sonar reception is impaired by engines, spinning turbines, shafts, screws, and various equipment housed in the aft end of the boats.

USS *BREMERTON*

The attack center was deathly quiet when Commander Lamar Joiner stuck his head in, then continued to the submarine's cramped control room. A third-generation submariner, Joiner had followed his grandfather and father through the Naval Academy and straight into the submarine service.

An athletic and gregarious man by nature, the husky skipper with the ice-blue eyes was respected by his officers and crewmen. Some of his famous exploits, both ashore and at sea, rivaled those of his legendary father. The Captain knew his crew almost as well as he knew his three children. He took pride in remembering the names of their wives and most of their offspring.

Joiner looked at his watch. It was time for the next watch-standers to relieve the duty crewmen so they could get some chow and a few hours of sack time. Later, when *Bremerton* reached her patrol area near *Kitty Hawk,* the crew would have to operate with more vigilance.

Now level at 240 feet beneath the surface of the strait, Joiner was grateful to see the water getting deeper. The passage through the crowded and narrow southern end of the strait had been nerve-racking and time-consuming. His navigator had winced on a number of occasions when he thought they were going to plow into the bottom of the shallow areas.

Deeper water also meant more reliable acoustic returns because the convergence zones allowed the sonar to detect targets at much longer ranges. Shallow water has an adverse effect on convergence-zone propagation, and the scattering of sound across the bottom makes detections extremely difficult.

In the sonar room, fresh faces stared at the luminescent glow from their scopes, while the helmsmen in the control room guided the submarine with yokes similar to those in the cockpit of an airliner.

Joiner patiently waited until the new watch-standers manned their stations, then glanced at the seasoned officer of the deck. "I have the conn."

The OD nodded. "Captain has the conn."

Noting their current depth, Joiner decided to ascend to 150 feet and evaluate the boundary layer between the cold, deep water and the warm surface water.

"Make your depth one hundred fifty feet," Joiner ordered with a smile creasing his lips.

Unlike some skippers who descended to a certain depth and never deviated, Lamar Joiner enjoyed maneuvering the fast-attack boats and seeing the enthusiasm on the faces of the officers and men.

"One hundred fifty feet, aye," the young diving officer replied with an authoritative voice. "Helm five degrees up on the planes."

The petty officer at the diving controls acknowledged the command, and the submarine commenced a slow ascent.

Leveling at 150 feet, *Bremerton* was close to the thermocline layer. Below this nearly isothermal layer, the water temperature decreased rapidly with depth, forming a shallow thermocline.

The drastic temperature change, combined with the associated changes in salinity, causes sound waves to refract when they travel obliquely through the layer. This refraction of sound is important in the sonar detection of submarines, and Lamar Joiner was considered a master at using the properties of salinity and temperature variance to conceal his boat.

"Left ten degrees rudder," Joiner said evenly. "New course three-one-zero."

After his instructions were repeated, Joiner waited until the submarine was steady-on the new course. "Engine room, conn. All ahead two-thirds."

"All ahead two-thirds, aye."

Lamar Joiner was proud of his crew and extremely confident in the reliable and redundant systems incorporated in his fast-attack submarine. From the sophisticated fire-control and weapons-launch systems to the propulsion and ship-control elements, *Bremerton* and her sister 688 boats were the best-built submarines in the world.

The only thing that bothered Joiner, and something he had never discussed at length with anyone, was the high-speed handling characteristics of the Los Angeles–class SSNs. It was common knowledge throughout the submarine community that the 688s were difficult to control at high speeds.

The stories were varied and colorful, but all of them had elements of the same troubling problems of significant pitching moments or tendencies to snap-roll like an airplane. Joiner had discounted most of the embellished anecdotes until his first cruise in *Cincinnati.*

After a series of high-speed evasive maneuvers during a routine training mission, the attack sub had suddenly pitched down while traveling at 27 knots. Joiner, along with a number of other crew members, had come to Jesus before the skipper regained control of the boat.

The frightening excursion had plunged the speeding submarine to a hazardous depth near the point where the creaking hull would have been crushed by seawater pressure. They also missed, by a margin of 110 feet, ramming the bow into the seafloor. When *Cincinnati* started ascending, everyone on board had a new sense of respect for the word *luck*.

From that horrifying moment, Joiner became a true believer in the instability factor and had not forgotten the incident. He often thought about the consequences of an uncontrolled pitch-up at high speed. In his dreams, Joiner could see a charter fishing boat being tossed through the air as his submarine shot out of the water.

"Conn, sonar," squawked the bulkhead-mounted speaker. "We have a contact bearing three-two-zero. Sounds like a freighter passing right to left . . . fourteen thousand yards."

"Very well," Joiner replied as he checked his course and speed. "Left ten degrees rudder. New course three-zero-zero."

Although Joiner felt no immediate threat, he reverted to the standard operating procedures that he had used for years. He would pass close to the freighter in order to mask the loud sounds of his fast-moving submarine. He didn't have the liberty of making a slow, quiet cruise to join the carrier battle group.

However, the Captain wasn't aware that the conventional submarine *Harushio* was directly behind *Bremerton* and accelerating in the attack sub's cone of silence.

30

THE WHITE HOUSE

The President stood by the windows in the Oval Office and stared at the three groundskeepers who were working on a section of the freshly mowed lawn. The dreary, overcast gray sky matched his gloomy spirits.

The United States, according to the latest news reports from around the world, was being acclaimed with great enthusiasm by some, while the majority of people screamed epithets at the Americans for being a swaggering superpower bully.

In related news on the major television networks, the shipping traffic that normally used the Strait of Malacca had dropped dramatically. Many civilian vessels were heading to secure harbors until the waterway was deemed safe to traverse. Others continued to use the strait in spite of the obvious dangers.

The President finally turned and walked from his office, stopping briefly in his secretary's small compartment to wish her a happy birthday, then entered the Cabinet room and greeted the top officials in his Administration.

After everyone was seated, the President turned to his Defense Secretary. "Bryce, I understand we have more complications in the South China Sea area?" The statement became a question.

"I'm afraid so," Mellongard reluctantly answered and donned his eyeglasses. "Our latest satellite- and photo-intelligence information indicates a large number of warships converging near the mouth of the strait, and many ships have entered the strait. These are in addition to the growing number of Japanese vessels that are spreading through the area."

No one made a sound while SECDEF took a drink of water, then continued the morning briefing.

"We now have confirmation—as of the past hour—that surface combatants from China, India, Indonesia, Malaysia, Pakistan, Taiwan, New Zealand, and Sri Lanka are in close proximity to the strait."

Mellongard looked at the color-coded briefing cards that had been prepared for him. "Due to the congestion on the water and in the airspace over the strait, our biggest problem is making proper identification of our allies, possible adversaries, and the neutrals using the waterway and airspace.

"Another factor plaguing us," he half-muttered, "is the onslaught of media people. In spite of our warnings, the airspace over the strait is saturated with chartered airplanes and helicopters full of reporters."

"What about mines?" the President asked, thinking about the hazards of mine warfare in the traffic-choked sea-lane. "I don't want to see our ships get pinned in by mines."

"We are focusing," Mellongard answered with a distant look, "on all aspects of mine countermeasures, including bringing in more Sea Dragons to bolster our efforts. *Essex* and her group are expected to enter the northern area of the strait by this evening—Washington time."

Bryce Mellongard eyed the men around the long table. "In response to the increasing threats to our expeditionary task force, we've also added more P-3 aircraft to our maritime patrol efforts.

"In order to sustain our forces afloat"—Mellongard leaned

back and pocketed his reading glasses—"we are increasing our logistics-support system and diverting more replenishment ships to the strait and the Java Sea."

The President glanced around the room and saw nothing but looks of concern. "Gentlemen, as you may be aware, I've been involved in a marathon of discussions with the leaders of our allies in the Asian and Oceanian regions.

"For the most part"—he paused and looked directly at his Secretary of State—"our international friends support our position, and they're looking forward—as much as we are—to our talks with the Japanese." He was openly lying and everyone knew it.

The President let his gaze drift from person to person. "We have to find out who is responsible for these acts of terrorism, and we have to work with the Japanese to stop the violence in our cities and mend our political differences."

"Mr. President . . ." the CIA Director said while he rolled a pencil between his hands.

"General Holcomb . . ."

All eyes shifted to the former two-star general.

"A number of my top people—the best analysts in the Agency," he ventured in his polished Bostonian accent, "believe that Pakistan and India will use this situation as an excuse to do some damage to each other."

The President heard a low rumbling from the swollen rain clouds. "General, there isn't much we can do about their problems at the moment."

Paul Holcomb inwardly cringed. *Whatever you say, Chief,* he thought.

"As the world focuses on this crisis with Japan," the President went on, "everyone has to make his or her decision about what is right and what is wrong."

The silence in the room was palpable.

"Our position is well defined"—the President stared down Holcomb—"and I stick by it. If someone else wants to wade into the fray, that's their prerogative, but we can't afford to get involved in regional power clashes until we sort through this mess with the Japanese."

Holcomb absently dropped his pencil and returned the President's cold stare. "There's something you—all of us—had better think about."

The President tossed a look at Bryce Mellongard before turning his attention to the suddenly outspoken Director of the Agency. "You have the floor, General."

"We have just received documented evidence," Holcomb declared with a hint of smugness, "that at least two—and possibly three—Iranian Kilo-class submarines have entered the Strait of Malacca.

"A Washington-based official from the People's Mojahedin of Iran made the announcement early this morning," he said boldly, "and the Iranian Defense Minister confirmed it to my people less than an hour ago."

The President, who was concerned about *Kitty Hawk* and her escort ships, glanced at the Defense Secretary. "Bryce, have we been getting any sonar contacts with Kilo-class submarines in the strait—or any other type of sub?"

Mellongard, who was always reluctant to speak freely in front of a group, leaned on the edge of the conference table. "Yes, but it wasn't an Iranian. It was the *Sindhuvijay* and it surfaced as soon as we began tracking it."

"Where's the sub now?" Bud Tidwell asked.

"The last report I received," Mellongard said without looking up, "indicated that it was on the surface and returning to port in India."

The President faced SECDEF. "Bryce, do you think we'll have any trouble locating the Iranian subs, if, in fact, they're in the strait at this time?"

"We shouldn't have any problem," Mellongard replied with complete confidence. "If they're in the strait, we'll find them and stay on their backs."

31

TOKYO, JAPAN

Steve Wickham held the phone receiver to his ear and looked out a third-floor window toward the Kasumigaseki Building in downtown Tokyo. A gleaming *Shinkansen* superexpress bullet train sped through the center of the bustling city as he concluded his call to Langley. He lingered a moment, absorbed by the sight of the crowded, noisy streets and sidewalks. If he closed his eyes, the sounds wouldn't be distinguishable from the din of New York City or Chicago.

He retraced his steps and entered the compact sushi restaurant, then glanced at Susan and her friend before he took a seat at the end of the low counter. They were still sitting at a tiny alcove in the corner of the restaurant. The intense, skinny young man was talking rapidly but softly. Susan calmly jotted notes while she listened and occasionally nodded her head in agreement.

Hiroshi Okubo had originally agreed to discuss his investigative findings with both Susan and Steve. But between Okubo's call to Susan and the subsequent meeting at the restaurant, the insurance-fraud investigator had decided that he didn't want to talk directly to Steve.

Glad that the restaurant was almost empty at this hour, Wickham ordered a rice patty and patiently waited.

A few minutes later, Steve watched Susan take the initiative to bring the conversation to an end. When he saw her rise and thank her informant, Steve swiveled around to greet them. Hiroshi Okubo graciously bowed and then smiled when Wickham returned the gesture.

"Steve," Susan quietly said when her friend left the restaurant, "let's take a walk."

"That interesting, huh?"

"Indeed."

The temperature was slowly getting cooler when Steve and Susan left the train station and entered the main entrance to Ueno Park. Deciding to explore Lake Shinobazu, renowned for its colorful lotus blossoms, they set off around the spectacularly manicured perimeter.

She fell in step and glanced at Steve. "I forgot to tell you something."

"What?" he asked, cautiously examining the grounds of the large park.

"We'll have seven or eight Bureau agents—all of them Japanese-Americans—working with us in a few days."

"Great," Steve replied with genuine enthusiasm. "The sooner the better as far as I'm concerned."

"Any news from the Agency?"

"Nothing new about this case," he freely admitted, "but then again, I haven't really pried or said much because I don't have any idea who is setting us up."

"I understand," she said flatly. "This whole thing frustrates me as much as it does you."

"I know," Steve replied with a perfunctory smile before he glanced over his shoulder to see if anyone appeared to be trailing them. "The showdown in the Strait of Malacca is growing out of control. A number of the Agency's best analysts think that we should quietly glide out of there before we get waylaid."

She looked up at him with a sense of vulnerability. "It's coming back to haunt us, isn't it?"

"What?"

"Our military has been cut too far, and we're going to pay a price for it."

"Oh, yeah," he replied in exasperation. "We'll have to get our asses kicked by some two-bit military power before the light will begin to glow in Washington."

They walked in silence, both taking the impending hostilities between the Japanese and the Americans very personally. The image of a military confrontation with Japan, after more than half a century of peace, seemed surrealistic and incomprehensible to both of them.

"Hiroshi," Susan said at last, "went into his main data-bank and discovered that the records at Tokio Marine and Fire had been altered."

"Which records?"

"The official documentation that connected the insurance company to the *Matsumi Maru* fleet during the time frame when number seven collided with the Navy destroyer."

"That seems almost impossible," Steve commented and gave her a perplexed look. "Unless you've got someone working for you who is inside the organization."

"Nothing is impossible," she countered dryly, "when you're dealing with Japan's endless saga of political and business scandals. The politicians and senior executives manage to air their dirty laundry—payoffs, corruption, lying, and infighting—on a routine basis."

"Well"—he chuckled and shook his head—"the Japanese don't have the market cornered on graft and corruption. Take a look at our political system if you want to see blatant lying and open thievery."

"At any rate," she continued while they followed the paved path along the shoreline, "Hiroshi used his contacts at Tokio Marine and Fire to get the computer code to access the files that track the financial settlements."

"He *must* be well respected."

"And trusted. He placed himself in a delicate position for us."

"What'd he find?" Steve asked.

"Copies of two checks," she explained enthusiastically, "that were issued as a settlement from Tokio Marine and Fire to the owner of the *Matsumi Maru* fleet."

Steve was incredulous. "You're kidding me."

"No, I'm not kidding."

"That easy?"

She shook her head. "It wasn't that easy. The checks had gone to a holding company, which ceased to exist shortly after the ships had been sold. It was simply a shell game with a box number and some fancy stationery."

"The same method of operation," he inquired, thinking about the mansion on Oahu, "that we found in Hawaii?"

"For the most part." Susan cast her gaze across the picturesque lake. "Hiroshi vaguely remembered seeing the name of the holding company from a previous investigation. He searched his files for hours, then gave up and called me late last night."

"Let me guess," Steve automatically said. "He wanted the names of the holding companies involved in the Pearl Harbor scheme?"

"Yes," she answered and stopped walking, then turned to look at Steve. "He found a connection that frightened him—really frightened him."

Wickham's brow arched in question, creating lines on his forehead. "Connection?"

She quietly nodded. "After cross-referencing the company names I gave him with the enterprise that owned the ships, Hiroshi found monetary ties to the headquarters of a major Japanese corporation.

"The man who owns the company," Susan continued with a tremor of excitement, "is Tadashi Matsukawa."

A flash of recognition crossed Steve's face. "The billionaire who is methodically buying a sizable investment in our Congress."

"One and the same," she confirmed in a voice laced with concern. "Hiroshi was terrified when he made the discovery—really panic-stricken."

Steve closed his eyes and grimaced, then looked up. "He erased the files."

"Yes—because he knows too much about Matsukawa," Susan explained reluctantly, "and he knew that Matsukawa didn't have any idea that the fragment of evidence linking him to the Pearl Harbor attack was still in the computer system. Every other connection to Hawaii had been thoroughly purged."

Wickham vigorously rubbed his hands together in the chilled air. "Well, we know the master of concealment made a mistake, but proving it may be difficult."

"From the files," Susan went on, "Hiroshi saw that Matsukawa is a major shareholder in Tokio Marine and Fire"—she paused and lowered her eyes—"and that's how Matsukawa gained direct access to the computer records."

Susan felt a pang of guilt sweep over her. "Hiroshi was afraid that his unauthorized entry into the system might be traced, so he obliterated the evidence and scrambled his record of entry."

"Shit," Wickham said lightly and turned to Susan. "Sorry."

"Forget it."

Sunk in their disappointment, they walked to an empty park bench and sat down.

"Steve," she began quietly, "Hiroshi told me that Matsukawa is known to be a merciless, unforgiving bastard who many believe has killed—or arranged to have killed—a number of people who have opposed him."

"I wouldn't doubt that for a second," Wickham said while he studied the other park visitors. *Why do I suddenly have an uneasy feeling?*

"Two of his senior members of management," Susan went on, "who openly argued with him on separate occasions, have died in mysterious accidents. Insiders are convinced that Matsukawa had them killed. He is one of the most powerful and brutal men in Japan, and he has connections with the elite, including the Prime Minister."

"That's what I understand," Steve replied in hushed tones, "from the intel briefs I've read about him. We have to assume that Matsukawa is the person behind the attacks in Hawaii and Los Angeles, not to mention the other incidents."

"I don't have any doubt," Susan said venomously. "We have to figure out a way to expose him for what he is . . . before the U.S. goes head-to-head with Japan."

"We'll work on it, trust me."

Susan looked up at the sky for a few moments. "We can thank Hiroshi for giving us the big break we needed."

"No question about it," Steve conceded.

Susan's compassion for Hiroshi Okubo's feelings was genuine and readily apparent. "He did us a giant favor, and now he fears for his life if things go wrong. Hiroshi didn't expect to find what he uncovered. We owe him the consideration to keep his name out of this."

"I agree with you. We'll be very cautious." He respected Susan's allegiance to her friend. "Why don't you meet him again and explain that as far as we're concerned, he doesn't exist?"

She turned and smiled. "I told him that before we left the restaurant."

"Good," he responded earnestly, then felt a moment of concern. "We're dealing with a shrewd operator. We can't nail Matsukawa if we don't have some solid evidence to connect him to the assault at Pearl."

"What do you suggest?" she inquired and reached into her jacket pocket for a pair of gloves.

"We'll see . . ." he trailed off for a moment, "if we can't interview Matsukawa for *The Wall Street Journal*."

Susan froze, then swung around and gave him a wide-eyed stare. "What are you talking about?"

"We're going to become journalists," he answered and cracked a smile. "Egoists like Matsukawa generally like to pontificate to the media, especially if it's a major publication and the subject happens to be about the global situation as the interviewee sees it."

"More specifically, the current strained relationship between Japan and the United States," Susan added while she slipped her hands into her gloves. "I'm sure that would be a hot topic."

"Exactly. We'll make an appointment with Matsukawa and see what we can glean if he takes the bait. At least it will offer us an opportunity to provide some firsthand information to our agencies. Now that we know what we're looking for, who knows what we might find?"

"Steve," she said under her breath, "you better be careful. Matsukawa isn't careless. What if his office calls the *Journal* to verify the legitimacy of the interview request?"

He glanced at his watch. "I'll arrange it with someone I can trust at Langley. Tony will have one of our people go to the *Journal,* make the request, then stand by to verify it until we've completed our chat with him. We'll do it completely out of the normal loop at Langley, so the informer shouldn't get wind of our plan."

He saw the fear and uncertainty in her eyes. "Relax. It's fine."

"That may be easy for you to say," Susan murmured, "but this is unexplored territory for me."

"I can trust Tony," Steve reassured her, "and the Agency has thousands of contacts who front for the CIA, including a number of newspapers, so he'll get it done—even if it takes a couple of days to set it up."

Susan gave him a long, suspicious look. "When the article doesn't appear in the paper—when Matsukawa inquires about the interview—then what?"

"The paper denies it requested an interview," Steve answered matter-of-factly, "and blames the misunderstanding on a hoax. Routine procedure."

She gave him a double take. "I need a drink."

"I'm buying," he offered and rose to his feet.

Susan started to rise, then abruptly grabbed his hand. "Sit

down," she demanded, "and don't turn around. He's over by the aquarium."

Steve sat down and studied her wide eyes. "Is he next to it or out in the open?"

"Next to it," she answered and withdrew crew cut's 9-millimeter Taurus from under her jacket. "He's standing by the southwest corner."

"Okay," he said calmly and forced himself not to turn and look. "Let's walk toward the aquarium and see if he tries to—"

"He knows I saw him," Susan interrupted. "He's heading toward the monorail!"

Steve drew his Beretta and leaped up. "Come on!"

They raced after the fleeing man, then dove for the ground when he turned and fired at them. The hordes of people waiting to board the monorail began screaming and running away.

When the hit man headed for the monorail station, Steve and Susan chased him, and again had to sprawl on the grass when he began firing at them.

"You sonuvabitch," Steve swore to himself and squeezed the trigger three times, then stopped when he saw the man stagger backwards and clutch his upper leg.

Susan and Steve jumped up and ran after the wounded man as he limped toward the now-vacated station.

Reacting from instinct, Susan paused and took aim a second before the Asian turned to fire. She pumped two rounds into his upper torso, then fired again and missed.

Steve reached the hit man as he tried to drag himself into the monorail station. He kicked Susan's stolen Smith & Wesson out of the man's hand and aimed squarely at his face. "Don't move or I'll blow your fuckin' head off!"

32

USS KITTY HAWK

The windswept seas had calmed and a gentle rain washed the flight deck of the carrier. An unusual atmospheric disturbance had recently passed over the Strait of Malacca, leaving the ship and her escorts in dismal weather conditions.

On the flag bridge, Rear Admiral Isaac Landesman monitored the brightly clad men on the flight deck as they prepared for the second launch of the day. He had a great deal of respect for the youngsters who regularly worked twelve to sixteen hours a day, seven days a week, during flight operations.

Landesman would not admit it to anyone, but he was concerned about the foul weather and the experience level of some of the new pilots. Sixteen of the twenty-three aircraft scheduled for the next launch cycle carried live ordnance, and four of the planes with bombs and rockets were being flown by "nuggets"—qualified but inexperienced aviators.

While the pilots started their engines and the flight crews went through their checklists, the battle group commander raised his binoculars and studied the hazy horizon. He moved his head slowly, scanning the freighters and tankers before he stopped and watched two ASW helicopters in the distance.

Both of the SH-60 Seahawks appeared to be using their dipping sonars in an effort to detect foreign submarines. While one of the slate-gray helos was actually listening for intruders, the other one was trailing a wire and communicating with the attack sub *La Jolla*.

Isaac Landesman continued his vigilant sweep of the shipping lanes, focusing on the Japanese Maritime Defense Force flagship *Hayasa* and her escorts as they sailed toward the southern end of the strait.

Flanked by two Asagiri-class destroyers, the Aegis destroyer was 1,500 yards behind the minesweepers *Hikoshima* and *Yurishima*. Estimating the distance of the ships to be approximately four nautical miles, the Admiral noticed that the replenishment oiler was not with the small flotilla.

When the first aircraft began to taxi forward to the number-two catapult, Landesman lowered his binoculars and concentrated on the flight-deck personnel. He watched the yellow-shirted catapult officer walk to the deck-edge operator and kneel to talk to him.

A moment later, Landesman saw a flash in his peripheral vision. He turned his head and froze in stunned silence. Trailing a white plume of smoke from its launch canister on the *Hayasa*, the antiship missile was headed straight for *Kitty Hawk*. Landesman started to shout an order at the instant he heard, "Man your battle stations! Man your battle stations! This is not a drill!"

Landesman watched helplessly while the Harpoon missile's radar altimeter and computer guided the surface-to-surface missile at the desired sea-skimming height. The maneuver was designed to thwart the Vulcan Phalanx 20-millimeter Close-In Weapons System mounted aboard many ships.

The powerful CIWS defensive system incorporates two radars that provide information to an on-board computer to constantly correlate the target track and the CIWS projectile stream. Angular error is automatically calculated to correct the next burst as the system rapidly eliminates the difference between the tracks of the incoming and outgoing weapons.

CIWS is a last-ditch defense that spews a heavy volume of fire from a six-barrel Gatling gun. If an antiship missile is barely above the water, it makes radar acquisition more difficult for the Vulcan Phalanx system.

Seconds after the launch, the missile's frequency-agile homing radar locked on to the carrier and commanded a sudden pitch-up to place the weapon in an excellent position to strike the carrier from above. The maneuver also defeated the rapid-firing CIWS gun.

The air-warfare officer aboard the Aegis guided-missile cruiser *Chancellorsville* was paralyzed when the alarms sounded and he recognized that a missile had been fired at *Kitty Hawk*. He was in radio contact with the tactical-action officer aboard the *Hayasa* and was about to key his microphone when the console speaker blasted out a frantic call.

"*Jiko! Jiko!*" the excited voice screamed, then repeated himself in English: "Accident! Accident!"

A statement from an overzealous junior officer had been misinterpreted, resulting in the launching of the powerful antiship missile.

Although *Chancellorsville*'s air-warfare officer missed a few of the Japanese words, the agonizing confession continued in a thin and high-pitched voice. "Accidental launching! Accidental launching! *Machigai!* Mistake—our mistake."

The AWO suddenly recalled when crew members of the aircraft carrier USS *Saratoga* accidentally fired two Sea Sparrow missiles that hit the Turkish destroyer *Muavenet* during a NATO exercise in the Aegean Sea. The incident killed five men, including the Captain of the warship.

The stunned air-warfare officer broadcast an order to the other American ships.

"Weapons hold! Weapons hold!" the officer shouted while he tried to sort through the situation. "I repeat—weapons hold! Stand by."

The Japanese antiship weapon rocketed skyward before the Texas Instruments active radar system changed the setting of the cruciform rear fins. The missile made a high-g pitch-over and targeted its large prey.

Christ Almighty, Landesman thought while the missile arched down toward the congested flight deck, *what the hell are they doing? They have to be crazy!*

The Admiral saw a blur of desperate men race for the sanctuary of the ship's island structure a second before the Harpoon hit an F/A-18 Hornet loaded with fuel and ordnance. The blinding flash and thunderous explosion shattered the windows on the flag bridge and blew twenty-eight sailors over the side of the stricken flattop.

Shocked by the jolting blast and violent concussion, Landesman stumbled backwards and tripped over an aide who tried to break the Admiral's fall. Collapsing heavily to the steel deck, Landesman felt his left wrist snap as he heard and felt a series of powerful explosions that shook the carrier from bow to stern.

With the help of his stunned aide, the battle-group commander forced himself up and lurched toward his chair overlooking the flight deck. He was appalled at the fire-swept carnage taking place in front of his eyes. Dazed men, some of whom were trying to extinguish their burning clothes, were crawling on their hands and knees in an effort to escape the fireball.

The F/A-18 Hornet's internal fuel tanks and wing-mounted drop tanks had erupted, spreading flames to other aircraft next to the destroyed fighter/attack airplane. The brisk wind sweeping over the deck caused the superheated inferno to spread rapidly, engulfing scores of airplanes in a huge, roiling conflagration.

The searing mass of flames detonated 1,000-pound bombs, 500-pound bombs, rockets, and other ordnance, ripping apart more aircraft and spilling thousands of gallons of blazing jet fuel. Another round of deafening explosions blew holes in the armored flight deck and sent debris and shrapnel ricocheting off adjacent airplanes.

A missile ignited under the wing of a Tomcat and shot

straight into the fuselage of an A-6 Intruder that was taxiing forward out of the fire. The aircraft blew apart a moment after a 1,000-pound bomb was heaved over the side by a host of sailors. The singed bomb exploded when it hit the sea, throwing a wall of water over the firefighters who were standing on the lowered flight-deck elevator.

The entire aft section of the carrier deck was swallowed by the raging fire and billowing black smoke when Landesman saw the first ejection seat blast upward and arc over the fantail. Seconds later, more ejection seats fired through the boiling flames as the trapped pilots and naval flight officers fought for their lives.

Landesman could feel the ship slowing and turning as a frantic pilot jockeyed his burning F-14 Tomcat toward a clear area at the edge of the deck. Like the other aviators, he was afraid that he and his RIO might come down in the inferno if they ejected in the middle of the deck.

The fighter accelerated in afterburner until the nosewheel swept over the side of the ship. At that point, the radar intercept officer initiated their ejection sequence, which fired his seat first. The pilot shot free of the scorched cockpit just as the nose of the Tomcat hit the water.

Landesman was reaching for his direct line to the captain's bridge when the flight-deck emergency-washdown system activated. Water spewed over the length of the crowded deck, but the downpour had little effect as more devastating explosions set a row of fuel-laden jets ablaze. The Admiral had never encountered anything that compared to the magnitude of destruction he was witnessing. Likewise, he had never seen such bravery and self-sacrifice in his long naval career.

"Captain . . ." Carl Witowski breathlessly answered Landesman's call.

"Jinks, what have we got from damage control?"

An explosion interrupted Witowski's reply. "We've got a lot of men trapped belowdecks, and flaming fuel is running into the spaces and hangar bay."

"Keep me advised," Landesman ordered and involuntarily flinched when another giant explosion rocked the ship.

"Yes, sir," the devastated skipper mechanically shot back. "It doesn't look good, but *Cowpens* is coming alongside to assist."

"Jinks," Landesman advised while he surveyed the burning flight deck, "I'm going to get a message off to CINCPAC." He hung up the receiver.

Out of the corner of his eye the Admiral saw an officer and two enlisted men toss a loose bomb over the side of the carrier. He turned to watch the three men as they approached another bomb that was rapidly being surrounded by flames. The officer was spraying the 500-pounder with a fire extinguisher when the bomb exploded. Landesman stared in horror and disbelief when the three men simply disappeared.

33

USS BREMERTON

Lamar Joiner was shaving in his cramped stateroom when he heard and felt the first detectable rumble. Curious, he stopped for a moment and waited for another hint of the unusual sound. The only noise was the deep hum of the ventilation ducts.

He dismissed the faint, rolling sound as an anomaly and placed the razor next to his cheek. Joiner again paused when he sensed another low, resonant sound. *It's real, but I can't identify the sound or the source.*

He knew they were rapidly approaching the rendezvous coordinates to take up station with the carrier task force, but the only sounds he expected to hear were the high-frequency pitch of ship's screws.

The communications speaker suddenly came to life.

"Cap'n, officer of the deck, sir," the smooth, confident voice said evenly.

Joiner quickly wiped the shaving cream from his face and toggled the speaker switch.

"Captain," Joiner replied with an uncomfortable feeling in the pit of his stomach. After many years of submarine duty, his intuitive feelings were generally correct.

"Sir, sonar is picking up some strange returns—like depth charges going off."

Joiner tossed the hand towel on the tiny sink. "I'll be in sonar for a couple of minutes if you need me."

"Aye aye, Cap'n."

After hurriedly donning his dark overalls, Joiner walked down the narrow passageway leading to the sonar room. He entered the dim, quiet space and looked at the data on the display screen.

"Mornin', Captain," the senior operator said without taking his eyes off the sonar console.

"Good morning," Joiner replied in a hushed voice and looked over the Petty Officer's shoulder.

The latest contact, other than ships in the crowded strait, was a vertical line on the console. Whatever the source, the loud sounds were coming from far away and the bearing was remaining constant.

"What have you got?" Joiner asked the senior operator as he studied the returns on his sonar screen.

"Sir, like I told the OD, the sounds have the characteristic trait of depth charges." The man slowly shook his head in frustration. "Something exploded in the water—at least twice—dead on the bow."

The Captain studied the display for a brief moment. He agreed with the Petty Officer, but he had grave reservations about the unusual sounds.

Joiner looked at his watch. *Bremerton* wasn't scheduled to go to periscope depth to receive the latest satellite radio transmissions, but Joiner needed information before he continued toward the strange sounds.

"I'll be in conn."

"Yessir." The sonar operator glanced at Joiner. "We'll stay on it, sir, till we have it figured out."

"Very well," Joiner responded and stepped out of the confined space. He thought about the perplexing sounds while he made his way to the control room. *If someone is dropping depth charges, I sure as hell don't want to blunder into the middle of the kill zone.*

Joiner walked into the control room and approached the officer of the deck at the navigation chart behind the periscope stand.

"What do you think, Frenchie?"

The Lieutenant absently tapped the chart with the end of his pencil. "Cap'n, I know it's early to go to PD, but we're getting mighty close to the *Hawk,* and I think we need some fresh info."

Joiner was about to answer when he, the Lieutenant, and the chief of the watch heard and felt another tremor reverberate through the attack submarine.

"Frenchie," Joiner said, "let's get between the shipping channels and take her up to periscope depth."

"Aye aye, sir."

ANDREWS AIR FORCE BASE, MARYLAND

The President had just boarded Air Force One when he received the word about the errant Japanese missile and the ensuing conflagration on *Kitty Hawk.*

He and Scott Eaglehoff had sequestered themselves in the communications compartment while the big Boeing took off and turned on course to Anchorage.

Refusing his usual evening cocktail, the President opted for a Pepsi while they waited for a conference call with the Joint Chiefs of Staff, the civilian Secretaries of the armed forces, the National Security Advisor, and prominent members of the security council. He also wanted to confer with his Vice President, who had been on an extended visit to European countries.

"Sonuva-*bitch,*" the President swore to himself and shoved his glass out of the way. "Accident?" he posed a question and then answered it himself: "Bullshit!"

"Sir," Eaglehoff began cautiously, "we've seen a number of accidents at sea over the years. It's possible that this catastrophe was accidental. Men and machinery sometimes fail, and I think we have to take it at face value."

The President glanced at his closest adviser and scowled in his unique way. "You can never take the Japanese at face value," he half-muttered and tapped his fingers on his desk.

Eaglehoff let the uneasy silence settle over the compartment before he spoke. "I think we have to remember the *Stark* incident, the *Iowa* disaster, the *Vincennes* debacle—people make mistakes and things fail.

"I sure as hell remember the *Forrestal* and *Enterprise* fires," Eaglehoff asserted. "I was on the *Forrestal* when it happened."

Both aircraft carriers suffered devastating fires during the Vietnam War when Zuni rockets attached to F-4 Phantoms accidentally ignited during prelaunch conditions.

The President brushed off Eaglehoff's remarks. "Do we have a casualty list yet?"

"No, sir. It's too soon to get anything that's accurate."

A buzz interrupted the President's response. He lifted the receiver and began issuing orders to the men and women gathered in the War Room at the Pentagon.

KITTY HAWK

The ship was dead in the water as flames and dense smoke spewed from the flight deck and the aircraft elevator doors leading to the hangar bay. Her escorts, except for the cruiser *Chancellorsville,* were alongside the mammoth carrier.

"It's fine," Isaac Landesman insisted as the ship's senior physician adjusted the sling for the Admiral's left arm. Although his wrist was broken, he wasn't going to sick bay for further treatment until the carrier was out of danger.

The weary doctor mumbled a few words and hurried below to help the multitude of burned and injured sailors and officers. The ship's hospital and dispensary were filled to capacity, forcing the medical team to use nearby spaces for the overflow of injured men.

Landesman surveyed the flight deck and felt sick to his stomach. The fire was still raging on the aft section of the deck, and damage-control reports indicated the blaze had spread to berthing compartments and the hangar bay from the last expansion joint to the fantail.

Although many aircraft had been shoved over the side of the ship, Landesman could see the charred remains of eighteen planes scattered around the blackened flight deck. He also counted twelve gaping holes where bombs secured underneath attack aircraft had detonated.

Forward on the flight deck, he counted thirteen aircraft that were not damaged. Those planes, plus a dozen on the forward section of the hangar bay, were the only salvageable aircraft left from the original eighty-seven planes on board, not counting the aircraft that were airborne when the missile hit *Kitty Hawk*.

The crews waiting to land had been diverted to Singapore, where they would refuel and provide a constant combat air patrol over the U.S. ships.

Both *Independence* and *Lincoln* were steaming toward the strait to offer assistance to the *Hawk* and her escorts. Aircraft from both carriers would supplement the planes from the damaged ship.

Landesman watched the guided missile cruisers *Worden* and *Leahy* while the crew assisted in the firefighting effort. The sailors from the cruiser *Cowpens* had successfully rescued the men in the water and were also attacking the blaze.

The *Hayasa* offered help, but was asked to stand clear near the *Chancellorsville*. The distraught Captain of the Japanese Aegis destroyer had requested an opportunity to meet with the battle-group commander and the Captain of *Kitty Hawk*. Landesman had approved the request, explaining that he was welcome once the fire had been extinguished.

Landesman peered down at the valiant crewmen who were battling the fire. The wet and exhausted sailors were surrounded by the crushed and burnt fuselages of several aircraft. The significance of the tragedy was difficult to fathom. Landesman lowered his head and said a silent prayer for the safety of his men.

USS *BREMERTON*

Commander Lamar Joiner turned toward the control-room sonar console and watched a sloping trace appear on the red display screen. He studied the readout for a few seconds and then examined the navigational chart that displayed the north- and southbound Strait of Malacca traffic lanes.

"Sonar, Captain," he said with an edge to his voice. "We've got a contact bearing three-four-zero."

"Conn, sonar, aye," the sonar Chief Petty Officer crisply replied. "The contact is a surface vessel now bearing three-three-zero—seven thousand yards."

"Very well."

The target was passing to the portside and would not be a factor during the ascent to periscope depth.

"Conn, sonar. I hold several faint contacts bearing zero-one-zero. Surface screws turning at low RPM."

"Sonar, Captain. Keep me informed."

"Aye aye, sir."

The minutes passed slowly while they proceeded toward the rendezvous with the carrier group. News travels at the speed of lightning aboard a submarine, and the 127 sailors and officers of the nuclear-powered boat sensed that something was amiss. Their normally confident and relaxed skipper was restive and the men noticed the subtle change in his behavior.

Finally, Joiner looked around the cramped control room and exchanged glances with the chief of the watch and the sober-faced diving officer. The helmsman and sternplanesman were strapped tightly to their seats, and the officer of the deck was waiting for his orders. It was time to surface and the CO was moving more slowly than usual.

Checking the inertial navigation coordinates for the third

time in ten minutes, Joiner was surprised when another tremor ran through the hull of the submarine.

"Conn, sonar." The pitch of the Chief's voice suddenly changed. "Something detonated bearing zero-one-zero—in close proximity to the sounds of the screws."

"Sonar, Captain," Joiner responded while he tried to hide the ominous feeling that was slowly engulfing him. "Could you tell if the explosion was on the surface or if we're dealing with depth charges?"

"I couldn't tell, sir."

"Very well."

Joiner noticed the looks of concern from everyone in the control room. He wiped a bead of sweat from his temple and turned to face the officer of the deck.

"Let's go to periscope depth."

"Aye aye, sir."

The OOD issued orders to the helmsman and the diving officer, then spoke to the chief sonarman. "Sonar, conn. Ascending to PD."

"Sonar, aye."

A moment later the OOD raised the periscope and stepped aside for the Captain. Whenever *Bremerton* surfaced, Joiner was always at the primary periscope.

The deck inclined slightly as the fast-attack submarine rose toward the surface of the strait. Working with the precision of a surgical team, the ship-control watch-standers steadied the boat at the prescribed depth. Their reputations were on the line every time *Bremerton* maneuvered.

"Periscope depth," the OOD announced with a hint of trepidation in his tone. This was the first time he had ever seen his skipper tense.

Joiner grasped the periscope handgrips and embraced the scope and optic module. He started to rotate the periscope at the same time he saw a dark, billowing smoke cloud in the distance. He stopped in place and stared at the distant flotilla of ships. The island superstructure of the burning carrier towered above the other vessels.

"*Kitty Hawk* is on fire," Joiner observed while he remained transfixed in amazement. He watched a giant crane on wheels shove a burning jet fighter over the side and then vanish in the dense smoke. "They must have had a helluva crash on the aft flight deck."

Although he was concerned about the unfolding tragedy on the carrier, he felt a personal sense of relief. "We've been hearing explosions caused by the fire. Probably ordnance that was thrown over the side."

A low murmur ran through the control room as the collective tension began to dissipate. They finally had an answer to the threatening mystery, and the news flashed through the submarine in an instant.

Joiner began to rotate the periscope to sweep the horizon, then stood immobilized in shocked disbelief when he saw the *Arafura Sea*. He was staring straight at the bow of a 260,000-ton supertanker carrying 77 million gallons of crude oil. The 1,132-foot behemoth, which was propelled by 37,400-shaft horsepower, was outside the normal shipping lanes in order to get a closer look at *Kitty Hawk*. The *Arafura Sea* was only seconds from colliding with the hapless *Bremerton*.

"Emergency deep! Emergency deep!" Joiner shouted in horror to the officer of the deck as he snapped the periscope grips up and quickly lowered the scope. "Rig for collision! Rig for flooding! This is not a drill!"

Everyone leaped into action while a depth-control tank was being flooded. They had to force the submarine into a steep diving angle in the next few seconds or face certain death beneath the colossal ship.

The frightened CO glanced up at the overhead. "We've got a tanker right on top of us."

Joiner's mind raced, thinking first about how he broke one of his cardinal rules. He had paused to look at something before he swung the periscope all the way around to check for surface vessels and other obstacles. He would have relieved a junior officer for an infraction of that magnitude.

Along with his fellow submariners, Joiner knew only too

well the dangers of dealing with the supertankers. Sonar often didn't detect the big ships, and there were many sea stories about close calls with the enormous vessels.

The huge volume of crude oil stored between the bow and the engine compartment in the stern of the tankers completely absorbed the engine and screw sounds. The latest generation of stretched supertankers was stealthily quiet and extremely dangerous to submarines.

Joiner was praying and counting down the seconds when the 260,000-ton oil tanker plowed into the side of the small attack submarine. Drawing seventy-six feet of water and traveling at 15.2 knots, the tanker's tremendous kinetic energy crushed the sub like a roll of aluminum foil.

The double hull of *Bremerton* was severed behind the conning tower. Joiner was thrown across the control room and slammed into a bulkhead. He momentarily heard screams of agony as the lights went out and the forward half of the submarine rolled inverted. He tumbled end over end, then tasted blood and gasped for air as the cool seawater poured over him and his crew.

Both halves of the doomed submarine plunged to the bottom of the strait while the crew of the supertanker shrugged off the slight shudder that rippled through their ship. They would not become aware of the damage to the bow until they made a port call in Taiwan.

34

THE SUBMARINE HARUSHIO

Like his crewmen, Commander Shigezo Takagi experienced a moment of paralysis when he heard the crunching sounds from the destruction of the American attack submarine. Takagi rushed into the sonar compartment, grabbed a set of earphones, then listened to *Bremerton* as the sub purged air and sank to the floor of the waterway. The sound of quadrillions of air bubbles rising to the surface was intermingled with popping and scraping noises.

The startling destruction of the hunter-killer submarine caused *Harushio*'s short, chunky skipper to relive his worst nightmare. On rare occasions, usually before a deep dive, he dreamed about being trapped in a sub and helplessly sinking to the bottom of the ocean.

Takagi was confused by the fact that *Bremerton* had suffered a massive structural failure and his crew had not heard an explosion or picked up the sound of a torpedo or the screws from a ship. The only audible noises had been generated by the propeller from the American attack boat and the distant explosive sounds that reminded him of depth charges.

Shigezo Takagi had never experienced the terror of having depth charges dropped on him, but he had not forgotten the recorded sounds of an actual attack that had been played over and over in submarine school.

Shaken by the disastrous event, Takagi listened until the two sections of *Bremerton* impacted the bottom of the strait, then returned to the control room and talked with his second-in-command, Lieutenant Commander Oda Kanjiro.

"Let's step into my stateroom," Takagi said under his breath and turned to go to his cabin. He didn't like to discuss important matters in front of his men.

Kanjiro wordlessly followed the CO down the narrow passageway and into the tiny sleeping compartment that was Takagi's sanctuary.

The CO quietly shut the door and leaned against the smooth bulkhead. He could always count on the man he was recommending to become the next Commanding Officer of *Harushio*. "Do you have an opinion, Oda?"

"We didn't hear a direct hit," Kanjiro observed and shrugged one shoulder, "so they may have collided with another submarine. We heard scraping and crunching sounds, and two distinct masses hit the bottom, so there may have been two submarines involved in the accident."

"That's possible," the skipper said at last, "but we didn't hear any other screws—not a single thing except the cluttered background noises from the distant ships."

Kanjiro folded his bony arms and frowned. "Let's take things in order, if you don't mind."

"Go ahead," Takagi said and closely studied the bright young officer.

"I think something hit the American sub . . ." Kanjiro trailed off, then continued. "What hit it is the unknown factor."

"Or," Takagi quickly interjected, "the American could have hit something they didn't hear, like a large submerged obstacle, another submarine, or a new type of quiet weapon we don't know anything about."

As always, Kanjiro nodded in deference to his CO. It was a habit he had learned early in his naval career. "Someone may have a torpedo similar to our new Sea Ferret."

"It might be extremely large," Takagi began, considering the various possibilities, "superfast, and capable of piercing the skin—actually puncturing the double hull of a submarine."

The frown returned to Kanjiro's face. "We don't know what happened, and we don't know if someone initiated an attack or if it was simply an accident."

"That's true," Takagi conceded, reviewing his sailing orders and the fact that his commander had been adamant about being aggressive. He had told Takagi not to hesitate to attack if he felt uncomfortable. The sub skipper also thought about his ultimate responsibility to Japan and the oath he had taken as an officer.

"Sir, I respectfully recommend," Kanjiro offered with measured confidence, "that we immediately close on the American fleet and prepare for battle."

Shigezo Takagi listened to his trusted second-in-command while he silently considered using the Sea Ferrets. The state-of-the-art torpedoes didn't use a conventional propeller, relying instead on the use of magnetohydrodynamics to supply the propulsion for the stealthy weapon.

Using the advanced technology of MHD, which is similar to a jet engine without a turbine, Sea Ferret had an open tube running the length of the torpedo. The long tube was surrounded by a ferro-liquid in a thin-sealed sleeve. A high-density, pulsing magnetic field produced tremendous sympathetic vibrations in the ferro-liquid.

This action caused a traveling wave, which resulted in the seawater in the tube being pumped out the back of the weapon. Sea Ferret was literally pulled through the water at a speed of 33 knots without making any perceptible sound.

"I'm in agreement that we should approach the Americans," Shigezo Takagi said and took in his friend's expression of delight. "Rig the ship for supersilent running and continue on our present course."

Kanjiro showed a moment of hesitation before he mustered the courage to speak. "Sir, do you want to seek permission to attack before we get too close?"

Takagi gave him a look that would freeze salt water. "I am my own authority."

"Yes, sir," Kanjiro replied in his practiced show of cordial respectfulness. One did not question the Captain of a Japanese maritime vessel, especially Commander Shigezo Takagi.

"Load and energize our two Sea Ferrets," Takagi ordered before Kanjiro could turn to leave, "and call the men to battle stations."

"Yes, sir," Kanjiro replied with a determined look on his face.

Alone in his darkened stateroom, Commander Shigezo Takagi sat in quiet meditation and experienced the heightened spiritual awareness and somatic calm of divine revelation. Like the other 10 million Japanese adherents of Zen Buddhism, the submarine commander thrived on experiencing the enlightenment and mental tranquillity that fostered spontaneity and fearlessness.

The practice of Zen gave Takagi a feeling of breaking through the boundaries of ordinary everyday logical thought. The special edge of ecstatic contemplation carried Takagi beyond the limits of divine incomprehensibility into the world of revelation.

He searched the depths of his mind, unraveling the unfathomable mysteries it contained. Revelation, as he had discovered over the years, transcended the categories of reason and rational thought.

At last Takagi turned on the soft, red-filtered light over his small writing desk and reached into the drawer that contained his personal belongings. He retrieved a faded, yellowed picture and stared at the photograph of his parents and late grandparents. His grandparents had died from radiation sickness less than three weeks after their modest home in Hiroshima was destroyed by the first atomic bomb dropped on Japan.

Using the single phone circuit to contact the submarine's control room, Takagi asked Oda Kanjiro to return to his stateroom.

Seconds later the devoted officer gently tapped on the door and entered the cabin. "Yes, sir?"

With total aplomb, Takagi looked up at Kanjiro. "My orders stipulate that I am free to use whatever measures necessary to protect *Harushio* in the event of a threat."

Beaming with pleasure, Kanjiro nodded in agreement. "I understand, sir."

"We are in a situation that I feel is extremely dangerous—the attack-sub incident and the unexplained explosions—so I have the responsibility to protect my crew."

Kanjiro felt a sense of elation, but he was cautious. "If we attack the Americans, they'll saturate the strait with ASW coverage."

Takagi worked his jaw muscles. "They will have a difficult time because of all the traffic. We will be okay."

"I have no doubt, sir."

"Set both torpedoes," Takagi calmly ordered, "to seek and destroy at a depth of ten-point-two meters. I'm going after their carrier."

Kanjiro swallowed and felt the adrenaline pump through his veins. "Yes, sir," he answered exuberantly. "Seek and destroy at a depth of ten-point-two meters."

From studying the displacements and dimensions of the American warships, the CO knew the depth of the vessel's keels below the waterline. The *Kitty Hawk* drew close to thirty-seven feet of water, while *Chancellorsville* and *Cowpens,* the Aegis guided-missile cruisers, drew approximately thirty-one feet. Takagi would try to thread the needle and bag a U.S. carrier with the two stealth torpedoes he had been allocated.

"Continue to close on the American task force, but don't go any closer than nine thousand meters," Takagi ordered and glanced at the navigation readout next to his bunk, "then prepare to go to periscope depth."

Kanjiro gave him a nod. "Yes, sir."

"Any questions?"

"No, sir, no questions," Kanjiro said clearly and stepped out of the austere stateroom.

Shigezo Takagi stared at the picture of his parents and grandparents for a few minutes, then turned out his light and rolled into the built-in berth. He rehearsed the attack in his mind. *The first order of business is to launch the torpedoes, then we'll quietly sail for the sanctity of the South China Sea. No one will know that we've been here, and I will have fulfilled my command responsibility in a high-threat environment.*

A few minutes later, the skipper turned on his side and dozed peacefully.

35

TOKYO INTERNATIONAL AIRPORT, NARITA, JAPAN

Prime Minister Genshiro Koyama stormed out of the sleek Aérospatiale helicopter and marched straight for the Boeing 747-400 VIP transport. Followed by his personal retinue and eight security specialists, Koyama ignored the crowd of well-wishers and journalists as he hurriedly boarded the lustrous jumbo jet.

The powerful turbine engines were spinning to life when Koyama entered the conference area where Foreign Minister Nagumo Katsumoto calmly waited along with one of Koyama's aides. He smiled and shifted in his chair in order to ease the pain in his curved spine.

"How could this possibly happen?" Koyama exclaimed in his raspy voice as he tossed his coat across the end of the table. "How could anyone—especially the commander of an Aegis destroyer—be so stupid?"

The courteous and restrained expert on foreign affairs remained quiet, allowing the agitated Prime Minister to vent his anger and frustration while his aide placed Koyama's coat in the closet.

"Japan is in the middle of an inherently unstable strategic position," Koyama said bitterly, "and an idiot shoots a missile at an American carrier." His taut neck muscles and darkened features reflected his rage. "He will never again step foot on a Japanese military ship."

Katsumoto was aware that Defense Minister Yutaka Isida had relieved the commanding officer of *Hayasa* of his duties and ordered an investigation into the tragic accident. The former commander of the destroyer and his tactical action officer were being flown to Tokyo for interrogation. The *Hayasa*'s ex–commanding officer would be fortunate if the powers in Tokyo merely threw him out of the military.

Koyama and Katsumoto felt the specially configured government 747 begin to roll as it taxied toward the duty runway. All air traffic bound for Tokyo International would be vectored to distant holding patterns or held in place on the ground until the Prime Minister was safely airborne and out of the local flying area.

Koyama leaned over and stared out the window at the scores of onlookers and media representatives before turning to the Foreign Minister. "The ship—the carrier—is still on fire and the loss of life is staggering."

"It was an accident," Katsumoto responded in his low-key manner. "The Americans must know that. I'm sure they've thought about some of their own embarrassing incidents. They've had their share of blunders over the years."

Koyama was not about to be appeased by the unflappable Foreign Minister. "The newspapers and magazines are full of headlines about the global fears and deep suspicions about our military reinventing itself, and—and"—he sputtered in his grating voice—"and then one of our finest Aegis commanders shoots a missile at an American aircraft carrier—and reminds the world of Japan's violent past."

"He didn't do it on purpose," Katsumoto said in his calm, measured style.

"What difference does it make?" Koyama barked. "The end result makes us look incompetent."

"It makes us look human. Everyone makes mistakes from

time to time, and this was obviously a mistake—a bad one, but still a human error."

"The timing," Koyama hissed, "could not have been worse in light of the current events."

Katsumoto sipped his warm tea and waited for an opportunity to speak calmly with Koyama. "We have offered our deepest apologies to the Americans, and we must trust that responsible people will understand the circumstances."

"I don't think you clearly understand the situation," Koyama suddenly blurted, which prompted the aide to discreetly step out of the soundproof meeting room. "We've got an arms race going on—a major arms race—that is rapidly gaining momentum throughout Asia."

Nagumo Katsumoto didn't respond to the cutting remark. When he was a young man attending Tokyo University, he had taught himself the self-discipline not to be lured into fruitless arguments with upset or inebriated people.

The Prime Minister cast a glance out the window. "The instability is becoming more obvious by the day, and I'm deeply concerned about the security of our military forces.

"And all of this," Koyama boldly went on, "at a time when Japan is in a downward spiral into slower business growth and constant restructuring.

"We can eventually correct our business deficiencies," the Prime Minister said cryptically, "but our most important concern at the moment is how our Asian neighbors view our military image while the U.S. continues to shrink its forces in the region."

"I'm quite aware of the problems our country faces," Katsumoto said evenly, "and we must understand and deal with the fact that emotions and feelings of insecurity are always stirred when the balance of power swings from one side of the pendulum to the other."

With a disgusted look, Koyama pushed himself back in his thickly padded chair. "The cycle of mistrust and open animosity between the U.S. and Japan, along with the fears of our

Asian neighbors, are forcing us to repeat the same things we had to do in the first half of the century."

Katsumoto sighed and leaned back to ease the discomfort in his lower back. "It isn't 'us' or 'we.' "

"You can't change the inevitable," Koyama snapped and lighted a cigarette. "Despite years of lying to each other, nothing has changed the fundamental feelings between the Japanese and the American people. If we had mutual trust, no one would worry about the size of our military forces."

The Foreign Minister let his head rest on the back of his chair and serenely closed his eyes. "The majority of Japanese *know* they're superior to anyone else on this planet—especially to the Americans—and most Americans *believe* they're superior to anyone who doesn't have their collective power and money. So the hostility goes on because we can't blend as basic human beings."

"Don't count Japan out," the Prime Minister said contemptuously as the airplane began its takeoff roll.

BENEATH THE STRAIT OF MALACCA

Commander Shigezo Takagi was startled awake when Oda Kanjiro gently touched his shoulder. The skipper groaned and rolled over, then switched on the dull red light and swung his legs over the side of the bunk.

"We are in position at nine thousand meters, sir," Kanjiro reported in a hushed voice. "Both torpedoes are active and sonar holds no close contacts."

"That is a good omen," Takagi said excitedly and quickly slipped his feet into the soft, padded sock-shoes the crew wore while on patrol. "Take us to periscope depth and lock in a solution on the carrier."

"Yes sir," Kanjiro responded quietly and turned toward the crowded control room.

A contact's course, range, and speed were calculated to determine the target's bearing rate—the "solution" for the torpedo shot.

Takagi sat still for a last moment of contemplation. His mind was clear and he felt comfortable with the pleasure he would derive from his inner calling. He looked forward to avenging his grandparents and the atrocious way the Americans had killed them.

Shigezo Takagi felt a visceral impulse toward the course of action he had set in motion, and the driving force was accompanied by a strong conviction of divine influence. *Harushio* was in harm's way and it was his responsibility to protect her and his crew.

The CO patiently waited until the depth readout next to his navigational data window indicated that *Harushio* was stabilized at periscope depth, then he calmly rose from his bed and walked to the control room.

All eyes turned to Takagi when he stepped through the hatch and approached the periscope.

"Sir," Kanjiro whispered, "we have a solution on a ship, but we don't think it's the carrier. The signature is different and sonar hasn't been able to locate the carrier."

"Keep trying."

Kanjiro obediently nodded and toggled the switch to raise the periscope before he glanced at the array of lights on the status board. "We are making two knots, outer torpedo doors are open, tubes one and two are flooded, and the fire-control system is up and ready."

"Excellent," Takagi replied as he grabbed the handgrips and quickly rotated the periscope 360 degrees, then reversed his crablike shuffle to take in the flotilla of American ships. "We're clear—no surface threats."

He was astonished to see *Kitty Hawk* burning while her escort ships were assisting with the firefighting efforts. Takagi was elated and felt a sudden sense of relief when he recognized where the strange explosions had originated.

"The carrier is dead in the water," he whispered to Kanjiro.

"It's on fire. That's why we can't get a signature—the screws aren't turning. There's only one ship moving, and it's a guided-missile cruiser."

The executive officer pursed his lips and smiled. "The sounds—the explosions we've been hearing—must have come from the carrier."

Takagi acknowledged his exec and stared at the blazing air-craft carrier. He was confident the Sea Ferrets would be enough to sink the beleaguered ship. The conventional 2,800-pound shaped charge explosive in each weapon was enough to blast a gaping hole in the hull of the carrier.

Harushio's CO felt a tingling sensation shoot through his chest. "This is a perfect opportunity. They'll most likely think a fire-related explosion sank the carrier."

Takagi tilted his head and looked at the glowing lights on the status board. The gyroscope, sonar transducer, and computer system in each torpedo was on line. The weapons were "hot" and ready for immediate use as soon as the final launch-code was punched into the complex fire-control system. The fire-control computer was constantly providing a solution to *Chancellorsville,* the guided-missile cruiser that was maneuvering around the burning carrier.

"The contact is turning." Takagi paused and waited to see what the Aegis cruiser would do next. "He's circling the carrier like a mother hen."

He timed the slow-moving cruiser as it completed a circle around *Kitty Hawk,* then glanced at the weapons' projected running time to the target. Takagi calculated the opportune firing time in order to have the pair of Sea Ferrets arrive at the cruiser when it was directly between the submarine and the huge carrier.

Hopefully, the CO thought while he nervously walked the periscope through another 360-degree sweep, *the torpedoes will go under the keel of the destroyer and hit the carrier as they start turning back toward their programmed sound signature.*

"Run the code for both tubes," Takagi ordered in a voice barely above a whisper.

"Run the code—both tubes," Kanjiro relayed to the fire-control team, "and stand by to execute."

Seconds passed before the twin amber lights illuminated on the status board.

"Both torpedoes are ready," Kanjiro tensely declared.

Takagi studied the destroyer and counted the seconds it took to turn 90 degrees. "Solution update."

A fire-control technician tapped three buttons on his console and looked at the exec. "Solution input."

"Weapons ready, sir," Kanjiro reported with a resolute expression and cast a look at the blinking lights on the status board. "Don't fail us," he said to himself.

"Stand by," Takagi calmly advised.

The junior officer on the fire-control team reached up and carefully placed his safety-interlock contact switches in the off position. "Weapons armed, sir."

"Very well."

Takagi hesitated for a brief moment and experienced the serenity of a mind completely at ease. "Fire One."

Everyone stared at the status board as the compressed-air charge hurtled the first Sea Ferret out of the specially designed launch tube.

All hands simultaneously felt the sudden pressure-pulse in their middle ears.

Along with his crew, Takagi plugged his nostrils and purged his eustachian tubes to equalize the air pressure on both sides of his tympanic membranes.

"Tube One fired, Captain."

"Stand by," Takagi replied in a clear voice. His trembling fingers were the only visible indications of the temporary increase in activity in his central nervous system.

The Sea Ferret rapidly accelerated out of the mass of air bubbles as the onboard computer double-checked its systems and the functions of the external control surfaces. A split second after the compatibility check, the weapon's active sonar sent out a wave of sound energy to initially locate and track the designated target. After the stealthy torpedo was stabilized on course, the passive sonar locked on the sound signature of the American cruiser.

"Fire Two," Takagi ordered and immediately lowered the periscope. His responsibility was finished as far as he was concerned; now it was up to the Sea Ferrets to complete the mission and avenge a small slice of Japan's honor.

The second torpedo plunged out of the tube and the crew again cleared their ears.

"Tube Two fired, Captain."

"Right full rudder," the CO said hastily and looked directly in Kanjiro's widened eyes. "Level at sixty-five meters and set course for the South China Sea."

"Yes, sir," he replied with a happy expression.

36

KITTY HAWK

The crew remained at general quarters while hundreds of sailors and Marines fought the flight-deck blaze and the secondary fires belowdeck. *Hawk*'s escort vessels continued to spray water on the burning ship while exhausted officers and men struggled together in an effort to clear the remaining weapons from the four-and-a-half-acre flight deck.

Though tired, hungry, and soggy, the men were methodically throwing bombs, rockets, ammunition, and other ordnance over the side of the ship, then staggering back into the heat and smoke to search for more explosives before the ammo could cook off and start more fires.

Rear Admiral Isaac Landesman looked down at the blackened and scorched deck where part of the raging inferno had been contained. Thousands of pieces of aircraft and firefighting gear lay strewn in a tangled mess on the wet, slippery flight deck.

Landesman lowered his head. *God, give us the courage and strength to overcome this tragedy. Please don't let—*

"Excuse me, sir." The carrier group commander's aide interrupted the silent prayer.

Landesman turned to see the sadness written on the junior officer's face.

"What is it, Tom?"

"Damage control has confirmed at least twenty-nine casualties in the berthing spaces directly below the flight deck." The JO looked down, fighting the ache inside. "They never had a chance."

Landesman inspected the jagged holes in the steel deck near the two remaining arresting-gear cables. "Below where the bombs went off?"

"Yes, sir."

The Admiral was about to speak when a devastating explosion rocked the big carrier from fantail to bow.

Stunned, Landesman glanced aft as a huge geyser of water shot skyward and engulfed the deck-edge platform used by the squadron landing-signal officers. "That must be ordnance from belowdeck!"

The aide stepped to the window. "It looks like something went off on the hangar bay."

When the spray had cleared, the sailors who had been holding a hose near the LSO platform were gone.

Landesman was sure the trio of firefighters had been blown over the side of the carrier. He reached for his handset to initiate the man-overboard rescue exercise, then stopped in midsentence when another horrendous blast near the bow shook the mighty warship.

Momentarily speechless, Landesman realized that *Kitty Hawk* was being torpedoed.

HARUSHIO

Standing behind the senior sonar technician, Commander Shigezo Takagi heard both Sea Ferrets detonate. He felt a strange mixture of elation tempered by pessimism. Seconds later, he turned to his XO. "I hit something, but I don't know if it was the carrier."

"I've got a feeling it was the carrier," Oda Kanjiro said with unrestrained enthusiasm. "What a shot!"

After what seemed like an eternity, the sonar operator stared at his display and made the announcement Takagi had been waiting to hear.

"Sir," he reported in a hushed voice, "I've got a solid contact from one of the cruisers."

Takagi turned to his second-in-command and smiled broadly. "If the torpedoes ran at the proper depth, we hit the carrier."

Oda Kanjiro returned the smile. "Sir, our Sea Ferrets ran true. I'm positive we got the carrier."

KEIO PLAZA INTER-CONTINENTAL HOTEL

Steve rinsed his mouth and placed his toothbrush in its plastic container while he thought about the hassle he and Susan had gone through with the Japanese law-enforcement officials. Shigeki Okamoto had died at the scene, and the first police officers who arrived had arrested Susan and Steve and confiscated their weapons.

After numerous phone calls to the headquarters of the FBI and CIA, along with a blizzard of paperwork, Steve and Susan were finally given back their personal weapons and released from custody.

Wickham took a swig of mouthwash and thought about Tadashi Matsukawa. *The man is getting away with murder.* He looked in the mirror and studied the tiny scar above his upper lip, then spat the mouthwash in the basin. *Hell, the sonuvabitch has been getting away with every crime in the book for years. We've got to find a way to corner him.*

The telephone rang and Steve went to answer it while he dried his mouth.

"Wickham."

"Steve," Susan inquired with a touch of concern in her voice, "are you up and around?"

"Sure. Are you okay?"

"I'm fine, but I just saw a report that one of our aircraft carriers was hit by a missile from a Japanese ship. It—a Harpoon missile, I think—apparently landed on the flight deck and caused a huge fire and numerous explosions."

The fateful news surprised and angered him. "What happened to cause them to fire a missile at us?"

"I really don't know. It's a breaking story."

She paused a moment. "Are you dressed?"

"Well, I'm in my warm-up rags." He looked down at his jogging pants. "Come on over and we'll turn on CNN."

"I'll be there in a minute." Her voice was tight and she nervously hesitated. "CNN isn't on the air—at least not in our hotel."

"Interesting."

"I thought so."

"The door'll be open."

"Okay."

Steve opened the door a few inches and a minute later Susan quietly knocked on it and slipped inside.

"What's happening?" he asked while she locked the door.

"From what I could gather from the local news," she began as her delicate fragrance drifted to him, "the Japanese claim that one of their destroyers accidentally fired a missile at our ship."

"Accidentally?" Steve asked with a dubious look.

"That's what the local stations are reporting. The carrier *Kitty Hawk* is on fire and there seems to be some confusion about how badly the ship is damaged. A senior officer, who is currently flying over the scene, said the fire appears to be out of control."

Steve shook his head. "It sounds like they're in trouble—big trouble."

"Do you think they'll lose the carrier?"

"That's possible."

"There's speculation from the Pentagon," Susan told him, "that *Kitty Hawk* was hit by torpedoes after the missile struck the flight deck, but they don't have confirmation at this time."

"Torpedoed?" Steve asked with a look of disbelief.

"Yes. The local media said that U.S. military-intelligence reports suggested that Iranian submarines are operating near our forces."

"That's probably speculation," Steve suggested while his every instinct warned against it. "They're trying to divert attention away from the so-called accidental missile launch."

"Possibly." Susan decided not to say anything else, since it was obvious that Steve didn't believe the Japanese version of the missile accident. "I also heard that British Airways and United Airlines have discontinued service to Osaka and Tokyo."

Steve grew silent and gazed out the window. "Yeah. I heard last night that Singapore Airlines, Cathay Pacific, and Malaysia Airlines have stopped flying into certain areas, and that many cruise ships are bypassing port calls in the South China Sea."

"Well," Susan said with a grim look on her face, "my prophecy about a war between the U.S. and Japan may be imminent."

"Susan," Steve explained, "there's something I didn't mention when we were discussing the possibility of an armed conflict between the two countries."

"Oh, really?"

"Yes," Steve replied uneasily. "The CIA located and published a document produced by a Japanese think tank that outlined what the Japanese military would do today in a sneak attack on the U.S."

"I'm not surprised," she said matter-of-factly. "The Japanese must have studied that scenario from every possible angle. They don't see any way to avoid a fight in the long run."

Wickham drooped his head in resignation. "I'm afraid this confrontation is going to get ugly."

Susan's face reflected the sadness she felt. "This whole mess . . . is an exercise in stupidity."

Steve had an unsettling fear that gnawed at him. "It doesn't look like either side is going to give in and back away."

She sat quietly for a few moments and then stared at the far wall. "What do you make of this missile accident—or do you think it was a well-planned attack?"

"I really don't have any idea," he admitted, "but the whole thing sounds very suspicious to me, especially the part about being torpedoed after the missile landed on the flight deck. Something isn't in focus here, but I don't have any facts to draw from."

Susan turned and studied his expression for a moment. "Do you think the Iranians would risk shooting torpedoes at one of our carriers?"

A look of bewilderment crossed his face. "I wish I knew."

The phone rang and Steve answered it while Susan turned on the television and selected a local station. She was astonished by the latest-breaking story. A U.S. nuclear-attack submarine was missing and presumed lost in the general area of the Strait of Malacca.

Susan clicked to a different station that was broadcasting in English. "Steve." She pointed to the screen.

"Pentagon officials have confirmed that a submarine is missing," the commentator declared and turned to the representative of the Commander in Chief, U.S. Pacific Fleet.

"Captain Tyler, can you tell us the name of the submarine and what type of mission it was conducting when they lost contact with the sub?"

The former Captain of the Ohio-class ballistic-missile submarine *Michigan* was wary, and it showed in his eyes. "I'm afraid I can't comment on the name of the submarine or its mission at this time. However, for the record, I would like to set something straight."

He cleared his throat, then glanced at the camera and faced the reporter. "The submarine failed to make a radio report at a specific time, and we are attempting to contact the boat as I speak. We do not consider the submarine lost until we have expended all search efforts."

The correspondent persevered with unflagging energy. "Captain, what methods do you normally use to make contact with a submerged submarine?"

"Our standard command-and-control procedures."

While the camera was directed toward him, the Navy submarine expert glimpsed the reporter mouth the word *relax*.

"Captain, in the event of a nuclear threat or national crisis, can you tell us what steps are involved in communicating the message to the submerged submarines?"

"Sure," he answered and turned toward the camera. "Faced with a major confrontation, any instructions—orders, if you will—to commence our government's Single Integrated Operational Plan would originate with the National Command Authority.

"Instructions from the highest level would then be issued by the National Military Command Center, providing it had not been destroyed. Otherwise the orders would come from the Alternate NMCC, or, in the event it had been neutralized, from the National Emergency Airborne Command Post—KNEE-CAP—the Flying White House as it's called in the military."

The reporter was beginning to acquire the information he wanted to convey to his audience. "How do you go about actually transmitting the messages to the subs when they're underwater?"

"We can use defense satellites to send telemetry," the submariner replied with more confidence, "but that requires at least part of the boat to break the surface, so we have to limit that method to mainly peacetime conditions."

The correspondent gave him a reassuring nod.

"Extremely low-frequency radio waves is another means of communicating," the officer went on. "The subs can receive messages at depths of over three hundred feet, but the drawback of the ELF system is the very low data rate compared with the satellite and TACAMO systems."

The reporter quickly seized the opportunity to extract more in-depth information rather than resort to the usual dull questions. "Would you mind explaining what TACAMO stands for and how it works?"

"TACAMO"—the Captain grinned self-consciously—"is an acronym for our Take Charge And Move Out E-6A communication aircraft. The airplanes, which are rebuilt ex-airline Boeing 707s, use very-low-frequency radio transmissions to communicate with the submarines. The aircraft use an extremely long trailing wire antenna to transmit while the airplane banks in a continuous tight circle with the wire submerged directly below."

Quickly shifting his train of thought, the correspondent attempted to get the Captain to speculate or acknowledge something not previously disclosed by the Pentagon. "Are the two incidents related—the missing submarine and the fire onboard the *Kitty Hawk*?"

"We have no way of knowing," the submariner replied, obviously uncomfortable about the line of questioning. "When we locate the submarine, we'll be able to piece together the events that led to the current situation."

Steve, who had been half-listening to the report, placed the phone receiver down and joined Susan. "Did they say that one of our submarines has sunk in the strait?"

"It's missing," Susan answered without taking her eyes off the television set.

Wickham stared at the screen and turned to her. "What the hell is going on out there?"

"The beginning of a war," she replied in a soft voice.

Steve gave her a strange look, then noticed the trim submariner kept rubbing his hands together. "He doesn't sound too convincing—the sub skipper."

"Yeah, he's definitely nervous," she observed. "Was that the Agency?"

"That was Tony—my friend from the Agency." Steve smiled. "We have an appointment to interview Matsukawa."

37

AIR FORCE ONE

Shortly after Air Force One passed over the westernmost boundary between British Columbia and the Yukon Territories, the accommodating air-traffic controllers allowed the flight crew to begin a shallow descent in preparation for a precision instrument approach to Elmendorf Air Force Base.

In a constant effort to provide a smooth and safe flight, the pilots closely monitored the airspeed and rate of descent as they prepared to execute the ILS approach.

Hand-flying the airplane, the seasoned transport-aircraft commander kept the electronic localizer and glide slope "nailed" from the outer marker to the point where he saw the approach lights, then began the transition to the landing attitude.

The gleaming presidential Boeing 747-200B emerged from the ragged overcast and made a typically smooth Air Force One landing and rollout. The bird colonel occupying the left seat in the cockpit exited the wet runway and slowly taxied the jet toward the ramp space designated for the most famous plane in the free world.

In the combination conference and family dining room, the President sat with his senior staffers, including his Chief of

Staff, the Secretaries of State and Defense, the National Security
Advisor, the top deputy of the National Security Council, and
the Chairman of the Foreign Intelligence Advisory Board, who
happened to be a former Chairman of the Joint Chiefs of Staff.
The conversation had been spirited and to the point during the
last half of the flight.

Although a large delegation of dignitaries and well-wishers
had assembled on the parking ramp to greet the Commander in
Chief of the United States, the President and his senior advisers
were in no hurry to leave the warmth and comfort of the blue
and white jumbo jet.

The President hunched over the table and stared at his Defense Secretary. "Bryce, I think it's time to take off the gloves
and stand our ground. We now have confirmation that *Kitty
Hawk* was torpedoed, and the Joint Chiefs suspect that *Bremerton* may have suffered the same fate."

Mellongard, who looked abnormally pale, shrugged. "What
do you suggest, sir?"

"Goddammit, you're the defense expert!" the President
flared. "You've been in constant contact with the Chairman
and the Joint Chiefs, and we have spent the past two and a half
hours discussing the issues—from *Kitty Hawk* to the missing
submarine. I want a recommendation from *you*, for Christ's
sake!"

A few seconds passed while Mellongard considered remind-
ing the President that it was he who was responsible for the
logjam in the crowded strait and the ensuing military tragedies
that had occurred. The volatile situation in the Strait of
Malacca was exactly the set of circumstances Mellongard had
worked so diligently to avoid.

"Sir, I think we need to proceed cautiously, and consider
withdrawing the rest of our forces from the strait before the
situation becomes more—"

"Admiral," the President suddenly blurted to his Chairman
of the Foreign Intelligence Advisory Board, "even though you
aren't the Chairman of the Joint Chiefs anymore, you're a

military expert and former submariner. I'd like a straight opinion from you."

"Yes, sir," the Admiral responded while he avoided glancing at the Defense Secretary.

"In your estimation," the President said evenly, "what happened to our submarine?"

The Admiral furrowed his brow and put on his eyeglasses, then looked at his notes for a second.

"Mr. President, I'm convinced the boat—or what's left of it—is lying on the bottom of the strait."

A hush settled over the conference room before the President finally spoke.

"Explain to us how you arrived at your conclusion."

"First, the strait isn't deep enough to crush the hull, so we can eliminate that possibility."

The President nodded.

"Secondly, if they experienced a major emergency, the Captain would have surfaced and made contact with the *Kitty Hawk* battle group and COMSUBPAC at Pearl Harbor."

"What if it was a catastrophic emergency," the President suggested, "like being hit by a torpedo?"

The retired Admiral leaned back and mulled the question for a moment. "If, for whatever reason, the submarine was damaged to the point it couldn't surface, the crew could send up a radio buoy, along with other means of pinpointing their position and situation."

"Don't they have a way of escaping from the sub?" Bud Tidwell asked.

The Admiral turned to the Secretary of State. "Yes, sir. If the boat is resting in reasonably shallow water, they could use the escape trunk."

The President leaned on the conference table and stared at the Admiral for a few seconds. "Since we don't know the location of the sub, we don't know the depth of the water."

"Unfortunately, that's true, sir."

The Admiral moved his coffee cup to the side and looked at

the President. "That's what leads me to believe the boat and all hands perished from some catastrophic incident, which could have been a torpedo. What really happened is only speculation at this point, and we may never know the truth."

A female Marine lieutenant colonel quietly eased through the entrance to the compartment and leaned near Bryce Mellongard's ear, then retraced her steps and closed the door.

All eyes focused on the Defense Secretary.

Mellongard sagged and then wanly looked up at the brooding President. "*Kitty Hawk* is sinking and the Captain has ordered his crew to abandon ship."

The President gave him a blank stare while the magnitude of the unfolding disaster became more clear. He was appalled at the loss of the supercarrier, and his personal self-defense mechanism took over to protect his mounting anxiety.

"Bryce," the President said with his jaw clenched, "I want another carrier in the strait as soon as possible, and I want an all-out ASW effort. Understand?"

Mellongard, stinging from the embarrassment of being treated like he was willfully neglecting his responsibilities, became cold and caustic.

"Mr. President," SECDEF said with unusual conviction, "I would strongly advise against further military involvement in the strait."

The President's hoarse voice cut through the air like a razor-sharp sword. "Secretary Mellongard, the subject is not open for discussion."

Mellongard's eyes widened and his face turned dark red as he faced the possibility of being relieved from his position. He had to keep his mouth shut and comply if he wanted to salvage his political future.

"Yes, sir," he said as steadily as possible.

"The next incident"—the President pointed his index finger for emphasis—"whether it's labeled accidental or not, is to be met with swift and decisive retaliation."

Mellongard returned the President's glare. "I will see to it, you can rest assured."

"If our ASW people," the President went on, "detect anything foreign under the water, I want it sunk. I want a thorough and ongoing submarine hunt."

"I fully understand," Mellongard replied as boldly as possible, then thought about the best way to cover his ass if things didn't go well. *I'll use a leak to let the press know I was against the President's actions in the strait. We're headed for a shooting war....*

"We've lost a carrier and a submarine," the President said firmly, "and I'm not going to stand by and see our military credibility go in the tank."

He looked at the rest of his staff, then turned back to Mellongard. "Not when I'm getting ready to confront the Japanese about their growing military strength."

USS *CHANCELLORSVILLE*

Windblown after the helicopter ride from *Kitty Hawk,* Rear Admiral Isaac Landesman stood on the bridge of the Aegis guided-missile cruiser and watched the last of the sailors and officers depart the blazing carrier.

Captain Carl Witowski, who remained onboard the huge flattop until he was assured that all hands had left the ship, was the last man to leave the doomed carrier.

Only a small area of the flight deck near the bow was visible to Landesman. The rest of the listing ship was burning furiously and the stern was beginning to settle lower and lower in the water. The once mighty carrier would soon be relegated to a watery grave.

Landesman followed the flight of the helicopter carrying "Jinks" Witowski and reflected on the incidents that had led to the order to abandon ship. *Who fired the two torpedoes? And why? If none of the ASW equipment detected the torpedoes, they must have been stealth technology. And the Iranians don't have that capability....*

Casting a look at the other vessels in the flotilla, Landesman was appreciative of all the rescue efforts put forth by the military and civilian ships. Even *Hayasa,* the Japanese flagship that inadvertently started the initial conflagration, was bursting from the bulkheads with American sailors and Marines.

Landesman had been impressed by the extraordinary help from the Japanese officers and seamen. They had displayed professionalism and resolve during the long ordeal, and their ship handling had been precise and snappy.

Twenty-five minutes later, Landesman and Witowski sadly watched the *Hawk* slip sternfirst below the surface of the strait. Emotionally, they had lost a close member of their collective family.

THE ANCHORAGE HILTON

The President and his senior staff assembled in the lounge at the Top of the World rooftop restaurant with Prime Minister Genshiro Koyama and the other participants in the summit meeting. The painful, inexplicable events of the past few days dampened the occasion, causing the Japanese delegation to be more cautious than usual.

Forty-five minutes had been allocated for cocktails and informal discussions before the dignitaries were scheduled to have gourmet cuisine prepared by select Japanese and White House chefs.

Taking advantage of the local waters, the cooks had decided to showcase Alaskan salmon, cod, herring, halibut, and pollack, as well as king, Tanner, and Dungeness crabs. A wide variety of European wines, and sake, would be served during the meal.

The entire restaurant and lounge area was off limits to hotel guests, and security was extremely tight. A large contingent of Secret Service agents worked quietly and efficiently with their Japanese counterparts to ensure the safety of their leaders.

Off to the side of the other men, Genshiro Koyama and the President greeted each other with restrained skepticism. They bowed politely and shook hands, then admired the panoramic view of Anchorage and the beautiful mountains that surrounded the city.

The atmosphere was tense and the initial awkwardness caused their casual conversation to be stilted. A moment later, each man was subtly handed his favorite libation.

"Prime Minister Koyama," the President began, then smiled with apparent innocent enthusiasm, "I'm very pleased to have this opportunity to visit with you."

Koyama observed the carefully rehearsed politeness in the voice of the American. Ambassador Koji Hagura had thoroughly schooled the Harvard MBA about the intricacies and craftiness of the American President.

"I share your feelings," the fiercely proud man replied in his raspy voice, "and look forward to a meaningful dialogue with you and your staff." What Koyama didn't say was that he loathed the American President.

38

TOKYO

The sun was shining brightly when Steve and Susan left their hotel in Nishi Shinjuku and entered the train and subway station. Nineteen minutes later, they stepped out of the train at Central Station and walked toward Matsukawa's office building in the Marunouchi business quarter.

They had grilled each other with a series of questions they planned to ask Tadashi Matsukawa, and each carried a spiral-bound notebook. Susan and Steve had no idea what they might find, but they felt confident that some incriminating evidence was bound to surface. He had to be involved in more ways than one. The fact that he'd kept his trail so well hidden was in itself proof. Matsukawa was, in effect, a ruthless murderer; the worst terrorist of them all.

ANCHORAGE

The President was irritated by the last-minute decision to honor the Alaskan Governor and the local Mayor by taking an early-morning windshield tour of Cook Inlet and the surrounding area. He and Prime Minister Koyama rode together, but the

Governor's incessant narration prevented them from having an opportunity to discuss anything significant.

When the limousines returned to the hotel, the President discreetly signaled to his Chief of Staff.

Scott Eaglehoff quickly fell in step with his boss. "Yes, sir?"

"Make sure there aren't any more surprise excursions or ceremonies," the President ordered in a quiet voice. "I want to focus on substance and keep it there."

"I'll take care of it," Eaglehoff responded and headed for Ambassador Koji Hagura, the man who had been responsible for the spontaneous trip.

He knew Hagura meant well and was trying to create a friendlier environment for the discussions, but the President wanted to get to the core of the issues, deal with them, then move on to other major problems.

When the early lunch was over, Prime Minister Koyama and the President led their senior staff members into a large conference room.

Bud Tidwell and Bryce Mellongard followed their Commander in Chief to the single long table in the center of the room.

Prime Minister Koyama, accompanied by Foreign Minister Nagumo Katsumoto and Ambassador Koji Hagura, joined the Americans and sat down while the security team left the conference room.

The formal atmosphere reflected a sense of seclusion, tranquillity, and simplicity, but the undercurrent of tension and false harmony was felt by everyone.

The President's Chief of Staff, the Chairman of the Foreign Intelligence Advisory Board, the National Security Advisor, and the top deputy of the National Security Council were meeting in another room with Special Envoy Yamagata Isoroku and other members of the Japanese delegation.

When the formalities were concluded, the President decided to skip some of the less pressing problems and begin with the difficult issues they had to resolve.

"Prime Minister Koyama, Minister Katsumoto, Ambassador

Hagura, I'd like to move forward on our agenda and discuss some topics that must be addressed and resolved to the satisfaction of everyone."

Trim and impeccably dressed as usual, Koyama allowed his irritation to show before he recovered and gave the President a narrow smile. The Prime Minister was not a person who easily adjusted to changes in schedules or prearranged formats.

Katsumoto and Hagura showed no emotion, while Tidwell and Mellongard smiled inwardly. The two Secretaries were accustomed to the President's penchant for cutting through the chaff and going straight to the heart of problems.

Koyama and Hagura looked puzzled while Katsumoto appeared to be his normal, unflappable self. They had been prepared to discuss the unprecedented events in the Strait of Malacca and were caught off guard by the unexpected turn of events.

"The recent incident at Pearl Harbor," the President began slowly, "was the beginning of an escalation of events that has culminated in this meeting. We are working diligently to uncover the perpetrators of the attacks, and we trust that Japan will fully cooperate with U.S. officials during the investigations."

Prime Minister Koyama allowed only a brief frown to indicate his irritation. He steeled himself and stared down the President of the United States. "We can't do anything about the past until we know who is behind the assaults, so we must deal with the present and the future."

He's a cocky little bastard, the President thought while he displayed his disarming smile. "I'm glad we agree."

Bud Tidwell cleared his throat, ready to employ his special negotiating skills, but his boss quietly stalled him with a light tap on the sleeve of his suit.

Koyama's natural skepticism surfaced and he sensed that the President was being clever and deceptive. "Why are you threatening Japan with an oil-tanker blockade?"

MARUNOUCHI BUSINESS QUARTER

The hectic pace of the bottom floor of the office building gave way to a quiet calm when Susan and Steve walked out of the elevator on the top level of the structure.

Susan's confidence was beginning to ebb. She was well schooled in following precise rules and guidelines and functioning within certain parameters of authority, but operating outside her jurisdiction made her uncomfortable.

"Steve," she began when her restless fear began to surface, "our first four agents are due to arrive tomorrow. Maybe we should wait until we have everyone in place."

He gave her a comforting look. "Take it easy. We're simply going to interview the guy today. We'll wait until we have backup before we go for the jugular."

Unconvinced, Susan maintained her superficial barrier of calm. "Okay. I'm going to follow your lead," she said under her breath as they approached the receptionist.

"Just relax and be yourself," he replied out of the corner of his mouth.

Steve withdrew a business card from the inside pocket of his suit and handed it to the gracious woman.

"We're from *The Wall Street Journal* and we have an appointment with Mr. Matsukawa," he announced while the receptionist looked at the counterfeit card and smiled.

She spoke softly into her small lip-microphone and then escorted them to the entrance to the executive suites.

The wooden sliding doors appeared to open by themselves and a smiling Tadashi Matsukawa bowed slightly and extended his hand to Steve. "Please come in."

"Eric Thomas," Wickham replied as Matsukawa quickly turned his attention to Susan.

He had a gleam in his eye when he warmly clasped her hand.

"Yoshiko Ohira." Susan smiled confidently. "We appreciate the opportunity to interview you."

"It is *my* pleasure," Matsukawa beamed and ushered them into his office, then motioned toward the two plush chairs canted toward each other in front of his large glass desk. "Please have a seat."

Matsukawa couldn't take his eyes off Susan. She looked truly beautiful. He slowly walked around the unique desk and sat down in his mink-fur chair.

Steve glanced out at the Kokyo Gaien square, then studied the Imperial Palace and the massive walls that surround it and the palace gardens.

Susan was surprised by the open concept of the luxurious executive offices. Once inside the primary entrance, glass partitions divided the interior structure of the offices. The openness was in contrast to the traditional design of most of the American offices she had seen.

"On behalf of the *Journal*," Steve said cheerfully, "we thank you for fitting us into your busy schedule."

Keeping his eyes on Susan, Matsukawa gave Wickham a disinterested look. "I'm always happy to accommodate my American friends."

Steve forced himself to display a convincing smile. *I'll bet you are, you slimeball.*

"We have a few routine biographical questions that we need to ask before—" Steve froze in place when he saw the look on Susan's face.

Wickham instinctively turned and saw someone walk into the adjacent office. His eyes grew large when he suddenly recognized the short, bespectacled Japanese man who had answered the door at the mansion in Hawaii.

"Yoshiko," Steve exclaimed as he turned back to her, "are you having another attack?"

Susan spontaneously lowered her head and clutched at her stomach. "Yes . . ." She groaned convincingly.

Matsukawa appeared to be dumbfounded while he stared at Susan. "Are you going to be okay?"

After she had seen the man who could identify them, Susan's

pale expression was real. "I'm afraid not." She winced and kept her head down.

Steve's mind raced as he jumped from his chair and turned his back to Mishima Takahashi in an attempt to shield Susan from his view.

"I'm sorry . . ." Steve muttered hurriedly and helped Susan to her feet. "Yoshiko is suffering from an acute intestinal disorder and we thought she was well enough to do the interview."

"I must apologize for the inconvenience," Susan murmured weakly and turned her head away from Takahashi. "It strikes so suddenly."

"Certainly," Matsukawa said. He pushed himself away from his desk and rose to walk them to the door. "We'll reschedule the interview when you're feeling better."

"That would be great," Steve replied briskly and saw Takahashi stop and stare at them for a few seconds. A moment later the senior executive rushed for his door. The deception was over.

39

ANCHORAGE

Pragmatically, the President decided to take a stronger stance since the Prime Minister appeared to be intent on taking command of the meeting. Flanked by Bud Tidwell and Bryce Mellongard, he decided to take on the caustic Japanese leader in a one-on-one battle.

"Prime Minister Koyama," the President's voice resonated through the conference room, "we aren't threatening *anyone* with a tanker blockade, and we understand about the accident that caused the chain reaction aboard the *Kitty Hawk*. That's why we're sending another carrier into the strait to stabilize the region as quickly as possible."

Koyama's sullen face gave away his feelings. The President was lying and everyone at the table knew it.

"The growing dissension," the President continued forcefully, "between our countries is—in my opinion—not inextricable. If we are willing to work together, which I'm confident that we can, then we'll be able to resolve some of the complex issues that face our nations."

Koyama gave the President a contemptuous sneer while Foreign Minister Nagumo Katsumoto nodded his agreement to the proposal to ease tensions between the two countries. Ambassador Hagura remained quiet, but his rubbery face indicated that he liked the idea of compromise.

"The fundamental issues," Genshiro Koyama said just as forcefully, "are fueled by American arrogance and broken agreements. We are not underlings to anyone—including the United States."

You have the unmitigated gall to mention broken agreements, the President almost said before he regained his composure.

Feeling more determined than ever, the President glanced at Hagura and Katsumoto. Both statesmen were quiet and reserved. Neither showed any visible signs of hostility.

"Gentlemen"—the President flashed his most disarming smile—"I propose that we take a short break—say, fifteen to twenty minutes—then we'll reconvene."

Before anyone could react, he rose and started around the end of the table while the other men shoved back their chairs and got to their feet.

"Prime Minister Koyama," the President said warmly, "may I have a word with you in private?"

Koyama hesitated until Katsumoto and Hagura walked away with the two Americans, then turned to the President. "Whatever you wish."

"I think it would be helpful," the President went on in a conciliatory gesture, "if we could spend a few minutes together."

Koyama gave him a dismissive shrug.

"Why don't we go to the lounge at the rooftop restaurant," the President suggested. "Security still has it sealed from the public."

"The lounge will be fine," Koyama agreed and noticed Secretary Mellongard hurrying back to the President. "I'll meet you there."

"I'll only be a minute," the President assured the brusque politician and turned to his Defense Secretary.

"Sir," Mellongard began in a guarded tone, "one of our cruisers forced an Iranian submarine—the *Taregh*—to the surface near where *Kitty Hawk* went down."

The President showed no emotion. "Did our ASW folks know it was Iranian?"

"No, but they knew from the sound signature that it was a Kilo-class boat and surmised that it was Iranian."

"And?" he prompted.

"Our people," Mellongard went on without enthusiasm, "tracked the suspicious target with a helicopter for almost an hour before *Cowpens* fired an Asroc missile at the contact. The submarine, which is slightly damaged, surfaced about two to three minutes later."

"Is there any indication"—the President began to walk out of the room—"that it may have torpedoed *Kitty Hawk*?"

"Not yet, sir. Admiral Landesman is attempting to get permission to have a boarding party search the sub for any indication that they fired torpedoes."

"Bryce"—the President lowered his voice—"tell the Admiral that he has my permission to do whatever he needs to do. I want an answer about the torpedoes and I want to find out if the Iranians were involved in sinking the carrier."

"Yes, sir."

"You and Bud keep everyone entertained until I get back."

Mellongard nodded. "Will do."

TOKYO

Steve and Susan knew they didn't have a second to waste as they ran for the elevator. The CIA agent glanced back when they heard Takahashi yell for the security detail. The small, dapper man who had been in charge of the brutal attack at Pearl Harbor sounded panic-stricken.

Steve was jabbing the elevator door button when he saw Takahashi race into the chairman's office.

Tadashi Matsukawa, initially paralyzed by the sudden confusion surrounding him, was shocked by the disclosure of the true identities of his two visitors. He cursed himself for waiting to murder Takahashi. Now, if he didn't kill the two agents, he was tied directly to the Pearl Harbor massacre.

Matsukawa quickly reached into his desk and withdrew a stainless-steel 9-millimeter Sig Sauer and rushed into the hallway.

"Call security!" he bellowed at the receptionist. "Get security up here!"

The frightened woman triggered an alarm that began howling throughout the building, prompting Steve to take Susan by the arm. "We've got to go down the stairs!"

They raced to the end of the hallway and instinctively ducked when two rounds ricocheted off the wall near the stairwell. Steve looked back and saw Matsukawa and the receptionist vanish behind her counter—Takahashi had disappeared.

Steve pushed Susan around the corner and into the staircase, then reached under his coat and drew his Beretta from the small of his back.

"Start down and I'll cover you!" he yelled and squeezed off three rounds at Matsukawa as the billionaire scrambled back to the safety of the counter.

Steve spun around to follow Susan, almost knocking her down. "Let's go! *Move!*"

"They're coming up the stairs," she told him in a strained voice and yanked her Smith & Wesson from her purse. "We better identify ourselves."

"It won't do any good." He fired a round down the hallway. "Matsukawa owns these guys! They don't give a shit who we are!"

Another shot rang out from the hallway as the alarm system wailed with a pulsating, high-pitched warble.

"Sonuvabitch," Steve swore under his breath and glanced at the short flight of stairs leading to the top of the building.

"We've got to try the roof. Maybe there's a fire escape."

"If there isn't," Susan protested, "we'll be trapped."

"We don't have many choices. Get up to the roof and I'll cover you."

He fired twice while Susan scurried up the steep steps. The door leading to the roof was locked.

"We can't get out," she yelled as she struggled with the lock. "We've got to take our chances and go back down!"

Wickham leaped up the steps and took a quick look at the obstacle that was blocking their path.

"Stand back," he barked while he braced himself against the railing and kicked the door as hard as he could. He kicked again, then in desperation another time when he heard the excited voices getting louder.

"Hold this," Steve said stiffly as he handed Susan his weapon and used his hands to brace himself. He leaped up and smashed the stubborn door with both feet, crashing to the stairs when the door flew open.

Susan handed him his Beretta as they rushed outside to see if there was any means of escape. It was quickly apparent that there was only one way down, short of jumping off the roof, and that was the same way they had come up.

"We're trapped," Steve said bitterly, "and these goons aren't going to allow us to give up. Trust me."

THE TOP-OF-THE-WORLD LOUNGE

An eerie silence hung in the room after the Secret Service agents and their Japanese counterparts replaced the barricade to the restaurant and lounge. The two leaders, who shared a sense of anxiety and animosity, sat down at a table overlooking the spectacular mountains.

"Prime Minister Koyama," the President began earnestly, "we need to reach an agreement about a couple of major issues or this conference will be seen as a waste of everyone's time and energy. We've got to bring our people and our countries closer together."

Genshiro Koyama stared into the distance for a long moment

before turning to the President. "Your major concern is our expanding military, is that not correct?"

"That's true," he answered slowly, "and we're not the only ones who are becoming alarmed. With the decline of U.S. and Russian activity in Southeast Asia, the waters of the China Sea, the northeast Indian Ocean, and the western Pacific have become a more complex operating environment."

The President saw a glimmer of annoyance flash across Koyama's rigid face.

"We're trying to organize," the President explained, "a Western Pacific Naval Alliance, similar to our NATO allies in the North Atlantic region. We see Japan as a cornerstone of this type of coalition."

The President paused, hoping Koyama might embrace the idea. The Prime Minister gave the impression of being bored.

"However," the President said at last, "there's a perplexing issue to deal with before we can pour the foundation for the alliance. As I said, many countries, including the members of the Association of Southeast Asian Nations, are worried about the growing military forces of Japan."

"They should be worried about their own affairs," Koyama snapped, "and leave Japan to our own designs."

Angered by the bruising confrontation, the President felt his pulse rise. "Regardless of how you feel, we're going to have to deal with this military problem."

Koyama's eyes narrowed and he glowered at the American President. The gesture sent an undercurrent of tension through the room. "*We* will make the decisions about our military," he hissed.

"You know there's a lot of sensitivity attached to the issue," the President said firmly, "and I'm determined to alleviate the problem."

Koyama's raspy voice became harsh. "As *you* know, we've been reviewing the 1946 Constitution. We feel that certain changes have to be made in the interest of Japan."

"That's what concerns us," the President replied as pleasantly as possible.

"Mr. President," Koyama shot back indignantly, "the Japanese people resent being ruled by a document written by foreigners. We should have a military to match our status as world leaders, and the Emperor should be declared the head of state, not just an empty symbol, as required by the postwar constitution."

"Prime Minister Koyama," the President said politely in an effort to show sincerity and concern, "before we discuss a review of Japan's constitution, I'm going to put my cards on the table."

Koyama's dark eyes reflected the contempt he felt toward Americans in general and this President in particular.

"I was reading about Japanese military exploits," the President declared with a friendly smile, "and discovered a basic philosophy about camouflage that I hadn't realized before."

The Prime Minister became wary and exuded a sense of growing irritation.

"If you only move an inch at a time," the President went on with a touch of a drawl, "you can move great distances before the enemy realizes you've even moved. It apparently takes the mind a while to triangulate the clever subterfuge."

Koyama suddenly looked disgusted. "And you believe that's how Japan again became a military power." He fixed his eyes on the man he had grown to despise.

"Let's just say that we haven't been as diligent as we should have been," the President countered dryly, "and your country has taken advantage of the situation and ignored the constitutional ban on the existence of a military in Japan."

Both men studied each other during the uncomfortable silence.

"Calling a growing military power"—the President carefully selected his words—"a Self-Defense Force, to skirt the word 'military' and circumvent the constitution, is exactly what has happened, and everyone has looked the other way."

"Are you suggesting," Koyama grumbled loudly, "that we stop expanding our military capability?"

"No," the President answered calmly and looked at the mountain scenery.

"Then I suggest we return to the conference room," Koyama said in his coarse rasp, "and expedite this meeting."

The President's demeanor changed from that of a pleasant gentleman to a person who was clearly combative. "I'm not saying that you should put a cap on the Japanese military. What I *am* saying is that we will continue to help defend Japan as long as we agree to the size and scope of your military forces."

For a long moment there was another period of silence in the lounge, sending a renewed level of tension through the empty room. The Prime Minister wasn't sure he had understood what the American had said.

"Our position is very straightforward," the President announced provocatively. "Our government—and many of our allies—are going to ensure that Japan does not become a global military power."

40

MARUNOUCHI BUSINESS DISTRICT

The first Japanese security guard to reach the top of the stairway was accompanied by a snarling, snapping, gray and black German shepherd.

"Susan," Steve cautioned in a steady voice, "don't make any quick or threatening moves."

She remained silent while they inched backwards toward the edge of the building.

The uniformed guard raised his gun. Steve had no choice. He shot the man twice in the chest and the barking Alsatian charged him.

"Steve!" Susan cried out as she fired at a second security guard. He staggered a half-dozen steps and fell to his knees, then rolled onto his side and lay still.

Wickham shot at the dog and missed. He raised his left arm to protect his throat and backed near the edge of the roof as the enraged animal leaped at him.

He squatted slightly, then thrust himself upward and twisted sideways, catapulting the dog over the side of the building.

Susan stopped in midstride as Steve frantically waved his arms to catch his balance while he teetered on the edge of the roof. As he felt himself going over, Wickham spun around and desperately grabbed for the cement edging.

"Hang on!" Susan yelled as she rushed to help him. A split second later, she caught a glimpse of Matsukawa as he stepped through the door and onto the roof.

They exchanged shots before she rolled behind an air-conditioning unit.

Wickham was struggling to hoist himself up on the roof when Matsukawa ran over to him and raised his Sig Sauer to shoot the CIA agent in the head.

Susan crawled from behind the air-conditioning machinery and pumped three rounds into Matsukawa's side. The businessman screamed and cursed in agony as he crumbled to the roof, then fell over the edge of the building.

With her heart in her throat, Susan raced over to Wickham as he painfully pulled himself up and threw a leg over the concrete lip on the roof, then crawled to safety.

"Give me your badge and your gun!" Steve ordered Susan while he jumped to his feet and ran to the nearer of the two wounded security officers.

"What are you talking about?" Susan demanded while Wickham rolled the mortally wounded man onto his stomach and yanked the handcuffs and key from his service belt.

"You're now in my custody"—he was breathing heavily— "and we're going to get the hell out of here!"

"Have you gone crazy?"

"Turn around," he barked and clamped her arms behind her with the handcuffs. "I've got the key in my pocket."

"Steve," she said curtly, "I don't like this idea."

"Come on!" he commanded and placed Susan's badge in his shirt pocket as he marched her toward the entrance to the stairway. "We have to get creative if we're going to survive."

"I hope," she fumed in a guttural voice, "that you know what the hell you're doing."

"That makes it unanimous."

She gave him a quick glance. "You *are* crazy."

Wickham fired three shots down the hallway to force everyone to run for cover, then jammed his Beretta into the small of his back and dropped Susan's weapon into his jacket pocket.

"Let's go," he exclaimed and grabbed Susan tightly by the upper arm to steady her while they bounded down the steps. "Hopefully, the guards won't have our description yet—so play it like a fugitive."

Susan lost her balance and Steve caught her before she stumbled facefirst into a wall. "Careful!"

"Steve, I feel helpless . . ."

"That's the image we want to project."

A few seconds later, they collided with a security guard and two policemen as all five tried to force their way through the stairwell entry on the ground floor.

Steve yanked Susan's badge out and flashed it in front of the three men while they gawked at the two strangers and backed away in stunned silence.

"Captain Rodzwicky," Steve said boldly, "Special Operations. I've captured one of the saboteurs, but there are three or four others loose on the top two floors.

"They're armed and dangerous," Steve continued loudly, "and the ringleader is a small man in a dark-gray suit with light-gray pinstripes."

Susan's eyes grew large and she looked at Steve. *That's what the man who was in Hawaii is wearing.*

"Be careful," Wickham cautioned and shoved Susan past the officers.

"Thank you, Captain," one of the policemen said formally while the other two men acknowledged the information and warning with a nod and slight bow.

"Excuse me, mate! Step aside!" Steve said to the onlookers as he deftly unlocked Susan's handcuffs and led her through the confused crowd.

"Gangway, lads," he said in his best Australian accent while he pocketed the handcuffs and flashed Susan's badge. "Police, mate. Make room! Now clear the way!"

When they reached the street, Steve and Susan heard a shot ring out. They paused and looked up toward the roof. Two security guards were pointing at them. One was talking into a portable transceiver.

"Stay calm, okay?" He clutched Susan's badge.

"What are my choices?"

They rushed out in the middle of traffic and Steve leaped in front of a taxi and held up the badge.

"Stop! Stop!" he shouted while they ran to the driver's window as the cab skidded to a halt.

"We have an emergency," Steve said and motioned for the two businessmen in the backseat to get out. "We must get to the nearest hospital as quickly as possible!"

The startled men got out of the back of the taxi and stood there in silence while Susan and Steve jumped in and the driver floored the accelerator.

"Steve," she said, staring through the windshield. "I can't believe you did—"

Susan's joyous relief was abruptly cut off by a round that penetrated the roof of the cab.

"Drive!" Steve ordered while he grabbed Susan and covered her with his body. *"Isoideiru!* Hurry!"

The frightened driver barely glanced up at his shattered roof as he skillfully weaved his way through the congested traffic. He hunched over the steering wheel and never once looked in the rearview mirror at his passengers.

"Are you okay?" Steve asked when he finally helped Susan to a sitting position.

"I think so," she replied weakly and slumped in the seat. "I don't know whether to thank you"—she looked up and shook her head—"or shoot you."

Steve shrugged with nervous fatigue. "Don't make any rash decisions. We're not out of this yet."

"May I ask just one small question?" Susan said while he returned her badge and Smith & Wesson.

"Sure"—he smiled uncomfortably—"if it isn't too personal."

"How have you managed to live this long?"

"Careful planning," Steve replied and motioned for the driver to pull over.

Wickham gave the shocked and confused man a generous tip and they walked a half block and caught another taxi to take them to the Keio Plaza Hotel.

"Susan," Steve began when the cab pulled into traffic, "we'll brief our people about who was behind the attack at Pearl Harbor, then check out of the hotel. We need to get out of the country and let the heavy hitters in Washington take over."

"I agree with that assessment." She noticed that her hands were trembling.

"Yeah," Steve replied with a grin of embarrassment. "It got a little crazy, but what do you do when the suspect from Hawaii walks into the office next to you . . . and looks through the glass partition?"

"Don't be so hard on yourself," Susan chided him while she clasped her hands together. "We didn't have any other options, except drawing our weapons and eventually being surrounded by Matsukawa's security personnel."

"Surrounded and shot. Thanks for what you did back there."

An odd silence settled between them before she finally spoke. "Your quick thinking saved both of us."

"Well," he responded, "I'd have to describe it as shifting into survival mode."

Susan allowed a tiny smile and grasped his hand. "I think we're a good team."

Steve gently squeezed her hand. "A great team."

They stared into each other's eyes, keeping their warm feelings bottled inside so their collective vulnerability wouldn't show.

Steve finally broke the spell. "When I contact Langley, I'll make arrangements to have the military pick us up at Atsugi, then we'll go to the air base for security reasons."

"Atsugi?"

"It's a U.S. Navy airfield just west of Yokohama. We'll be safe there."

"I still think I'll shoot you," she observed with a quiet laugh, "and save you the trouble of waiting for someone else to put you out of your misery."

41

ANCHORAGE

Genshiro Koyama felt light-headed and feared that he might be on the verge of having a major stroke. Small black dots drifted to and fro in his field of vision and his balance was strangely off center. *You bastard,* he thought as he studied the American President. *When your country is bankrupt and the remnants of your carrier battle groups are rusting in storage, Japan will own America.*

"Prime Minister Koyama," the President went on with a renewed determination not to taunt the highly respected Japanese leader. "In the best interest of both of our countries and our combined allies and trading partners, we want to help make Japan's military strong enough to be a deterrent to would-be aggressors, yet not a threat to the global balance of power."

Koyama was only half listening to the man he considered to be an incompetent, dangerous fool. The Prime Minister firmly believed that the American President had developed a loud, irritating bark to offset his rubber teeth.

"We are going to increase our protective commitment," the President continued in a calm, relaxed manner, "to ensure that Japan has adequate U.S. military support in Southeast Asia."

Koyama finally found his voice. "I'm afraid you're deluding yourself about making the decisions on how large Japan's military forces are going to be."

The heavy mood, combined with the opposing personalities and tough talk, were threatening to shatter the fragile alliance of the former bitter enemies.

"I wouldn't have made the statement," the President said emphatically, "if I had any doubt about the outcome of the policy I intend to pursue."

The irascible Japanese politician scowled with anger and gave himself time to think. His contempt was further aroused by his indignation at losing face, and the American detected the emotion.

"Japan regained its independence in 1952," Koyama growled, "and *we* will decide what is in the best interest of our country and military."

The President struggled to hold himself in check. "Prime Minister Koyama, you're going out on a dangerous limb, and it's not all that strong."

Koyama bolted forward in his chair and flared his nostrils. "The days of dancing to the whims of the White House are over," the ruffled Prime Minister spat venomously, "and you better get used to it."

Now it was time for the American to measure his words before he opened his mouth.

"What we're going to have to get used to," the President responded evenly, "is helping each other through difficult times and agreeing to what is in the best interest of the whole world—not just Japan or the United States."

"We will not be dictated to by America," Koyama replied in a low voice, "or by anyone else, for that matter."

"The facts may be distasteful," the President conceded in a voice laced with canned sadness, "but Japan has had a taste of sobriety—a taste of reality, if you will—from the boom days of the eighties to the difficult days of the nineties."

The President fixed Koyama in his stare. "There are certain

steps we must take to ease the concerns of our neighbors, and one of the first tasks is a realignment of the Japanese military structure."

The Prime Minister coldly returned the unblinking stare and leaned toward the man who was causing him a great deal of mental anguish and personal humiliation. "We will not reduce our military forces to suit the U.S., and I am not going to discuss the issue."

With his decision announced, Koyama leaned back and shifted in his chair.

Cocking his head to the side, the President gazed at the distant mountains and turned to Koyama. "There isn't an option available to Japan, and I'm confident that the United Nations and world opinion will be on our side.

"As partners," he continued, "we can reduce your active military in an orderly fashion and store much of the inventory to be used as replacements in the future."

The President peacefully folded his hands. "Or we can do it for you . . . by whatever means are necessary. It's your choice."

The years of Genshiro Koyama's deep-seated antagonism toward America boiled to the surface and overflowed. With fire in his eyes, he fought to control his emotions and keep his anger to himself while he considered the future.

"Ultimately," the Prime Minister spat, "we will prevail—and America will answer to Japan."

Epilogue

Working with the Japanese National Police Agency, FBI investigators were able to interrogate Mishima Takahashi after he confessed his involvement in the assault at Pearl Harbor and the JAL crash landing at Los Angeles International Airport.

The dethroned senior executive also implicated another Matsukawa Corporation top manager who had directed the attacks staged by the Chukaku-Ha terrorist group.

With his face twisted in an agonizing expression of sadness and guilt, Mishima Takahashi voluntarily appeared on Japanese television and admitted his part in the diabolical scheme. Less than three weeks later, Takahashi was sentenced to spend his life in confinement.

In a face-saving gesture, the Matsukawa Corporation paid over 1.8 million yen to each of the passengers and the families of the victims aboard the *Star of Honolulu* and Japan Air Lines Flight 62. In addition, the company donated the mansion to the state of Hawaii and established a generous scholarship fund at the University of Hawaii.

Using the information they had gained from Mishima Takahashi, FBI agents were able to link Bryce Mellongard and

Senator Frank Brazzell, the powerful Chairman of the House Armed Services Committee, to Tadashi Matsukawa.

The tenacious Attorney General shifted into high gear and Washington hummed with investigations and legal wrangling. When the fallout settled around the Beltway, new faces appeared at the helms of the House Appropriations Committee, House Science and Technology Committee, the Committee on Foreign Investment, the House Ways and Means Committee, and the Secretary of Defense was replaced by a retired Army general.

Known only to Matsukawa, the leak in the Central Intelligence Agency went undiscovered. The senior official, who had amassed a small fortune by providing classified information to the wealthy businessman, retired three months after Matsukawa died.

Despite a lengthy argument with Japanese law-enforcement officials, the identities of the two American agents who were involved in Matsukawa's death were kept secret.

After two weeks of extensive debriefings in Washington, Susan happily joined Steve for a twelve-night cruise to the Mediterranean. The amorous relationship, which had blossomed during the relaxing vacation, continued to develop after they returned from the trip.

Susan applied for a transfer to the Washington area and was reassigned to the FBI headquarters.

The President of the United States, gambling that Tokyo would not retaliate after the bitter encounter in Alaska, vowed to take a tougher stance on trade issues with Japan. Tired of the frivolous squabbles over endless details in the trade dispute, the President took a no-holds-barred approach to dealing with the Japanese government.

Using the Matsukawa scandal as political leverage, he increased import duties on various Japanese products and promised another round of antidumping lawsuits aimed at Japanese automakers.

•　　•　　•

After the Japanese submarine *Harushio* returned to port, Lieutenant Commander Oda Kanjiro had a change of heart and reported the Sea Ferret torpedo attack on the burning and defenseless American carrier.

Under intense questioning, Commander Shigezo Takagi initially grew defensive about his actions, then brazenly admitted firing the stealth torpedoes at *Kitty Hawk*. Consumed with rage, Takagi fervently cited his responsibilities to his country, to his devoted crew members, and to his submarine.

Takagi was immediately relieved of his command and placed under military arrest.

Defiant to the end, the ardent practitioner of Zen Buddhism and follower of *Sun Tzu*—The Art of War—committed hara-kiri by disemboweling himself with a screwdriver he had deftly slipped into his sock when he was escorted from *Harushio*.

Prime Minister Koyama, stunned by the Matsukawa revelation, publicly expressed sorrow over the horrible incidents that had been perpetrated by the Japanese billionaire. Behind the scenes, Genshiro Koyama grudgingly manufactured an air of conciliation and cooperation with the White House.

However, Japanese military research and development, including the production of an arsenal of nuclear weapons, continued unabated behind a façade of civilian-related enterprises.

The President and his advisers were unaware of the seed they had planted in the Japanese Prime Minister and his staunchest supporters. The feelings of humiliation and utter frustration galvanized the Japanese leaders into a core of driven men.

Koyama and his colleagues were determined to set Japan on a course to defeat and rule America, regardless of how many generations it would take to position themselves. The Prime Minister and other powerful Japanese leaders became obsessed with the ambitious dream, and dedicated their lives to the day America would become a Japanese colony.

REMEMBER PEARL HARBOR—KEEP AMERICA ALERT

—The motto of the Pearl Harbor Survivors Association